THE WORLD'S CLASSICS

THE STRANGE CASE OF DR JEKYLL AND MR HYDE AND WEIR OF HERMISTON

ROBERT LOUIS STEVENSON, only child of Thomas Stevenson, engineer and lighthouse keeper, and Margaret Balfour, daughter of a Scots minister, was born in Edinburgh in 1850. In 1871 he exchanged the study of engineering for the law. From 1876 he pursued a full-time literary career, beginning as an essayist and travel-writer with the publication of *An Inland Voyage* (1878), *Edinburgh: Picturesque Notes* (1878), *Travels with a Donkey in the Cévennes* (1879) and *Virginibus Puerisque* (1881). Stevenson is probably best remembered for *Treasure Island* (his first widespread success, 1883), *Kidnapped* and *Dr Jekyll and Mr Hyde* (both published in 1886). Ill health, and temperament, prompted Stevenson to travel widely on the Continent and in the South Seas, where he settled in 1889–90 until his death in Samoa on 3 December 1894. He was working on *Weir of Hermiston* on the day he died.

EMMA LETLEY is currently Visiting Lecturer at the Roehampton Institute in London. She has edited R. L. Stevenson's *The Master of Ballantrae*, *Treasure Island* and *Kidnapped* and *Catriona* for The World's Classics (1983, 1985, 1986).

THE WORLD'S CLASSICS

ROBERT LOUIS STEVENSON

The Strange Case of Dr Jekyll and Mr Hyde

and

Weir of Hermiston

Edited with an Introduction by

EMMA LETLEY

Oxford New York

OXFORD UNIVERSITY PRESS

Oxford University Press, Walton Street, Oxford OX2 6DP
Oxford New York Toronto
Delhi Bombay Calcutta Madras Karachi
Kuala Lumpur Singapore Hong Kong Tokyo
Nairobi Dar es Salaam Cape Town
Melbourne Auckland Madrid

and associated companies in
Berlin Ibadan

Oxford is a trade mark of Oxford University Press

First published as a World's Classics paperback 1987

British Library Cataloguing in Publication Data
Data available

Library of Congress Cataloging in Publication Data
Stevenson, Robert Louis, 1850 1894.
The strange case of Dr. Jekyll and Mr. Hyde and
Weir of Hermiston.
(The World's classics)
I. Letley, Emma. II. Stevenson, Robert Louis,
1850-1894. Weir of Hermiston. III. Title.
PR5482.L48 1987 823'.8 86 23524
ISBN 0-19-281740 X (pbk.)

9 10 8

Printed in Great Britain by
BPC Paperbacks Ltd
Aylesbury, Bucks

CONTENTS

Introduction vii

Note on the Texts xxvi

Select Bibliography xxvii

A Chronology of Robert Louis Stevenson xxix

THE STRANGE CASE OF DR JEKYLL AND MR HYDE 1

WEIR OF HERMISTON 77

Appendix A: The Continuation of Weir of Hermiston 195

Appendix B: A Chapter on Dreams 198

Explanatory Notes 211

Glossary 224

INTRODUCTION

> Nothing Mr. Stevenson has written as yet has so strongly impressed us with the versatility of his very original genius as this sparsely-printed little shilling volume. (*The Times*, 25 January 1886)

> Stevenson's 'Weir of Hermiston' certainly promised to be the best of his novels . . . (*Athenaeum*, 23 May 1896)[1]

Jekyll and Hyde was published in 1886 and gained Stevenson international acclaim: a prime example of his strengths as a writer at the outset of a relatively short literary career, the book introduces themes and preoccupations that remained with Stevenson throughout his life, themes that have become part of the consciousness of many generations of readers. *Weir of Hermiston* was the novel upon which he was working on the day of his death; promising to be 'the best of his novels', it explores and refines issues that were first brought to light by him in *Jekyll and Hyde*.

Stevenson was born in Edinburgh in 1850, the son of Thomas Stevenson, a well-known harbour and lighthouse engineer, and was educated at the Edinburgh Academy and University. Even in his early years, he suffered from that ill health (respiratory disorders) that was to trouble him throughout his life. Initially he had intended to follow his father's profession and study engineering but then he decided to read for the Bar and was admitted in 1875. He did not, however, practise as a barrister but kept to his decision, made in 1871, to pursue a full-time literary career. In spite of the success of *Treasure Island* (1883), *Kidnapped* (1886) and *Jekyll and Hyde* (1886), he was not self-supporting as a writer at this stage of his career; and he was not in fact financially independent until his father's death in 1887. Both his temperament and his constitution prompted Stevenson to travel widely. In 1879, he went to the United States (following

[1] Paul Maixner (ed.), *Robert Louis Stevenson: The Critical Heritage* (1981), pp. 205, 465.

Fanny Osbourne whom he had met in France in 1876 and whom he married in 1880) and he spent parts of the subsequent years at Davos in Switzerland and by the Mediterranean. As a wedding present to his new daughter-in-law, Thomas Stevenson bought the house in Bournemouth, 'Skerryvore' (named after one of the most famous of Scottish lighthouses built by Stevenson's uncle), where Fanny and Louis lived from 1886 to 1887. It was here that he wrote *Jekyll and Hyde*, *Kidnapped* and a number of short stories. After his father's death in 1887, Stevenson left Britain, travelled with his mother and Fanny, made a trip to America and then cruised around the Pacific. In 1888–9 the family settled at Vailima in Samoa where he wrote *Weir of Hermiston* and where he died in December 1894.

The move to Bournemouth and to 'Skerryvore' was in some ways both disquieting for and uncharacteristic of Stevenson: as his stepson, Lloyd Osbourne, comments, 'Stevenson, in the word he hated most of all, had become the "burgess" of his former jeers. Respectability, dullness, and similar villas encompassed him for miles in every direction.'[2] Yet, perhaps, this place, an appropriate setting for a respectable Jekyll, was instrumental in Stevenson's story of duality, offering a marked contrast to his own active, subversive inner life.

Different accounts of the story's genesis exist. Lloyd comments:

> One day he [R.L.S.] came down to luncheon in a very preoccupied frame of mind; hurried through his meal—an unheard-of thing for him to do—and on leaving said he was working with extraordinary success on a new story that had come to him in a dream, and that he was not to be interrupted or disturbed even if the house caught fire.[3]

The importance to Stevenson of dreams in his work is clear, too, from the essay 'A Chapter on Dreams' (see Appendix B, pp. 198–209 below) where he describes the vital assistance he receives from his 'unseen collaborators', the 'Little People' who give him inspiration whilst he is asleep.

[2] Lloyd Osbourne, 'Stevenson at Thirty-Seven', Tusitala Edition, V, vii.
[3] Ibid., p. ix.

Lloyd goes on to report how, for three days, a hush fell on the house until Stevenson appeared with the first draft to read aloud. Lloyd himself was spell-bound; Fanny, however, initially silent, ventured to comment that Louis had 'missed the point . . . missed the allegory; had made it merely a story—a magnificent bit of sensationalism—when it should have been a masterpiece.' At first Stevenson was extremely angry but then he came to see the justness of Fanny's criticism, burned the manuscript and, during the next three days, wrote it again. As Lloyd says, 'it was an astounding feat . . . sixty-four thousand words in six days'.[4]

A slightly different account is given in Balfour's *Life*, where the author states that Fanny wrote:

> . . . pointing out her chief objection—that it was really an allegory, whereas he had treated it purely as if it were a story. In the first draft Jekyll's nature was bad all through, and the Hyde change was worked only for the sake of a disguise. She gave the paper to her husband and left the room. After a while his bell rang; on her return she found him sitting up in bed (the clinical thermometer in his mouth), pointing with a long denunciatory finger to a pile of ashes. He had burned the entire draft. Having realised that he had taken the wrong point of view, that the tale was an allegory and not another 'Markheim' he at once destroyed his manuscript, acting not out of pique, but from a fear that he might be tempted to make use of it, and not re-write the whole from a new standpoint.[5]

The dream, combined with pressing financial circumstances, was the immediate inspiration for *Jekyll and Hyde*; but other elements had been with Stevenson for the greater part of his life and contributed to the story. Since boyhood he had been fascinated by that notorious Scots character Deacon Brodie, cabinet-maker by day, robber by night. A bookcase and a chest of drawers crafted by the Deacon in his daytime self occupied their place in the young Louis's (he was always called Louis, pronounced with the 's') room in Edinburgh. The Deacon was thus one of the earliest 'double' characters to have fired his imagination. Then, in adult life, Fanny reports that her husband was 'deeply impressed by a paper he read in a

[4] Ibid., pp. x, xi.

[5] Graham Balfour, *The Life of Robert Louis Stevenson* (1901), II, 13.

French scientific journal on sub-consciousness', and that this paper and Deacon Brodie 'gave the germ of the idea that afterwards developed into the play, was used again in the story of *Markheim*, and finally, in a hectic fever following a hemorrhage of the lungs, culminated in the dream of Jekyll and Hyde.'[6] Then, too, there had been *The Travelling Companion*, an earlier version of the Jekyll theme destroyed by Stevenson as 'a foul, gross, bitter ugly daub . . . a carrion tale!'[7] It was, perhaps, a tale that could have been the literary production of a character (or self) like Mr Hyde.

Jekyll and Hyde is the portrait of a double consciousness, of a 'divided self'; it is a study that is both universal and characteristically Scottish, the product of a peculiarly Scots 'divided consciousness' to use Edwin Muir's well-known notion.[8] Fascinated by the idea of the double as found in the life and strategies of Deacon Brodie, Stevenson himself also lead something of a double life in the strict, Calvinistic confines of nineteenth-century bourgeois Edinburgh: as a student and young man in the city he and his friend, Charles Baxter, would use a benign doubleness to deal with the pressures of high bourgeois existence; they assumed the liberating roles of Johnson and Thomson, heavy-drinking, convivial, blasphemous iconoclasts, whose sense of humour would have been a little too strong for the Stevensons' Heriot Row drawing-room. David Daiches has commented that the Johnson-Thomson (sometimes Johnstone-Thomson) play was, for Stevenson, 'associated with the whole Jekyll-and-Hyde syndrome';[9] in these masks they could full-bloodedly enjoy those pleasures denied to Stevenson and Baxter, and to Dr Jekyll.

The motif of the double is crucial, too, to Scottish fiction where it is linked specifically with the idea of diabolic possession as well as with that division of the self resulting from the harsher and more repressive forms of Calvinism. James Hogg's *Confessions of a Justified Sinner* (1824) is the

[6] Mrs R. L. Stevenson, 'Prefatory Note', Tusitala Edition, V, xvi.

[7] Roger G. Swearingen, *The Prose Writings of Robert Louis Stevenson: A Guide* (1980), p. 62. See also, 'A Chapter on Dreams', p. 208 below.

[8] Edwin Muir, *Scott and Scotland: The Predicament of the Scottish Writer*, Introduction by Allan Massie (Edinburgh, 1982), p. 9f.

[9] David Daiches, *Literature and Gentility in Scotland* (Edinburgh, 1982), p. 82.

most brilliant realization of the theme in the early part of the century with its portrayal of doubleness not only in content but also in narrative method: the story is divided between an 'editor' and the 'sinner' himself; and there are some particularly effective Scots interventions which insist upon a non-rational, alternative, possibly diabolic interpretation of the events recorded as well as the rational response offered by the editor. From Stevenson's own work, the Scots story 'The Merry Men' (1887) offers the portrait of Gordon Darnaway, a man divided and possessed, as, vampire-like, he derives fresh life from the many shipwrecks he witnesses on the dangerous Scottish coastline where he has made his home; in *The Master of Ballantrae* (1889) Stevenson takes the idea of doubleness and possession and presents them within a study of fraternal relationship and rivalry between the brothers James and Henry Durie; in the 'Tale of Tod Lapraik' in *Catriona* (1893) there is a prime example of Stevenson's interest in the double motif with its characterization of Tod, part-weaver, part-incubus. In non-Scots tales, too, the double motif develops in Stevenson's *œuvre*, in stories such as 'Markheim' and 'Olalla'; but it is in *Jekyll* that we find the strongest and earliest realization of the theme.

Jekyll and Hyde is in many ways a characteristically nineteenth-century text: on one level it is a clear response to the constrictions of Scottish Victorianism and to bourgeois Edinburgh; it also has a firm place in the century's literature of the double alongside works such as Dostoevsky's *The Double* (1846) and Wilde's *Dorian Grey* (1891). As Rosemary Jackson has commented in her study of fantasy, 'fantasies of recidivism (a relapse into crime) multiplied in Victorian England after the publication of Darwin's *Origin of Species* (1859) . . . Recidivism and regression to bestial levels are common post-Darwinian fantasies.'[10] A few years before *Jekyll and Hyde*, another Scottish writer, George MacDonald, included this interchange in his children's story, *The Princess and Curdie* (1883):

> '. . . Have you ever heard what some philosophers say—that men were all animals once?'

[10] Rosemary Jackson, *Fantasy: The Literature of Subversion* (1981), p. 116.

'. . . But there is another thing that is of the greatest consequence—this: that all men, if they do not take care, go down the hill to the animals' country; that many men are actually, all their lives, going to be beasts. People knew it once, but it is long since they forgot it.'[11]

This story, with its horror of the man who is 'travelling beastwards', is characteristically fearful of a Darwinian regression: MacDonald negotiates with such a fear by means of a benign (and at times saccharine) religious belief. Stevenson confronts the Darwinian elements directly in *Jekyll and Hyde*, employing a very striking cluster of images stressing the bestial and animalistic: Hyde is described as 'hissing' like a snake (p. 18); he is a nameless 'thing' (p. 45); moves 'like a monkey' (p. 47); acts with 'mere animal terror' (p. 48) and is seen after one transformation 'sorely contorted and still twitching' (p. 49); and Jekyll awakes one morning, when the metamorphoses have become uncontrollable, to find 'a swart growth of hair' on his hand, the mark of Hyde (p. 67); later, Jekyll describes his double as 'the animal within me licking the chops of memory' (p. 71) and a 'caged' and 'apelike' creature that cannot be denied (p. 75). As the narrative progresses the animal imagery increases and the post-Darwinian nightmare intensifies until, in Jekyll's 'Statement', the images reach their most fearful. The legal framework (the 'Statement') cannot contain the disquieting material of the nightmare regression; it is Jekyll, of course, who sees Hyde most emphatically in bestial terms rather than the other characters who have some experience of his alter ego.

A story of a divided self, *Jekyll and Hyde* is also an excellent example of literary fantasy: critical discussions of fantasy have laid especial stress on the key importance of subversion. Roger Caillois, for example, writes: 'The fantastic is always a break in the acknowledged order, an irruption of the inadmissable within the changeless everyday legality.'[12] This applies well to Stevenson's 'shilling shocker': on its surface *Jekyll and Hyde*

[11] George MacDonald, *The Princess and Curdie* (1883: Harmondsworth, Middlesex, 1966), p. 69.

[12] Roger Caillois, *Images, Images* (1965), p. 15, as quoted in Jackson, op. cit., p. 21.

records a break with legality in the manner the story is structured, divided initially between two characters who are pillars of Reason and Establishment—Utterson, the lawyer, and Lanyon, the Doctor, with Enfield as the third narrator. Neither Utterson nor Lanyon is able to assimilate the events of the story into his known reality; at the end of the first chapter both try to retreat from the 'bad story' (p. 11); they agree to close the matter, implying that they would, were it possible, close the path to a new kind of awareness upon which they have embarked. The story, however, does not allow them this kind of control.

The first section is a masterpiece of narrative unease, an effect at which Stevenson excels. The building itself, by virtue of its windowless state, promotes this impression; the cheque is signed with an unmentionable name; Hyde resists specific description and there is a supernatural suggestion about his undefined comings and goings. As a doctor carrying out 'unscientific' researches, Jekyll literally upsets Lanyon's sense of order and rightness, whilst the irregularities of his will disquiet the lawyer. Thus Jekyll's actions challenge these pillars of bourgeois society and, at the same time, question the reader's rational assumptions.

Unease and uncertainty, too, are caused by the nature of the men who are called upon to tell the story, to bear witness. As Masao Miyoshi has pointed out, Utterson has a past that is not blameless; he also lacks fellow-feeling and avoids asking uncomfortable questions. Similarly, Lanyon avoids distressing issues by a very closely-guarded, cautious control. Thus, 'The important men of the book, then, are all unmarried, intellectually barren, emotionally stifled, joyless.'[13] They are also men who only partly understand the events in which they are implicated; they do not understand the 'bad story', and it is this, so foreign to his lived life, that ultimately undermines and kills Dr Lanyon as his life is 'shaken to its roots' (p. 59) and he dies. Stevenson consistently, throughout his work, exploits daring narrative structures; the split narrative of *Jekyll and Hyde* looks forward to the more full-ranging narrative experiments of *The Master of Ballantrae* (1889),

[13] Masao Miyoshi, *The Divided Self* (New York, 1969), p. 297.

recalls the divisions of *Treasure Island* (1883) and links with those of *Kidnapped* (1886) and *Catriona* (1893).

In the latter, David Balfour in a moment of intense disillusion about the ways of the political world, and the unjust conduct of the trial of James of the Glens (James Mhor) at Inverary in 1752, comments: 'James was hanged . . . He had been hanged by fraud and violence, and the world wagged along, and there was not a pennyweight of difference; and the villains of that horrid plot were decent, kind, respectable fathers of families, who went to kirk and took the sacrament!'[14] It was this duality (whether in the form of a split between an outer surface and an inner reality or between a social façade and private role) that was to preoccupy Stevenson throughout his literary life from his youthful acquaintance with Deacon Brodie's 'Double Life' onwards; he makes the young David Balfour experience duality in *Kidnapped* and, to a greater extent, in *Catriona*; and it is a preoccupation that comes to the fore in *Weir of Hermiston*, a book that has justly been described as Stevenson's 'last word on duality' in every sense.[15]

An important link between *Jekyll* and *Weir* comes in the portrayal of the father-son relationship: Hyde is very much Jekyll's creation, his son and creature, in the tradition of other Gothic fantasies such as Mary Shelley's *Frankenstein* (1818). 'Jekyll had more than a father's interest; Hyde had more than a son's indifference' (p. 68), writes Jekyll in his 'Statement' and this pairing is consolidated in the text (see notes e.g. to pp. 64, 75). It is here, as well as in the portrayal of Scotland and a Scottish sensibility, that the autobiographical relevance of the two texts comes to the fore. Stevenson's relationship with Thomas Stevenson, although affectionate, was often uneasy, and 'the thunderbolt of paternal anger' was all too painfully on occasion aimed at the son's attitudes and actions. There was, for instance, the great crisis with his father about the Society formed by Louis, Bob Stevenson, Charles Baxter and others, whose constitution

[14] *Catriona*, Swanston Edition, XI, 197.

[15] Edwin M. Eigner, *Robert Louis Stevenson and Romantic Tradition* (Princeton, 1965), p. 227.

opened with the words, 'Disregard everything our parents taught us.'[16] Filial relationships, with varying degrees of tension and distress, recur throughout Stevenson's fiction in, for instance, *The House of Eld*, *The Story of a Lie*, *The Strange Adventures of John Nicholson* and *The Wrecker*, as well as very centrally in *The Master of Ballantrae* and, last of all, in *Weir*.

In *Kidnapped* and *Catriona*, Stevenson drew the portrait of a fine 'Scots character' in David Balfour, a young man with whom he himself had something considerable in common; but David's father was dead and buried at the outset of his son's adventures; and it was not until *Weir*, written in Samoa shortly before his own death, that Stevenson engaged with a young man like himself in a difficult paternal relationship—Archie Weir, son of Lord Hermiston. In October 1892, he started work on the novel, telling Sidney Colvin that its title 'ought' to be 'Braxfield' (after Robert MacQueen, Lord Braxfield, the inspiration for Hermiston) but that, since such a title was 'impossible', it would be called one of a number of alternatives, possibly *Weir of Hermiston*. He tells Colvin, too, that the book is set in the areas about 'Hermiston in the Lammermuirs and in Edinburgh' in the year 1812.[17] On 1 December 1892, he writes to Baxter:

> . . . I have a novel on the stocks to be called *The Justice-Clerk* [another possible title for *Weir*]. It is pretty Scotch, the Grand Premier is taken from Braxfield—(Oh, by the by, send me Cockburn's *Memorials*)—and some of the story is—well—queer. The heroine is seduced by one man, and finally disappears with the other man who shot him . . . Mind you, I expect *The Justice-Clerk* to be my masterpiece. My Braxfield is already a thing of beauty and a joy for ever, and so far as he has gone *far* my best character.[18]

[16] See Daiches, *Literature and Gentility* op. cit., p. 82.

[17] Letter to Sidney Colvin, 28 October 1892, Swanston Edition, XXV, 260.

[18] Letter to Charles Baxter, 1 December 1892, Swanston Edition, XXV, 270–1. W. E. Henley points out that the name Weir would have been specially significant for R.L.S. as being that of the legendary Scottish Major Weir (*c.* 1600–70) who was an extremely religious man, a Lieutenant in the army sent by the Covenanters to protect the Ulster Colonists in 1650 and later a Major in Lanark's army: he was secretly engaged in a number of crimes and, believed to be a warlock, was burned in 1670 together with his sister. For Henley's comment, see E. V. Lucas, *The Colvins and Their Friends* (1928), pp. 247–48.

Intermittent work on the book went on towards the end of 1892 and throughout 1893, but sustained writing of *Weir* did not really get under way until early in 1894 and, even then, there were interruptions whilst Stevenson worked on *St Ives*, the adventures of a French prisoner held captive in Edinburgh Castle during the Napoleonic Wars. In a letter to Colvin of February 1894, Stevenson describes having re-read his story, *The Ebb-Tide*: 'It gives me great hope, as I see I *can* work in that constipated, mosaic manner, which is what I have to do just now with *Weir of Hermiston*.'[19] On 6 February, Isobel Strong (Stevenson's step-daughter and his amanuensis) recorded in her Journal that she and Louis had been working for several days on the novel; then, there was one more hiatus whilst they continued with the adventures of St Ives; and finally, in September 1894, Isobel reported that they had been working 'like steam-engines' on *Weir*.[20]

On 3 December, the day of Stevenson's death, Lloyd writes that, 'He wrote hard all that morning of the last day; his half-finished book, Hermiston, he judged the best he had ever written, and the sense of successful effort made him buoyant and happy as nothing else could.'[21] At this time, Charles Baxter was en route for Samoa; when he returned to Britain he took the unfinished manuscript with him. Edited by Sidney Colvin, it appeared in four instalments in the magazine *Cosmopolis* from January to April 1896, and the first book edition appeared in the same year.

The book that Stevenson felt promised to be his best attracted mixed responses: friends of whom Colvin asked advice about its publication were uniformly enthusiastic; W. E. Henley and Henry James both felt that *Weir* was worthy of immediate publication; J. M. Barrie commented that 'here it seems to me that he *has* done it, here is the big book'.[22] Arnold Bennett remarked in his journal, 'The mere writing of "Weir of Hermiston" surpasses all

[19] Letter to Sidney Colvin, February 1894, Swanston Edition, XXV, 383.
[20] Swearingen, op. cit., p. 175.
[21] Lloyd Osbourne, 'Account of the Death and Burial of R. L. Stevenson', Tusitala Edition, XXXV, 185.
[22] E. V. Lucas, op. cit., p. 248.

Stevenson's previous achievement.'[23] Contemporary reviewers, however, were more chary: some objected to the publication of a fragment; there were criticisms of Colvin's handling of the ending; the thorough-going Scottishness of the novel provoked some hostility; and there was a tendency to agree with E. Purcell who wrote: 'Rich as it is in those perfections of which Stevenson was a supreme master, "Weir of Hermiston" would never have been a great novel, for a great novel he could never have written.' He adds more generously, however, 'The great novel never emerged, but in its stead what a roll of successes, and in such various styles!'[24]

Weir may not indeed be the finished masterpiece envisaged by critics such as Purcell but, even in its fragmentary state, it has its own individual 'roll of successes'; it is an intense and, at times, brilliant portrayal of duality and division, both personal and public, a fitting conclusion to a career that was early on distinguished by *Jekyll and Hyde*. Stevenson himself said that the novel was 'pretty Scotch'; Sidney Colvin concluded his note on the book saying that 'Surely no son of Scotland has died leaving with his last breath a worthier tribute to the land he loved.'[25] *Weir*, above all, is a text that asks the reader to consider what being 'pretty Scotch' meant to Stevenson, to join him in addressing a question that he could consider with maturity only at a distance of several thousand miles, in Samoa. Some years earlier he had dealt with 'The Scot Abroad' in his book *The Silverado Squatters* (1883): 'Scotland is indefinable; it has no unity except upon the map. Two languages, many dialects, innumerable forms of piety, and countless local patriotisms and prejudices, part us among ourselves more widely than the extreme east and west of that great continent of America.'[26] In *Weir*, Stevenson sets his exploration of personal division and rebellion (portrayed in the son, Archie) against a background of national and historical division. Of all Stevenson's work, *Weir* is most aware of Scottishness, of Scotland's languages and dialects,

[23] Maixner (ed.), op. cit., p. 465.
[24] Ibid., pp. 474, 475.
[25] Sidney Colvin, 'Editorial Note', *Weir of Hermiston* (1896), p. 286.
[26] 'The Scot Abroad', *The Silverado Squatters*, Swanston Edition, II, 194.

history and literary heritage (at times, the novel reads like a roll call of honour of the great literati of the past); and it is in *Weir* that he gives this awareness its most mature and fullest expression. If we look simply at the opening of the book we note at once that Stevenson sets the scene with reference to some of the most turbulent and divided times of Scottish history—the Covenanting period. With a few telling allusions, the reader is reminded of one of the most tortured of Scotland's religious splits, the results of the 'innumerable forms of piety' in the land.

The opening, too, lays stress on those characters about whom history has been strongly divided, men who have called forth widely differing responses: Claverhouse who, in folk memory and some fiction, is 'bloody Clavers' but who is also commemorated in Scotland's song as 'Bonnie Dundee'; and George MacKenzie, known by many as 'bloody MacKenzie' but who was also a reputed literary figure, the founder of the Advocates' Library in Edinburgh (today, the National Library of Scotland) and a much more complex personality than his sobriquet suggests. Such characters demand a response that appreciates their duality; and this is, above all, the case, too, with Judge Hermiston, modelled on Braxfield, a man whose name 'smack[ed] of the gallows' but who also had 'a sneaking kindness for any unpopular person'.[27] It is for Archie in the novel to try to come to terms with the contradictions of a father who is 'the brutal judge and the industrious, dispassionate student' (p. 108).

Historical and political divisions are matched in the text by an exploration of division in the literary world. Among others, the book draws on two Scottish figures who are profoundly associated with duality on a number of different levels: James Hogg and Robert Burns. In life, both these men exploited a kind of duality in creating a mask, a consciously-constructed persona to suit their audiences. Burns presented himself both as a 'professional Don Juan' and as literary darling of Edinburgh bourgeois society; Hogg created himself both as raw, Ettrick shepherd and as aspiring, genteel litterateur; and

[27] 'Some Portraits by Raeburn', *Virginibus Puerisque*, Swanston Edition, II, 389.

what is more both wrote in these and other, variant guises in full knowledge of what they were doing.[28] Both writers, too, have aroused very different reactions, as diverse as those prompted by political men such as Claverhouse and MacKenzie. We could say that *Jekyll and Hyde* is a simplification or reduction (I mean the notion, not the book itself, which is extremely consciously and artistically constructed) of the much more subtle dualities explored in *Weir of Hermiston*.

It would seem then that Scottishness and doubleness, division and duality are synonymous in Stevenson's work, that the ideas coincide on political, historical and literary levels. It is an idea that is registered very strongly indeed in the language and the linguistic divisions of the novel. Judge Braxfield was distinguished in his own time by his Scots. Henry Cockburn describes him thus (in *Memorials*, the book which Stevenson asked Baxter to send him in Samoa whilst he was working on *Weir*):

> But the giant of the bench was Braxfield. His very name makes people start yet.
>
> Strong built and dark, with rough eyebrows, powerful eyes, threatening lips, and a low growling voice, he was like a formidable blacksmith. His accent and his dialect were exaggerated Scotch; his language, like his thoughts, short, strong, and conclusive.
>
> .. .. ..
>
> Illiterate and without any taste for refined enjoyment, strength of understanding, which gave him power without cultivation, only encouraged him to a more contemptuous disdain of all natures less coarse than his own. Despising the growing improvement of manners, he shocked the feelings even of an age, which, with more of the formality, had far less of the substance of decorum than our own. [He refers to the first half of the nineteenth century.][29]

The broad Scots of Hermiston, Stevenson's version of

[28] See also Emma Letley, '"The Management of the Tongue": Hogg's Literary Uses of Scots', *Papers Given at the Second Conference of the James Hogg Society* (forthcoming, 1987).

[29] Henry Cockburn, *Memorials of His Time*, ed. Harry A. Cockburn (Edinburgh, 1909), pp. 104–5.

Braxfield, is an important part of *his* resistance to the 'growing improvement of manners' of his time. In Stevenson's own youth, too, the use of broad Scots was itself a gesture of defiance against genteel, Edinburgh values. The masks employed by him and Baxter of Johnstone and Thomson often involved such broad Scots, as here when Johnstone writes to 'Thomson in Gaol': 'Ye've been, since ever 'at I kent ye, a drunkard, a whoremonger, a blasphemer, and mair that I wouldnae like to name, you bein' whaur ye are and your letters likely opened.'[30]

Archie Weir in the novel is linguistically the opposite of the young Stevenson: his rebellion against his father is expressed in English; it is only as a child that he speaks Scots apart from very occasional lapses towards the end of the fragment. With his mother he employs Scots forms as he tries to understand the logic of Hermiston's position; if judging is a sin, how is it that his father is a judge:

> 'I can't see it,' said the little Rabbi, and wagged his head.
> Mrs Weir abounded in commonplace replies.
> 'No, I canna see it,' reiterated Archie. 'And I'll tell you what, Mamma, I don't think you and me's justifeed in staying with him.' (p. 92)

Despite his mother's remonstrances, Archie still clings to the idea that his father is 'crooool' (p. 92).

The 'pretty Scotch' quality of the book is clearly seen here, as elsewhere, in the language. In childhood conversations with his mother, Scots is established as Archie's language of intimacy with her; the language in its pronunciation features is also a sign that he has at least some affinity with his broad Scots father (an affinity that persists, although without linguistic signs, in his manhood however hard he may try to deny it). With the death of Jean Rutherford, the constant 'tender' influence on Archie's life is denied; she leaves him with 'a shivering delicacy, unequally mated with potential violence' (p. 98). It is this duality that causes the tragedy of Archie Weir; and it is the legacy of genteel tenderness from

[30] *RLS: Stevenson's Letters to Charles Baxter*, ed. De Lancey Ferguson and Marshall Waingrow (1956), p. 143.

his mother that prompts him to reject his father as gross and vulgar. The tension is dramatized in this passage:

The father, with a grand simplicity, either spoke of what interested himself, or maintained an unaffected silence. The son turned in his head for some topic that should be quite safe, that would spare him fresh evidences either of my lord's inherent grossness or of the innocence of his inhumanity; treading gingerly the ways of intercourse, like a lady gathering up her skirts in a by-path. (pp. 101–2)

Scots is linked with this 'grand simplicity', with the natural, and with expansiveness and, in Archie's view, with vulgarity and the low speech of 'sculduddery'. By contrast, English is associated with a carefully-contrived safety, a fear of and retreat from deep emotion, an emphasis on the aesthetic and a veneer of conventional politeness. Part of Archie's reaction against his father is his 'translation' of his mother's primary characteristic of tenderness into the more refined language. One example from the well-known Duncan Jopp chapter shows the intensified tension between father and son and the use of a particularly effective piece of 'translation'. Archie tries to justify himself for his outburst about the sentence passed on Jopp, calling it ' "a hideous business" '. Hermiston's reply translates his son's term, making it seem paltry and inadequate: ' "Heedious! I never gave twa thoughts to heediousness, I have no call to be bonny" ' (p. 113). Hermiston's scorn, expressed by means of the accentuated vowel sounds, dismisses Archie's aesthetic objections; by translating 'hideous' into not being 'bonny', Hermiston implies that his son's comments are mean-minded and effete. This negative association of English is intensified with the appearance of Frank Innes, 'Mephistopheles'. His language is appropriate for an intruder; but English is also associated with the Satanic in Stevenson's work as it is too in that of James Hogg. In Hogg's *Confessions of a Justified Sinner* (1824), the double, Gil Martin, speaks English in a strongly Scots environment, stressing his dangerous lack of local roots. Karl Miller has pointed out that Hogg spoke of the literati (and anglicized Scots) Wilson and Lockhart as 'two devils'; and Wilson wrote of the 'Mephistopheles tricks' he had played on

Hogg.[31] In this tradition, Innes's English is a definite danger sign, a reflection of his scorn of Scots and the culture implied by Scots speech. His very occasional Scots (see Notes, p. 180) is used with Archie merely as part of a denigrating pun, his playing with the Scots tongue an image of the way he plays cruelly with Archie and Christina. Overall the tension between the two languages helps to maintain the necessary artistic balance between rational sympathy and imaginative power. For all his coarseness and indeed his cruelty, the Judge has an essential valour that even Archie has to acknowledge; moreover, he is surely right in his rejection of his son's defence in the matter of the Duncan Jopp incident; Archie has, after all, betrayed a filial bond on account of a question of style; it is an aesthetic objection pushed to the point of cruelty. Stevenson was firm in his belief about the need for sympathy in the treatment of a character such as Braxfield/Hermiston and the Scots in tension with English promotes this sympathy.

On the Scots side of the Scots-English tension in the text is also the elder Kirstie, housekeeper at Hermiston. A number of critics of *Weir* were much impressed by the advance they found in the book in terms of Stevenson's ability to draw convincing female characters. This was never his strong point in his earlier work: his great successes lived without female interest (in *Jekyll and Hyde* there is almost no female presence except for a very brief appearance of the servant who witnesses the murder of Sir Danvers Carew, pp. 25–6); but in his more mature work, Stevenson begins to draw fully-rounded female characters. J. M. Barrie was one critic who commented approvingly upon this point:

> The rest is what I always supposed he could do, but I never believed he could do the women. The mother is more surprising to me than Braxfield [Hermiston], and the two Kirsties also. He seemed hitherto to be afraid of himself when writing of women, to doubt his own sincerity, so to speak. Catriona was an exquisite child and Barbara Grant [in *Catriona*] a fine treatment from the outside; but here he gets 'into' the very heart of woman, best of all in the last paragraph . . .[32]

[31] Karl Miller, *Cockburn's Millennium* (1975), p. 198.
[32] E. V. Lucas, op. cit., p. 248.

The elder Kirstie is drawn, in particular, as a foil to the insidious Frank Innes; her disgust about him is expressed vividly as she resists his intrusion into the house at Hermiston:

'There's no a hair on ayther o' the Weirs that hasna mair spunk and dirdum to it than what he has in his hale dwaibly body! Settin' up his snash to me! Let him gang to the black toon where he's mebbe wantit—birling in a curricle—wi' pimatum on his heid—making a mess o' himsel' wi' nesty hizzies—a fair disgrace!" ' (pp. 170–1)

Kirstie's Scots here contrasts with Innes's gentrified English; and she differs further from him in her advice to Archie about the acute problems of his relationship with Christina (p. 185f) and her anxiety about his situation, combined with her jealousy about being supplanted in his affections by her niece. Frank's and Kirstie's parallel advice sets English dissembling against Scots affection. This is a variation of Stevenson's linguistic strategy where he sets up a tension between Scots and English so that English emerges as an inadequate language and Scots comes off as both morally and imaginatively more powerful.

Stevenson's success in creating the character of the elder Kirstie and her relationship with Archie is found very strongly in the scene where she pleads with him not to jeopardize her niece's life and his own future happiness:

'Promise me ae thing,' she cried in a sharp voice. 'Promise me ye'll never do naething without telling me.'

'No, Kirstie, I canna promise ye that,' he replied. 'I have promised enough, God kens!' (p. 189)

The 'lapse' into Scots signals the coming crisis in Archie's and Christina's relationship: and the Scots itself suggests that here Archie regains something of the spontaneous feeling of his boyhood as he employs the Scots speech forms earlier used with his mother. His feeling for Christina, however, cannot remain unthreatened by himself; in order to make the break with her, he has to adopt a rational attitude; and in the final chapter of *Weir* in its existing fragment, Archie, after a night of reflection, returns to his habitual (in adulthood) anglicized mode (p. 193). Like David Balfour in *Catriona*, with his safe retreats into dry, legal works at emotionally awkward moments,[33] Archie becomes the 'schoolmaster' and speaks in 'cold, convincing sentences'—*English* sentences which recall the linguistic situations of many Scots fictional characters forced into an English style. The counterpointing of Archie's cold English and Christina's angry, Scots pleading dramatizes the tension between them: it also stresses Archie's attempt to hold on to the certainties he associates with his anglicized reason and underlines the impossibility of their relationship. The fragment ends as the 'curtains of boyhood' rise before him as, for the first time, he sees 'the ambiguous face of woman as she is' (p. 194). The same could, perhaps, be said of Stevenson himself. It is the first time he has appreciated in fiction the full complexities of woman's 'ambiguous face'. In *Catriona* the heroine and Barbara Grant are living, appealing characters but their ambiguity is unrealized by David Balfour. In *Weir*, both Stevenson and Archie come to appreciate this quality.

Although it is only a fragment, an 'unfinished romance', *Weir* successfully presents in Archie a hero divided psychologically, nationally and linguistically—a very Scottish kind of hero, the creation of a writer from a nation that very much likes to present itself as subject to that 'divided consciousness' identified by Muir. (This is, by the way, a self-dramatization as deliberate and self-conscious as those literary masks invented for themselves by writers such as Burns and Hogg.) One commentator on the novel, J. D. Scott, suggested that both *Weir* and George Douglas Brown's *The House with the Green Shutters* (1901) were, in different ways, attempts to 'realize the demoniac quality of the national character, to unfasten the bonds of religion, respectability, sentimentality and success, which hold it down, to find out what the Scot—the minister, the Edinburgh lawyer, the city financier, and the chief engineer—really is.'[34] There is here more than simply a point of comparison between two anti-Kailyard novelists who were intent on countering the saccharine view of Scotland

[33] *Catriona* (1893), p. 284f.

[34] J. D. Scott, 'The Myth of Lord Braxfield', *Horizon*, XIII, 307 (May 1946).

peddled by writers such as Crockett, MacLaren and (at times) Barrie. It was Stevenson's life-long project to realize in fiction the 'ambiguous face' of the Scottish national character and his own connections with that character. He is not Archie Weir but, like Archie, he too was the product of many divisions; their dramatization in *Weir* makes a fitting conclusion to a literary career that had, only eight years previously, exploded with the success of *The Strange Case of Dr Jekyll and Mr Hyde*.

NOTE ON THE TEXTS

THE texts are those of the first British book editions; *Jekyll and Hyde* was first published by Longmans, Green in 1886 and *Weir of Hermiston* by Cassell in 1896. In *Weir* a number of misprints appeared in the first edition which were subsequently amended in the Edinburgh Edition of 1896 [EE]: in these cases I have used the EE readings. Stevenson's essay 'A Chapter on Dreams' is reproduced from the first edition of *Across the Plains* (Cassell, 1892).

The Glossary of Scots words in *Weir* has been prepared for this edition.

The existence of an explanatory note is indicated in the text by an asterisk.

SELECT BIBLIOGRAPHY

(*Place of publication is London unless stated otherwise.*)

BIBLIOGRAPHY

George H. Ford (ed.), *Victorian Fiction: A Second Guide to Research* (Cambridge, Mass., 1978) [includes a chapter on R.L.S. by Robert Kiely].

George L. McKay, *The Stevenson Library of Edwin J. Beinecke*, 6 vols. (New Haven, 1958).

W. F. Prideaux, *Bibliography of Robert Louis Stevenson* (1903; revised edition, 1917).

Roger G. Swearingen, *The Prose Writings of Robert Louis Stevenson: a Guide* (1980).

EDITIONS

Collected Editions of the works of R.L.S. include:

The Edinburgh Edition, ed. Sidney Colvin (1894–8).

The Pentland Edition, with bibliographical notes by Edmund Gosse (1906–7).

The Swanston Edition, with an Introduction by Andrew Lang (1911–12).

The Vailima Edition, ed. Lloyd Osbourne, with Prefatory Notes by Fanny van de Grift Stevenson (1922–3).

The Tusitala Edition (1923–4).

LETTERS

Vailima Letters (1895).

The Letters of Robert Louis Stevenson to His Family and Friends, ed. Sidney Colvin (1899; new edition, 1911).

Henry James and Robert Louis Stevenson: A Record of Friendship and Criticism, ed. Janet Adam Smith (1948).

RLS: Stevenson's Letters to Charles Baxter, ed. De Lancey Ferguson and Marshall Waingrow (New Haven, 1956).

BIOGRAPHY

Graham Balfour, *The Life of Robert Louis Stevenson* (1901).
Jenni Calder, *RLS: A Life Study* (1980).
Elsie Noble Caldwell, *Last Witness for Robert Louis Stevenson* (Norman, Oklahoma, 1960).
David Daiches, *Robert Louis Stevenson and His World* (1973).
J. C. Furnas, *Voyage to Windward* (1951).
J. A. Hammerton, *Stevensoniana: An Anecdotal Life and Appreciation of Robert Louis Stevenson* (Edinburgh; revised edition, 1910).
James Pope Hennessy, *Robert Louis Stevenson* (1974).

CRITICISM AND HISTORICAL BACKGROUND

Jenni Calder (ed.), *Stevenson and Victorian Scotland* (Edinburgh, 1981).
David Daiches, *Literature and Gentility in Scotland* (Edinburgh, 1982).
— *Stevenson and The Art of Fiction* (New York, 1951).
— *Robert Louis Stevenson* (Glasgow, 1947).
Edwin M. Eigner, *Robert Louis Stevenson and Romantic Tradition* (Princeton, 1965).
Andrew Jefford, 'Dr Jekyll and Professor Nabokov: Reading a Reading' in Noble.
W. D. Lyell, 'The Real Weir of Hermiston'; an address delivered to the Glasgow Juridical Society (Edinburgh, 1903).
Paul Maixner (ed.), *Robert Louis Stevenson: The Critical Heritage* (1981).
Karl Miller, *Cockburn's Millennium* (1975).
— *Doubles* (1985).
Masao Miyoshi, *The Divided Self* (New York, 1969).
Andrew Noble (ed.), *Robert Louis Stevenson* (1983) [Noble].
J. D. Scott, 'Novelist-Philosophers: R. L. Stevenson and G. D. Brown: The Myth of Lord Braxfield', *Horizon*, XIII, 298–310 (May 1946).
K. G. Simpson, 'Author and Narrator in *Weir of Hermiston*' in Noble.

MISCELLANEOUS

Alanna Knight, *Robert Louis Stevenson Treasury* (1985).
George L. McKay, *Some Notes on Robert Louis Stevenson, His Finances and His Agents and Publishers* (New Haven, 1958).

A CHRONOLOGY OF ROBERT LOUIS STEVENSON

1850 Born in Edinburgh, 13 November.

1862–3 Excursions with his parents to Germany, the Riviera and Italy.

1867 Enters Edinburgh University to study engineering.

1871 Makes decision to abandon engineering and study law.

1872 Passes preliminary examinations for the Scottish Bar.

1873 Crisis with his father over his agnosticism; following this, and a bout of ill health, goes to Suffolk to stay with his Balfour cousins. Meets Frances Sitwell, one of the most important influences on his life until his marriage. Beginning of his friendship with Sidney Colvin. Further ill health sends R.L.S. south to France at the end of the year.

1874 At Menton in France. Returns to Edinburgh in May and resumes reading for the Bar. Contributes to the *Cornhill Magazine*.

1875 Meets W. E. Henley in Edinburgh. Called to the Scottish Bar but does not practise as a barrister. Visits France and joins his cousin, Bob Stevenson, at the artists' colony at Barbizon, Fontainebleau (1875–6); contributes to *Vanity Fair* and the *Academy*.

1876 Makes a canoe trip around the canals of northern France, later to be recorded in *An Inland Voyage*. Meets Fanny Osbourne, a married woman with two children, from Indiana.

1877 Divides time between Edinburgh, London and Fontainebleau.

1878 Fanny returns to her husband in California and, eventually, divorce proceedings begin. R.L.S. goes on travels with his donkey, Modestine, in the Cévennes. Publication of *Edinburgh: Picturesque Notes* and *An Inland Voyage*.

1879 Divides times between London, Scotland and France. Very ill in March and April. Sets off on journey to join Fanny in America. *Travels with a Donkey* published.

1880 Marries Fanny in San Francisco in May. They stay in the Californian mountains and then return to Scotland. Publication of *Deacon Brodie*, R.L.S.'s first play in collaboration with W. E. Henley, and a drama which, in part, looks forward to *Jekyll and Hyde.*

1881 At Braemar, begins *Treasure Island* which is completed later in the same year at Davos in Switzerland. Begins 'The Travelling Companion', a forerunner of *Jekyll and Hyde*, later destroyed by R.L.S. Publication of *Virginibus Puerisque.*

1882 At Davos, then R.L.S. and Fanny move to Hyères, France, their main home from March 1883 to July 1884. Publication of *Familiar Studies of Men and Books* and *New Arabian Nights.*

1883 Publication of *The Silverado Squatters* and *Treasure Island.*

1884 Illness at Nice in January and further serious ill health in May. The Stevensons return to England at about the same time as an outbreak of cholera at Hyères. They go to Bournemouth, their home from September of this year until August 1887. Publication of *Austin Guinea* and *Beau Austin*, both in collaboration with W. E. Henley.

1885 Moves to 'Skerryvore', Bournemouth (the house was a wedding present from Thomas Stevenson to his daughter-in-law). Henry James spends a long visit in Bournemouth. Publication of *A Child's Garden of Verses*; *Prince Otto*; *More New Arabian Nights*; *The Dynamiter* (with Fanny); and *Macaire* (with W. E. Henley). Towards the end of this year, writes *The Strange Case of Dr Jekyll and Mr Hyde.*

1886 Publication of *Jekyll and Hyde* in January, followed by *Kidnapped.*

1887 Thomas Stevenson dies in May. In August, R.L.S. sails for America with his mother, Fanny and Lloyd. Very enthusiastic reception of R.L.S. in New York due to the immense success in America of *Jekyll and Hyde.* Stays at Saranac in the Adirondack Mountains. Publication of *The Merry Men and Other Tales and Fables*; *Memories and Portraits*; and *A Memoir of Fleeming Jenkin.*

1888 Scribner's, Stevenson's American publishers, commission a volume on the South Seas. Voyage on the yacht *Casco* to the Marquesas, the Paumotus, Tahiti, and then to Hawaii. Publication of *The Black Arrow* and *The Misadventures of John Nicholson.* 'A Chapter on Dreams' appeared in *Scribner's Magazine* in October.

1889 Mrs Thomas Stevenson returns to Scotland. R.L.S., Fanny and Lloyd remain in Honolulu. Voyage on the trading schooner *Equator* to the Gilbert Islands and then to Samoa. Publication of *The Wrong Box*, with Lloyd, and *The Master of Ballantrae*. Buys an estate at Upolu, Samoa.

1890 A third voyage in the trading steamer *Janet Nicholl*, in the Eastern and Western pacific. Ill health, including a serious haemorrhage, leads the Stevensons to realize that R.L.S. can never again leave a tropical climate. In October, they take up residence at Upolu. Publication of *In the South Seas* and *Ballads*.

1892 Becomes involved in Samoan politics. Publication of *A Footnote to History, Across the Plains* (includes 'A Chapter on Dreams') and *The Wrecker*. In October, has drawn up an outline of *Weir of Hermiston*.

1893 War breaks out in Samoa. Stevenson supports Mataafa. Visits Honolulu. Publication of *Island Nights' Entertainments* and *Catriona*. Works intermittently on *Weir of Hermiston*. Also on *St Ives*.

1894 The tribe of Mataafa build 'The Road of Loving Hearts' in gratitude to R.L.S. for helping their cause. Publication of *The Ebb Tide*. Returns to work on *Weir of Hermiston* in February, and again in September and November. Works also on *St Ives*. On 3 December works all morning on *Weir* and dies later that day of a cerebral haemorrhage.

1896 *Weir of Hermiston* posthumously published; serialized in *Cosmopolis*, January–April 1896. *St Ives* serialized *Pall Mall Magazine*, November 1896–7.

1897 *St Ives* published (American book edition; British book edition 1898).

schooner *Equator* to the Gilbert Islands and then to Samoa. Publication of *The Wrong Box*, with Lloyd, and *The Master of Ballantrae*. Buys an estate at Upolu, Samoa.

1890 A third voyage in the trading steamer *Janet Nicoll* in the Eastern and Western pacific. Ill health, including a serious haemorrhage, leads the Stevensons to realize that R.L.S. can never again leave a tropical climate. In October, they take up residence at Upolu. Publication of *In the South Seas* and *Ballads*.

1892 Becomes involved in Samoan politics. Publication of *A Footnote to History*, *Across the Plains* (includes 'A Chapter on Dreams') and *The Wrecker*. In October has drawn up an outline of *Weir of Hermiston*.

1893 War breaks out in Samoa. Stevenson supports Mataafa. Visits Honolulu. Publication of *Island Nights' Entertainments* and *Catriona*. Works intermittently on *Weir of Hermiston*. Also on *St Ives*.

1894 The tribe of Mataafa build 'The Road of Loving Hearts' in gratitude to R.L.S. for helping their cause. Publication of *The Ebb Tide*. Returns to work on *Weir of Hermiston* in February and again in September and November. Works also on *St Ives*. On 3 December works all morning on *Weir* and dies later that day of a cerebral haemorrhage.

1896 *Weir of Hermiston* posthumously published, serialized in *Cosmopolis*, January–April 1896. *St Ives* serialized *Pall Mall Magazine*, November 1896–7.

1897 *St Ives* published (American book edition; British book edition 1898).

The Strange Case of Dr Jekyll and Mr Hyde

TO

KATHARINE DE MATTOS*

It's ill to loose the bands that God decreed to bind;
Still will we be the children of the heather and the wind.
Far away from home, O it's still for you and me
That the broom is blowing bonnie in the north countrie.

CONTENTS

STORY OF THE DOOR 7
SEARCH FOR MR HYDE 14
DR JEKYLL WAS QUITE AT EASE 22
THE CAREW MURDER CASE 25
INCIDENT OF THE LETTER 30
REMARKABLE INCIDENT OF DR LANYON 35
INCIDENT AT THE WINDOW 39
THE LAST NIGHT 41
DR LANYON'S NARRATIVE 53
HENRY JEKYLL'S FULL STATEMENT OF THE CASE 60

THE

STRANGE CASE

OF

DR JEKYLL AND MR HYDE

STORY OF THE DOOR

MR UTTERSON the lawyer was a man of a rugged countenance, that was never lighted by a smile; cold, scanty and embarrassed in discourse; backward in sentiment; lean, long, dusty, dreary and yet somehow lovable. At friendly meetings, and when the wine was to his taste, something eminently human beaconed from his eye; something indeed which never found its way into his talk, but which spoke not only in these silent symbols of the after-dinner face, but more often and loudly in the acts of his life. He was austere with himself; drank gin when he was alone, to mortify a taste for vintages; and though he enjoyed the theatre, had not crossed the doors of one for twenty years. But he had an approved tolerance for others; sometimes wondering, almost with envy, at the high pressure of spirits involved in their misdeeds; and in any extremity inclined to help rather than to reprove. 'I incline to Cain's heresy,'* he used to say quaintly: 'I let my brother go to the devil in his own way.' In this character, it was frequently his fortune to be the last reputable acquaintance and the last good influence in the lives of down-going men. And to such as these, so long as they came about his chambers, he never marked a shade of change in his demeanour.

No doubt the feat was easy to Mr Utterson; for he was undemonstrative at the best, and even his friendships seemed to be founded in a similar catholicity of good-nature. It is the mark of a modest man to accept his friendly circle ready-made from the hands of opportunity; and that was the lawyer's way. His friends were those of his own blood or those whom he had known the longest; his affections, like ivy, were the growth of time, they implied no aptness in the object. Hence, no doubt, the bond that united him to Mr Richard Enfield, his distant kinsman, the well-known man about town. It was a nut to crack for many, what these two could see in each other or what subject they could find in common. It was reported by those who encountered them in their Sunday walks, that they said nothing, looked singularly dull, and would hail with obvious relief the appearance of a friend. For all that, the two men put the greatest store by these excursions, counted them the chief jewel of each week, and not only set aside occasions of pleasure, but even resisted the calls of business, that they might enjoy them uninterrupted.

It chanced on one of these rambles that their way led them down a by-street in a busy quarter of London. The street was small and what is called quiet, but it drove a thriving trade on the week-days. The inhabitants were all doing well, it seemed, and all emulously hoping to do better still, and laying out the surplus of their gains in coquetry; so that the shop fronts stood along that thoroughfare with an air of invitation, like rows of smiling saleswomen. Even on Sunday, when it veiled its more florid charms and lay comparatively empty of passage, the street shone out in contrast to its dingy neighbourhood, like a fire in a forest; and with its freshly painted shutters, well-polished brasses and general cleanliness and gaiety of note, instantly caught and pleased the eye of the passenger.

Two doors from one corner, on the left hand going east, the line was broken by the entry of a court; and just at that point, a certain sinister block of building thrust forward its gable on the street. It was two storeys high; showed no window, nothing but a door on the lower storey and a blind forehead of discoloured wall on the upper; and bore in every feature, the marks of prolonged and sordid negligence. The door, which was equipped with neither bell nor knocker, was blistered and distained. Tramps slouched into the recess and struck matches on the panels; children kept shop upon the steps; the schoolboy had tried his knife on the mouldings; and for close on a generation, no one had appeared to drive away these random visitors or to repair their ravages.

Mr Enfield and the lawyer were on the other side of the by-street; but when they came abreast of the entry, the former lifted up his cane and pointed.

'Did you ever remark that door?' he asked; and when his companion had replied in the affirmative, 'It is connected in my mind,' added he, 'with a very odd story.'

'Indeed?' said Mr Utterson, with a slight change of voice, 'and what was that?'

'Well, it was this way,' returned Mr Enfield: 'I was coming home from some place at the end of the world, about three o'clock of a black winter morning, and my way lay through a part of town where there was literally nothing to be seen but lamps. Street after street, and all the folks asleep—street after street, all lighted up as if for a procession and all as empty as a church—till at last I got into that state of mind when a man listens and listens and begins to long for the sight of a policeman. All at once, I saw two figures: one a little man who was stumping along eastward at a good walk, and the other a girl of maybe eight or ten who was running as hard as she was able down a cross street. Well, sir, the two ran into one another naturally enough at the corner; and then came the horrible part of the thing; for the man trampled calmly over the child's body and left her screaming on the ground. It sounds nothing to hear, but it was hellish to see. It wasn't like a man; it was like some damned Juggernaut.* I gave a view halloa, took to my heels, collared my gentleman, and brought him back to where there was already quite a group about the screaming child. He was perfectly cool and made no resistance, but gave me one look, so ugly that it brought out the sweat on me like running. The people who had turned out were the girl's own family; and pretty soon, the doctor, for whom she had been sent, put in his appearance. Well, the child was not much the worse, more frightened, according to the Sawbones; and there you might have supposed would be an end to it. But there was one curious circumstance. I had taken a loathing to my gentleman at first sight. So had the child's family, which was only natural. But the doctor's case was what struck me. He was the usual cut and dry apothecary, of no particular age and colour, with a strong Edinburgh accent, and about as emotional as a bagpipe. Well, sir, he was like the rest of us; every time he looked at my prisoner, I saw that Sawbones turn sick and white with the desire to kill him. I knew what was in his mind, just as he knew what was in mine; and killing being out of the question, we did the next best. We told the man we could and would make such a scandal out of this, as should make his name stink from one end of London to the other. If he had any friends or any credit, we undertook that he should lose them. And all the time, as we were pitching it in red hot, we were keeping the women off him as best we could, for they were as wild as harpies. I never saw a circle of such hateful faces; and there was the man in the middle, with a kind of black, sneering coolness—frightened too, I could see that—but carrying it off, sir, really like Satan. 'If you choose to make capital out of this accident,' said he, 'I am naturally helpless. No gentleman but wishes to avoid a scene,' says he. 'Name your figure.' Well, we screwed him up to a hundred pounds for the child's family; he would have clearly liked to stick out; but there was something about the lot of us that meant mischief, and at last he struck. The next thing was to get the money; and where do you think he carried us but to that place with the door?—whipped out a key, went in, and presently came back with the matter of ten pounds in gold and a cheque for the balance on Coutts's, drawn payable to bearer and signed with a name that I can't mention, though it's one of the points of my story, but it was a name at least very well known and often printed. The figure was stiff; but the signature was good for more than that, if it was only genuine. I took the liberty of pointing out to my gentleman that the whole business looked apocryphal, and that a man does not, in real life, walk into a cellar door at four in the morning and come out of it with another man's cheque for close upon a hundred pounds. But he was quite easy and sneering. 'Set your mind at rest,' says he, 'I will stay with you till the banks open and cash the cheque myself.' So we all set off, the doctor, and the child's father, and our friend and myself, and passed the rest of the night in my chambers; and next day, when we had breakfasted, went in a body to the bank. I gave in the cheque myself, and said I had every reason to believe it was a forgery. Not a bit of it. The cheque was genuine.'

'Tut-tut,' said Mr Utterson.

'I see you feel as I do,' said Mr Enfield. 'Yes, it's a bad story. For my man was a fellow that nobody could have to do with, a really damnable man; and the person that drew the cheque is the very pink of the proprieties, celebrated too, and (what makes it worse) one of your fellows who do what they call good. Black mail, I suppose; an honest man paying through the nose for some of the capers of his youth. Black Mail House is what I call that place with the door, in consequence. Though even that, you know, is far from explaining all,' he added, and with the words fell into a vein of musing.

From this he was recalled by Mr Utterson asking rather suddenly: 'And you don't know if the drawer of the cheque lives there?'

'A likely place isn't it?' returned Mr Enfield. 'But I happen to have noticed his address; he lives in some square or other.'

'And you never asked about—the place with the door?' said Mr Utterson.

'No, sir: I had a delicacy,' was the reply. 'I feel very strongly about putting questions; it partakes too much of the style of the day of judgment. You start a question, and it's like starting a stone. You sit quietly on the top of a hill; and away the stone goes, starting others; and presently some bland old bird (the last you would have thought of) is knocked on the head in his own back garden and the family have to change their name. No, sir, I make it a rule of mine: the more it looks like Queer Street,* the less I ask.'

'A very good rule, too,' said the lawyer.

'But I have studied the place for myself,' continued Mr Enfield. 'It seems scarcely a house. There is no other door, and nobody goes in or out of that one but, once in a great while, the gentleman of my adventure. There are three windows looking on the court on the first floor; none below; the windows are always shut but they're clean. And then there is a chimney which is generally smoking; so somebody must live there. And yet it's not so sure; for the buildings are so packed together about that court, that it's hard to say where one ends and another begins.'

The pair walked on again for a while in silence; and then 'Enfield,' said Mr Utterson, 'that's a good rule of yours.'

'Yes, I think it is,' returned Enfield.

'But for all that,' continued the lawyer, 'there's one point I want to ask: I want to ask the name of that man who walked over the child.'

'Well,' said Mr Enfield, 'I can't see what harm it would do. It was a man of the name of Hyde.'

'Hm,' said Mr Utterson. 'What sort of a man is he to see?'

'He is not easy to describe. There is something wrong with his appearance; something displeasing, something downright detestable. I never saw a man I so disliked, and yet I scarce know why. He must be deformed somewhere; he gives a strong feeling of deformity, although I couldn't specify the point. He's an extraordinary looking man, and yet I really can name nothing out of the way. No, sir; I can make no hand of it; I can't describe him. And it's not want of memory; for I declare I can see him this moment.'

Mr Utterson again walked some way in silence and obviously under a weight of consideration. 'You are sure he used a key?' he inquired at last.

'My dear sir . . .' began Enfield, surprised out of himself.

'Yes, I know,' said Utterson; 'I know it must seem strange. The fact is, if I do not ask you the name of the other party, it is because I know it already. You see, Richard, your tale has gone home. If you have been inexact in any point, you had better correct it.'

'I think you might have warned me,' returned the other with a touch of sullenness. 'But I have been pedantically exact, as you call it. The fellow had a key; and what's more, he has it still. I saw him use it, not a week ago.'

Mr Utterson sighed deeply but said never a word; and the young man presently resumed. 'Here is another lesson to say nothing,' said he. 'I am ashamed of my long tongue. Let us make a bargain never to refer to this again.'

'With all my heart,' said the lawyer. 'I shake hands on that, Richard.'

SEARCH FOR MR HYDE

THAT evening, Mr Utterson came home to his bachelor house in sombre spirits and sat down to dinner without relish. It was his custom of a Sunday, when this meal was over, to sit close by the fire, a volume of some dry divinity on his reading desk, until the clock of the neighbouring church rang out the hour of twelve, when he would go soberly and gratefully to bed. On this night, however, as soon as the cloth was taken away, he took up a candle and went into his business room. There he opened his safe, took from the most private part of it a document endorsed on the envelope as Dr Jekyll's Will, and sat down with a clouded brow to study its contents. The will was holograph, for Mr Utterson, though he took charge of it now that it was made, had refused to lend the least assistance in the making of it; it provided not only that, in case of the decease of Henry Jekyll, M.D., D.C.L., LL.D., F.R.S., &c., all his possessions were to pass into the hands of his 'friend and benefactor Edward Hyde,' but that in case of Dr Jekyll's 'disappearance or unexplained absence for any period exceeding three calendar months,' the said Edward Hyde should step into the said Henry Jekyll's shoes without further delay* and free from any burthen or obligation, beyond the payment of a few small sums to the members of the doctor's household. This document had long been the lawyer's eyesore. It offended him both as a lawyer and as a lover of the sane and customary sides of life, to whom the fanciful was the immodest. And hitherto it was his ignorance of Mr Hyde that had swelled his indignation; now, by a sudden turn, it was his knowledge. It was already bad enough when the name was but a name of which he could learn no more. It was worse when it began to be clothed upon with detestable attributes; and out of the shifting, insubstantial mist that had so long baffled his eye, there leaped up the sudden, definite presentment of a fiend.

'I thought it was madness,' he said, as he replaced the obnoxious paper in the safe, 'and now I begin to fear it is disgrace.'

With that he blew out his candle, put on a great coat and set forth in the direction of Cavendish Square, that citadel of medicine, where his friend, the great Dr Lanyon, had his house and received his crowding patients. 'If anyone knows, it will be Lanyon,' he had thought.

The solemn butler knew and welcomed him; he was subjected to no stage of delay, but ushered direct from the door to the dining-room where Dr Lanyon sat alone over his wine. This was a hearty, healthy, dapper, red-faced gentleman, with a shock of hair prematurely white, and a boisterous and decided manner. At sight of Mr Utterson, he sprang up from his chair and welcomed him with both hands. The geniality, as was the way of the man, was somewhat theatrical to the eye; but it reposed on genuine feeling. For these two were old friends, old mates both at school and college, both thorough respecters of themselves and of each other, and, what does not always follow, men who thoroughly enjoyed each other's company.

After a little rambling talk, the lawyer led up to the subject which so disagreeably preoccupied his mind.

'I suppose, Lanyon,' said he, 'you and I must be the two oldest friends that Henry Jekyll has?'

'I wish the friends were younger,' chuckled Dr Lanyon. 'But I suppose we are. And what of that? I see little of him now.'

'Indeed?' said Utterson. 'I thought you had a bond of common interest.'

'We had,' was the reply. 'But it is more than ten years since Henry Jekyll became too fanciful for me. He began to go wrong, wrong in mind; and though of course I continue to take an interest in him for old sake's sake as they say, I see and I have seen devilish little of the man. Such unscientific balderdash,' added the doctor, flushing suddenly purple, 'would have estranged Damon and Pythias.'*

This little spirt of temper was somewhat of a relief to Mr Utterson. 'They have only differed on some point of science,' he thought; and being a man of no scientific passions (except in the matter of conveyancing) he even added: 'It is nothing worse than that!' He gave his friend a few seconds to recover his composure, and then approached the question he had come to put. 'Did you ever come across a protégé of his—one Hyde?' he asked.

'Hyde?' repeated Lanyon. 'No. Never heard of him. Since my time.'

That was the amount of information that the lawyer carried back with him to the great, dark bed on which he tossed to and fro, until the small hours of the morning began to grow large. It was a night of little ease to his toiling mind, toiling in mere darkness and besieged by questions.

Six o'clock struck on the bells of the church that was so conveniently near to Mr Utterson's dwelling, and still he was digging at the problem. Hitherto it had touched him on the intellectual side alone; but now his imagination also was engaged or rather enslaved; and as he lay and tossed in the gross darkness of the night and the curtained room, Mr Enfield's tale went by before his mind in a scroll of lighted pictures. He would be aware of the great field of lamps of a nocturnal city; then of the figure of a man walking swiftly; then of a child running from the doctor's; and then these met, and that human Juggernaut trod the child down and passed on regardless of her screams. Or else he would see a room in a rich house, where his friend lay asleep, dreaming and smiling at his dreams; and then the door of that room would be opened, the curtains of the bed plucked apart, the sleeper recalled, and lo! there would stand by his side a figure to whom power was given, and even at that dead hour, he must rise and do its bidding. The figure in these two phases haunted the lawyer all night; and if at any time he dozed over, it was but to see it glide more stealthily through sleeping houses, or move the more swiftly and still the more swiftly, even to dizziness, through wider labyrinths of lamplighted city, and at every street corner crush a child and leave her screaming. And still the figure had no face by which he might know it; even in his dreams, it had no face, or one that baffled him and melted before his eyes; and thus it was that there sprang up and grew apace in the lawyer's mind a singularly strong, almost an inordinate, curiosity to behold the features of the real Mr Hyde. If he could but once set eyes on him, he thought the mystery would lighten and perhaps roll altogether away, as was the habit of mysterious things when well examined. He might see a reason for his friend's strange preference or bondage (call it which you please) and even for the startling clauses of the will. And at least it would be a face worth seeing: the face of a man who was without bowels of mercy: a face which had but to show itself to raise up, in the mind of the unimpressionable Enfield, a spirit of enduring hatred.

From that time forward, Mr Utterson began to haunt the door in the by-street of shops. In the morning before office hours, at noon when business was plenty and time scarce, at night under the face of the fogged city moon, by all lights and at all hours of solitude or concourse, the lawyer was to be found on his chosen post.

'If he be Mr Hyde,' he had thought, 'I shall be Mr Seek.'

And at last his patience was rewarded. It was a fine dry night; frost in the air; the streets as clean as a ballroom floor; the lamps, unshaken by any wind, drawing a regular pattern of light and shadow. By ten o'clock, when the shops were closed, the by-street was very solitary and, in spite of the low growl of London from all round, very silent. Small sounds carried far; domestic sounds out of the houses were clearly audible on either side of the roadway; and the rumour of the approach of any passenger preceded him by a long time. Mr Utterson had been some minutes at his post, when he was aware of an odd, light footstep drawing near. In the course of his nightly patrols, he had long grown accustomed to the quaint effect with which the footfalls of a single person, while he is still a great way off, suddenly spring out distinct from the vast hum and clatter of the city. Yet his attention had never before been so sharply and decisively arrested; and it was with a strong, superstitious prevision of success that he withdrew into the entry of the court.

The steps drew swiftly nearer, and swelled out suddenly louder as they turned the end of the street. The lawyer, looking forth from the entry, could soon see what manner of man he had to deal with. He was small and very plainly dressed, and the look of him, even at that distance, went somehow strongly against the watcher's inclination. But he made straight for the door, crossing the roadway to save time; and as he came, he drew a key from his pocket like one approaching home.

Mr Utterson stepped out and touched him on the shoulder as he passed. 'Mr Hyde, I think?'

Mr Hyde shrank back with a hissing intake of the breath. But his fear was only momentary; and though he did not look the lawyer in the face, he answered coolly enough: 'That is my name. What do you want?'

'I see you are going in,' returned the lawyer. 'I am an old friend of Dr Jekyll's—Mr Utterson of Gaunt Street—you must have heard my name; and meeting you so conveniently, I thought you might admit me.'

'You will not find Dr Jekyll; he is from home,' replied Mr Hyde, blowing in the key. And then suddenly, but still without looking up, 'How did you know me?' he asked.

'On your side,' said Mr Utterson, 'will you do me a favour?'

'With pleasure,' replied the other. 'What shall it be?'

'Will you let me see your face?' asked the lawyer.

Mr Hyde appeared to hesitate, and then, as if upon some sudden reflection, fronted about with an air of defiance; and the pair stared at each other pretty fixedly for a few seconds. 'Now I shall know you again,' said Mr Utterson. 'It may be useful.'

'Yes,' returned Mr Hyde, 'it is as well we have met; and *à propos*, you should have my address.' And he gave a number of a street in Soho.

'Good God!' thought Mr Utterson, 'can he too have been thinking of the will?' But he kept his feelings to himself and only grunted in acknowledgement of the address.

'And now,' said the other, 'how did you know me?'

'By description,' was the reply.

'Whose description?'

'We have common friends,' said Mr Utterson.

'Common friends?' echoed Mr Hyde, a little hoarsely. 'Who are they?'

'Jekyll, for instance,' said the lawyer.

'He never told you,' cried Mr Hyde, with a flush of anger. 'I did not think you would have lied.'

'Come,' said Mr Utterson, 'that is not fitting language.'

The other snarled aloud into a savage laugh; and the next moment, with extraordinary quickness, he had unlocked the door and disappeared into the house.

The lawyer stood awhile when Mr Hyde had left him, the picture of disquietude. Then he began slowly to mount the street, pausing every step or two and putting his hand to his brow like a man in mental perplexity. The problem he was thus debating as he walked, was one of a class that is rarely solved. Mr Hyde was pale and dwarfish, he gave an impression of deformity without any nameable malformation, he had a displeasing smile, he had borne himself to the lawyer with a sort of murderous mixture of timidity and boldness, and he spoke with a husky, whispering and somewhat broken voice; all these were points against him, but not all of these together could explain the hitherto unknown disgust, loathing and fear with which Mr Utterson regarded him. 'There must be something else,' said the perplexed gentleman. 'There *is* something more, if I could find a name for it. God bless me, the man seems hardly human! Something troglodytic, shall we say? or can it be the old story of Dr Fell?* or is it the mere radiance of a foul soul that thus transpires through, and transfigures, its clay continent? The last, I think; for O my poor old Harry Jekyll, if ever I read Satan's signature upon a face, it is on that of your new friend.'

Round the corner from the by-street, there was a square of ancient, handsome houses, now for the most part decayed from their high estate and let in flats and chambers to all sorts and conditions of men: map-engravers, architects, shady lawyers and the agents of obscure enterprises. One house, however, second from the corner, was still occupied entire; and at the door of this, which wore a great air of wealth and comfort, though it was now plunged in darkness except for the fan-light, Mr Utterson stopped and knocked. A well-dressed, elderly servant opened the door.

'Is Dr Jekyll at home, Poole?' asked the lawyer.

'I will see, Mr Utterson,' said Poole, admitting the visitor, as he spoke, into a large, low-roofed, comfortable hall, paved with flags, warmed (after the fashion of a country house) by a bright, open fire, and furnished with costly cabinets of oak. 'Will you wait here by the fire, sir? or shall I give you a light in the dining-room?'

'Here, thank you,' said the lawyer, and he drew near and leaned on the tall fender. This hall, in which he was now left alone, was a pet fancy of his friend the doctor's; and Utterson himself was wont to speak of it as the pleasantest room in London. But to-night there was a shudder in his blood; the face of Hyde sat heavy on his memory; he felt (what was rare with him) a nausea and distaste of life; and in the gloom of his spirits, he seemed to read a menace in the flickering of the firelight on the polished cabinets and the uneasy starting of the shadow on the roof. He was ashamed of his relief, when Poole presently returned to announce that Dr Jekyll was gone out.

'I saw Mr Hyde go in by the old dissecting room door, Poole,' he said. 'Is that right, when Dr Jekyll is from home?'

'Quite right, Mr Utterson, sir,' replied the servant. 'Mr Hyde has a key.'

'Your master seems to repose a great deal of trust in that young man, Poole,' resumed the other musingly.

'Yes, sir, he do indeed,' said Poole. 'We have all orders to obey him.'

'I do not think I ever met Mr Hyde?' asked Utterson.

'O, dear no, sir. He never *dines* here,' replied the butler. 'Indeed we see very little of him on this side of the house; he mostly comes and goes by the laboratory.'

'Well, good night, Poole.'

'Good night, Mr Utterson.'

And the lawyer set out homeward with a very heavy heart. 'Poor Harry Jekyll,' he thought, 'my mind misgives me he is in deep waters! He was wild when he was young; a long while ago to be sure; but in the law of God, there is no statute of limitations. Ay, it must be that; the ghost of some old sin, the cancer of some concealed disgrace; punishment coming, *pede claudo*,* years after memory has forgotten and self-love condoned the fault.' And the lawyer, scared by the thought, brooded awhile on his own past, groping in all the corners of memory, lest by chance some Jack-in-the-Box of an old iniquity should leap to light there. His past was fairly blameless; few men could read the rolls of their life with less apprehension; yet he was humbled to the dust by the many ill things he had done, and raised up again into a sober and fearful gratitude by the many that he had come so near to doing, yet avoided. And then by a return on his former subject, he conceived a spark of hope. 'This Master Hyde, if he were studied,' thought he, 'must have secrets of his own: black secrets, by the look of him; secrets compared to which poor Jekyll's worst would be like sunshine. Things cannot continue as they are. It turns me cold to think of this creature stealing like a thief to Harry's bedside; poor Harry, what a wakening! And the danger of it; for if this Hyde suspects the existence of the will, he may grow impatient to inherit. Ay, I must put my shoulder to the wheel—if Jekyll will but let me,' he added, 'if Jekyll will only let me.' For once more he saw before his mind's eye, as clear as a transparency, the strange clauses of the will.

DR JEKYLL WAS QUITE AT EASE

A FORTNIGHT later, by excellent good fortune, the doctor gave one of his pleasant dinners to some five or six old cronies, all intelligent, reputable men and all judges of good wine; and Mr Utterson so contrived that he remained behind after the others had departed. This was no new arrangement, but a thing that had befallen many scores of times. Where Utterson was liked, he was liked well. Hosts loved to detain the dry lawyer, when the light-hearted and the loose-tongued had already their foot on the threshold; they liked to sit awhile in his unobtrusive company, practising for solitude, sobering their minds in the man's rich silence after the expense and strain of gaiety. To this rule, Dr Jekyll was no exception; and as he now sat on the opposite side of the fire—a large, well-made, smooth-faced man of fifty, with something of a slyish cast perhaps, but every mark of capacity and kindness—you could see by his looks that he cherished for Mr Utterson a sincere and warm affection.

'I have been wanting to speak to you, Jekyll,' began the latter. 'You know that will of yours?'

A close observer might have gathered that the topic was distasteful; but the doctor carried it off gaily. 'My poor Utterson,' said he, 'you are unfortunate in such a client. I never saw a man so distressed as you were by my will; unless it were that hide-bound pedant, Lanyon, at what he called my scientific heresies. O, I know he's a good fellow—you needn't frown—an excellent fellow, and I always mean to see more of him; but a hide-bound pedant for all that; an ignorant, blatant pedant. I was never more disappointed in any man than Lanyon.'

'You know I never approved of it,' pursued Utterson, ruthlessly disregarding the fresh topic.

'My will? Yes, certainly, I know that,' said the doctor, a trifle sharply. 'You have told me so.'

'Well, I tell you so again,' continued the lawyer. 'I have been learning something of young Hyde.'

The large handsome face of Dr Jekyll grew pale to the very lips, and there came a blackness about his eyes. 'I do not care to hear more,' said he. 'This is a matter I thought we had agreed to drop.'

'What I heard was abominable,' said Utterson.

'It can make no change. You do not understand my position,' returned the doctor, with a certain incoherency of manner. 'I am painfully situated, Utterson; my position is a very strange—a very strange one. It is one of those affairs that cannot be mended by talking.'

'Jekyll,' said Utterson, 'you know me: I am a man to be trusted. Make a clean breast of this in confidence; and I make no doubt I can get you out of it.'

'My good Utterson,' said the doctor, 'this is very good of you, this is downright good of you, and I cannot find words to thank you in. I believe you fully; I would trust you before any man alive, ay, before myself, if I could make the choice; but indeed it isn't what you fancy; it is not so bad as that; and just to put your good heart at rest, I will tell you one thing: the moment I choose, I can be rid of Mr Hyde. I give you my hand upon that; and I thank you again and again; and I will just add one little word, Utterson, that I'm sure you'll take in good part: this is a private matter, and I beg of you to let it sleep.'

Utterson reflected a little looking in the fire.

'I have no doubt you are perfectly right,' he said at last, getting to his feet.

'Well, but since we have touched upon this business, and for the last time I hope,' continued the doctor, 'there is one point I should like you to understand. I have really a very great interest in poor Hyde. I know you have seen him; he told me so; and I fear he was rude. But I do sincerely take a great, a very great interest in that young man; and if I am taken away, Utterson, I wish you to promise me that you will bear with him and get his rights for him. I think you would, if you knew all; and it would be a weight off my mind if you would promise.'

'I can't pretend that I shall ever like him,' said the lawyer.

'I don't ask that,' pleaded Jekyll, laying his hand upon the other's arm; 'I only ask for justice; I only ask you to help him for my sake, when I am no longer here.'

Utterson heaved an irrepressible sigh. 'Well,' said he. 'I promise.'

THE CAREW MURDER CASE

NEARLY a year later, in the month of October 18—, London was startled by a crime of singular ferocity and rendered all the more notable by the high position of the victim. The details were few and startling. A maid servant living alone in a house not far from the river, had gone upstairs to bed about eleven. Although a fog rolled over the city in the small hours, the early part of the night was cloudless, and the lane, which the maid's window overlooked, was brilliantly lit by the full moon. It seems she was romantically given, for she sat down upon her box, which stood immediately under the window, and fell into a dream of musing. Never (she used to say, with streaming tears, when she narrated that experience) never had she felt more at peace with all men or thought more kindly of the world. And as she so sat she became aware of an aged and beautiful gentleman with white hair, drawing near along the lane; and advancing to meet him, another and very small gentleman, to whom at first she paid less attention. When they had come within speech (which was just under the maid's eyes) the older man bowed and accosted the other with a very pretty manner of politeness. It did not seem as if the subject of his address were of great importance; indeed, from his pointing, it sometimes appeared as if he were only inquiring his way; but the moon shone on his face as he spoke, and the girl was pleased to watch it, it seemed to breathe such an innocent and old-world kindness of disposition, yet with something high too, as of a well-founded self-content. Presently her eye wandered to the other, and she was surprised to recognise in him a certain Mr Hyde, who had once visited her master and for whom she had conceived a dislike. He had in his hand a heavy cane, with which he was trifling; but he answered never a word, and seemed to listen with an ill-contained impatience. And then all of a sudden he broke out in a great flame of anger, stamping with his foot, brandishing the cane, and carrying on (as the maid described it) like a madman. The old gentleman took a step back, with the air of one very much surprised and a trifle hurt; and at that Mr Hyde broke out of all bounds and clubbed him to the earth. And next moment, with ape-like fury, he was trampling his victim under foot, and hailing down a storm of blows, under which the bones were audibly shattered and the body jumped upon the roadway. At the horror of these sights and sounds, the maid fainted.

It was two o'clock when she came to herself and called for the police. The murderer was gone long ago; but there lay his victim in the middle of the lane, incredibly mangled. The stick with which the deed had been done, although it was of some rare and very tough and heavy wood, had broken in the middle under the stress of this insensate cruelty; and one splintered half had rolled in the neighbouring gutter—the other, without doubt, had been carried away by the murderer. A purse and a gold watch were found upon the victim; but no cards or papers, except a sealed and stamped envelope, which he had been probably carrying to the post, and which bore the name and address of Mr Utterson.

This was brought to the lawyer the next morning, before he was out of bed; and he had no sooner seen it, and been told the circumstances, than he shot out a solemn lip. 'I shall say nothing till I have seen the body,' said he; 'this may be very serious. Have the kindness to wait while I dress.' And with the same grave countenance he hurried through his breakfast and drove to the police station, whither the body had been carried. As soon as he came into the cell, he nodded.

'Yes,' said he, 'I recognise him. I am sorry to say that this is Sir Danvers Carew.'

'Good God, sir,' exclaimed the officer, 'is it possible?' And the next moment his eye lighted up with professional ambition. 'This will make a deal of noise,' he said. 'And perhaps you can help us to the man.' And he briefly narrated what the maid had seen, and showed the broken stick.

Mr Utterson had already quailed at the name of Hyde; but when the stick was laid before him, he could doubt no longer: broken and battered as it was, he recognised it for one that he had himself presented many years before to Henry Jekyll.

'Is this Mr Hyde a person of small stature?' he inquired.

'Particularly small and particularly wicked-looking, is what the maid calls him,' said the officer.

Mr Utterson reflected; and then, raising his head, 'If you will come with me in my cab,' he said, 'I think I can take you to his house.'

It was by this time about nine in the morning, and the first fog of the season. A great chocolate-coloured pall lowered over heaven, but the wind was continually charging and routing these embattled vapours; so that as the cab crawled from street to street, Mr Utterson beheld a marvellous number of degrees and hues of twilight; for here it would be dark like the back-end of evening; and there would be a glow of a rich, lurid brown, like the light of some strange conflagration; and here, for a moment, the fog would be quite broken up, and a haggard shaft of daylight would glance in between the swirling wreaths. The dismal quarter of Soho seen under these changing glimpses, with its muddy ways, and slatternly passengers, and its lamps, which had never been extinguished or had been kindled afresh to combat this mournful rëinvasion of darkness, seemed, in the lawyer's eyes, like a district of some city in a nightmare. The thoughts of his mind, besides, were of the gloomiest dye; and when he glanced at the companion of his drive, he was conscious of some touch of that terror of the law and the law's officers, which may at times assail the most honest.

As the cab drew up before the address indicated, the fog lifted a little and showed him a dingy street, a gin palace, a low French eating house, a shop for the retail of penny numbers and twopenny salads, many ragged children huddled in the doorways, and many women of many different nationalities passing out, key in hand, to have a morning glass; and the next moment the fog settled down again upon that part, as brown as umber, and cut him off from his blackguardly surroundings. This was the home of Henry Jekyll's favourite; of a man who was heir to a quarter of a million sterling.

An ivory-faced and silvery-haired old woman opened the door. She had an evil face, smoothed by hypocrisy; but her manners were excellent. Yes, she said, this was Mr Hyde's, but he was not at home; he had been in that night very late, but had gone away again in less than an hour; there was nothing strange in that; his habits were very irregular, and he was often absent; for instance, it was nearly two months since she had seen him till yesterday.

'Very well then, we wish to see his rooms,' said the lawyer; and when the woman began to declare it was impossible, 'I had better tell you who this person is,' he added. 'This is Inspector Newcomen of Scotland Yard.'

A flash of odious joy appeared upon the woman's face. 'Ah!' said she, 'he is in trouble! What has he done?'

Mr Utterson and the inspector exchanged glances. 'He don't seem a very popular character,' observed the latter. 'And now, my good woman, just let me and this gentleman have a look about us.'

In the whole extent of the house, which but for the old woman remained otherwise empty, Mr Hyde had only used a couple of rooms; but these were furnished with luxury and good taste. A closet was filled with wine; the plate was of silver, the napery elegant; a good picture hung upon the walls, a gift (as Utterson supposed) from Henry Jekyll,* who was much of a connoisseur; and the carpets were of many piles and agreeable in colour. At this moment, however, the rooms bore every mark of having been recently and hurriedly ransacked; clothes lay about the floor, with their pockets inside out; lockfast drawers stood open; and on the hearth there lay a pile of gray ashes, as though many papers had been burned. From these embers the inspector disinterred the butt end of a green cheque book, which had resisted the action of the fire; the other half of the stick was found behind the door; and as this clinched his suspicions, the officer declared himself delighted. A visit to the bank, where several thousand pounds were found to be lying to the murderer's credit, completed his gratification.

'You may depend upon it, sir,' he told Mr Utterson: 'I have him in my hand. He must have lost his head, or he never would have left the stick or, above all, burned the cheque book. Why, money's life to the man. We have nothing to do but wait for him at the bank, and get out the handbills.'

This last, however, was not so easy of accomplishment; for

Mr Hyde had numbered few familiars—even the master of the servant maid had only seen him twice; his family could nowhere be traced; he had never been photographed; and the few who could describe him differed widely, as common observers will. Only on one point, were they agreed; and that was the haunting sense of unexpressed deformity with which the fugitive impressed his beholders.

INCIDENT OF THE LETTER

IT was late in the afternoon, when Mr Utterson found his way to Dr Jekyll's door, where he was at once admitted by Poole, and carried down by the kitchen offices and across a yard which had once been a garden, to the building which was indifferently known as the laboratory or the dissecting rooms. The doctor had bought the house from the heirs of a celebrated surgeon; and his own tastes being rather chemical than anatomical, had changed the destination of the block at the bottom of the garden. It was the first time that the lawyer had been received in that part of his friend's quarters; and he eyed the dingy windowless structure with curiosity, and gazed round with a distasteful sense of strangeness as he crossed the theatre, once crowded with eager students now lying gaunt and silent, the tables laden with chemical apparatus, the floor strewn with crates and littered with packing straw, and the light falling dimly through the foggy cupola. At the further end, a flight of stairs mounted to a door covered with red baize; and through this Mr Utterson was at last received into the doctor's cabinet. It was a large room, fitted round with glass presses, furnished, among other things, with a cheval-glass and a business table, and looking out upon the court by three dusty windows barred with iron. The fire burned in the grate; a lamp was set lighted on the chimney shelf, for even in the houses the fog began to lie thickly; and there, close up to the warmth. sat Dr Jekyll, looking deadly sick. He did not rise to meet his visitor, but held out a cold hand and bade him welcome in a changed voice.

'And now,' said Mr Utterson, as soon as Poole had left them, 'you have heard the news?'

The doctor shuddered 'They were crying it in the square,' he said. 'I heard them in my dining room.'

'One word,' said the lawyer. 'Carew was my client, but so are you, and I want to know what I am doing. You have not been mad enough to hide this fellow?'

'Utterson, I swear to God,' cried the doctor. 'I swear to God

I will never set eyes on him again. I bind my honour to you that I am done with him in this world. It is all at an end. And indeed he does not want my help; you do not know him as I do; he is safe, he is quite safe; mark my words, he will never more be heard of.'

The lawyer listened gloomily; he did not like his friend's feverish manner. 'You seem pretty sure of him,' said he; 'and for your sake, I hope you may be right. If it came to a trial, your name might appear.'

'I am quite sure of him,' replied Jekyll; 'I have grounds for certainty that I cannot share with anyone. But there is one thing on which you may advise me. I have—I have received a letter; and I am at a loss whether I should show it to the police. I should like to leave it in your hands, Utterson; you would judge wisely I am sure; I have so great a trust in you.'

'You fear, I suppose, that it might lead to his detection?' asked the lawyer.

'No,' said the other. 'I cannot say that I care what becomes of Hyde; I am quite done with him. I was thinking of my own character, which this hateful business has rather exposed.'

Utterson ruminated awhile; he was surprised at his friend's selfishness, and yet relieved by it. 'Well,' said he, at last, 'let me see the letter.'

The letter was written in an odd, upright hand and signed 'Edward Hyde': and it signified, briefly enough, that the writer's benefactor, Dr Jekyll, whom he had long so unworthily repaid for a thousand generosities, need labour under no alarm for his safety as he had means of escape on which he placed a sure dependence. The lawyer liked this letter well enough; it put a better colour on the intimacy than he had looked for; and he blamed himself for some of his past suspicions.

'Have you the envelope?' he asked.

'I burned it,' replied Jekyll, 'before I thought what I was about. But it bore no postmark. The note was handed in.'

'Shall I keep this and sleep upon it?' asked Utterson.

'I wish you to judge for me entirely,' was the reply. 'I have lost confidence in myself.'

'Well, I shall consider,' returned the lawyer. 'And now one

word more: it was Hyde who dictated the terms in your will about that disappearance?'

The doctor seemed seized with a qualm of faintness; he shut his mouth tight and nodded.

'I knew it,' said Utterson. 'He meant to murder you. You have had a fine escape.'

'I have had what is far more to the purpose,' returned the doctor solemnly: 'I have had a lesson—O God, Utterson, what a lesson I have had!' And he covered his face for a moment with his hands.

On his way out, the lawyer stopped and had a word or two with Poole. 'By the by,' said he, 'there was a letter handed in to-day: what was the messenger like?' But Poole was positive nothing had come except by post; 'and only circulars by that,' he added.

This news sent off the visitor with his fears renewed. Plainly the letter had come by the laboratory door; possibly, indeed, it had been written in the cabinet; and if that were so, it must be differently judged, and handled with the more caution. The newsboys, as he went, were crying themselves hoarse along the footways: 'Special edition. Shocking murder of an M.P.' That was the funeral oration of one friend and client; and he could not help a certain apprehension lest the good name of another should be sucked down in the eddy of the scandal. It was, at least, a ticklish decision that he had to make; and self-reliant as he was by habit, he began to cherish a longing for advice. It was not to be had directly; but perhaps, he thought, it might be fished for.

Presently after, he sat on one side of his own hearth, with Mr Guest, his head clerk, upon the other, and midway between, at a nicely calculated distance from the fire, a bottle of a particular old wine that had long dwelt unsunned in the foundations of his house. The fog still slept on the wing above the drowned city, where the lamps glimmered like carbuncles; and through the muffle and smother of these fallen clouds, the procession of the town's life was still rolling in through the great arteries with a sound as of a mighty wind. But the room was gay with firelight. In the bottle the acids were long ago resolved; the imperial dye had softened with time, as the colour grows richer in stained windows; and the glow of hot autumn afternoons on hillside vineyards, was ready to be set free and to disperse the fogs of London. Insensibly the lawyer melted. There was no man from whom he kept fewer secrets than Mr Guest; and he was not always sure that he kept as many as he meant. Guest had often been on business to the doctor's; he knew Poole; he could scarce have failed to hear of Mr Hyde's familiarity about the house; he might draw conclusions: was it not as well, then, that he should see a letter which put that mystery to rights? and above all since Guest, being a great student and critic of handwriting, would consider the step natural and obliging? The clerk, besides, was a man of counsel; he would scarce read so strange document without dropping a remark; and by that remark Mr Utterson might shape his future course.

'This is a sad business about Sir Danvers,' he said.

'Yes, sir, indeed. It has elicited a great deal of public feeling,' returned Guest. 'The man, of course, was mad.'

'I should like to hear your views on that,' replied Utterson. 'I have a document here in his handwriting; it is between ourselves, for I scarce know what to do about it; it is an ugly business at the best. But there it is; quite in your way: a murderer's autograph.'

Guest's eyes brightened, and he sat down at once and studied it with passion. 'No, sir,' he said; 'not mad; but it is an odd hand.'

'And by all accounts a very odd writer,' added the lawyer.

Just then the servant entered with a note.

'Is that from Doctor Jekyll, sir?' inquired the clerk. 'I thought I knew the writing. Anything private, Mr Utterson?'

'Only an invitation to dinner. Why? do you want to see it?'

'One moment. I thank you, sir;' and the clerk laid the two sheets of paper alongside and sedulously compared their contents. 'Thank you, sir,' he said at last, returning both; 'it's a very interesting autograph.'

There was a pause, during which Mr Utterson struggled with himself. 'Why did you compare them, Guest?' he inquired suddenly.

'Well, sir,' returned the clerk, 'there's a rather singular

resemblance; the two hand are in many points identical: only differently sloped.'

'Rather quaint,' said Utterson.

'It is, as you say, rather quaint,' returned Guest.

'I wouldn't speak of this note, you know,' said the master.

'No, sir,' said the clerk. 'I understand.'

But no sooner was Mr. Utterson alone that night, than he locked the note into his safe where it reposed from that time forward. 'What!' he thought. 'Henry Jekyll forge for a murderer!' And his blood ran cold in his veins.

REMARKABLE INCIDENT OF DOCTOR LANYON

TIME ran on; thousands of pounds were offered in reward, for the death of Sir Danvers was resented as a public injury; but Mr Hyde had disappeared out of the ken of the police as though he had never existed. Much of his past was unearthed, indeed, and all disreputable: tales came out of the man's cruelty, at once so callous and violent, of his vile life, of his strange associates, of the hatred that seemed to have surrounded his career; but of his present whereabouts, not a whisper. From the time he had left the house in Soho on the morning of the murder, he was simply blotted out; and gradually, as time drew on, Mr Utterson began to recover from the hotness of his alarm, and to grow more at quiet with himself. The death of Sir Danvers was, to his way of thinking, more than paid for by the disappearance of Mr Hyde. Now that that evil influence had been withdrawn, a new life began for Dr Jekyll. He came out of his seclusion, renewed relations with his friends, became once more their familiar guest and entertainer; and whilst he had always been known for charities, he was now no less distinguished for religion. He was busy, he was much in the open air, he did good; his face seemed to open and brighten, as if with an inward consciousness of service; and for more than two months, the doctor was at peace.

On the 8th of January Utterson had dined at the doctor's with a small party; Lanyon had been there; and the face of the host had looked from one to the other as in the old days when the trio were inseparable friends. On the 12th, and again on the 14th, the door was shut against the lawyer. 'The doctor was confined to the house,' Poole said, 'and saw no one.' On the 15th, he tried again, and was again refused; and having now been used for the last two months to see his friend almost daily, he found this return of solitude to weigh upon his spirits. The fifth night, he had in Guest to dine with him; and the sixth he betook himself to Doctor Lanyon's.

There at least he was not denied admittance; but when he came in, he was shocked at the change which had taken place in the doctor's appearance. He had his death-warrant written legibly upon his face. The rosy man had grown pale; his flesh had fallen away; he was visibly balder and older; and yet it was not so much these tokens of a swift physical decay that arrested the lawyer's notice, as a look in the eye and quality of manner that seemed to testify to some deep-seated terror of the mind. It was unlikely that the doctor should fear death; and yet that was what Utterson was tempted to suspect. 'Yes,' he thought; 'he is a doctor, he must know his own state and that his days are counted; and the knowledge is more than he can bear.' And yet when Utterson remarked on his ill-looks, it was with an air of great firmness that Lanyon declared himself a doomed man.

'I have had a shock,' he said, 'and I shall never recover. It is a question of weeks. Well, life has been pleasant; I liked it; yes, sir, I used to like it. I sometimes think if we knew all, we should be more glad to get away.'

'Jekyll is ill, too,' observed Utterson. 'Have you seen him?'

But Lanyon's face changed, and he held up a trembling hand. 'I wish to see or hear no more of Doctor Jekyll,' he said in a loud, unsteady voice. 'I am quite done with that person; and I beg that you will spare me any allusion to one whom I regard as dead.'

'Tut-tut,' said Mr Utterson; and then after a considerable pause, 'Can't I do anything?' he inquired. 'We are three very old friends, Lanyon; we shall not live to make others.'

'Nothing can be done,' returned Lanyon; 'ask himself.'

'He will not see me,' said the lawyer.

'I am not surprised at that,' was the reply. 'Some day, Utterson, after I am dead, you may perhaps come to learn the right and wrong of this. I cannot tell you. And in the meantime, if you can sit and talk with me of other things, for God's sake, stay and do so; but if you cannot keep clear of this accursed topic, then, in God's name, go, for I cannot bear it.'

As soon as he got home, Utterson sat down and wrote to Jekyll, complaining of his exclusion from the house, and asking the cause of this unhappy break with Lanyon; and the next day brought him a long answer, often very pathetically worded, and sometimes darkly mysterious in drift. The quarrel with Lanyon was incurable. 'I do not blame our old friend,' Jekyll wrote, 'but I share his view that we must never meet. I mean from henceforth to lead a life of extreme seclusion; you must not be surprised, nor must you doubt my friendship, if my door is often shut even to you. You must suffer me to go my own dark way. I have brought on myself a punishment and a danger that I cannot name. If I am the chief of sinners, I am the chief of sufferers also. I could not think that this earth contained a place for sufferings and terrors so unmanning; and you can do but one thing, Utterson, to lighten this destiny, and that is to respect my silence.' Utterson was amazed; the dark influence of Hyde had been withdrawn, the doctor had returned to his old tasks and amities; a week ago, the prospect had smiled with every promise of a cheerful and an honoured age; and now in a moment, friendship, and peace of mind and the whole tenor of his life were wrecked. So great and unprepared a change pointed to madness; but in view of Lanyon's manner and words, there must lie for it some deeper ground.

A week afterwards Dr Lanyon took to his bed, and in something less than a fortnight he was dead. The night after the funeral, at which he had been sadly affected, Utterson locked the door of his business room, and sitting there by the light of a melancholy candle, drew out and set before him an envelope addressed by the hand and sealed with the seal of his dead friend. 'PRIVATE: for the hands of J. G. Utterson ALONE and in case of his predecease *to be destroyed unread*,' so it was emphatically superscribed; and the lawyer dreaded to behold the contents. 'I have buried one friend to-day,' he thought: 'what if this should cost me another?' And then he condemned the fear as a disloyalty, and broke the seal. Within there was another enclosure, likewise sealed, and marked upon the cover as 'not to be opened till the death or disappearance of Dr Henry Jekyll.' Utterson could not trust his eyes. Yes, it was disappearance; here again, as in the mad will which he had long ago restored to its author, here again were the idea of a disappearance and the name of Henry Jekyll bracketed. But in the will, that idea had sprung from the sinister suggestion of the man Hyde; it was set there with a purpose all too plain and horrible. Written by the hand of Lanyon, what should it mean? A great curiosity came on the trustee, to disregard the prohibition and dive at once to the bottom of these mysteries; but professional honour and faith to his dead friend were stringent obligations; and the packet slept in the inmost corner of his private safe.

It is one thing to mortify curiosity, another to conquer it; and it may be doubted if, from that day forth, Utterson desired the society of his surviving friend with the same eagerness. He thought of him kindly; but his thoughts were disquieted and fearful. He went to call indeed; but he was perhaps relieved to be denied admittance; perhaps, in his heart, he preferred to speak with Poole upon the doorstep and surrounded by the air and sounds of the open city, rather than to be admitted into that house of voluntary bondage, and to sit and speak with its inscrutable recluse. Poole had, indeed, no very pleasant news to communicate. The doctor, it appeared, now more than ever confined himself to the cabinet over the laboratory, where he would sometimes even sleep; he was out of spirits, he had grown very silent, he did not read; it seemed as if he had something on his mind. Utterson became so used to the unvarying character of these reports, that he fell off little by little in the frequency of his visits.

INCIDENT AT THE WINDOW

IT chanced on Sunday, when Mr Utterson was on his usual walk with Mr Enfield, that their way lay once again through the bystreet; and that when they came in front of the door, both stopped to gaze on it.

'Well,' said Enfield, 'that story's at an end at least. We shall never see more of Mr Hyde.'

'I hope not,' said Utterson. 'Did I ever tell you that I once saw him, and shared your feeling of repulsion?'

'It was impossible to do the one without the other,' returned Enfield. 'And by the way what an ass you must have thought me, not to know that this was a back way to Dr Jekyll's! It was partly your own fault that I found it out, even when I did.'

'So you found it out, did you?' said Utterson. 'But if that be so, we may step into the court and take a look at the windows. To tell you the truth, I am uneasy about poor Jekyll; and even outside, I feel as if the presence of a friend might do him good.'

The court was very cool and a little damp, and full of premature twilight, although the sky, high up overhead, was still bright with sunset. The middle one of the three windows was half way open; and sitting close beside it, taking the air with an infinite sadness of mien, like some disconsolate prisoner, Utterson saw Dr Jekyll.

'What! Jekyll!' he cried. 'I trust you are better.'

'I am very low, Utterson,' replied the doctor drearily, 'very low. It will not last long, thank God.'

'You stay too much indoors,' said the lawyer. 'You should be out, whipping up the circulation like Mr Enfield and me. (This is my cousin—Mr Enfield—Dr Jekyll.) Come now; get your hat and take a quick turn with us.'

'You are very good,' sighed the other. 'I should like to very much; but no, no, no, it is quite impossible; I dare not. But indeed, Utterson, I am very glad to see you; this is really a great pleasure; I would ask you and Mr Enfield up, but the place is really not fit.'

'Why then,' said the lawyer, good-naturedly, 'the best thing we can do is to stay down here and speak with you from where we are.'

'That is just what I was about to venture to propose,' returned the doctor with a smile. But the words were hardly uttered, before the smile was struck out of his face and succeeded by an expression of such abject terror and despair, as froze the very blood of the two gentlemen below. They saw it but for a glimpse, for the window was instantly thrust down; but that glimpse had been sufficient and they turned and left the court without a word. In silence, too, they traversed the bystreet; and it was not until they had come into a neighbouring thoroughfare, where even upon a Sunday there were still some stirrings of life, that Mr Utterson at last turned and looked at his companion. They were both pale; and there was an answering horror in their eyes.

'God forgive us, God forgive us,' said Mr Utterson.

But Mr Enfield only nodded his head very seriously, and walked on once more in silence.

THE LAST NIGHT

MR UTTERSON was sitting by his fireside one evening after dinner, when he was surprised to receive a visit from Poole.

'Bless me, Poole, what brings you here?' he cried; and then taking a second look at him, 'What ails you?' he added, 'is the doctor ill?'

'Mr Utterson,' said the man, 'there is something wrong.'

'Take a seat, and here is a glass of wine for you,' said the lawyer. 'Now, take your time, and tell me plainly what you want.'

'You know the doctor's ways, sir,' replied Poole, 'and how he shuts himself up. Well, he's shut up again in the cabinet; and I don't like it, sir—I wish I may die if I like it. Mr Utterson, sir, I'm afraid.'

'Now, my good man,' said the lawyer, 'be explicit. What are you afraid of?'

'I've been afraid for about a week,' returned Poole, doggedly disregarding the question; 'and I can bear it no more.'

The man's appearance amply bore out his words; his manner was altered for the worse; and except for the moment when he had first announced his terror, he had not once looked the lawyer in the face. Even now, he sat with the glass of wine untasted on his knee, and his eyes directed to a corner of the floor. 'I can bear it no more,' he repeated.

'Come,' said the lawyer, 'I see you have some good reason, Poole; I see there is something seriously amiss. Try to tell me what it is.'

'I think there's been foul play,' said Poole, hoarsely.

'Foul play!' cried the lawyer, a good deal frightened and rather inclined to be irritated in consequence. 'What foul play? What does the man mean?'

'I daren't say, sir,' was the answer; 'but will you come along with me and see for yourself?'

'Mr Utterson's only answer was to rise and get his hat and great coat; but he observed with wonder the greatness of the relief that appeared upon the butler's face, and perhaps with no less, that the wine was still untasted when he set it down to follow.

It was a wild, cold, seasonable night of March, with a pale moon, lying on her back as though the wind had tilted her, and a flying wrack of the most diaphanous and lawny texture. The wind made talking difficult, and flecked the blood into the face. It seemed to have swept the streets unusually bare of passengers, besides; for Mr Utterson thought he had never seen that part of London so deserted. He could have wished it otherwise; never in his life had he been conscious of so sharp a wish to see and touch his fellow-creatures; for struggle as he might, there was borne in upon his mind a crushing anticipation of calamity. The square, when they got there, was all full of wind and dust, and the thin trees in the garden were lashing themselves along the railing. Poole, who had kept all the way a pace or two ahead, now pulled up in the middle of the pavement, and in spite of the biting weather, took off his hat and mopped his brow with a red pocket-handkerchief. But for all the hurry of his coming, these were not the dews of exertion that he wiped away, but the moisture of some strangling anguish; for his face was white and his voice, when he spoke, harsh and broken.

'Well, sir,' he said, 'here we are, and God grant there be nothing wrong.'

'Amen, Poole,' said the lawyer.

Thereupon the servant knocked in a very guarded manner; the door was opened on the chain; and a voice asked from within, 'Is that you, Poole?'

'It's all right,' said Poole. 'Open the door.'

The hall, when they entered it, was brightly lighted up; the fire was built high; and about the hearth the whole of the servants, men and women, stood huddled together like a flock of sheep. At the sight of Mr Utterson, the housemaid broke into hysterical whimpering; and the cook, crying out 'Bless God! it's Mr Utterson,' ran forward as if to take him in her arms.

'What, what? Are you all here?' said the lawyer peevishly. 'Very irregular, very unseemly; your master would be far from pleased.'

'They're all afraid,' said Poole.

Blank silence followed, no one protesting; only the maid lifted up her voice and now wept loudly.

'Hold your tongue!' Poole said to her, with a ferocity of accent that testified to his own jangled nerves; and indeed, when the girl had so suddenly raised the note of her lamentation, they had all started and turned towards the inner door with faces of dreadful expectation. 'And now,' continued the butler, addressing the knife-boy, 'reach me a candle, and we'll get this through hands at once.' And then he begged Mr Utterson to follow him, and led the way to the back garden.

'Now, sir,' said he, 'you come as gently as you can. I want you to hear, and I don't want you to be heard. And see here, sir, if by any chance he was to ask you in, don't go.'

Mr Utterson's nerves, at this unlooked-for termination, gave a jerk that nearly threw him from his balance; but he re-collected his courage and followed the butler into the laboratory building and through the surgical theatre, with its lumber of crates and bottles, to the foot of the stair. Here Poole motioned him to stand on one side and listen; while he himself, setting down the candle and making a great and obvious call on his resolution, mounted the steps and knocked with a somewhat uncertain hand on the red baize of the cabinet door.

'Mr Utterson, sir, asking to see you,' he called; and even as he did so, once more violently signed to the lawyer to give ear.

A voice answered from within: 'Tell him I cannot see anyone,' it said complainingly.

'Thank you, sir,' said Poole, with a note of something like triumph in his voice; and taking up his candle, he led Mr Utterson back across the yard and into the great kitchen, where the fire was out and the beetles were leaping on the floor.

'Sir,' he said, looking Mr Utterson in the eyes, 'was that my master's voice?'

'It seems much changed,' replied the lawyer, very pale, but giving look for look.

'Changed? Well, yes, I think so,' said the butler. 'Have I been twenty years in this man's house, to be deceived about his voice? No, sir; master's made away with; he was made away with, eight days ago, when we heard him cry out upon the name of God: and *who's* in there instead of him, and *why* it stays there, is a thing that cries to Heaven, Mr Utterson!'

'This is a very strange tale, Poole; this is rather a wild tale, my man,' said Mr Utterson, biting his finger. 'Suppose it were as you suppose, supposing Dr Jekyll to have been—well, murdered, what could induce the murderer to stay? That won't hold water; it doesn't commend itself to reason.'

'Well, Mr Utterson, you are a hard man to satisfy, but I'll do it yet,' said Poole. 'All this last week (you must know) him, or it, or whatever it is that lives in that cabinet, has been crying night and day for some sort of medicine and cannot get it to his mind. It was sometimes his way—the master's, that is—to write his orders on a sheet of paper and throw it on the stair. We've had nothing else this week back; nothing but papers, and a closed door, and the very meals left there to be smuggled in when nobody was looking. Well, sir, every day, ay, and twice and thrice in the same day, there have been orders and complaints, and I have been sent flying to all the wholesale chemists in town. Every time I brought the stuff back, there would be another paper telling me to return it, because it was not pure, and another order to a different firm. This drug is wanted bitter bad, sir,* whatever for.'

'Have you any of these papers?' asked Mr Utterson.

Poole felt in his pocket and handed out a crumpled note, which the lawyer, bending nearer to the candle, carefully examined. Its contents ran thus: 'Dr Jekyll presents his compliments to Messrs. Maw. He assures them that their last sample is impure and quite useless for his present purpose. In the year 18—, Dr J. purchased a somewhat large quantity from Messrs. M. He now begs them to search with the most sedulous care, and should any of the same quality be left, to forward it to him at once. Expense is no consideration. The importance of this to Dr J. can hardly be exaggerated.' So far the letter had run composedly enough, but here with a sudden splutter of the pen, the writer's emotion had broken loose. 'For God's sake,' he had added, 'find me some of the old.'

'This is a strange note,' said Mr Utterson; and then sharply, 'How do you come to have it open?'

'The man at Maw's was main angry, sir, and he threw it back to me like so much dirt,' returned Poole.

'This is unquestionably the doctor's hand, do you know?' resumed the lawyer.

'I thought it looked like it,' said the servant rather sulkily; and then, with another voice, 'But what matters hand of write,' he said. 'I've seen him!'

'Seen him?' repeated Mr Utterson. 'Well?'

'That's it!' said Poole. 'It was this way. I came suddenly into the theatre from the garden. It seems he had slipped out to look for this drug or whatever it is; for the cabinet door was open, and there he was at the far end of the room digging among the crates. He looked up when I came in, gave a kind of cry, and whipped upstairs into the cabinet. It was but for one minute that I saw him, but the hair stood upon my head like quills. Sir, if that was my master, why had he a mask upon his face? If it was my master, why did he cry out like a rat, and run from me? I have served him long enough. And then . . .' the man paused and passed his hand over his face.

'These are all very strange circumstances,' said Mr Utterson, 'but I think I begin to see daylight. Your master, Poole, is plainly seized with one of those maladies that both torture and deform the sufferer; hence, for aught I know, the alteration of his voice; hence the mask and his avoidance of his friends; hence his eagerness to find this drug, by means of which the poor soul retains some hope of ultimate recovery—God grant that he be not deceived! There is my explanation; it is sad enough, Poole, ay, and appalling to consider; but it is plain and natural, hangs well together and delivers us from all exorbitant alarms.'

'Sir,' said the butler, turning to a sort of mottled pallor, 'that thing was not my master, and there's the truth. My master'—here he looked round him and began to whisper—'is a tall fine build of a man, and this was more of a dwarf.' Utterson attempted to protest. 'O, sir,' cried Poole, 'do you think I do not know my master after twenty years? do you think I do not know where his head comes to in the cabinet door, where I saw him every morning of my life? No, sir, that thing in the mask was never Doctor Jekyll—God knows what it was, but it was never Doctor Jekyll; and it is the belief of my heart that there was murder done.'

'Poole,' replied the lawyer, 'if you say that, it will become my duty to make certain. Much as I desire to spare your master's feelings, much as I am puzzled by this note which seems to prove him to be still alive, I shall consider it my duty to break in that door.'

'Ah, Mr Utterson, that's talking!' cried the butler.

'And now comes the second question,' resumed Utterson: 'Who is going to do it?'

'Why, you and me, sir,' was the undaunted reply.

'That is very well said,' returned the lawyer; 'and whatever comes of it, I shall make it my business to see you are no loser.'

'There is an axe in the theatre,' continued Poole; 'and you might take the kitchen poker for yourself.'

The lawyer took that rude but weighty instrument into his hand, and balanced it. 'Do you know, Poole,' he said, looking up, 'that you and I are about to place ourselves in a position of some peril?'

'You may say so, sir, indeed,' returned the butler.

'It is well, then, that we should be frank,' said the other. 'We both think more than we have said; let us make a clean breast. This masked figure that you saw, did you recognise it?'

'Well, sir, it went so quick, and the creature was so doubled up, that I could hardly swear to that,' was the answer. 'But if you mean, was it Mr Hyde?—why, yes, I think it was! You see, it was much of the same bigness; and it had the same quick light way with it; and then who else could have got in by the laboratory door? You have not forgot, sir, that at the time of the murder he had still the key with him? But that's not all. I don't know, Mr Utterson, if ever you met this Mr Hyde?'

'Yes,' said the lawyer, 'I once spoke with him.'

'Then you must know as well as the rest of us that there was something queer about that gentleman—something that gave a man a turn—I don't know rightly how to say it, sir, beyond this: that you felt it in your marrow kind of cold and thin.'

'I own I felt something of what you describe,' said Mr Utterson.

'Quite so, sir,' returned Poole. 'Well, when that masked thing like a monkey jumped from among the chemicals and whipped into the cabinet, it went down my spine like ice. O, I know it's not evidence, Mr Utterson; I'm book-learned enough for that; but a man has his feelings, and I give you my bible-word it was Mr Hyde!'

'Ay, ay,' said the lawyer. 'My fears incline to the same point. Evil, I fear, founded—evil was sure to come—of that connection. Ay, truly, I believe you; I believe poor Harry is killed; and I believe his murderer (for what purpose, God alone can tell) is still lurking in his victim's room. Well, let our name be vengeance. Call Bradshaw.'

The footman came at the summons, very white and nervous.

'Pull yourself together, Bradshaw,' said the lawyer. 'This suspense, I know, is telling upon all of you; but it is now our intention to make an end of it. Poole, here, and I are going to force our way into the cabinet. If all is well, my shoulders are broad enough to bear the blame. Meanwhile, lest anything should really be amiss, or any malefactor seek to escape by the back, you and the boy must go round the corner with a pair of good sticks, and take your post at the laboratory door. We give you ten minutes, to get to your stations.'

As Bradshaw left, the lawyer looked at his watch. 'And now, Poole, let us get to ours,' he said; and taking the poker under his arm, he led the way into the yard. The scud had banked over the moon, and it was now quite dark. The wind, which only broke in puffs and draughts into that deep well of building, tossed the light of the candle to and fro about their steps, until they came into the shelter of the theatre, where they sat down silently to wait. London hummed solemnly all around; but nearer at hand, the stillness was only broken by the sound of a footfall moving to and fro along the cabinet floor.

'So it will walk all day, sir,' whispered Poole; 'ay, and the better part of the night. Only when a new sample comes from the chemist there's a bit of a break. Ah, it's an ill-conscience that's such an enemy to rest! Ah, sir, there's blood foully shed in every step of it! But hark again, a little closer—put your heart in your ears, Mr Utterson, and tell me, is that the doctor's foot?'

The steps fell lightly and oddly, with a certain swing, for all they went so slowly; it was different indeed from the heavy creaking tread of Henry Jekyll. Utterson sighed. 'Is there never anything else?' he asked.

Poole nodded. 'Once,' he said. 'Once I heard it weeping!'

'Weeping? how that?' said the lawyer, conscious of a sudden chill of horror.

'Weeping like a woman or a lost soul,' said the butler. 'I came away with that upon my heart, that I could have wept too.'

But now the ten minutes drew to an end. Poole disinterred the axe from under a stack of packing straw; the candle was set upon the nearest table to light them to the attack; and they drew near with bated breath to where that patient foot was still going up and down, up and down, in the quiet of the night.

'Jekyll,' cried Utterson, with a loud voice, 'I demand to see you.' He paused a moment, but there came no reply. 'I give you fair warning, our suspicions are aroused, and I must and shall see you,' he resumed; 'if not by fair means then by foul—if not of your consent, then by brute force!'

'Utterson,' said the voice, 'for God's sake, have mercy!'

'Ah, that's not Jekyll's voice—it's Hyde's!' cried Utterson. 'Down with the door, Poole.'

Poole swung the axe over his shoulder; the blow shook the building, and the red baize door leaped against the lock and hinges. A dismal screech, as of mere animal terror, rang from the cabinet. Up went the axe again, and again the panels crashed and the frame bounded; four times the blow fell; but the wood was tough and the fittings were of excellent workmanship; and it was not until the fifth, that the lock burst in sunder and the wreck of the door fell inwards on the carpet.

The besiegers, appalled by their own riot and the stillness that had succeeded, stood back a little and peered in. There lay the cabinet before their eyes in the quiet lamplight, a good fire glowing and chattering on the hearth, the kettle singing its thin strain, a drawer or two open, papers neatly set forth on the business table, and nearer the fire, the things laid out for tea; the quietest room, you would have said and, but for the glazed presses full of chemicals, the most commonplace that night in London.

Right in the midst there lay the body of a man sorely contorted and still twitching. They drew near on tiptoe, turned it on its back and beheld the face of Edward Hyde. He was dressed in clothes far too large for him, clothes of the doctor's bigness; the cords of his face still moved with a semblance of life, but life was quite gone; and by the crushed phial in the hand and the strong smell of kernels that hung upon the air, Utterson knew that he was looking on the body of a self-destroyer.

'We have come too late,' he said sternly, 'whether to save or punish. Hyde is gone to his account; and it only remains for us to find the body of your master.'

The far greater proportion of the building was occupied by the theatre, which filled almost the whole ground story and was lighted from above, and by the cabinet, which formed an upper story at one end and looked upon the court. A corridor joined the theatre to the door on the bystreet; and with this, the cabinet communicated separately by a second flight of stairs. There were besides a few dark closets and a spacious cellar. All these they now thoroughly examined. Each closet needed but a glance, for all were empty and all, by the dust that fell from their doors, had stood long unopened. The cellar, indeed, was filled with crazy lumber, mostly dating from the times of the surgeon who was Jekyll's predecessor; but even as they opened the door, they were advertised of the uselessness of further search, by the fall of a perfect mat of cobweb which had for years sealed up the entrance. Nowhere was there any trace of Henry Jekyll, dead or alive.

Poole stamped on the flags of the corridor. 'He must be buried here,' he said, hearkening to the sound.

'Or he may have fled,' said Utterson, and he turned to examine the door in the bystreet. It was locked; and lying near by on the flags, they found the key, already stained with rust.

'This does not look like use,' observed the lawyer.

'Use!' echoed Poole. 'Do you not see, sir, it is broken? much as if a man had stamped on it.'

'Ay,' continued Utterson, 'and the fractures, too, are rusty.' The two men looked at each other with a scare. 'This is beyond me, Poole,' said the lawyer. 'Let us go back to the cabinet.'

They mounted the stair in silence, and still with an occasional awestruck glance at the dead body, proceeded more thoroughly to examine the contents of the cabinet. At one table, there were traces of chemical work, various measured heaps of some white salt being laid on glass saucers, as though for an experiment in which the unhappy man had been prevented.

'That is the same drug that I was always bringing him,' said Poole; and even as he spoke, the kettle with a startling noise boiled over.

This brought them to the fireside, where the easy chair was drawn cosily up, and the tea things stood ready to the sitter's elbow, the very sugar in the cup. There were several books on a shelf; one lay beside the tea things open, and Utterson was amazed to find it a copy of a pious work, for which Jekyll had several times expressed a great esteem, annotated, in his own hand, with startling blasphemies.

Next, in the course of their review of the chamber, the searchers came to the cheval glass, into whose depths they looked with an involuntary horror. But it was so turned as to show them nothing but the rosy glow playing on the roof, the fire sparkling in a hundred repetitions along the glazed front of the presses, and their own pale and fearful countenances stooping to look in.

'This glass have seen some strange things, sir,' whispered Poole.

'And surely none stranger than itself,' echoed the lawyer in the same tones. 'For what did Jekyll'—he caught himself up at the word with a start, and then conquering the weakness: 'what could Jekyll want with it?' he said.

'You may say that!' said Poole.

Next they turned to the business table. On the desk among the neat array of papers, a large envelope was uppermost, and bore, in the doctor's hand, the name of Mr Utterson. The lawyer unsealed it, and several enclosures fell to the floor. The first was a will, drawn in the same eccentric terms as the one which he had returned six months before, to serve as a testament in case of death and as a deed of gift in case of disappearance; but in place of the name of Edward Hyde, the lawyer, with indescribable amazement, read the name of Gabriel John Utterson. He looked at Poole, and then back at the paper, and last of all at the dead malefactor stretched upon the carpet.

'My head goes round,' he said. 'He has been all these days in possession; he had no cause to like me; he must have raged to see himself displaced; and he has not destroyed this document.'

He caught up the next paper; it was a brief note in the doctor's hand and dated at the top. 'O Poole!' the lawyer cried, 'he was alive and here this day. He cannot have been disposed of in so short a space, he must be still alive, he must have fled! And then, why fled? and how? and in that case, can we venture to declare this suicide? O, we must be careful. I foresee that we may yet involve your master in some dire catastrophe.'

'Why don't you read it, sir?' asked Poole.

'Because I fear,' replied the lawyer solemnly. 'God grant I have no cause for it!' And with that he brought the paper to his eyes and read as follows.

'My dear Utterson,—When this shall fall into your hands, I shall have disappeared, under what circumstances I have not the penetration to foresee, but my instinct and all the circumstances of my nameless situation tell me that the end is sure and must be early. Go then, and first read the narrative which Lanyon warned me he was to place in your hands; and if you care to hear more, turn to the confession of

'Your unworthy and unhappy friend,

'HENRY JEKYLL.'

'There was a third enclosure?' asked Utterson.

'Here, sir,' said Poole, and gave into his hands a considerable packet sealed in several places.

The lawyer put it in his pocket. 'I would say nothing of this paper. If your master has fled or is dead, we may at least save his credit. It is now ten; I must go home and read these documents in quiet; but I shall be back before midnight, when we shall send for the police.'

They went out, locking the door of the theatre behind them; and Utterson, once more leaving the servants gathered about the fire in the hall, trudged back to his office to read the two narratives in which this mystery was now to be explained.

DOCTOR LANYON'S NARRATIVE

ON the ninth of January, now four days ago, I received by the evening delivery a registered envelope, addressed in the hand of my colleague and old school-companion, Henry Jekyll. I was a good deal surprised by this; for we were by no means in the habit of correspondence; I had seen the man, dined with him, indeed, the night before; and I could imagine nothing in our intercourse that should justify the formality of registration. The contents increased my wonder; for this is how the letter ran:

'10th December, 18—

'Dear Lanyon,—You are one of my oldest friends; and although we may have differed at times on scientific questions, I cannot remember, at least on my side, any break in our affection. There was never a day when, if you had said to me, "Jekyll, my life, my honour, my reason, depend upon you," I would not have sacrificed my fortune or my left hand to help you. Lanyon, my life, my honour, my reason, are all at your mercy; if you fail me to-night, I am lost. You might suppose, after this preface, that I am going to ask you for something dishonourable to grant. Judge for yourself.

'I want you to postpone all other engagements for to-night—ay, even if you were summoned to the bedside of an emperor; to take a cab, unless your carriage should be actually at the door; and with this letter in your hand for consultation, to drive straight to my house. Poole, my butler, has his orders; you will find him waiting your arrival with a locksmith. The door of my cabinet is then to be forced; and you are to go in alone; to open the glazed press (letter E) on the left hand, breaking the lock if it be shut; and to draw out, *with all its contents as they stand*, the fourth drawer from the top or (which is the same thing) the third from the bottom. In my extreme distress of mind, I have a morbid fear of misdirecting you; but even if I am in error, you may know the right drawer by its contents: some powders, a phial and a paper book. This drawer I beg of you to carry back with you to Cavendish Square exactly as it stands.

'That is the first part of the service: now for the second. You should be back, if you set out at once on the receipt of this, long before midnight; but I will leave you that amount of margin, not only in the fear of one of those obstacles that can neither be prevented nor foreseen, but because an hour when your servants are in bed is to be preferred for what will then remain to do. At midnight, then, I have to ask you to be alone in your consulting room, to admit with your own hand into the house a man who will present himself in my name, and to place in his hands the drawer that you will have brought with you from my cabinet. Then you will have played your part and earned my gratitude completely. Five minutes, afterwards, if you insist upon an explanation, you will have understood that these arrangements are of capital importance; and that by the neglect of one of them, fantastic as they must appear, you might have charged your conscience with my death or the shipwreck of my reason.

'Confident as I am that you will not trifle with this appeal, my heart sinks and my hand trembles at the bare thought of such a possibility. Think of me at this hour, in a strange place, labouring under a blackness of distress that no fancy can exaggerate, and yet well aware that, if you will but punctually serve me, my troubles will roll away like a story that is told. Serve me, my dear Lanyon, and save

'Your friend,

'H. J.

'P.S. I had already sealed this up when a fresh terror struck upon my soul. It is possible that the post office may fail me, and this letter not come into your hands until to-morrow morning. In that case, dear Lanyon, do my errand when it shall be most convenient for you in the course of the day; and once more expect my messenger at midnight. It may then already be too late; and if that passes without event, you will know that you have seen the last of Henry Jekyll.'

Upon the reading of this letter, I made sure my colleague was insane; but till that was proved beyond the possibility of doubt, I felt bound to do as he requested. The less I understood of this farrago, the less I was in a position to judge of its importance; and an appeal so worded could not be set aside without a grave responsibility. I rose accordingly from table, got into a hansom, and drove straight to Jekyll's house. The butler was awaiting my arrival; he had received by the same post as mine a registered letter of instruction and had sent at once for a locksmith and a carpenter. The tradesmen came while we were yet speaking; and we moved in a body to old Dr Denman's surgical theatre from which (as you are doubtless aware) Jekyll's private cabinet is most conveniently entered. The door was very strong, the lock excellent; the carpenter avowed he would have great trouble and have to do much damage, if force were to be used; and the locksmith was near despair. But this last was a handy fellow, and after two hours' work, the door stood open. The press marked E was unlocked; and I took out the drawer, had it filled up with straw and tied in a sheet, and returned with it to Cavendish Square.

Here I proceeded to examine its contents. The powders were neatly enough made up, but not with the nicety of the dispensing chemist; so that it was plain they were of Jekyll's private manufacture; and when I opened one of the wrappers, I found what seemed to me a simple, crystalline salt of a white colour. The phial, to which I next turned my attention, might have been about half-full of a blood-red liquor, which was highly pungent to the sense of smell and seemed to me to contain phosphorus and some volatile ether. At the other ingredients, I could make no guess. The book was an ordinary version book and contained little but a series of dates. These covered a period of many years, but I observed that the entries ceased nearly a year ago and quite abruptly. Here and there a brief remark was appended to a date, usually no more than a single word: 'double' occurring perhaps six times in a total of several hundred entries; and once very early in the list and followed by several marks of exclamation, 'total failure!!!' All this, though it whetted my curiosity, told me little that was definite. Here were a phial of some tincture, a paper of some salt, and the record of a series of experiments that had led (like too many of Jekyll's investigations) to no end of practical usefulness. How could the presence of these articles in my house affect either the honour, the sanity, or the life of my flighty colleague? If his messenger could go to one place, why could he not go to another? And even granting some impediment, why was this gentleman to be received by me in secret? The more I reflected, the more convinced I grew that I was dealing with a case of cerebral disease; and though I dismissed my servants to bed, I loaded an old revolver that I might be found in some posture of self-defence.

Twelve o'clock had scarce rung out over London, ere the knocker sounded very gently on the door. I went myself at the summons, and found a small man crouching against the pillars of the portico.

'Are you come from Dr Jekyll?' I asked.

He told me 'yes' by a constrained gesture; and when I had bidden him enter, he did not obey me without a searching backward glance into the darkness of the square. There was a policeman not far off, advancing with his bull's eye open; and at the sight, I thought my visitor started and made greater haste.

These particulars struck me, I confess, disagreeably; and as I followed him into the bright light of the consulting room, I kept my hand ready on my weapon. Here, at last, I had a chance of clearly seeing him. I had never set eyes on him before, so much was certain. He was small, as I have said; I was struck besides with the shocking expression of his face, with his remarkable combination of great muscular activity and great apparent debility of constitution, and—last but not least—with the odd, subjective disturbance caused by his neighbourhood. This bore some resemblance to incipient rigor, and was accompanied by a marked sinking of the pulse. At the time, I set it down to some idiosyncratic, personal distaste, and merely wondered at the acuteness of the symptoms; but I have since had reason to believe the cause to lie much deeper in the nature of man, and to turn on some nobler hinge than the principle of hatred.

This person (who had thus, from the first moment of his entrance, struck in me what I can only describe as a disgustful curiosity) was dressed in a fashion that would have made an ordinary person laughable: his clothes, that is to say, although they were of rich and sober fabric, were enormously too large for him in every measurement—the trousers hanging on his legs and rolled up to keep them from the ground, the waist of the coat below his haunches, and the collar sprawling wide upon his shoulders. Strange to relate, this ludicrous accoutrement was far from moving me to laughter. Rather, as there was something abnormal and misbegotten in the very essence of the creature that now faced me—something seizing, surprising and revolting—this fresh disparity seemed but to fit in with and to reinforce it; so that to my interest in the man's nature and character, there was added a curiosity as to his origin, his life, his fortune and status in the world.

These observations, though they have taken so great a space to be set down in, were yet the work of a few seconds. My visitor was, indeed, on fire with sombre excitement.

'Have you got it?' he cried. 'Have you got it?' And so lively was his impatience that he even laid his hand upon my arm and sought to shake me.

I put him back, conscious at his touch of a certain icy pang along my blood. 'Come, sir,' said I. 'You forget that I have not yet the pleasure of your acquaintance. Be seated, if you please.' And I showed him an example, and sat down myself in my customary seat and with as fair an imitation of my ordinary manner to a patient, as the lateness of the hour, the nature of my prëoccupations, and the horror I had of my visitor, would suffer me to muster.

'I beg your pardon, Dr Lanyon,' he replied civilly enough. 'What you say is very well founded; and my impatience has shown its heels to my politeness. I come here at the instance of your colleague, Dr Henry Jekyll, on a piece of business of some moment; and I understood . . .' he paused and put his hand to his throat, and I could see, in spite of his collected manner, that he was wrestling against the approaches of the hysteria—'I understood, a drawer . . .'

But here I took pity on my visitor's suspense, and some perhaps on my own growing curiosity.

'There it is, sir,' said I, pointing to the drawer, where it lay on the floor behind a table and still covered with the sheet.

He sprang to it, and then paused, and laid his hand upon his heart; I could hear his teeth grate with the convulsive action of his jaws; and his face was so ghastly to see that I grew alarmed both for his life and reason.

'Compose yourself,' said I.

He turned a dreadful smile to me, and as if with the decision of despair, plucked away the sheet. At sight of the contents, he uttered one loud sob of such immense relief that I sat petrified. And the next moment, in a voice that was already fairly well under control, 'Have you a graduated glass?' he asked.

I rose from my place with something of an effort and gave him what he asked.

He thanked me with a smiling nod, measured out a few minims of the red tincture and added one of the powders. The mixture, which was at first of a reddish hue, began, in proportion as the crystals melted, to brighten in colour, to effervesce audibly, and to throw off small fumes of vapour. Suddenly and at the same moment, the ebullition ceased and the compound changed to a dark purple, which faded again more slowly to a watery green. My visitor, who had watched these metamorphoses with a keen eye, smiled, set down the glass upon the table, and then turned and looked upon me with an air of scrutiny.

'And now,' said he, 'to settle what remains. Will you be wise? will you be guided? will you suffer me to take this glass in my hand and to go forth from your house without further parley? or has the greed of curiosity too much command of you? Think before you answer, for it shall be done as you decide. As you decide, you shall be left as you were before, and neither richer nor wiser, unless the sense of service rendered to a man in mortal distress may be counted as a kind of riches of the soul. Or, if you shall so prefer to choose, a new province of knowledge and new avenues to fame and power shall be laid open to you, here, in this room, upon the instant; and your sight shall be blasted by a prodigy to stagger the unbelief of Satan.'*

'Sir,' said I, affecting a coolness that I was far from truly possessing, 'you speak enigmas, and you will perhaps not wonder that I hear you with no very strong impression of belief. But I have gone too far in the way of inexplicable services to pause before I see the end.'

'It is well,' replied my visitor. 'Lanyon, you remember your vows: what follows is under the seal of our profession. And now, you who have so long been bound to the most narrow and material views, you who have denied the virtue of transcendental medicine, you who have derided your superiors—behold!'

He put the glass to his lips and drank at one gulp. A cry followed; he reeled, staggered, clutched at the table and held on, staring with injected eyes, gasping with open mouth; and as I looked there came, I thought, a change—he seemed to swell—his face became suddenly black and the features seemed to melt and alter—and the next moment, I had sprung to my feet and leaped back against the wall, my arm raised to shield me from that prodigy, my mind submerged in terror.

'O God!' I screamed, and 'O God!' again and again; for there before my eyes—pale and shaken, and half fainting, and groping before him with his hands, like a man restored from death—there stood Henry Jekyll!

What he told me in the next hour, I cannot bring my mind to set on paper. I saw what I saw, I heard what I heard, and my soul sickened at it; and yet now when that sight has faded from my eyes, I ask myself if I believe it, and I cannot answer. My life is shaken to its roots; sleep has left me; the deadliest terror sits by me at all hours of the day and night; I feel that my days are numbered, and that I must die; and yet I shall die incredulous. As for the moral turpitude that man unveiled to me, even with tears of penitence, I cannot, even in memory, dwell on it without a start of horror. I will say but one thing, Utterson, and that (if you can bring your mind to credit it) will be more than enough. The creature who crept into my house that night was, on Jekyll's own confession, known by the name of Hyde and hunted for in every corner of the land as the murderer of Carew.

HASTIE LANYON.

HENRY JEKYLL'S FULL STATEMENT OF THE CASE

I WAS born in the year 18— to a large fortune, endowed besides with excellent parts, inclined by nature to industry, fond of the respect of the wise and good among my fellow-men, and thus, as might have been supposed, with every guarantee of an honourable and distinguished future. And indeed the worst of my fault was a certain impatient gaiety of disposition, such as has made the happiness of many, but such as I found it hard to reconcile with my imperious desire to carry my head high, and wear a more than commonly grave countenance before the public. Hence it came about that I concealed my pleasures; and that when I reached years of reflection, and began to look round me and take stock of my progress and position in the world, I stood already committed to a profound duplicity of life. Many a man would have even blazoned such irregularities as I was guilty of; but from the high views that I had set before me, I regarded and hid them with an almost morbid sense of shame. It was thus rather the exacting nature of my aspirations than any particular degradation in my faults, that made me what I was and, with even a deeper trench than in the majority of men, severed in me those provinces of good and ill which divide and compound man's dual nature. In this case, I was driven to reflect deeply and inveterately on that hard law of life, which lies at the root of religion and is one of the most plentiful springs of distress. Though so profound a double-dealer, I was in no sense a hypocrite; both sides of me were in dead earnest; I was no more myself when I laid aside restraint and plunged in shame, than when I laboured, in the eye of day, at the furtherance of knowledge or the relief of sorrow and suffering. And it chanced that the direction of my scientific studies, which led wholly towards the mystic and the transcendental, reacted and shed a strong light on this consciousness of the perennial war among my members. With every day, and from both sides of my intelligence, the moral and the intellectual, I thus drew steadily nearer to that truth, by whose partial discovery I have been doomed to such a dreadful shipwreck: that man is not truly one, but truly two. I say two, because the state of my own knowledge does not pass beyond that point. Others will follow, others will outstrip me on the same lines; and I hazard the guess that man will be ultimately known for a mere polity of multifarious, incongruous and independent denizens. I for my part, from the nature of my life, advanced infallibly in one direction and in one direction only. It was on the moral side, and in my own person, that I learned to recognise the thorough and primitive duality of man; I saw that, of the two natures that contended in the field of my consciousness, even if I could rightly be said to be either, it was only because I was radically both; and from an early date, even before the course of my scientific discoveries had begun to suggest the most naked possibility of such a miracle, I had learned to dwell with pleasure, as a beloved daydream, on the thought of the separation of these elements. If each, I told myself, could but be housed in separate identities, life would be relieved of all that was unbearable; the unjust might go his way, delivered from the aspirations and remorse of his more upright twin; and the just could walk steadfastly and securely on his upward path, doing the good things in which he found his pleasure, and no longer exposed to disgrace and penitence by the hands of this extraneous evil. It was the curse of mankind that these incongruous faggots were thus bound together—that in the agonised womb of consciousness, these polar twins should be continuously struggling. How, then, were they dissociated?

I was so far in my reflections when, as I have said, a side light began to shine upon the subject from the laboratory table. I began to perceive more deeply than it has ever yet been stated, the trembling immateriality, the mist-like transience, of this seemingly so solid body in which we walk attired. Certain agents I found to have the power to shake and to pluck back that fleshly vestment, even as a wind might toss the curtains of a pavilion. For two good reasons, I will not enter deeply into this scientific branch of my confession. First, because I have been made to learn that the doom and burthen of our life is bound forever on man's shoulders, and when the attempt is made to cast it off, it but returns upon us with more unfamiliar and more awful pressure. Second, because as my narrative will make alas! too evident, my discoveries were incomplete. Enough, then, that I not only recognised my natural body for the mere aura and effulgence of certain of the powers that made up my spirit, but managed to compound a drug by which these powers should be dethroned from their supremacy, and a second form and countenance substituted, none the less natural to me because they were the expression, and bore the stamp, of lower elements in my soul.

I hesitated long before I put this theory to the test of practice. I knew well that I risked death; for any drug that so potently controlled and shook the very fortress of identity, might by the least scruple of an overdose or at the least inopportunity in the moment of exhibition, utterly blot out that immaterial tabernacle which I looked to it to change. But the temptation of a discovery so singular and profound, at last overcame the suggestions of alarm. I had long since prepared my tincture; I purchased at once, from a firm of wholesale chemists, a large quantity of a particular salt which I knew, from my experiments, to be the last ingredient required; and late one accursed night, I compounded the elements, watched them boil and smoke together in the glass, and when the ebullition had subsided, with a strong glow of courage, drank off the potion.

The most racking pangs succeeded: a grinding in the bones, deadly nausea, and a horror of the spirit that cannot be exceeded at the hour of birth or death. Then these agonies began swiftly to subside, and I came to myself as if out of a great sickness. There was something strange in my sensations, something indescribably new and, from its very novelty, incredibly sweet. I felt younger, lighter, happier in body; within I was conscious of a heady recklessness, a current of disordered sensual images running like a mill race in my fancy, a solution of the bonds of obligation, an unknown but not an innocent freedom of the soul. I knew myself, at the first breath of this new life, to be more wicked, tenfold more wicked, sold a slave to my original evil; and the thought, in that moment, braced and delighted me like wine. I stretched out my hands, exulting in the freshness of these sensations; and in the act, I was suddenly aware that I had lost in stature.

There was no mirror, at that date, in my room; that which stands beside me as I write, was brought there later on and for the very purpose of these transformations. The night, however, was far gone into the morning—the morning, black as it was, was nearly ripe for the conception of the day—the inmates of my house were locked in the most rigorous hours of slumber; and I determined, flushed as I was with hope and triumph, to venture in my new shape as far as to my bedroom. I crossed the yard, wherein the constellations looked down upon me, I could have thought, with wonder, the first creature of that sort that their unsleeping vigilance had yet disclosed to them; I stole through the corridors, a stranger in my own house; and coming to my room, I saw for the first time the appearance of Edward Hyde.

I must here speak by theory alone, saying not that which I know, but that which I suppose to be most probable. The evil side of my nature, to which I had now transferred the stamping efficacy, was less robust and less developed than the good which I had just deposed. Again, in the course of my life, which had been, after all, nine tenths a life of effort, virtue and control, it had been much less exercised and much less exhausted. And hence, as I think, it came about that Edward Hyde was so much smaller, slighter and younger than Henry Jekyll. Even as good shone upon the countenance of the one, evil was written broadly and plainly on the face of the other. Evil besides (which I must still believe to be the lethal side of man) had left on that body an imprint of deformity and decay. And yet when I looked upon that ugly idol in the glass, I was conscious of no repugnance, rather of a leap of welcome. This, too, was myself. It seemed natural and human. In my eyes it bore a livelier image of the spirit, it seemed more express and single, than the imperfect and divided countenance, I had been hitherto accustomed to call mine. And in so far I was doubtless right. I have observed that when I wore the semblance of Edward Hyde, none could come near to me at first without a visible misgiving of the flesh. This, as I take it, was because all human beings, as we meet them, are commingled out of good and evil: and Edward Hyde, alone in the ranks of mankind, was pure evil.

I lingered but a moment at the mirror: the second and conclusive experiment had yet to be attempted; it yet remained to be seen if I had lost my identity beyond redemption and must flee before daylight from a house that was no longer mine; and hurrying back to my cabinet, I once more prepared and drank the cup, once more suffered the pangs of dissolution, and came to myself once more with the character, the stature and the face of Henry Jekyll.

That night I had come to the fatal cross roads. Had I approached my discovery in a more noble spirit, had I risked the experiment while under the empire of generous or pious aspirations, all must have been otherwise, and from these agonies of death and birth,* I had come forth an angel instead of a fiend. The drug had no discriminating action; it was neither diabolical nor divine; it but shook the doors of the prisonhouse of my disposition; and like the captives of Philippi,* that which stood within ran forth. At that time my virtue slumbered; my evil, kept awake by ambition, was alert and swift to seize the occasion; and the thing that was projected was Edward Hyde. Hence, although I had now two characters as well as two appearances, one was wholly evil, and the other was still the old Henry Jekyll, that incongruous compound of whose reformation and improvement I had already learned to despair. The movement was thus wholly toward the worse.

Even at that time, I had not yet conquered my aversion to the dryness of a life of study. I would still be merrily disposed at times; and as my pleasures were (to say the least) undignified, and I was not only well known and highly considered, but growing towards the elderly man, this incoherencey of my life was daily growing more unwelcome. It was on this side that my new power tempted me until I fell in slavery. I had but to drink the cup, to doff at once the body of the noted professor, and to assume, like a thick cloak, that of Edward Hyde. I smiled at the notion; it seemed to me at the time to be humorous; and I made my preparations with the most studious care. I took and furnished that house in Soho, to which Hyde was tracked by the police; and engaged as housekeeper a creature whom I well knew to be silent and unscrupulous. On the other side, I announced to my servants that a Mr Hyde (whom I described) was to have full liberty and power about my house in the square; and to parry mishaps, I even called and made myself a familiar object, in my second character. I next drew up that will to which you so much objected; so that if anything befell me in the person of Doctor Jekyll, I could enter on that of Edward Hyde without pecuniary loss. And thus fortified, as I supposed, on every side, I began to profit by the strange immunities of my position.

Men have before hired bravos to transact their crimes, while their own person and reputation sat under shelter. I was the first that ever did so for his pleasures. I was the first that could thus plod in the public eye with a load of genial respectability, and in a moment, like a schoolboy, strip off these lendings and spring headlong into the sea of liberty. But for me, in my impenetrable mantle, the safety was complete. Think of it—I did not even exist! Let me but escape into my laboratory door, give me but a second or two to mix and swallow the draught that I had always standing ready; and whatever he had done, Edward Hyde would pass away like the stain of breath upon a mirror; and there in his stead, quietly at home, trimming the midnight lamp in his study, a man who could afford to laugh at suspicion, would be Henry Jekyll.

The pleasures which I made haste to seek in my disguise were, as I have said, undignified; I would scarce use a harder term. But in the hands of Edward Hyde, they soon began to turn towards the monstrous. When I would come back from these excursions, I was often plunged into a kind of wonder at my vicarious depravity. This familiar that I called out of my own soul, and sent forth alone to do his good pleasure, was a being inherently malign and villainous; his every act and thought centered on self; drinking pleasure with bestial avidity from any degree of torture to another; relentless like a man of stone. Henry Jekyll stood at times aghast before the acts of Edward Hyde; but the situation was apart from ordinary laws, and insidiously relaxed the grasp of conscience. It was Hyde, after all, and Hyde alone, that was guilty. Jekyll was no worse; he woke again to his good qualities seemingly unimpaired; he would even make haste, where it was possible, to undo the evil done by Hyde. And thus his conscience slumbered.

Into the details of the infamy at which I thus connived (for even now I can scarce grant that I committed it) I have no design of entering; I mean but to point out the warnings and the successive steps with which my chastisement approached. I met with one accident which, as it brought on no consequence, I shall no more than mention. An act of cruelty to a child aroused against me the anger of a passer by, whom I recognised the other day in the person of your kinsman; the doctor and the child's family joined him; there were moments when I feared for my life; and at last, in order to pacify their too just resentment, Edward Hyde had to bring them to the door, and pay them in a cheque drawn in the name, of Henry Jekyll. But this danger was easily eliminated from the future, by opening an account at another bank in the name of Edward Hyde himself; and when, by sloping my own hand backward, I had supplied my double with a signature, I thought I sat beyond the reach of fate.

Some two months before the murder of Sir Danvers, I had been out for one of my adventures, had returned at a late hour, and woke the next day in bed with somewhat odd sensations. It was in vain I looked about me; in vain I saw the decent furniture and tall proportions of my room in the square; in vain that I recognised the pattern of the bed curtains and the design of the mahogany frame; something still kept insisting that I was not where I was, that I had not wakened where I seemed to be, but in the little room in Soho where I was accustomed to sleep in the body of Edward Hyde. I smiled to myself, and, in my psychological way, began lazily to inquire into the elements of this illusion, occasionally, even as I did so, dropping back into a comfortable morning doze. I was still so engaged when, in one of my more wakeful moments, my eye fell upon my hand. Now the hand of Henry Jekyll (as you have often remarked) was professional in shape and size: it was large, firm, white and comely. But the hand which I now saw, clearly enough, in the yellow light of a mid-London morning, lying half shut on the bed clothes, was lean, corded, knuckly, of a dusky pallor and thickly shaded with a swart growth of hair. It was the hand of Edward Hyde.

I must have stared upon it for near half a minute, sunk as I was in the mere stupidity of wonder, before terror woke up in my breast as sudden and startling as the crash of cymbals; and bounding from my bed, I rushed to the mirror. At the sight that met my eyes, my blood was changed into something exquisitely thin and icy. Yes, I had gone to bed Henry Jekyll, I had awakened Edward Hyde. How was this to be explained? I asked myself; and then, with another bound of terror—how was it to be remedied? It was well on in the morning; the servants were up; all my drugs were in the cabinet—a long journey, down two pair of stairs, through the back passage, across the open court and through the anatomical theatre, from where I was then standing horror-struck. It might indeed be possible to cover my face; but of what use was that, when I was unable to conceal the alteration in my stature? And then with an overpowering sweetness of relief, it came back upon my mind that the servants were already used to the coming and going of my second self. I had soon dressed, as well as I was able, in clothes of my own size: had soon passed through the house, where Bradshaw stared and drew back at seeing Mr Hyde at such an hour and in such a strange array; and ten minutes later, Dr Jekyll had returned to his own shape and was sitting down, with a darkened brow, to make a feint of breakfasting.

Small indeed was my appetite. This inexplicable incident, this reversal of my previous experience, seemed, like the Babylonian finger on the wall,* to be spelling out the letters of my judgment; and I began to reflect more seriously than ever before on the issues and possibilities of my double existence. That part of me which I had the power of projecting, had lately been much exercised and nourished; it had seemed to me of late as though the body of Edward Hyde had grown in stature, as though (when I wore that form) I were conscious of a more generous tide of blood; and I began to spy a danger that, if this were much prolonged, the balance of my nature might be permanently overthrown, the power of voluntary change be forfeited, and the character of Edward Hyde become irrevocably mine. The power of the drug had not been always equally displayed. Once, very early in my career, it had totally failed me; since then I had been obliged on more than one occasion to double, and once, with infinite risk of death, to treble the amount; and these rare uncertainties had cast hitherto the sole shadow on my contentment. Now, however, and in the light of that morning's accident, I was led to remark that whereas, in the beginning, the difficulty had been to throw off the body of Jekyll, it had of late, gradually but decidedly transferred itself to the other side. All things therefore seemed to point to this: that I was slowly losing hold of my original and better self, and becoming slowly incorporated with my second and worse.

Between these two, I now felt I had to choose. My two natures had memory in common, but all other faculties were most unequally shared between them. Jekyll (who was composite) now with the most sensitive apprehensions, now with a greedy gusto, projected and shared in the pleasures and adventure of Hyde; but Hyde was indifferent to Jekyll, or but remembered him as the mountain bandit remembers the cavern in which he conceals himself from pursuit. Jekyll had more than a father's interest; Hyde had more than a son's indifference.* To cast in my lot with Jekyll, was to die to those appetites which I had long secretly indulged and had of late begun to pamper. To cast it in with Hyde, was to die to a thousand interests and aspirations, and to become, at a blow and forever, despised and friendless. The bargain might appear unequal; but there was still another consideration in the scales; for while Jekyll would suffer smartingly in the fires of abstinence, Hyde would be not even conscious of all that he had lost. Strange as my circumstances were, the terms of this debate are as old and commonplace as man; much the same inducements and alarms cast the die for any tempted and trembling sinner; and it fell out with me, as it falls with so vast a majority of my fellows, that I chose the better part and was found wanting in the strength to keep to it.

Yes, I preferred the elderly and discontented doctor, surrounded by friends and cherishing honest hopes; and bade a resolute farewell to the liberty, the comparative youth, the light step, leaping pulses and secret pleasures, that I had enjoyed in the disguise of Hyde. I made this choice perhaps with some unconscious reservation, for I neither gave up the house in Soho, nor destroyed the clothes of Edward Hyde, which still lay ready in my cabinet. For two months, however, I was true to my determination; for two months, I led a life of such severity as I had never before attained to, and enjoyed the compensations of an approving conscience. But time began at last to obliterate the freshness of my alarm; the praises of conscience began to grow into a thing of course; I began to be tortured with throes and longings, as of Hyde struggling after freedom; and at last, in an hour of moral weakness, I once again compounded and swallowed the transforming draught.

I do not suppose that, when a drunkard reasons with himself upon his vice, he is once out of five hundred times affected by the dangers that he runs through his brutish, physical insensibility; neither had I, long as I had considered my position, made enough allowance for the complete moral insensibility and insensate readiness to evil, which were the leading characters of Edward Hyde. Yet it was by these that I was punished. My devil had been long caged, he came out roaring. I was conscious, even when I took the draught, of a more unbridled, a more furious propensity to ill. It must have been this, I suppose, that stirred in my soul that tempest of impatience with which I listened to the civilities of my unhappy victim; I declare at least, before God, no man morally sane could have been guilty of that crime upon so pitiful a provocation; and that I struck in no more reasonable spirit than that in which a sick child may break a plaything. But I had voluntarily stripped myself of all those balancing instincts, by which even the worst of us continues to walk with some degree of steadiness among temptations; and in my case, to be tempted, however slightly, was to fall.

Instantly the spirit of hell awoke in me and raged. With a transport of glee, I mauled the unresisting body, tasting delight from every blow; and it was not till weariness had begun to succeed, that I was suddenly, in the top fit of my delirium, struck through the heart by a cold thrill of terror. A mist dispersed; I saw my life to be forfeit; and fled from the scene of these excesses, at once glorying and trembling, my lust of evil gratified and stimulated, my love of life screwed to the topmost peg. I ran to the house in Soho, and (to make assurance doubly sure) destroyed my papers; thence I set out through the lamplit streets, in the same divided ecstasy of mind, gloating on my crime, light-headedly devising others in the future, and yet still hastening and still hearkening in my wake for the steps of the avenger. Hyde had a song upon his lips as he compounded the draught, and as he drank it, pledged the dead man. The pangs of transformation had not done tearing him, before Henry Jekyll, with streaming tears of gratitude and remorse, had fallen upon his knees and lifted his clasped hands to God. The veil of self-indulgence was rent from head to foot, I saw my life as a whole: I followed it up from the days of childhood, when I had walked with my father's hand, and through the self-denying toils of my professional life, to arrive again and again, with the same sense of unreality, at the damned horrors of the evening. I could have screamed aloud; I sought with tears and prayers to smother down the crowd of hideous images and sounds with which my memory swarmed against me; and still, between the petitions, the ugly face of my iniquity stared into my soul. As the acuteness of this remorse began to die away, it was succeeded by a sense of joy. The problem of my conduct was solved. Hyde was thenceforth impossible; whether I would or not, I was now confined to the better part of my existence; and O, how I rejoiced to think it! with what willing humility, I embraced anew the restrictions of natural life! with what sincere renunciation, I locked the door by which I had so often gone and come, and ground the key under my heel!

The next day, came the news that the murder had been overlooked, that the guilt of Hyde was patent to the world, and that the victim was a man high in public estimation. It was not only a crime, it had been a tragic folly. I think I was glad to know it; I think I was glad to have my better impulses thus buttressed and guarded by the terrors of the scaffold.

Jekyll was now my city of refuge; let but Hyde peep out an instant, and the hands of all men would be raised to take and slay him.

I resolved in my future conduct to redeem the past; and I can say with honesty that my resolve was fruitful of some good. You know yourself how earnestly in the last months of last year, I laboured to relieve suffering; you know that much was done for others, and that the days passed quietly, almost happily for myself. Nor can I truly say that I wearied of this beneficent and innocent life; I think instead that I daily enjoyed it more completely; but I was still cursed with my duality of purpose; and as the first edge of my penitence wore off, the lower side of me, so long indulged, so recently chained down, began to growl for license.* Not that I dreamed of resuscitating Hyde; the bare idea of that would startle me to frenzy: no, it was in my own person, that I was once more tempted to trifle with my conscience; and it was as an ordinary secret sinner, that I at last fell before the assaults of temptation.

There comes an end to all things; the most capacious measure is filled at last; and this brief condescension to my evil finally destroyed the balance of my soul. And yet I was not alarmed; the fall seemed natural, like a return to the old days before I had made my discovery. It was a fine, clear, January day, wet under foot where the frost had melted, but cloudless overhead; and the Regent's park was full of winter chirruppings and sweet with Spring odours. I sat in the sun on a bench; the animal within me licking the chops of memory; the spiritual side a little drowsed, promising subsequent penitence, but not yet moved to begin. After all, I reflected I was like my neighbours; and then I smiled, comparing myself with other men, comparing my active goodwill with the lazy cruelty of their neglect. And at the very moment of that vainglorious thought, a qualm came over me, a horrid nausea and the most deadly shuddering. These passed away, and left me faint; and then as in its turn the faintness subsided, I began to be aware of a change in the temper of my thoughts, a greater boldness, a contempt of danger, a solution of the bonds of obligation. I looked down; my clothes hung formlessly on my shrunken limbs; the hand that lay on my knee was corded and hairy. I was once more Edward Hyde. A moment before I had been safe of all men's respect, wealthy, beloved—the cloth laying for me in the dining room at home; and now I was the common quarry of mankind, hunted, houseless, a known murderer, thrall to the gallows.

My reason wavered, but it did not fail me utterly. I have more than once observed that, in my second character, my faculties seemed sharpened to a point and my spirits more tensely elastic; thus it came about that, where Jekyll perhaps might have succumbed, Hyde rose to the importance of the moment. My drugs were in one of the presses of my cabinet; how was I to reach them? That was the problem that (crushing my temples in my hands) I set myself to solve. The laboratory door I had closed. If I sought to enter by the house, my own servants would consign me to the gallows. I saw I must employ another hand, and thought of Lanyon. How was he to be reached? how persuaded? Supposing that I escaped capture in the streets, how was I to make my way into his presence? and how should I, an unknown and displeasing visitor, prevail on the famous physician to rifle the study of his colleague, Dr Jekyll? Then I remembered that of my original character, one part remained to me: I could write my own hand; and once I had conceived that kindling spark, the way that I must follow became lighted up from end to end.

Thereupon, I arranged my clothes as best I could, and summoning a passing hansom, drove to an hotel in Portland street, the name of which I chanced to remember. At my appearance (which was indeed comical enough, however tragic a fate these garments covered) the driver could not conceal his mirth. I gnashed my teeth upon him with a gust of devilish fury; and the smile withered from his face—happily for him—yet more happily for myself, for in another instant I had certainly dragged him from his perch. At the inn, as I entered, I looked about me with so black a countenance as made the attendants tremble; not a look did they exchange in my presence; but obsequiously took my orders, led me to a private room, and brought me wherewithal to write. Hyde in dange of his life was a creature new to me: shaken with inordinate anger, strung to the pitch of murder, lusting to inflict pain. Yet the creature was astute; mastered his fury with a great effort of the will; composed his two important letters, one to Lanyon and one to Poole; and that he might receive actual evidence of their being posted, sent them out with directions that they should be registered.

Thenceforward, he sat all day over the fire in the private room, gnawing his nails; there he dined, sitting alone with his fears, the waiter visibly quailing before his eye; and thence, when the night was fully come, he set forth in the corner of a closed cab, and was driven to and fro about the streets of the city. He, I say—I cannot say, I.* That child of Hell had nothing human; nothing lived in him but fear and hatred. And when at last, thinking the driver had begun to grow suspicious, he discharged the cab and ventured on foot, attired in his misfitting clothes, an object marked out for observation, into the midst of the nocturnal passengers, these two base passions raged within him like a tempest. He walked fast, hunted by his fears, chattering to himself, skulking through the less frequented thoroughfares, counting the minutes that still divided him from midnight. Once a woman spoke to him, offering, I think, a box of lights. He smote her in the face, and she fled.

When I came to myself at Lanyon's, the horror of my old friend perhaps affected me somewhat: I do not know; it was at least but a drop in the sea to the abhorrence with which I looked back upon these hours. A change had come over me. It was no longer the fear of the gallows, it was the horror of being Hyde that racked me. I received Lanyon's condemnation partly in a dream; it was partly in a dream that I came home to my own house and got into bed. I slept after the prostration of the day, with a stringent and profound slumber which not even the nightmares that wrung me could avail to break. I awoke in the morning shaken, weakened, but refreshed. I still hated and feared the thought of the brute that slept within me, and I had not of course forgotten the appalling dangers of the day before; but I was once more at home, in my own house and close to my drugs; and gratitude for my escape shone so strong in my soul that it almost rivalled the brightness of hope.

I was stepping leisurely across the court after breakfast, drinking the chill of the air with pleasure, when I was seized again with those indescribable sensations that heralded the change; and I had but the time to gain the shelter of my cabinet, before I was once again raging and freezing with the passions of Hyde. It took on this occasion a double dose to recall me to myself; and alas, six hours after, as I sat looking sadly in the fire, the pangs returned, and the drug had to be re-administered. In short, from that day forth it seemed only by a great effort as of gymnastics, and only under the immediate stimulation of the drug, that I was able to wear the countenance of Jekyll. At all hours of the day and night, I would be taken with the premonitory shudder; above all, if I slept, or even dozed for a moment in my chair, it was always as Hyde that I awakened. Under the strain of this continually impending doom and by the sleeplessness to which I now condemned myself, ay, even beyond what I had thought possible to man, I became, in my own person, a creature eaten up and emptied by fever, languidly weak both in body and mind, and solely occupied by one thought: the horror of my other self. But when I slept, or when the virtue of the medicine wore off, I would leap almost without transition (for the pangs of transformation grew daily less marked) into the possession of a fancy brimming with images of terror, a soul boiling with causeless hatreds, and a body that seemed not strong enough to contain the raging energies of life. The powers of Hyde seemed to have grown with the sickliness of Jekyll. And certainly the hate that now divided them was equal on each side. With Jekyll, it was a thing of vital instinct. He had now seen the full deformity of that creature that shared with him some of the phenomena of consciousness, and was co-heir with him to death: and beyond these links of community, which in themselves made the most poignant part of his distress, he thought of Hyde, for all his energy of life, as of something not only hellish but inorganic. This was the shocking thing; that the slime of the pit seemed to utter cries and voices; that the amorphous dust gesticulated and sinned; that what was dead, and had no shape, should usurp the offices of life. And this again, that that insurgent horror was knit to him closer than a wife, closer than an eye; lay caged in his flesh, where he heard it mutter and felt it struggle to be born; and at every hour of weakness, and in the confidence of slumber, prevailed against him, and deposed him out of life. The hatred of Hyde for Jekyll, was of a different order. His terror of the gallows drove him continually to commit temporary suicide, and return to his subordinate station of a part instead of a person; but he loathed the necessity, he loathed the despondency into which Jekyll was now fallen, and he resented the dislike with which he was himself regarded. Hence the apelike tricks that he would play me, scrawling in my own hand blasphemies on the pages of my books, burning the letters and destroying the portrait of my father;* and indeed, had it not been for his fear of death, he would long ago have ruined himself in order to involve me in the ruin. But his love of life is wonderful; I go further: I, who sicken and freeze at the mere thought of him, when I recall the abjection and passion of this attachment, and when I know how he fears my power to cut him off by suicide, I find it in my heart to pity him.

It is useless, and the time awfully fails me, to prolong this description; no one has ever suffered such torments, let that suffice; and yet even to these, habit brought—no, not alleviation—but a certain callousness of soul, a certain acquiescence of despair; and my punishment might have gone on for years, but for the last calamity which has now fallen, and which has finally severed me from my own face and nature. My provision of the salt, which had never been renewed since the date of the first experiment, began to run low. I sent out for a fresh supply, and mixed the draught; the ebullition followed, and the first change of colour, not the second; I drank it and it was without efficiency. You will learn from Poole how I have had London ransacked; it was in vain; and I am now persuaded that my first supply was impure, and that it was that unknown impurity which lent efficacy to the draught.

About a week has passed, and I am now finishing this statement under the influence of the last of the old powders. This, then, is the last time, short of a miracle, that Henry Jekyll can think his own thoughts or see his own face (now how sadly altered!) in the glass. Nor must I delay too long to bring my writing to an end; for if my narrative has hitherto escaped destruction, it has been by a combination of great prudence and great good luck. Should the throes of change take me in the act of writing it, Hyde will tear it in pieces; but if some time shall have elapsed after I have laid it by, his wonderful selfishness and circumscription to the moment will probably save it once again from the action of his apelike spite. And indeed the doom that is closing on us both, has already changed and crushed him. Half an hour from now, when I shall again and forever reindue that hated personality, I know how I shall sit shuddering and weeping in my chair, or continue, with the most strained and fearstruck ecstasy of listening, to pace up and down this room (my last earthly refuge) and give ear to every sound of menace. Will Hyde die upon the scaffold? or will he find the courage to release himself at the last moment? God knows; I am careless; this is my true hour of death, and what is to follow concerns another than myself. Here then, as I lay down the pen and proceed to seal up my confession, I bring the life of that unhappy Henry Jekyll to an end.

Weir of Hermiston

AN UNFINISHED ROMANCE

TO MY WIFE

I saw rain falling and the rainbow drawn
On Lammermuir. Hearkening I heard again
In my precipitous city beaten bells
Winnow the keen sea wind. And here afar,
Intent on my own race and place, I wrote.
  Take thou the writing: thine it is. For who
Burnished the sword, blew on the drowsy coal,
Held still the target higher, chary of praise
And prodigal of counsel—who but thou?
So now, in the end, if this the least be good,
If any deed be done, if any fire
Burn in the imperfect page, the praise be thine.

CONTENTS

Dedication 79

Introductory 83

I. LIFE AND DEATH OF MRS WEIR 84

II. FATHER AND SON 97

III. IN THE MATTER OF THE HANGING OF DUNCAN JOPP 103

IV. OPINIONS OF THE BENCH 117

V. WINTER ON THE MOORS:

1. AT HERMISTON 125

2. KIRSTIE 128

3. A BORDER FAMILY 131

VI. A LEAF FROM CHRISTINA'S PSALM-BOOK 146

VII. ENTER MEPHISTOPHELES 168

VIII. A NOCTURNAL VISIT 183

IX. AT THE WEAVER'S STONE 190

INTRODUCTORY

IN the wild end of a moorland parish, far out of the sight of any house, there stands a cairn among the heather, and a little by east of it, in the going down of the braeside, a monument with some verses half defaced. It was here that Claverhouse* shot with his own hand the Praying Weaver of Balweary,* and the chisel of Old Mortality* has clinked on that lonely gravestone. Public and domestic history have thus marked with a bloody finger this hollow among the hills; and since the Cameronian* gave his life there, two hundred years ago, in a glorious folly, and without comprehension or regret, the silence of the moss has been broken once again by the report of firearms and the cry of the dying.

The Deil's Hags was the old name. But the place is now called Francie's Cairn.* For a while it was told that Francie walked. Aggie Hogg met him in the gloaming by the cairnside, and he spoke to her, with chattering teeth, so that his words were lost. He pursued Rob Todd (if any one could have believed Robbie) for the space of half a mile with pitiful entreaties. But the age is one of incredulity; these superstitious decorations speedily fell off; and the facts of the story itself, like the bones of a giant buried there and half dug up, survived, naked and imperfect, in the memory of the scattered neighbours. To this day, of winter nights, when the sleet is on the window and the cattle are quiet in the byre, there will be told again, amid the silence of the young and the additions and corrections of the old, the tale of the Justice-Clerk and of his son, young Hermiston, that vanished from men's knowledge; of the two Kirsties and the Four Black Brothers of the Cauldstaneslap; and of Frank Innes, 'the young fool advocate,' that came into these moorland parts to find his destiny.

CHAPTER I

LIFE AND DEATH OF MRS WEIR

THE Lord Justice-Clerk* was a stranger in that part of the country; but his lady wife was known there from a child, as her race had been before her. The old 'riding Rutherfords of Hermiston,' of whom she was the last descendant, had been famous men of yore, ill neighbours, ill subjects, and ill husbands to their wives though not their properties. Tales of them were rife for twenty miles about; and their name was even printed in the page of our Scots histories, not always to their credit. One bit the dust at Flodden;* one was hanged at his peel door by James the Fifth;* another fell dead in a carouse with Tom Dalyell;* while a fourth (and that was Jean's own father) died presiding at a Hell-Fire Club,* of which he was the founder. There were many heads shaken in Crossmichael at that judgment; the more so as the man had a villainous reputation among high and low, and both with the godly and the worldly. At that very hour of his demise, he had ten going pleas before the Session, eight of them oppressive. And the same doom extended even to his agents; his grieve, that had been his right hand in many a left-hand business, being cast from his horse one night and drowned in a peat-hag on the Kye-skairs; and his very doer (although lawyers have long spoons) surviving him not long, and dying on a sudden in a bloody flux.

In all these generations, while a male Rutherford was in a saddle with his lads, or brawling in a change-house, there would be always a white-faced wife immured at home in the old peel or the later mansion-house. It seemed this succession of martyrs bided long, but took their vengeance in the end, and that was in the person of the last descendant, Jean. She bore the name of the Rutherfords, but she was the daughter of their trembling wives. At the first she was not wholly without charm. Neighbours recalled in her, as a child, a strain of elfin wilfulness, gentle little mutinies, sad little gaieties, even a morning gleam of beauty that was not to be fulfilled. She withered in the growing, and (whether it was the sins of her sires or the sorrows of her mothers) came to her maturity depressed, and, as it were, defaced; no blood of life in her, no grasp or gaiety; pious, anxious, tender, tearful, and incompetent.

It was a wonder to many that she had married—seeming so wholly of the stuff that makes old maids. But chance cast her in the path of Adam Weir, then the new Lord-Advocate,* a recognised, risen man, the conqueror of many obstacles, and thus late in the day beginning to think upon a wife. He was one who looked rather to obedience than beauty, yet it would seem he was struck with her at the first look. 'Wha's she?' he said, turning to his host; and, when he had been told, 'Ay,' says he, 'she looks menseful. She minds me——'; and then, after a pause (which some have been daring enough to set down to sentimental recollections), 'Is she releegious?' he asked, and was shortly after, at his own request, presented. The acquaintance, which it seems profane to call a courtship, was pursued with Mr Weir's accustomed industry, and was long a legend, or rather a source of legends, in the Parliament House. He was described coming, rosy with much port, into the drawing-room, walking direct up to the lady, and assailing her with pleasantries, to which the embarrassed fair one responded, in what seemed a kind of agony, 'Eh, Mr Weir!' or 'O, Mr Weir!' or 'Keep me, Mr Weir!' On the very eve of their engagement, it was related that one had drawn near to the tender couple, and had overheard the lady cry out, with the tones of one who talked for the sake of talking, 'Keep me, Mr Weir, and what became of him?' and the profound accents of the suitor reply, 'Haangit, mem, haangit.'* The motives upon either side were much debated. Mr Weir must have supposed his bride to be somehow suitable; perhaps he belonged to that class of men who think a weak head the ornament of women—an opinion invariably punished in this life. Her descent and her estate were beyond question. Her wayfaring ancestors and her litigious father had done well by Jean. There was ready money and there were broad acres, ready to fall wholly to the husband, to lend dignity to his descendants, and to himself a title, when he should be called upon the Bench. On the side of Jean, there was perhaps some fascination of curiosity as to this unknown male animal that approached her with the roughness of a ploughman and the *aplomb* of an advocate. Being so trenchantly opposed to all she knew, loved, or understood, he may well have seemed to her the extreme, if scarcely the ideal, of his sex. And besides, he was an ill man to refuse. A little over forty at the period of his marriage, he looked already older, and to the force of manhood added the senatorial dignity of years; it was, perhaps, with an unreverend awe, but he was awful. The Bench, the Bar, and the most experienced and reluctant witness, bowed to his authority—and why not Jeannie Rutherford?

The heresy about foolish women is always punished, I have said, and Lord Hermiston began to pay the penalty at once. His house in George Square was wretchedly ill-guided; nothing answerable to the expense of maintenance but the cellar, which was his own private care. When things went wrong at dinner, as they continually did, my lord would look up the table at his wife: 'I think these broth would be better to sweem in than to sup.' Or else to the butler: 'Here, M'Killop, awa' wi' this Raadical gigot—tak' it to the French, man, and bring me some puddocks! It seems rather a sore kind of a business that I should be all day in Court haanging Raadicals, and get nawthing to my denner.' Of course this was but a manner of speaking, and he had never hanged a man for being a radical in his life; the law, of which he was the faithful minister, directing otherwise. And of course these growls were in the nature of pleasantry, but it was of a recondite sort; and uttered as they were in his resounding voice, and commented on by that expression which they called in the Parliament House 'Hermiston's hanging face'—they struck mere dismay into the wife. She sat before him speechless and fluttering; at each dish, as at a fresh ordeal, her eye hovered toward my lord's countenance and fell again; if he but ate in silence, unspeakable relief was her portion; if there were complaint, the world was darkened. She would seek out the cook, who was always her *sister in the Lord*. 'O, my dear, this is the most dreidful thing that my lord can never be contented in his own house!' she would begin; and weep and pray with the cook; and then the cook would pray with Mrs Weir; and the next day's meal would never be a penny the better—and the next cook (when she came) would be worse, if anything, but just as pious. It was often wondered that Lord Hermiston bore it as he did; indeed, he was a stoical old voluptuary, contented with sound wine and plenty of it. But there were moments when he overflowed. Perhaps half a dozen times in the history of his married life—'Here! tak' it awa,' and bring me a piece bread and kebbuck!' he had exclaimed, with an appalling explosion of his voice and rare gestures. None thought to dispute or to make excuses; the service was arrested; Mrs Weir sat at the head of the table whimpering without disguise; and his lordship opposite munched his bread and cheese in ostentatious disregard. Once only, Mrs Weir had ventured to appeal. He was passing her chair on his way into the study.

'O, Edom!' she wailed, in a voice tragic with tears, and reaching out to him both hands, in one of which she held a sopping pocket-handkerchief.

He paused and looked upon her with a face of wrath, into which there stole, as he looked, a twinkle of humour.

'Noansense!' he said. 'You and your noansense! What do I want with a Christian faim'ly? I want Christian broth! Get me a lass that can plain-boil a potato, if she was a whüre off the streets.' And with these words, which echoed in her tender ears like blasphemy, he had passed on to his study and shut the door behind him.

Such was the housewifery in George Square. It was better at Hermiston, where Kirstie Elliott, the sister of a neighbouring bonnet-laird, and an eighteenth cousin of the lady's, bore the charge of all, and kept a trim house and a good country table. Kirstie was a woman in a thousand, clean, capable, notable; once a moorland Helen, and still comely as a blood horse and healthy as the hill wind. High in flesh and voice and colour, she ran the house with her whole intemperate soul, in a bustle, not without buffets. Scarce more pious than decency in those days required, she was the cause of many an anxious thought and many a tearful prayer to Mrs

Weir. Housekeeper and mistress renewed the parts of Martha and Mary; and though with a pricking conscience, Mary reposed on Martha's strength as on a rock. Even Lord Hermiston held Kirstie in a particular regard. There were few with whom he unbent so gladly, few whom he favoured with so many pleasantries. 'Kirstie and me maun have our joke,' he would declare, in high good-humour, as he buttered Kirstie's scones, and she waited at table. A man who had no need either of love or of popularity, a keen reader of men and of events, there was perhaps only one truth for which he was quite unprepared: he would have been quite unprepared to learn that Kirstie hated him. He thought maid and master were well matched; hard, handy, healthy, broad Scots folk, without a hair of nonsense to the pair of them. And the fact was that she made a goddess and an only child of the effete and tearful lady; and even as she waited at table her hands would sometimes itch for my lord's ears.

Thus, at least, when the family were at Hermiston, not only my lord, but Mrs Weir too, enjoyed a holiday. Free from the dreadful looking-for of the miscarried dinner, she would mind her seam, read her piety books, and take her walk (which was my lord's orders), sometimes by herself, sometimes with Archie, the only child of that scarce natural union. The child was her next bond to life. Her frosted sentiment bloomed again, she breathed deep of life, she let loose her heart, in that society. The miracle of her motherhood was ever new to her. The sight of the little man at her skirt intoxicated her with the sense of power, and froze her with the consciousness of her responsibility. She looked forward, and, seeing him in fancy grow up and play his diverse part on the world's theatre, caught in her breath and lifted up her courage with a lively effort. It was only with the child that she forgot herself and was at moments natural; yet it was only with the child that she had conceived and managed to pursue a scheme of conduct. Archie was to be a great man and a good; a minister if possible, a saint for certain. She tried to engage his mind upon her favourite books, Rutherford's *Letters,** Scougal's *Grace Abounding,** and the like. It was a common practice of hers (and strange to remember now) that she would carry the child to the Deil's Hags, sit with him on the Praying Weaver's stone, and talk of the Covenanters till their tears ran down. Her view of history was wholly artless, a design in snow and ink; upon the one side, tender innocents with psalms upon their lips; upon the other, the persecutors, booted, bloody-minded, flushed with wine: a suffering Christ, a raging Beelzebub. *Persecutor* was a word that knocked upon the woman's heart; it was her highest thought of wickedness, and the mark of it was on her house. Her great-great-grandfather had drawn the sword against the Lord's anointed on the field of Rullion Green,* and breathed his last (tradition said) in the arms of the detestable Dalyell. Nor could she blind herself to this, that had they lived in those old days, Hermiston himself would have been numbered alongside of Bloody MacKenzie* and the politic Lauderdale* and Rothes,* in the band of God's immediate enemies. The sense of this moved her to the more fervour; she had a voice for that name of *persecutor* that thrilled in the child's marrow; and when one day the mob hooted and hissed them all in my lord's travelling carriage, and cried, 'Down with the persecutor! down with Hanging Hermiston!' and mamma covered her eyes and wept, and papa let down the glass and looked out upon the rabble with his droll formidable face, bitter and smiling, as they said he sometimes looked when he gave sentence, Archie was for the moment too much amazed to be alarmed, but he had scarce got his mother by herself before his shrill voice was raised demanding an explanation: why had they called papa a persecutor?

'Keep me, my precious!' she exclaimed. 'Keep me, my dear! this is poleetical. Ye must never ask me anything poleetical,* Erchie. Your faither is a great man, my dear, and it's no for me or you to be judging him. It would be telling us all, if we behaved ourselves in our several stations the way your faither does in his high office; and let me hear no more of any such disrespectful and undutiful questions! No that you meant to be undutiful, my lamb; your mother kens that—she kens it well, dearie!' And so slid off to safer topics, and left on the mind of the child an obscure but ineradicable sense of something wrong.

Mrs Weir's philosophy of life was summed in one expression—tenderness. In her view of the universe, which was all lighted up with a glow out of the doors of hell, good people must walk there in a kind of ecstasy of tenderness. The beasts and plants had no souls; they were here but for a day, and let their day pass gently! And as for the immortal men, on what black, downward path were many of them wending, and to what a horror of an immortality! 'Are not two sparrows,' 'Whosoever shall smite thee,' 'God Sendeth His rain,' 'Judge not, that ye be not judged'—these texts made her body of divinity; she put them on in the morning with her clothes and lay down to sleep with them at night; they haunted her like a favourite air, they clung about her like a favourite perfume. Their minister was a marrowy expounder of the law, and my lord sat under him with relish; but Mrs Weir respected him from far off; heard him (like the cannon of a beleaguered city) usefully booming outside on the dogmatic ramparts; and meanwhile, within and out of shot, dwelt in her private garden which she watered with grateful tears. It seems strange to say of this colourless and ineffectual woman, but she was a true enthusiast, and might have made the sunshine and the glory of a cloister. Perhaps none but Archie knew she could be eloquent; perhaps none but he had seen her—her colour raised, her hands clasped or quivering—glow with gentle ardour. There is a corner of the policy of Hermiston, where you come suddenly in view of the summit of Black Fell, sometimes like the mere grass top of a hill, sometimes (and this is her own expression) like a precious jewel in the heavens. On such days, upon the sudden view of it, her hand would tighten on the child's fingers, her voice rise like a song. '*I to the hills!*' she would repeat. 'And O, Erchie, are nae these like the hills of Naphtali?'* and her tears would flow.

Upon an impressionable child the effect of this continual and pretty accompaniment to life was deep. The woman's quietism and piety passed on to his different nature undiminished; but whereas in her it was a native sentiment, in him it was only an implanted dogma. Nature and the child's pugnacity at times revolted. A cad from the Potterrow once struck him in the mouth; he struck back, the pair fought it out in the back stable lane towards the Meadows, and Archie returned with a considerable decline in the number of his front teeth, and unregenerately boasting of the losses of the foe. It was a sore day for Mrs Weir; she wept and prayed over the infant backslider until my lord was due from Court, and she must resume that air of tremulous composure with which she always greeted him. The judge was that day in an observant mood, and remarked upon the absent teeth.

'I am afraid Erchie will have been fechting with some of they blagyard lads,' said Mrs Weir.

My lord's voice rang out as it did seldom in the privacy of his own house. 'I'll have nonn of that, sir!' he cried. 'Do you hear me?—nonn of that! No son of mine shall be speldering in the glaur with any dirty raibble.'

The anxious mother was grateful for so much support; she had even feared the contrary. And that night when she put the child to bed—'Now, my dear, ye see!' she said, 'I told you what your faither would think of it, if he heard ye had fallen into this dreidful sin; and let you and me pray to God that ye may be keepit from the like temptation or stren'thened to resist it!'

The womanly falsity of this was thrown away. Ice and iron cannot be welded; and the points of view of the Justice-Clerk and Mrs Weir were not less unassimilable. The character and position of his father had long been a stumbling-block to Archie, and with every year of his age the difficulty grew more instant. The man was mostly silent; when he spoke at all, it was to speak of the things of the world, always in a worldly spirit, often in language that the child had been schooled to think coarse, and sometimes with words that he knew to be sins in themselves. Tenderness was the first duty, and my lord was invariably harsh. God was love, the name of my lord (to all who knew him) was fear. In the world, as schematised for Archie by his mother, the place was marked for such a creature. There were some whom it was good to pity and well (though very likely useless) to pray for; they were named reprobates, goats, God's enemies, brands for the burning; and Archie tallied every mark of identification, and drew the inevitable private inference that the Lord Justice-Clerk was the chief of sinners.

The mother's honesty was scarce complete. There was one influence she feared for the child and still secretly combated; that was my lord's; and half unconsciously, half in a wilful blindness, she continued to undermine her husband with his son. As long as Archie remained silent, she did so ruthlessly, with a single eye to heaven and the child's salvation; but the day came when Archie spoke. It was 1801, and Archie was seven, and beyond his years for curiosity and logic, when he brought the case up openly. If judging were sinful and forbidden, how came papa to be a judge? to have that sin for a trade? to bear the name of it for a distinction?

'I can't see it,' said the little Rabbi, and wagged his head.

Mrs Weir abounded in commonplace replies.

'No, I canna see it,' reiterated Archie. 'And I'll tell you what, mamma, I don't think you and me's justifeed in staying with him.'*

The woman awoke to remorse; she saw herself disloyal to her man, her sovereign and bread-winner, in whom (with what she had of worldliness) she took a certain subdued pride. She expatiated in reply on my lord's honour and greatness; his useful services in this world of sorrow and wrong, and the place in which he stood, far above where babes and innocents could hope to see or criticise. But she had builded too well—Archie had his answers pat: Were not babes and innocents the type of the kingdom of heaven? Were not honour and greatness the badges of the world? And at any rate, how about the mob that had once seethed about the carriage?

'It's all very fine,' he concluded, 'but in my opinion, papa has no right to be it. And it seems that's not the worst yet of it. It seems he's called "the Hanging Judge"*—it seems he's crooool. I'll tell you what it is, mamma, there's a tex' borne in upon me: It were better for that man if a milestone were bound upon his back and him flung into the deepestmost pairts of the sea.'

'O, my lamb, ye must never say the like of that!' she cried. 'Ye're to honour faither and mother, dear, that your days may be long in the land. It's Atheists that cry out against him—

French Atheists, Erchie! Ye would never surely even yourself down to be saying the same thing as French Atheists? It would break my heart to think that of you. And O, Erchie, here arena *you* setting up to *judge*? And have ye no forgot God's plain command—the First with Promise, dear? Mind you upon the beam and the mote!'

Having thus carried the war into the enemy's camp, the terrified lady breathed again. And no doubt it is easy thus to circumvent a child with catchwords, but it may be questioned how far it is effectual. An instinct in his breast detects the quibble, and a voice condemns it. He will instantly submit, privately hold the same opinion. For even in this simple and antique relation of the mother and the child, hypocrisies are multiplied.

When the Court rose that year and the family returned to Hermiston, it was a common remark in all the country that the lady was sore failed. She seemed to loose and seize again her touch with life, now sitting inert in a sort of durable bewilderment, anon waking to feverish and weak activity. She dawdled about the lasses at their work, looking stupidly on; she fell to rummaging in old cabinets and presses, and desisted when half through; she would begin remarks with an air of animation and drop them without a struggle. Her common appearance was of one who has forgotten something and is trying to remember; and when she overhauled, one after another, the worthless and touching mementoes of her youth, she might have been seeking the clue to that lost thought. During this period, she gave many gifts to the neighbours and house lasses, giving them with a manner of regret that embarrassed the recipients.

The last night of all she was busy on some female work, and toiled upon it with so manifest and painful a devotion that my lord (who was not often curious) inquired as to its nature.

She blushed to the eyes. 'O, Edom, it's for you!' she said. 'It's slippers. I—I hae never made ye any.'

'Ye daft auld wife!' returned his lordship. 'A bonny figure I would be, palmering about in bauchles!'

The next day, at the hour of her walk, Kirstie interfered. Kirstie took this decay of her mistress very hard; bore her a grudge, quarrelled with railed upon her, the anxiety of a genuine love wearing the disguise of temper. This day of all days she insisted disrespectfully, with rustic fury, that Mrs Weir should stay at home. But, 'No, no,' she said, 'it's my lord's orders,' and set forth us usual. Archie was visible in the acre bog, engaged upon some childish enterprise, the instrument of which was mire; and she stood and looked at him a while like one about to call; then thought otherwise, sighed, and shook her head, and proceeded on her rounds alone. The house lasses were at the burnside washing, and saw her pass with her loose, weary, dowdy gait.

'She's a terrible feckless wife, the mistress!' said the one.

'Tut,' said the other, 'the wumman's seeck.'

'Weel, I canna see nae differ in her,' returned the first. 'A füshionless quean, a feckless carline.'

The poor creature thus discussed rambled a while in the grounds without a purpose. Tides in her mind ebbed and flowed, and carried her to and fro like seaweed. She tried a path, paused, returned, and tried another; questing, forgetting her quest; the spirit of choice extinct in her bosom, or devoid of sequency. On a sudden, it appeared as though she had remembered, or had formed a resolution, wheeled about, returned with hurried steps, and appeared in the dining-room, where Kirstie was at the cleaning, like one charged with an important errand.

'Kirstie?' she began, and paused; and then with conviction, 'Mr Weir isna speeritually minded, but he has been a good man to me.'

It was perhaps the first time since her husband's elevation that she had forgotten the handle to his name, of which the tender, inconsistent woman was not a little proud. And when Kirstie looked up at the speaker's face, she was aware of a change.

'Godsake, what's the maitter wi' ye, mem?' cried the housekeeper, starting from the rug.

'I do not ken,' answered her mistress, shaking her head. 'But he is not speeritually minded, my dear.'

'Here, sit down with ye! Godsake, what ails the wife?' cried Kirstie, and helped and forced her into the lord's own chair by the cheek of the hearth.

'Keep me, what's this?' she gasped. 'Kirstie, what's this? I'm frich'ened.'

They were her last words.

It was the lowering nightfall when my lord returned. He had the sunset in his back, all clouds and glory; and before him, by the wayside, spied Kirstie Elliott waiting. She was dissolved in tears, and addressed him in the high, false note of barbarous mourning, such as still lingers modified among Scots heather.

'The Lord peety ye, Hermiston! the Lord prepare ye!' she keened out. 'Weary upon me, that I should have to tell it!'

He reined in his horse and looked upon her with the hanging face.

'Has the French landit?' cried he.

'Man, man,' she said, 'is that a' ye can think of? The Lord prepare ye: the Lord comfort and support ye!'

'Is onybody deid?' says his lordship. 'It's no Erchie?'

'Bethankit, no!' exclaimed the woman startled into a more natural tone. 'Na, na, it's no sae bad as that. It's the mistress, my lord; she just fair flittit before my e'en. She just gi'ed a sab and was by wi' it. Eh, my bonny Miss Jeannie, that I mind sae weel!' And forth again upon that pouring tide of lamentation in which women of her class excel and overabound.

Lord Hermiston sat in the saddle beholding her. Then he seemed to recover command upon himself.

'Weel, it's something of the suddenest,' said he. 'But she was a dwaibly body from the first.'

And he rode home at a precipitate amble with Kirstie at his horse's heels.

Dressed as she was for her last walk, they had laid the dead lady on her bed. She was never interesting in life; in death she was not impressive; and as her husband stood before her, with his hands crossed behind his powerful back, that which he looked upon was the very image of the insignificant.

'Her and me were never cut out for one another,' he remarked at last. 'It was a daft-like marriage.' And then, with a most unusual gentleness of tone, 'Puir bitch,' said he, 'puir bitch!' Then suddenly: 'Where's Erchie?'

Kirstie had decoyed him to her room and given him 'a jeely-piece.'

'Ye have some kind of gumption, too,' observed the judge, and considered his housekeeper grimly. 'When all's said,' he added, 'I micht have done waur—I micht have been marriet upon a skirling Jezebel like you!'

'There's naebody thinking of you, Hermiston!' cried the offended woman. 'We think of her that's out of her sorrows. And could *she* have done waur? Tell me that, Hermiston—tell me that before her clay-cauld corp!'

'Weel, there's some of them gey an' ill to please,' observed his lordship.

CHAPTER II

FATHER AND SON

MY Lord Justice-Clerk was known to many; the man Adam Weir perhaps to none. He had nothing to explain or to conceal; he sufficed wholly and silently to himself; and that part of our nature which goes out (too often with false coin) to acquire glory or love, seemed in him to be omitted. He did not try to be loved, he did not care to be; it is probable the very thought of it was a stranger to his mind. He was an admired lawyer, a highly unpopular judge; and he looked down upon those who were his inferiors in either distinction, who were lawyers of less grasp or judges not so much detested. In all the rest of his days and doings, not one trace of vanity appeared; and he went on through life with a mechanical movement, as of the unconscious, that was almost august.

He saw little of his son. In the childish maladies with which the boy was troubled, he would make daily inquiries and daily pay him a visit, entering the sick-room with a facetious and appalling countenance, letting off a few perfunctory jests, and going again swiftly, to the patient's relief. Once, a court holiday falling opportunely, my lord had his carriage, and drove the child himself to Hermiston, the customary place of convalescence. It is conceivable he had been more than usually anxious, for that journey always remained in Archie's memory as a thing apart, his father having related to him from beginning to end, and with much detail, three authentic murder cases. Archie went the usual round of other Edinburgh boys, the high school and the college; and Hermiston looked on, or rather looked away, with scarce an affectation of interest in his progress. Daily, indeed, upon a signal after dinner, he was brought in, given nuts and a glass of port, regarded sardonically, sarcastically questioned. 'Well, sir, and what have you donn with you book to-day?' my lord might begin, and set him posers in law Latin. To a child just stumbling into Corderius, Papinian and Paul* proved quite invincible. But papa had memory of no other. He was not harsh to the little scholar, having a vast fund of patience learned upon the bench, and was at no pains whether to conceal or to express his disappointment. 'Well, ye have a long jaunt before ye yet!' he might observe, yawning, and fall back on his own thoughts (as like as not) until the time came for separation, and my lord would take the decanter and the glass, and be off to the back chambers looking on the Meadows, where he toiled on his cases till the hours were small. There was no 'fuller man' on the bench; his memory was marvellous, though wholly legal; if he had to 'advise' extempore, none did it better; yet there was none who more earnestly prepared. As he thus watched in the night, or sat at table and forgot the presence of his son, no doubt but he tasted deeply of recondite pleasures. To be wholly devoted to some intellectual exercise is to have succeeded in life; and perhaps only in law and the higher mathematics may this devotion be maintained, suffice to itself without reaction, and find continual rewards without excitement. This atmosphere of his father's sterling industry was the best of Archie's education. Assuredly it did not attract him; assuredly it rather rebutted and depressed. Yet it was still present, unobserved like the ticking of a clock, an arid ideal, a tasteless stimulant in the boy's life.

But Hermiston was not all of one piece. He was, besides, a mighty toper; he could sit at wine until the day dawned, and pass directly from the table to the bench with a steady hand and a clear head. Beyond the third bottle, he showed the plebeian in a larger print; the low, gross accent, the low, foul mirth, grew broader and commoner; he became less formidable, and infinitely more disgusting. Now, the boy had inherited from Jean Rutherford a shivering delicacy, unequally mated with potential violence. In the playing-fields, and amongst his own companions, he repaid a coarse expression with a blow; at his father's table (when the time came for him to join these revels) he turned pale and sickened in silence. Of all the guests whom he there encountered, he had toleration for only one: David Keith Carnegie, Lord Glenalmond. Lord Glenalmond was tall and emaciated, with long features and long delicate hands. He was often compared with the statue of Forbes of Culloden* in the Parliament House; and his blue eye, at more than sixty, preserved some of the fire of youth. His exquisite disparity with any of his fellow-guests, his appearance as of an artist and an aristocrat stranded in rude company, riveted the boy's attention; and as curiosity and interest are the things in the world that are the most immediately and certainly rewarded, Lord Glenalmond was attracted by the boy.

'And so this is your son, Hermiston?' he asked, laying his hand on Archie's shoulder. 'He's getting a big lad.'

'Hout!' said the gracious father, 'just his mother over again—daurna say boo to a goose!'

But the stranger retained the boy, talked to him, drew him out, found in him a taste for letters, and a fine, ardent, modest, youthful soul; and encouraged him to be a visitor on Sunday evenings in his bare, cold, lonely dining-room, where he sat and read in the isolation of a bachelor grown old in refinement. The beautiful gentleness and grace of the old judge, and the delicacy of his person, thoughts, and language, spoke to Archie's heart in its own tongue. He conceived the ambition to be such another; and, when the day came for him to choose a profession, it was in emulation of Lord Glenalmond, not of Lord Hermiston, that he chose the Bar. Hermiston looked on at this friendship with some secret pride, but openly with the intolerance of scorn. He scarce lost an opportunity to put them down with a rough jape; and, to say truth, it was not difficult, for they were neither of them quick. He had a word of contempt for the whole crowd of poets, painters, fiddlers, and their admirers, the bastard race of amateurs, which was continually on his lips. 'Signor Feedle-eerie!' he would say. 'O, for Goad's sake, no more of the Signor!'

'You and my father are great friends, are you not?' asked Archie once.

'There is no man that I more respect, Archie,' replied Lord Glenalmond. 'He is two things of price. He is a great lawyer, and he is upright as the day.'

'You and he are so different,' said the boy, his eyes dwelling on those of his old friend, like a lover's on his mistress's.

'Indeed so,' replied the judge; 'very different. And so I fear are you and he. Yet I would like it very ill if my young friend were to misjudge his father. He has all the Roman virtues: Cato and Brutus* were such; I think a son's heart might well be proud of such an ancestry of one.'

'And I would sooner he were a plaided herd,' cried Archie, with sudden bitterness.

'And that is neither very wise, nor I believe entirely true,' returned Glenalmond. 'Before you are done you will find some of these expressions rise on you like a remorse. They are merely literary and decorative; they do not aptly express your thought, nor is your thought clearly apprehended, and no doubt your father (if he were here) would say, "Signor Feedle-eerie!" '

With the infinitely delicate sense of youth, Archie avoided the subject from that hour. It was perhaps a pity. Had he but talked—talked freely—let himself gush out in words (the way youth loves to do and should), there might have been no tale to write upon the Weirs of Hermiston. But the shadow of a threat of ridicule sufficed; in the slight tartness of these words he read a prohibition; and it is likely that Glenalmond meant it so.

Besides the veteran, the boy was without confidant or friend. Serious and eager, he came through school and college, and moved among a crowd of the indifferent, in the seclusion of his shyness. He grew up handsome, with an open, speaking countenance, with graceful, youthful ways; he was clever, he took prizes, he shone in the Speculative Society.* It should seem he must become the centre of a crowd of friends; but something that was in part the delicacy of his mother, in part the austerity of his father, held him aloof from all. It is a fact, and a strange one, that among his contemporaries Hermiston's son was thought to be a chip of the old block. 'You're a friend of Archie Weir's?' said one to Frank Innes; and Innes replied, with his usual flippancy and more than his usual insight: 'I know Weir, but I never met Archie.' No one had met Archie, a malady most incident to only sons. He flew his private signal, and none heeded it; it seemed he was abroad in a world from which the very hope of intimacy was banished; and he looked round about him on the concourse of his fellow-students, and forward to the trivial days and acquaintances that were to come, without hope or interest.

As time went on, the tough and rough old sinner felt himself drawn to the son of his loins and sole continuator of his new family, with softnesses of sentiment that he could hardly credit and was wholly impotent to express. With a face, voice, and manner trained through forty years to terrify and repel, Rhadamanthus* may be great, but he will scarce be engaging. It is a fact that he tried to propitiate Archie, but a fact that cannot be too lightly taken; the attempt was so unconspicuously made, the failure so stoically supported. Sympathy is not due to these steadfast iron natures. If he failed to gain his son's friendship, or even his son's toleration, on he went up the great, bare staircase of his duty, uncheered and undepressed. There might have been more pleasure in his relations with Archie, so much he may have recognised at moments; but pleasure was a by-product of the singular chemistry of life, which only fools expected.

An idea of Archie's attitude, since we are all grown up and have forgotten the days of our youth, it is more difficult to convey. He made no attempt whatsoever to understand the man with whom he dined and breakfasted. Parsimony of pain, glut of pleasure, these are the two alternating ends of youth; and Archie was of the parsimonious. The wind blew cold out of a certain quarter—he turned his back upon it; stayed as little as was possible in his father's presence; and when there, averted his eyes as much as was decent from his father's face. The lamp shone for many hundred days upon these two at table—my lord, ruddy, gloomy, and unreverent; Archie with a potential brightness that was always dimmed and veiled in that society; and there were not, perhaps, in Christendom two men more radically strangers. The father, with a grand simplicity, either spoke of what interested himself, or maintained an unaffected silence. The son turned in his head for some topic that should be quite safe, that would spare him fresh evidences either of my lord's inherent grossness or of the innocence of his inhumanity; treading gingerly the ways of intercourse, like a lady gathering up her skirts in a by-path. If he made a mistake, and my lord began to abound in matter of offence, Archie drew himself up, his brow grew dark, his share of the talk expired; but my lord would faithfully and cheerfully continue to pour out the worst of himself before his silent and offended son.

'Well, it's a poor hert that never rejoices!' he would say, at the conclusion of such a nightmare interview. 'But I must get to my plew-stilts.' And he would seclude himself as usual in the back room, and Archie go forth into the night and the city quivering with animosity and scorn.

CHAPTER III

IN THE MATTER OF THE HANGING OF DUNCAN JOPP

IT chanced in the year 1813 that Archie strayed one day into the Judiciary Court. The macer made room for the son of the presiding judge. In the dock, the centre of men's eyes, there stood a whey-coloured, misbegotten caitiff, Duncan Jopp, on trial for his life. His story, as it was raked out before him in that public scene, was one of disgrace and vice and cowardice, the very nakedness of crime; and the creature heard and it seemed at times as though he understood—as if at times he forgot the horror of the place he stood in, and remembered the shame of what had brought him there. He kept his head bowed and his hands clutched upon the rail; his hair dropped in his eyes and at times he flung it back; and now he glanced about the audience in a sudden fellness of terror, and now looked in the face of his judge and gulped. There was pinned about his throat a piece of dingy flannel; and that it was perhaps that turned the scale in Archie's mind between disgust and pity. The creature stood in a vanishing point; yet a little while, and he was still a man, and had eyes and apprehension; yet a little longer, and with a last sordid piece of pageantry, he would cease to be. And here, in the meantime, with a trait of human nature that caught at the beholder's breath, he was tending a sore throat.

Over against him, my Lord Hermiston occupied the bench in the red robes of criminal jurisdiction, his face framed in the white wig. Honest all through, he did not affect the virtue of impartiality; this was no case for refinement; there was a man to be hanged, he would have said, and he was hanging him. Nor was it possible to see his lordship, and acquit him of gusto in the task. It was plain he gloried in the exercise of his trained faculties, in the clear sight which pierced at once into the joint of fact, in the rude, unvarnished gibes with which he demolished every figment of defence. He took his ease and jested, unbending in that solemn place with some of the freedom of the tavern; and the rag of man with the flannel round his neck was hunted gallowsward with jeers.

Duncan had a mistress, scarce less forlorn and greatly older than himself, who came up, whimpering and curtseying, to add the weight of her betrayal. My lord gave her the oath in his most roaring voice, and added an intolerant warning.

'Mind what ye say now, Janet,' said he. 'I have an e'e upon ye, I'm ill to jest with.'

Presently, after she was tremblingly embarked on her story, 'And what made ye do this, ye auld runt?' the Court interposed. 'Do ye mean to tell me ye was the panel's mistress?'

'If you please, ma loard,' whined the female.

'Godsake! ye made a bonny couple,' observed his lordship; and there was something so formidable and ferocious in his scorn that not even the galleries thought to laugh.

The summing up contained some jewels.

'These two peetiable creatures seem to have made up thegither, it's not for us to explain why.'—'The panel, who (whatever else he may be) appears to be equally ill set-out in mind and boady.'—'Neither the panel nor yet the old wife appears to have had so much common sense as even to tell a lie when it was necessary.' And in the course of sentencing, my lord had this *obiter dictum*:* 'I have been the means, under God, of haanging a great number, but never just such a disjaskit rascal as yourself.' The words were strong in themselves; the light and heat and detonation of their delivery, and the savage pleasure of the speaker in his task, made them tingle in the ears.

When all was over, Archie came forth again into a changed world. Had there been the least redeeming greatness in the crime, any obscurity, any dubiety, perhaps he might have understood. But the culprit stood, with his sore throat, in the sweat of his mortal agony, without defence or excuse: a thing to cover up with blushes: a being so much sunk beneath the zones of sympathy that pity might seem harmless. And the judge had pursued him with a monstrous, relishing gaiety, horrible to be conceived, a trait for nightmares. It is one thing to spear a tiger, another to crush a toad; there are aesthetics even of the slaughter-house; and the loathsomeness of Duncan Jopp enveloped and infected the image of his judge.

Archie passed by his friends in the High Street with incoherent words and gestures. He saw Holyrood* in a dream, remembrance of its romance awoke in him and faded; he had a vision of the old radiant stories, of Queen Mary* and Prince Charlie,* of the hooded stag,* of the splendour and crime, the velvet and bright iron of the past; and dismissed them with a cry of pain. He lay and moaned in the Hunter's Bog, and the heavens were dark above him and the grass of the field an offence. 'This is my father,' he said. 'I draw my life from him; the flesh upon my bones is his, the bread I am fed with is the wages of these horrors.' He recalled his mother, and ground his forehead in the earth. He thought of flight, and where was he to flee to? of other lives, but was there any life worth living in this den of savage and jeering animals?

The interval before the execution was like a violent dream. He met his father; he would not look at him, he could not speak to him. It seemed there was no living creature but must have been swift to recognise that imminent animosity; but the hide of the Justice-Clerk remained impenetrable. Had my lord been talkative, the truce could never have subsisted; but he was by fortune in one of his humours of sour silence; and under the very guns of his broadside, Archie nursed the enthusiasm of rebellion. It seemed to him, from the top of his nineteen years' experience, as if he were marked at birth to be the perpetrator of some signal action, to set back fallen Mercy, to overthrow the usurping devil that sat, horned and hoofed, on her throne. Seductive Jacobin figments, which he had often refuted at the Speculative, swam up in his mind and startled him as with voices: and he seemed to himself to walk accompanied by an almost tangible presence of new beliefs and duties.

On the named morning he was at the place of execution. He saw the fleering rabble, the flinching wretch produced. He looked on for a while at a certain parody of devotion, which seemed to strip the wretch of his last claim to manhood. Then followed the brutal instant of extinction, and the paltry dangling of the remains like a broken jumping-jack. He had been prepared for something terrible, not for this tragic meanness. He stood a moment silent, and then—'I denounce this God-defying murder,' he shouted; and his father, if he must have disclaimed the sentiment, might have owned the stentorian voice with which it was uttered.

Frank Innes dragged him from the spot. The two handsome lads followed the same course of study and recreation, and felt a certain mutual attraction, founded mainly on good looks. It had never gone deep; Frank was by nature a thin, jeering creature, not truly susceptible whether of feeling or inspiring friendship; and the relation between the pair was altogether on the outside, a thing of common knowledge and the pleasantries that spring from a common acquaintance. The more credit to Frank that he was appalled by Archie's outburst, and at least conceived the design of keeping him in sight, and, if possible, in hand, for the day. But Archie, who had just defied—was it God or Satan?—would not listen to the word of a college companion.

'I will not go with you,' he said. 'I do not desire your company, sir; I would be alone.'

'Here, Weir, man, don't be absurd,' said Innes, keeping a tight hold upon his sleeve. 'I will not let you go until I know what you mean to do with yourself; it's no use brandishing that staff.' For indeed at that moment Archie had made a sudden—perhaps a warlike—movement. 'This has been the most insane affair; you know it has. You know very well that I'm playing the good Samaritan. All I wish is to keep you quiet.'

'If quietness is what you wish, Mr Innes,' said Archie, 'and you will promise to leave me entirely to myself, I will tell you so much, that I am going to walk in the country and admire the beauties of nature.'

'Honour bright?' asked Frank.

'I am not in the habit of lying, Mr Innes,' retorted Archie. 'I have the honour of wishing you good-day.'

'You won't forget the Spec.?' asked Innes.

'The Spec.?' said Archie. 'O no, I won't forget the Spec.'

And the one young man carried his tortured spirit forth of

the city and all the day long, by one road and another, in an endless pilgrimage of misery; while the other hastened smilingly to spread the news of Weir's access of insanity, and to drum up for that night a full attendance at the Speculative, where further eccentric developments might certainly be looked for. I doubt if Innes had the least belief in his prediction; I think it flowed rather from a wish to make the story as good and the scandal as great as possible; not from any ill-will to Archie—from the mere pleasure of beholding interested faces. But for all that his words were prophetic. Archie did not forget the Spec.;* he put in an appearance there at the due time, and, before the evening was over, had dealt a memorable shock to his companions. It chanced he was the president of the night. He sat in the same room where the Society still meets—only the portraits were not there: the men who afterwards sat for them were then but beginning their career. The same lustre of many tapers shed its light over the meeting; the same chair, perhaps, supported him that so many of us have sat in since. At times he seemed to forget the business of the evening, but even in these periods he sat with a great air of energy and determination. At times he meddled bitterly, and launched with defiance those fines which are the precious and rarely used artillery of the president. He little thought, as he did so, how he resembled his father, but his friends remarked upon it, chuckling. So far, in his high place above his fellow-students, he seemed set beyond the possibility of any scandal; but his mind was made up—he was determined to fulfil the sphere of his offence. He signed to Innes (whom he had just fined, and who just impeached his ruling) to succeed him in the chair, stepped down from the platform, and took his place by the chimney-piece, the shine of many wax tapers from above illuminating his pale face, the glow of the great red fire relieving from behind his slim figure. He had to propose, as an amendment to the next subject in the case-book, 'Whether capital punishment be consistent with God's will or man's policy?'

A breath of embarrassment, of something like alarm, passed round the room, so daring did these words appear upon the lips of Hermiston's only son. But the amendment was not seconded; the previous question was promptly moved and unanimously voted, and the momentary scandal smuggled by. Innes triumphed in the fulfilment of his prophecy. He and Archie were now become the heroes of the night; but whereas every one crowded about Innes, when the meeting broke up, but one of all his companions came to speak to Archie.

'Weir, man! That was an extraordinary raid of yours!' observed this courageous member, taking him confidentially by the arm as they went out.

'I don't think it a raid,' said Archie grimly. 'More like a war. I saw that poor brute hanged this morning, and my gorge rises at it yet.'

'Hut-tut,' returned his companion, and, dropping his arm like something hot, he sought the less tense society of others.

Archie found himself alone. The last of the faithful—or was it only the boldest of the curious?—had fled. He watched the black huddle of his fellow-students draw off down and up the street, in whispering or boisterous gangs. And the isolation of the moment weighed upon him like an omen and an emblem of his destiny in life. Bred up in unbroken fear himself, among trembling servants, and in a house which (at the least ruffle in the master's voice) shuddered into silence, he saw himself on the brink of the red valley of war, and measured the danger and length of it with awe. He made a détour in the glimmer and shadow of the streets, came into the back stable lane, and watched for a long while the light burn steady in the Judge's room. The longer he gazed upon that illuminated window-blind, the more blank became the picture of the man who sat behind it, endlessly turning over sheets of process, pausing to sip a glass of port, or rising and passing heavily about his book-lined walls to verify some reference. He could not combine the brutal judge and the industrious, dispassionate student; the connecting link escaped him; from such a dual nature, it was impossible he should predict behaviour; and he asked himself if he had done well to plunge into a business of which the end could not be foreseen? and presently after, with a sickening decline of confidence, if he had done loyally to strike his father? For he had struck him—defied him twice over and before a cloud of witnesses—struck him a public buffet before crowds. Who had called him to judge his father in these precarious and high questions? The office was usurped. It might have become a stranger; in a son—there was no blinking it—in a son, it was disloyal. And now, between these two natures so antipathetic, so hateful to each other, there was depending an unpardonable affront: and the providence of God alone might foresee the manner in which it would be resented by Lord Hermiston.

These misgivings tortured him all night and arose with him in the winter's morning; they followed him from class to class, they made him shrinkingly sensitive to every shade of manner in his companions, they sounded in his ears through the current voice of the professor; and he brought them home with him at night unabated and indeed increased. The cause of this increase lay in a chance encounter with the celebrated Dr Gregory.* Archie stood looking vaguely in the lighted window of a book shop, trying to nerve himself for the approaching ordeal. My lord and he had met and parted in the morning as they had now done for long, with scarcely the ordinary civilities of life; and it was plain to the son that nothing had yet reached the father's ears. Indeed, when he recalled the awful countenance of my lord, a timid hope sprang up in him that perhaps there would be found no one bold enough to carry tales. If this were so, he asked himself, would he begin again? and he found no answer. It was at this moment that a hand was laid upon his arm, and a voice said in his ear, 'My dear Mr Archie, you had better come and see me.'

He started, turned round, and found himself face to face with Dr Gregory. 'And why should I come to see you?' he asked, with the defiance of the miserable.

'Because you are looking exceeding ill,' said the doctor, 'and you very evidently want looking after, my young friend. Good folk are scarce, you know; and it is not every one that would be quite so much missed as yourself. It is not every one that Hermiston would miss.'

And with a nod and a smile, the doctor passed on.

A moment after, Archie was in pursuit, and had in turn, but more roughly, seized him by the arm.

'What do you mean? what did you mean by saying that? What makes you think that Hermis—my father would have missed me?'

The doctor turned about and looked him all over with a clinical eye. A far more stupid man than Dr Gregory might have guessed the truth; but ninety-nine out of a hundred, even if they had been equally inclined to kindness, would have blundered by some touch of charitable exaggeration. The doctor was better inspired. He knew the father well; in that white face of intelligence and suffering, he divined something of the son; and he told, without apology or adornment, the plain truth.

'When you had the measles, Mr Archibald, you had them gey and ill; and I thought you were going to slip between my fingers,' he said. 'Well, your father was anxious. How did I know it? says you. Simply because I am a trained observer. The sign that I saw him make, ten thousand would have missed; and perhaps—*perhaps*, I say, because he's a hard man to judge of—but perhaps he never made another. A strange thing to consider! It was this. One day I came to him: "Hermiston," said I, "there's a change." He never said a word, just glowered at me (if ye 'll pardon the phrase) like a wild beast. "A change for the better," said I. And I distinctly heard him take his breath.'

The doctor left no opportunity for anticlimax ; nodding his cocked hat (a piece of antiquity to which he clung) and repeating 'Distinctly' with raised eyebrows, he took his departure, and left Archie speechless in the street.

The anecdote might be called infinitely little, and yet its meaning for Archie was immense. 'I did not know the old man had so much blood in him.' He had never dreamed this sire of his, this aboriginal antique, this adamantine Adam, had even so much of a heart as to be moved in the least degree for another—and that other himself, who had insulted him! With the generosity of youth, Archie was instantly under arms upon the other side: had instantly created a new image of Lord Hermiston, that of a man who was all iron without and all sensibility within. The mind of the vile jester, the tongue that had pursued Duncan Jopp with unmanly insults, the unbeloved countenance that he had known and feared for so long, were all forgotten; and he hastened home, impatient to confess his misdeeds, impatient to throw himself on the mercy of this imaginary character.

He was not to be long without a rude awakening. It was in the gloaming when he drew near the doorstep of the lighted house, and was aware of the figure of his father approaching from the opposite side. Little daylight lingered; but on the door being opened, the strong yellow shine of the lamp gushed out upon the landing and shone full on Archie, as he stood, in the old-fashioned observance of respect, to yield precedence. The Judge came without haste, stepping stately and firm; his chin raised, his face (as he entered the lamplight) strongly illumined, his mouth set hard. There was never a wink of change in his expression; without looking to the right or left, he mounted the stair, passed close to Archie, and entered the house. Instinctively, the boy, upon his first coming, had made a movement to meet him; instinctively, he recoiled against the railing, as the old man swept by him in a pomp of indignation. Words were needless; he knew all—perhaps more than all—and the hour of judgment was at hand.

It is possible that, in this sudden revulsion of hope, and before these symptoms of impending danger, Archie might have fled. But not even that was left to him. My lord, after hanging up his cloak and hat, turned round in the lighted entry, and made him an imperative and silent gesture with his thumb, and with the strange instinct of obedience, Archie followed him into the house.

All dinner-time there reigned over the Judge's table a palpable silence, and as soon as the solids were despatched he rose to his feet.

'M'Killup, tak' the wine into my room,' said he; and then to his son: 'Archie, you and me has to have a talk.'

It was at this sickening moment that Archie's courage, for the first and last time, entirely deserted him. 'I have an appointment,' said he.

'It'll have to be broken, then,' said Hermiston, and led the way into his study.

The lamp was shaded, the fire trimmed to a nicety, the table covered deep with orderly documents, the backs of law books made a frame upon all sides that was only broken by the window and the doors.

For a moment Hermiston warmed his hands at the fire, presenting his back to Archie; then suddenly disclosed on him the terrors of the Hanging Face.

'What's this I hear of ye?' he asked.

There was no answer possible to Archie.

'I'll have to tell ye, then,' pursued Hermiston. 'It seems ye've been skirling against the father that begot ye, and one of his Maijesty's Judges in this land; and that in the public street, and while an order of the Court was being executit. Forbye which, it would appear that ye've been airing your opeenions in a Coallege Debatin' Society'; he paused a moment: and then, with extraordinary bitterness, added: 'Ye damned eediot.'

'I had meant to tell you,' stammered Archie. 'I see you are well informed.'

'Muckle obleeged to ye,' said his lordship, and took his usual seat. 'And so you disapprove of Caapital Punishment?' he added.

'I am sorry, sir, I do,' said Archie.

'I am sorry, too,' said his lordship. 'And now, if you please, we shall approach this business with a little more parteecularity. I hear that at the hanging of Duncan Jopp—and, man! ye had a fine client there—in the middle of all the riff-raff of the ceety, ye thought fit to cry out, "This is a damned murder, and my gorge rises at the man that haangit him." '

'No, sir, these were not my words,' cried Archie.

'What were yer word, then?' asked the Judge.

'I believe I said, "I denounce it as a murder!" ' said the son. 'I beg your pardon—a God-defying murder. I have no wish to conceal the truth,' he added, and looked his father for a moment in the face.

'God, it would only need that of it next!' cried Hermiston. 'There was nothing about your gorge rising, then?'

'That was afterwards, my lord, as I was leaving the Speculative. I said I had been to see the miserable creature hanged, and my gorge rose at it.'

'Did ye, though?' said Hermiston. 'And I suppose ye knew who haangit him?'

'I was present at the trial, I ought to tell you that, I ought to explain. I ask your pardon beforehand for any expression that may seem undutiful. The position in which I stand is wretched,' said the unhappy hero, now fairly face to face with the business he had chosen. 'I have been reading some of your cases. I was present while Jopp was tried. It was a hideous business. Father, it was a hideous thing! Grant he was vile, why should you hunt him with a vileness equal to his own? It was done with glee—that is the word—you did it with glee; and I looked on, God help me! with horror.'

'You're a young gentleman that doesna approve of Caapital Punishment,' said Hermiston. 'Weel, I'm an auld man that does. I was glad to get Jopp haangit, and what for would I pretend I wasna? You're all for honesty, it seems; you couldn't even steik your mouth on the public street. What for should I steik mines upon the bench, the King's officer, bearing the sword, a dreid to evil-doers, as I was from the beginning, and as I will be to the end! Mair than enough of it! Heedious! I never gave twa thoughts to heediousness, I have no call to be bonny. I'm a man that gets through with my day's business, and let that suffice.'

The ring of sarcasm had died out of his voice as he went on; the plain words became invested with some of the dignity of the Justice-seat.

'It would be telling you if you could say as much,' the speaker resumed. 'But ye cannot. Ye've been reading some of my cases, ye say. But it was not for the law in them, it was to spy out your faither's nakedness, a fine employment in a son. You're splairging; you're running at lairge in life like a wild nowt. It's impossible you should think any longer of coming to the Bar. You're not fit for it; no splairger is. And another thing: son of mines or no son of mines, you have flung fylement in public on one of the Senators of the Coallege of Justice, and I would make it my business to see that ye were never admitted there yourself. There is a kind of a decency to be observit. Then comes the next of it—what am I to do with ye next? Ye'll have to find some kind of a trade, for I'll never support ye in idleset. What do ye fancy ye'll be fit for? The pulpit? Na, they could never get diveenity into that bloackhead. Him that the law of man whammles is no likely to do muckle better by the law of God. What would ye make of hell? Wouldna your gorge rise at that? Na, there's no room for splairgers under the fower quarters of John Calvin. What else is there? Speak up. Have ye got nothing of your own?'

'Father, let me go to the Peninsula,'* said Archie. 'That's all I'm fit for—to fight.'

'All? quo' he!' returned the Judge. 'And it would be enough too, if I thought it. But I'll never trust ye so near the French, you that's so Frenchifeed.'

'You do me injustice there, sir,' said Archie. 'I am loyal; I will not boast; but any interest I may have ever felt in the French——'

'Have ye been so loyal to me?' interrupted his father.

There came no reply.

'I think not,' continued Hermiston. 'And I would send no man to be a servant to the King, God bless him! that has proved such a shauchling son to his own faither. You can splairge here on Edinburgh street, and where's the hairm? It doesna play buff on me! And if there were twenty thousand eediots like yourself, sorrow a Duncan Jopp would hang the fewer. But there's no splairging possible in a camp; and if you were to go to it, you would find out for yourself whether Lord Well'n'ton approves of caapital punishment or not. You a sodger!' he cried, with a sudden burst of scorn. 'Ye auld wife, the sodgers would bray at ye like cuddies!'

As at the drawing of a curtain, Archie was aware of some illogicality in his position, and stood abashed. He had a strong impression, besides, of the essential valour of the old gentleman before him, how conveyed it would be hard to say.

'Well, have ye no other proposeetion?' said my lord again.

'You have taken this so calmly, sir, that I cannot but stand ashamed,' began Archie.

'I'm nearer voamiting, though, than you would fancy,' said my lord.

The blood rose to Archie's brow.

'I beg your pardon, I should have said that you had accepted my affront. . . . I admit it was an affront; I did not think to apologise, but I do, I ask your pardon; it will not be so again, I pass you my word of honour. . . . I should have said that I admired your magnanimity with—this—offender,' Archie concluded with a gulp.

'I have no other son, ye see,' said Hermiston. 'A bonny one I have gotten! But I must just do the best I can wi' him, and what am I to do? If ye had been younger, I would have wheepit ye for this rideeculous exhibeetion. The way it is, I have just to grin and bear. But one thing is to be clearly understood. As a faither, I must grin and bear it; but if I had been the Lord Advocate instead of the Lord Justice-Clerk, son or no son, Mr Erchibald Weir would have been in a jyle the night.'

Archie was now dominated. Lord Hermiston was coarse and cruel; and yet the son was aware of a bloomless nobility, an ungracious abnegation of the man's self in the man's office. At every word, this sense of the greatness of Lord Hermiston's spirit struck more home; and along with it that of his own impotence, who had struck—and perhaps basely struck—at his own father, and not reached so far as to have even nettled him.

'I place myself in your hands without reserve,' he said.

'That's the first sensible word I've had of ye the night,' said Hermiston. 'I can tell ye, that would have been the end of it, the one way or the other; but it's better ye should come there yourself, than what I would have had to hirstle ye. Weel, by my way of it—and my way is the best—there's just the one thing it's possible that ye might be with decency, and that's a laird. Ye'll be out of hairm's way at the least of it. If ye have to rowt, ye can rowt amang the kye; and the maist feck of the caapital punishment ye're like to come across 'll be guddling trouts. Now, I'm for no idle lairdies; every man has to work, if it's only at peddling ballants; to work, or to be wheeped, or to be haangit. If I set ye down at Hermiston, I'll have to see you work that place the way it has never been workit yet; ye must ken about the sheep like a herd; ye must be my grieve there, and I'll see that I gain by ye. Is that understood?'

'I will do my best,' said Archie.

'Well, then, I'll send Kirstie word the morn, and ye can go

yourself the day after,' said Hermiston. 'And just try to be less of an eediot!' he concluded, with a freezing smile, and turned immediately to the papers on his desk.

CHAPTER IV

OPINIONS OF THE BENCH

LATE the same night, after a disordered walk, Archie was admitted into Lord Glenalmond's dining-room, where he sat, with a book upon his knee, beside three frugal coals of fire. In his robes upon the bench, Glenalmond had a certain air of burliness: plucked of these, it was a may-pole of a man that rose unsteadily from his chair to give his visitor welcome. Archie had suffered much in the last days, he had suffered again that evening; his face was white and drawn, his eyes wild and dark. But Lord Glenalmond greeted him without the least mark of surprise or curiosity.

'Come in, come in,' said he. 'Come in and take a seat. Carstairs' (to his servant) 'make up the fire, and then you can bring a bit of supper,' and again to Archie, with a very trivial accent: 'I was half expecting you,' he added.

'No supper,' said Archie. 'It is impossible that I should eat.'

'Not impossible,' said the tall old man, laying his hand upon his shoulder, 'and, if you will believe me, necessary.'

'You know what brings me?' said Archie, as soon as the servant had left the room.

'I have a guess, I have a guess,' replied Glenalmond. 'We will talk of it presently—when Carstairs has come and gone, and you have had a piece of my good Cheddar cheese and a pull at the porter tankard: not before.'

'It is impossible I should eat,' repeated Archie.

'Tut, tut!' said Lord Glenalmond. 'You have eaten nothing to-day, and I venture to add, nothing yesterday. There is no case that may not be made worse: this may be a very disagreeable business, but if you were to fall sick and die, it would be still more so, and for all concerned—for all concerned.'

'I see you must know all,' said Archie. 'Where did you hear it?'

'In the mart of scandal, in the Parliament House,' said

Glenalmond. 'It runs riot below among the bar and the public, but it sifts up to us upon the bench, and rumour has some of her voices even in the divisions.'

Carstairs returned at this moment, and rapidly laid out a little supper; during which Lord Glenalmond spoke at large and a little vaguely on indifferent subjects, so that it might be rather said of him that he made a cheerful noise, than that he contributed to human conversation; and Archie sat upon the other side, not heeding him, brooding over his wrongs and errors.

But so soon as the servant was gone, he broke forth again at once. 'Who told my father? Who dared to tell him? Could it have been you?'

'No, it was not me,' said the Judge; 'although—to be quite frank with you, and after I had seen and warned you—it might have been me. I believe it was Glenkindie.'

'That shrimp!' cried Archie.

'As you say, that shrimp,' returned my lord; 'although really it is scarce a fitting mode of expression for one of the senators of the College of Justice. We were hearing the parties in a long, crucial case, before the fifteen; Creech was moving at some length for an infeftment; when I saw Glenkindie lean forward to Hermiston with his hand over his mouth and make him a secret communication. No one could have guessed its nature from your father; from Glenkindie, yes, his malice sparked out of him a little grossly. But your father, no. A man of granite. The next moment he pounced upon Creech. "Mr Creech," says he, "I'll take a look of that sasine," and for thirty minutes after,' said Glenalmond, with a smile, 'Messrs. Creech and Co. were fighting a pretty uphill battle, which resulted, I need hardly add, in their total rout. The case was dismissed. No, I doubt if ever I heard Hermiston better inspired. He was literally rejoicing *in apicibus juris*.'*

Archie was able to endure no longer. He thrust his plate away and interrupted the deliberate and insignificant stream of talk. 'Here,' he said, 'I have made a fool of myself, if I have not made something worse. Do you judge between us—judge between a father and a son. I can speak to you; it is not like . . . I will tell you what I feel and what I mean to do; and you shall be the judge,' he repeated.

'I decline jurisdiction,' said Glenalmond, with extreme seriousness. 'But, my dear boy, if it will do you any good to talk, and if it will interest you at all to hear what I may choose to say when I have heard you, I am quite at your command. Let an old man say it, for once, and not need to blush: I love you like a son.'

There came a sudden sharp sound in Archie's throat. 'Ay,'* he cried, 'and there it is! Love! Like a son! And how do you think I love my father?'

'Quietly, quietly,' says my lord.

'I will be very quiet,' replied Archie. 'And I will be baldly frank. I do not love my father; I wonder sometimes if I do not hate him. There's my shame; perhaps my sin; at least, and in the sight of God, not my fault. How was I to love him? He has never spoken to me, never smiled upon me; I do not think he ever touched me. You know the way he talks? You do not talk so, yet you can sit and hear him without shuddering, and I cannot. My soul is sick when he begins with it; I could smite him in the mouth. And all that's nothing. I was at the trial of this Jopp. You were not there, but you must have heard him often; the man's notorious for it, for being—look at my position! he's my father and this is how I have to speak of him—notorious for being a brute and cruel and a coward. Lord Glenalmond, I give you my word, when I came out of that Court, I longed to die—the shame of it was beyond my strength: but I—I—' he rose from his seat and began to pace the room in a disorder. 'Well, who am I? A boy, who have never been tried, have never done anything except this twopenny impotent folly with my father. But I tell you, my lord, and I know myself, I am at least that kind of a man—or that kind of a boy, if you prefer it—that I could die in torments rather than that any one should suffer as that scoundrel suffered. Well, and what have I done? I see it now. I have made a fool of myself, as I said in the beginning; and I have gone back, and asked my father's pardon, and placed myself wholly in his hands—and he has sent me to Hermiston,' with a wretched smile, 'for life, I suppose—and what can I say? he strikes me as having done quite right, and let me off better than I had deserved.'

'My poor, dear boy!' observed Glenalmond. 'My poor dear and, if you will allow me to say so, very foolish boy! You are only discovering where you are; to one of your temperament, or of mine, a painful discovery. The world was not made for us; it was made for ten hundred millions of men, all different from each other and from us; there's no royal road there, we just have to sclamber* and tumble. Don't think that I am at all disposed to be surprised; don't suppose that I ever think of blaming you; indeed I rather admire! But there fall to be offered one or two observations on the case which occur to me and which (if you will listen to them dispassionately) may be the means of inducing you to view the matter more calmly. First of all, I cannot acquit you of a good deal of what is called intolerance. You seem to have been very much offended because your father talks a little sculduddery after dinner, which it is perfectly licit for him to do, and which (although I am not very fond of it myself) appears to be entirely an affair of taste. Your father, I scarcely like to remind you, since it is so trite a commonplace, is older than yourself. At least, he is *major* and *sui juris*,* and may please himself in the matter of his conversation. And, do you know, I wonder if he might not have as good an answer against you and me? We say we sometimes find him *coarse*, but I suspect he might retort that he finds us always dull. Perhaps a relevant exception.'

He beamed on Archie, but no smile could be elicited.

'And now,' proceeded the Judge, 'for "Archibald on Capital Punishment." This is a very plausible academic opinion; of course I do not and I cannot hold it; but that's not to say that many able and excellent persons have not done so in the past. Possibly, in the past also, I may have a little dipped myself in the same heresy. My third client, or possibly my fourth, was the means of a return in my opinions. I never saw the man I more believed in; I would have put my hand in the fire, I would have gone to the cross for him; and when it came to trial he was gradually pictured before me, by undeniable probation, in the light of so gross, so cold-blooded, and so black-hearted a villain, that I had a mind to have cast my brief upon the table. I was then boiling against the man with even a more tropical temperature than I had been boiling for him.

But I said to myself: "No, you have taken up his case; and because you have changed your mind it must not be suffered to let drop. All that rich tide of eloquence that you prepared last night with so much enthusiasm is out of place, and yet you must not desert him, you must say something." So I said something, and I got him off. It made my reputation. But an experience of that kind is formative. A man must not bring his passions to the bar—or to the bench,' he added.

The story had slightly rekindled Archie's interest. 'I could never deny,' he began—'I mean I can conceive that some men would be better dead. But who are we to know all the springs of God's unfortunate creatures? Who are we to trust ourselves where it seems that God Himself must think twice before He treads, and to do it with delight? Yes, with delight. *Tigris ut aspera.**

'Perhaps not a pleasant spectacle,' said Glenalmond. 'And yet, do you know, I think somehow a great one.'

'I've had a long talk with him to-night,' said Archie.

'I was supposing so,' said Glenalmond.

'And he struck me—I cannot deny that he struck me as something very big,' pursued the son. 'Yes, he is big. He never spoke about himself; only about me. I suppose I admired him. The dreadful part——'

'Suppose we did not talk about that,' interrupted Glenalmond. 'You know it very well, it cannot in any way help that you should brood upon it, and I sometimes wonder whether you and I—who are a pair of sentimentalists—are quite good judges of plain men.'

'How do you mean?' asked Archie.

'*Fair* judges, I mean,' replied Glenalmond. 'Can we be just to them? Do we not ask too much? There was a word of yours just now that impressed me a little when you asked me who we were to know all the springs of God's unfortunate creatures. You applied that, as I understood, to capital cases only. But does it—I ask myself—does it not apply all through? Is it any less difficult to judge of a good man or of a half-good man, than of the worst criminal at the bar? And may not each have relevant excuses?'

'Ah, but we do not talk of punishing the good,' cried Archie.

'No, we do not talk of it,' said Glenalmond. 'But I think we do it. Your father, for instance.'

'You think I have punished him?' cried Archie.

Lord Glenalmond bowed his head.

'I think I have,' said Archie. 'And the worst is, I think he feels it! How much, who can tell, with such a being? But I think he does.'

'And I am sure of it,' said Glenalmond

'Has he spoken to you, then?' cried Archie.

'O no,' replied the judge.

'I tell you honestly,' said Archie, 'I want to make it up to him. I will go, I have already pledged myself to go to Hermiston. That was to him. And now I pledge myself to you, in the sight of God, that I will close my mouth on capital punishment and all other subjects where our views may clash, for—how long shall I say? when shall I have sense enough?—ten years. Is that well?'

'It is well,' said my lord.

'As far as it goes,' said Archie. 'It is enough as regards myself, it is to lay down enough of my conceit. But as regards him, whom I have publicly insulted? What am I to do to him? How do you pay attentions to a—an Alp like that?'

'Only in one way,' replied Glenalmond. 'Only by obedience, punctual, prompt, and scrupulous.'

'And I promise that he shall have it,' answered Archie. 'I offer you my hand in pledge of it.'

'And I take your hand as a solemnity,' replied the judge. 'God bless you, my dear, and enable you to keep your promise. God guide you in the true way, and spare your days, and preserve to you your honest heart.' At that, he kissed the young man upon the forehead in a gracious, distant, antiquated way; and instantly launched, with a marked change of voice, into another subject. 'And now, let us replenish the tankard; and I believe, if you will try my Cheddar again, you would find you had a better appetite. The Court has spoken, and the case is dismissed.'

'No, there is one thing I must say,' cried Archie. 'I must say it in justice to himself. I know—I believe faithfully, slavishly, after our talk—he will never ask me anything unjust. I am proud to feel it, that we have that much in common, I am proud to say it to you.'

The Judge, with shining eyes, raised his tankard. 'And I think perhaps that we might permit ourselves a toast,' said he. 'I should like to propose the health of a man very different from me and very much my superior—a man from whom I have often differed, who has often (in the trivial expression) rubbed me the wrong way, but whom I have never ceased to respect and, I may add, to be not a little afraid of. Shall I give you his name?'

'The Lord Justice-Clerk, Lord Hermiston,' said Archie, almost with gaiety; and the pair drank the toast deeply.

It was not precisely easy to re-establish, after these emotional passages, the natural flow of conversation. But the Judge eked out what was wanting with kind looks, produced his snuff-box (which was very rarely seen) to fill in a pause, and at last, despairing of any further social success, was upon the point of getting down a book to read a favourite passage, when there came a rather startling summons at the front door, and Carstairs ushered in my Lord Glenkindie, hot from a midnight supper. I am not aware that Glenkindie was ever a beautiful object, being short, and gross-bodied, and with an expression of sensuality comparable to a bear's. At that moment, coming in hissing from many potations, with a flushed countenance and blurred eyes, he was strikingly contrasted with the tall, pale, kingly figure of Glenalmond. A rush of confused thought came over Archie—of shame that this was one of his father's elect friends; of pride, that at the least of it Hermiston could carry his liquor; and last of all, of rage, that he should have here under his eyes the man that had betrayed him. And then that too passed away; and he sat quiet, biding his opportunity.

The tipsy senator plunged at once into an explanation with Glenalmond. There was a point reserved yesterday, he had been able to make neither head nor tail of it, and seeing lights in the house, he had just dropped in for a glass of porter—and at this point he became aware of the third person. Archie saw the cod's mouth and the blunt lips of Glenkindie gape at him for a moment, and the recognition twinkle in his eyes.

'Who's this?' said he. 'What? is this possibly you, Don Quickshot? And how are ye? And how's your father? And what's all this we hear of you? It seems you're a most extraordinary leveller, by all tales. No king, no parliaments, and your gorge rises at the macers, worthy men! Hoot, toot! Dear, dear me! Your father's son too! Most rideeculous!'

Archie was on his feet, flushing a little at the reappearance of his unhappy figure of speech, but perfectly self-possessed. 'My lord—and you, Lord Glenalmond, my dear friend,' he began, 'this is a happy chance for me, that I can make my confession and offer my apologies to two of you at once.'

'Ah, but I don't know about that. Confession? It'll be judeecial, my young friend,' cried the jocular Glenkindie. 'And I'm afraid to listen to ye. Think if ye were to make me a coanvert!'

'If you would allow me, my lord,' returned Archie, 'what I have to say is very serious to me; and be pleased to be humorous after I am gone!'

'Remember, I'll hear nothing against the macers!' put in the incorrigible Glenkindie.

But Archie continued as though he had not spoken. 'I have played, both yesterday and to-day, a part for which I can only offer the excuse of youth. I was so unwise as to go to an execution; it seems I made a scene at the gallows; not content with which, I spoke the same night in a college society against capital punishment. This is the extent of what I have done, and in case you hear more alleged against me, I protest my innocence. I have expressed my regret already to my father, who is so good as to pass my conduct over—in a degree, and upon the condition that I am to leave my law studies.' . . .

CHAPTER V

WINTER ON THE MOORS

1. *At Hermiston**

THE road to Hermiston runs for a great part of the way up the valley of a stream, a favourite with anglers and with midges, full of falls and pools, and shaded by willows and natural woods of birch. Here and there, but at great distances, a byway branches off, and a gaunt farmhouse may be descried above in a fold of the hill; but the more part of the time, the road would be quite empty of passage and the hills of habitation. Hermiston parish is one of the least populous in Scotland; and, by the time you came that length, you would scarce be surprised at the inimitable smallness of the kirk, a dwarfish, ancient place seated for fifty, and standing in a green by the burn-side among two-score gravestones. The manse close by, although no more than a cottage, is surrounded by the brightness of a flower-garden and the straw roofs of bees; and the whole colony, kirk and manse, garden and graveyard, finds harbourage in a grove of rowans, and is all the year round in a great silence broken only by the drone of the bees, the tinkle of the burn, and the bell on Sundays. A mile beyond the kirk the road leaves the valley by a precipitous ascent, and brings you a little after to the place of Hermiston, where it comes to an end in the back-yard before the coach-house. All beyond and about is the great field of the hills; the plover, the curlew, and the lark cry there; the wind blows as it blows in a ship's rigging, hard and cold and pure; and the hill-tops huddle one behind another like a herd of cattle into the sunset.

The house was sixty years old, unsightly, comfortable; a farmyard and a kitchen-garden on the left, with a fruit wall where little hard green pears came to their maturity about the end of October.

The policy (as who should say the park) was of some extent, but very ill reclaimed; heather and moorfowl had crossed the boundary wall and spread and roosted within; and it would have tasked a landscape gardener to say where policy ended and unpolicied nature began. My lord had been led by the influence of Mr Sheriff Scott* into a considerable design of planting; many acres were accordingly set out with fir, and the little feathery besoms gave a false scale and lent a strange air of a toy-shop to the moors. A great, rooty sweetness of bogs was in the air, and at all seasons an infinite melancholy piping of hill birds. Standing so high and with so little shelter, it was a cold, exposed house, splashed by showers, drenched by continuous rains that made the gutters to spout, beaten upon and buffeted by all the winds of heaven; and the prospect would be often black with tempest, and often white with the snows of winter. But the house was wind and weather proof, the hearths were kept bright, and the rooms pleasant with live fires of peat; and Archie might sit of an evening and hear the squalls bugle on the moorland, and watch the fire prosper in the earthy fuel, and the smoke winding up the chimney, and drink deep of the pleasures of shelter.

Solitary as the place was, Archie did not want neighbours. Every night, if he chose, he might go down to the manse and share a 'brewst' of toddy with the minister—a hare-brained ancient gentleman, long and light and still active, though his knees were loosened with age, and his voice broke continually in childish trebles—and his lady wife, a heavy, comely dame, without a word to say for herself beyond good-even and good-day. Harum-scarum, clodpole young lairds of the neighbourhood paid him the compliment of a visit. Young Hay of Romanes rode down to call, on his crop-eared pony; young Pringle of Drumanno came up on his bony grey. Hay remained on the hospitable field, and must be carried to bed; Pringle got somehow to his saddle about 3 A.M., and (as Archie stood with the lamp on the upper doorstep) lurched, uttered a senseless view-holloa, and vanished out of the small circle of illumination like a wraith. Yet a minute or two longer the clatter of his break-neck flight was audible, then it was cut off by the intervening steepness of the hill; and again, a great while after, the renewed beating of phantom horse-hoofs, far in the valley of the Hermiston, showed that the horse at least, if not his rider, was still on the homeward way.

There was a Tuesday club at the 'Crosskeys' in Crossmichael, where the young bloods of the country-side congregated and drank deep on a percentage of the expense, so that he was left gainer who should have drunk the most. Archie had no great mind to this diversion, but he took it like a duty laid upon him, went with a decent regularity, did his manfullest with the liquor, held up his head in the local jests, and got home again and was able to put up his horse, to the admiration of Kirstie and the lass that helped her. He dined at Driffel, supped at Windielaws. He went to the new year's ball at Huntsfield and was made welcome, and thereafter rode to hounds with my Lord Muirfell, upon whose name, as that of a legitimate Lord of Parliament, in a work so full of Lords of Session, my pen should pause reverently. Yet the same fate attended him here as in Edinburgh. The habit of solitude tends to perpetuate itself, and an austerity of which he was quite unconscious, and a pride which seemed arrogance, and perhaps was chiefly shyness, discouraged and offended his new companions. Hay did not return more than twice, Pringle never at all, and there came a time when Archie even desisted from the Tuesday Club, and became in all things—what he had had the name of almost from the first—the Recluse of Hermiston. High-nosed Miss Pringle of Drumanno and high-stepping Miss Marshall of the Mains were understood to have had a difference of opinion about him the day after the ball—he was none the wiser, he could not suppose himself to be remarked by these entrancing ladies. At the ball itself my Lord Muirfell's daughter, the Lady Flora, spoke to him twice, and the second time with a touch of appeal, so that her colour rose and her voice trembled a little in his ear, like a passing grace in music. He stepped back with a heart on fire, coldly and not ungracefully excused himself, and a little after watched her dancing with young Drumanno of the empty laugh, and was harrowed at the sight, and raged to himself that this was a world in which it was given to Drumanno to please, and to himself only to stand aside and envy. He seemed excluded, as of right, from the favour of such society—seemed to extinguish mirth wherever he came, and was quick to feel the wound, and desist, and retire into solitude. If he had but understood the figure he presented, and the impression he made on these bright eyes and tender hearts; if he had but guessed that the Recluse of Hermiston, young, graceful, well spoken, but always cold, stirred the maidens of the county with the charm of Byronism when Byronism was new,* it may be questioned whether his destiny might not even yet have been modified. It may be questioned, and I think it should be doubted. It was in his horoscope to be parsimonious of pain to himself, or of the chance of pain, even to the avoidance of any opportunity of pleasure; to have a Roman sense of duty, an instinctive aristocracy of manners and taste; to be the son of Adam Weir and Jean Rutherford.

2. *Kirstie*

Kirstie was now over fifty, and might have sat to a sculptor. Long of limb, and still light of foot, deep-breasted, robust-loined, her golden hair not yet mingled with any trace of silver, the years had but caressed and embellished her. By the lines of a rich and vigorous maternity, she seemed destined to be the bride of heroes and the mother of their children; and behold, by the iniquity of fate, she had passed through her youth alone, and drew near to the confines of age, a childless woman. The tender ambitions that she had received at birth had been, by time and disappointment, diverted into a certain barren zeal of industry and fury of interference. She carried her thwarted ardours into housework, she washed floors with her empty heart. If she could not win the love of one with love, she must dominate all by her temper. Hasty, wordy, and wrathful, she had a drawn quarrel with most of her neighbours, and with the others not much more than armed neutrality. The grieve's wife had been 'sneisty'; the sister of the gardener who kept house for him had shown herself 'upsitten'; and she wrote to Lord Hermiston about once a year demanding the discharge of the offenders, and justifying the demand by much wealth of detail. For it must not be supposed that the quarrel rested with the wife and did not take in the husband also—or with the gardener's sister, and did not speedily include the gardener himself. As the upshot of all this petty quarrelling and intemperate speech, she was practically excluded (like a lightkeeper on his tower) from the comforts of human association; except with her own indoor drudge, who, being but a lassie and entirely at her mercy, must submit to the shifty weather of 'the mistress's' moods without complaint, and be willing to take buffets or caresses according to the temper of the hour. To Kirstie, thus situate and in the Indian summer of her heart, which was slow to submit to age, the gods sent this equivocal good thing of Archie's presence. She had known him in the cradle and paddled him when he misbehaved; and yet, as she had not so much as set eyes on him since he was eleven and had his last serious illness, the tall, slender, refined, and rather melancholy young gentleman of twenty came upon her with the shock of a new acquaintance. He was 'Young Hermiston,' 'the laird himsel'': he had an air of distinctive superiority, a cold straight glance of his black eyes, that abashed the woman's tantrums in the beginning, and therefore the possibility of any quarrel was excluded. He was new, and therefore immediately aroused her curiosity; he was reticent, and kept it awake. And lastly he was dark and she fair, and he was male and she female, the everlasting fountains of interest.

Her feeling partook of the loyalty of a clanswoman, the hero-worship of a maiden aunt, and the idolatry due to a god. No matter what he had asked of her, ridiculous or tragic, she would have done it and joyed to do it. Her passion, for it was nothing less, entirely filled her. It was a rich physical pleasure to make his bed or light his lamp for him when he was absent, to pull off his wet boots or wait on him at dinner when he returned. A young man who should have so doted on the idea, moral and physical, of any woman, might be properly described as being in love, head and heels, and would have behaved himself accordingly. But Kirstie—though her heart leaped at his coming footsteps—though, when he patted her shoulder, her face brightened for the day—had not a hope or thought beyond the present moment and its perpetuation to the end of time. Till the end of time she would have had nothing altered, but still continue delightedly to serve her idol, and be repaid (say twice in the month) with a clap on the shoulder.

I have said her heart leaped—it is the accepted phrase. But rather, when she was alone in any chamber of the house, and heard his foot passing on the corridors, something in her bosom rose slowly until her breath was suspended, and as slowly fell again with a deep sigh, when the steps had passed and she was disappointed of her eyes' desire. This perpetual hunger and thirst of his presence kept her all day on the alert. When he went forth at morning, she would stand and follow him with admiring looks. As it grew late and drew to the time of his return, she would steal forth to a corner of the policy wall and be seen standing there sometimes by the hour together, gazing with shaded eyes, waiting the exquisite and barren pleasure of his view a mile off on the mountains. When at night she had trimmed and gathered the fire, turned down his bed, and laid out his night-gear—when there was no more to be done for the king's pleasure, but to remember him fervently in her usually very tepid prayers, and go to bed brooding upon his perfections, his future career, and what she should give him the next day for dinner—there still remained before her one more opportunity; she was still to take in the tray and say good-night. Sometimes Archie would glance up from his book with a preoccupied nod and a perfunctory salutation which was in truth a dismissal; sometimes—and by degrees more often—the volume would be laid aside, he would meet her coming with a look of relief; and the conversation would be engaged, last out the supper, and be prolonged till the small hours by the waning fire. It was no wonder that Archie was fond of company after his solitary days; and Kirstie, upon her side, exerted all the arts of her vigorous nature to ensnare his attention. She would keep back some piece of news during dinner to be fired off with the entrance of the supper tray, and form as it were the *lever de rideau** of the evening's entertainment. Once he had heard her tongue wag, she made sure of the result. From one subject to another she moved by insidious transitions, fearing the least silence, fearing almost to give him time for an answer lest it should slip into a hint of separation. Like so many people of her class, she was a brave narrator; her place was on the hearth-rug and she made it a rostrum, mimeing her stories as she told them, fitting them with vital detail, spinning them out with endless 'quo' he's' and 'quo' she's,' her voice sinking into a whisper over the supernatural or the horrific; until she would suddenly spring up in affected surprise, and pointing to the clock, 'Mercy, Mr Archie!' she would say, 'whatten a time o' night is this of it! God forgive me for a daft wife!' So it befell, by good management, that she was not only the first to begin these nocturnal conversations, but invariably the first to break them off; so she managed to retire and not to be dismissed.

3. *A Border Family*

Such an unequal intimacy has never been uncommon in Scotland, where the clan spirit survives; where the servant tends to spend her life in the same service, a helpmeet at first, then a tyrant, and at last a pensioner; where, besides, she is not necessarily destitute of the pride of birth, but is, perhaps, like Kirstie, a connection of her master's, and at least knows the legend of her own family, and may count kinship with some illustrious dead. For that is the mark of the Scot of all classes: that he stands in an attitude towards the past unthinkable to Englishmen, and remembers and cherishes the memory of his forebears, good or bad; and there burns alive in him a sense of identity with the dead even to the twentieth generation. No more characteristic instance could be found than in the family of Kirstie Elliott. They were all, and Kirstie the first of all, ready and eager to pour forth the particulars of their genealogy, embellished with every detail that memory had handed down or fancy fabricated; and, behold! from every ramification of that tree dangled a halter. The Elliotts themselves have had a chequered history; but these Elliotts deduced, besides, from three of the most unfortunate of the border clans—the Nicksons, the Ellwalds, and the Crozers. One ancestor after another might be seen appearing a moment out of the rain and the hill mist upon his furtive business, speeding home, perhaps, with a paltry booty of lame horses and lean kine, or squealing and dealing death in some moorland feud of the ferrets and the wild cats. One after another closed his obscure adventures in mid-air, triced up to the arm of the royal gibbet or the Baron's dule-tree. For the rusty blunderbuss of Scots criminal justice, which usually hurt nobody but jurymen, became a weapon of precision for the Nicksons, the Ellwalds, and the Crozers. The exhilaration of their exploits seemed to haunt the memories of their descendants alone, and the shame to be forgotten. Pride glowed in their bosoms to publish their relationship to 'Andrew Ellwald of the Laverockstanes, called "Unchancy Dand," who was justifeed wi' seeven mair of the same name at Jeddart in the days of King James the Sax.' In all this tissue of crime and misfortune, the Elliotts of Cauldstaneslap had one boast which must appear legitimate: the males were gallows-birds, born outlaws, petty thieves, and deadly brawlers; but, according to the same tradition, the females were all chaste and faithful. The power of ancestry on the character is not limited to the inheritance of cells. If I buy ancestors by the gross from the benevolence of Lyon King of Arms,* my grandson (if he is Scottish) will feel a quickening emulation of their deeds. The men of the Elliotts were proud, lawless, violent as of right, cherishing and prolonging a tradition. In like manner with the women. And the women, essentially passionate and reckless, who crouched on the rug, in the shine of the peat fire, telling these tales, had cherished through life a wild integrity of virtue.

Her father Gilbert had been deeply pious, a savage disciplinarian in the antique style, and withal a notorious smuggler. 'I mind when I was a bairn getting mony a skelp and being shoo'd to bed like pou'try,' she would say. 'That would be when the lads and their bit kegs were on the road. We've had the riffraff of two-three counties in our kitchen, mony's the time, betwix' the twelve and the three; and their lanterns would be standing in the forecourt, ay, a score o' them at once. But there was nae ungodly talk permitted at Cauldstaneslap; my faither was a consistent man in walk and conversation; just let slip an aith, and there was the door to ye! He had that zeal for the Lord, it was a fair wonder to hear him pray, but the faimily has aye had a gift that way.' This father was twice married, once to a dark woman of the old Ellwald stock, by whom he had Gilbert, presently of Cauldstaneslap; and, secondly, to the mother of Kirstie. 'He was an auld man when he married her, a fell auld man wi' a muckle voice—you could hear him rowting from the top o' the Kye-skairs,' she said; 'but for her, it appears she was a perfit wonder. It was gentle blood she had, Mr Archie, for it was your ain. The country-side gaed gyte about her and her gowden hair. Mines is no to be mentioned wi' it, and there's few weemen has mair hair than what I have, or yet a bonnier colour. Often would I tell my dear Miss Jeannie—that was your mother, dear, she was cruel ta'en up about her hair, it was unco tender, ye see—"Houts, Miss Jeannie," I would say, "just fling your washes and your French dentifrishes in the back o' the fire, for that's the place for them; and awa' down to a burn side, and wash yersel' in cauld hill water, and dry your bonny hair in the caller wind o' the muirs, the way that my mother aye washed hers, and that I have aye made it a practice to have wishen mines—just you do what I tell ye, my dear, and ye'll give me news of it! Ye'll have hair, and routh of hair, a pigtail as thick's my arm," I said, "and the bonniest colour like the clear gowden guineas, so as the lads in kirk'll no can keep their eyes off it!" Weel, it lasted out her time, puir thing! I cuttit a lock of it upon her corp that was lying there sae cauld. I'll show it ye some of thir days if ye're good. But, as I was sayin', my mither——'

On the death of the father there remained golden-haired Kirstie, who took service with her distant kinsfolk, the Rutherfords, and black-a-vised Gilbert, twenty years older, who farmed the Cauldstaneslap, married, and begot four sons between 1773 and 1784, and a daughter, like a postscript, in '97, the year of Camperdown and Cape St Vincent.* It seemed it was a tradition in the family to wind up with a belated girl. In 1804, at the age of sixty, Gilbert met an end that might be called heroic. He was due home from market any time from eight at night till five in the morning, and in any condition from the quarrelsome to the speechless, for he maintained to that age the goodly customs of the Scots farmer. It was known on this occasion that he had a good bit of money to bring home; the word had gone round loosely. The laird had shown his guineas, and if anybody had but noticed it, there was an ill-looking vagabond crew, the scum of Edinburgh, that drew out of the market long ere it was dusk and took the hill-road by Hermiston, where it was not to be believed that they had lawful business. One of the country-side, one Dickieson, they took with them to be their guide, and dear he paid for it! Of a sudden, in the ford of the Broken Dykes, this vermin clan fell on the laird, six to one, and him three parts asleep, having drunk hard. But it is ill to catch an Elliott. For a while, in the night and the black water that was deep as to his saddle-girths, he wrought with his staff like a smith at his stithy, and great was the sound of oaths and blows. With that the ambuscade was burst, and he rode for home with a pistol-ball in him, three knife wounds, the loss of his front teeth, a broken rib and bridle, and a dying horse. That was a race with death that the laird rode! In the mirk night, with his broken bridle and his head swimming, he dug his spurs to the rowels in the horse's side, and the horse, that was even worse off than himself, the poor creature! screamed out loud like a person as he went, so that the hills echoed with it, and the folks at Cauldstaneslap got to their feet about the table and looked at each other with white faces. The horse fell dead at the yard gate, the laird won the length of the house and fell there on the threshold. To the son that raised him he gave the bag of money. 'Hae,' said he. All the way up the thieves had seemed to him to be at his heels, but now the hallucination left him—he saw them again in the place of the ambuscade—and the thirst of vengeance seized on his dying mind. Raising himself and pointing with an imperious finger into the black night from which he had come, he uttered the single command, 'Brocken Dykes,' and fainted. He had never been loved, but he had been feared in honour. At that sight, at that word, gasped out at them from a toothless and bleeding mouth, the old Elliott spirit awoke with a shout in the four sons. 'Wanting the hat,' continues my author, Kirstie, whom I but haltingly follow, for she told this tale like one inspired, 'wanting guns, for there wasna twa grains o' pouder in the house, wi' nae mair weepons than their sticks into their hands, the fower o' them took the road. Only Hob, and that was the eldest, hunkered at the doorsill where the blood had rin, fyled his hand wi' it, and haddit it up to Heeven in the way o' the auld Border aith. "Hell shall have her ain again this nicht!" he raired, and rode forth upon his errand.' It was three miles to Broken Dykes, down hill, and a sore road. Kirstie has seen men from Edinburgh dismounting there in plain day to lead their horses. But the four brothers rode it as if Auld Hornie were behind and Heaven in front. Come to the ford, and there was Dickieson. By all tales, he was not dead, but breathed and reared upon his elbow, and cried out to them for help. It was at a graceless face that he asked mercy. As soon as Hob saw, by the glint of the lantern, the eyes shining and the whiteness of the teeth in the man's face, 'Damn you!' says he; 'ye hae your teeth, hae ye?' and rode his horse to and fro upon that human remnant. Beyond that, Dandie must dismount with the lantern to be their guide; he was the youngest son, scarce twenty at the time. 'A' nicht long they gaed in the wet heath and jennipers, and whaur they gaed they neither knew nor cared, but just followed the bluid-stains and the footprints o' their faither's murderers. And a' nicht Dandie had his nose to the grund like a tyke, and the ithers followed and spak' naething, neither black nor white. There was nae noise to be heard, but just the sough of the swalled burns, and Hob, the dour yin, risping his teeth as he gaed.' With the first glint of the morning they saw they were on the drove road, and at that the four stopped and had a dram to their breakfasts, for they knew that Dand must have guided them right, and the rogues could be but little ahead, hot foot for Edinburgh by the way of the Pentland Hills. By eight o'clock they had word of them—a shepherd had seen four men 'uncoly mishandled' go by in the last hour. 'That's yin a piece,' says Clem, and swung his cudgel. 'Five o' them!' says Hob. 'God's death, but the faither was a man! And him drunk!' And then there befell them what my author termed 'a sair misbegowk,' for they were overtaken by a posse of mounted neighbours come to aid in the pursuit. Four sour faces looked on the reinforcement. 'The Deil's broughten you!' said Clem, and they rode thenceforward in the rear of the party with hanging heads. Before ten they had found and secured the rogues, and by three of the afternoon, as they rode up the Vennel with their prisoners, they were aware of a concourse of people bearing in their midst something that dripped. 'For the boady of the saxt,' pursued Kirstie, 'wi' his head smashed like a hazelnit, had been a' that nicht in the chairge o' Hermiston Water, and it dunting it on the stanes, and grunding it on the shallows, and flinging the deid thing heels-ower-hurdie at the Fa's o' Spango; and in the first o' the day, Tweed had got a hold o' him and carried him off like a wind, for it was uncoly swalled, and raced wi' him, bobbing under brae-sides, and was long playing with the creature in the drumlie lynns under the castle, and at the hinder end of all cuist him up on the starling of Crossmichael brig. Sae there they were a'thegither at last (for Dickieson had been brought in on a cart long syne), and folk could see what mainner o' man my brither had been that had held his head again sax and saved the siller, and him drunk!' Thus died of honourable injuries and in the savour of fame Gilbert Elliott of the Cauldstaneslap; but his sons had scarce less glory out of the business. Their savage haste, the skill with which Dand had found and followed the trail, the barbarity to the wounded Dickieson (which was like an open secret in the county), and the doom which it was currently supposed they had intended for the others, struck and stirred popular imagination. Some century earlier the last of the minstrels might have fashioned the last of the ballads out of that Homeric fight and chase; but the spirit was dead, or had been reincarnated already in Mr Sheriff Scott, and the degenerate moorsmen must be content to tell the tale in prose, and to make of the 'Four Black Brothers' a unit after the fashion of the 'Twelve Apostles' or the 'Three Musketeers.'

Robert, Gilbert, Clement, and Andrew—in the proper Border diminutives, Hob, Gib, Clem, and Dand Elliott—these ballad heroes, had much in common; in particular, their high sense of the family and the family honour; but they went diverse ways, and prospered and failed in different businesses. According to Kirstie, 'they had a' bees in their bonnets but Hob.' Hob the laird was, indeed, essentially a decent man. An elder of the Kirk, nobody had heard an oath upon his lips, save, perhaps, thrice or so at the sheep-washing, since the chase of his father's murderers. The figure he had shown on that eventful night disappeared as if swallowed by a trap. He who had ecstatically dipped his hand in the red blood, he who had ridden down Dickieson, became, from that moment on, a stiff and rather graceless model of the rustic proprieties; cannily profiting by the high war prices, and yearly stowing away a little nest-egg in the bank against calamity; approved of and sometimes consulted by the greater lairds for the massive and placid sense of what he said, when he could be induced to say anything; and particularly valued by the minister, Mr Torrance, as a right-hand man in the parish, and a model to parents. The transfiguration had been for the moment only; some Barbarossa,* some old Adam of our ancestors, sleeps in all of us till the fit circumstance shall call it into action; and, for as sober as he now seemed, Hob had given once for all the measure of the devil that haunted him. He was married, and, by reason of the effulgence of that legendary night, was adored by his wife. He had a mob of little lusty, barefoot children who marched in a caravan the long miles to school, the stages of whose pilgrimage were marked by acts of spoliation and mischief, and who were qualified in the country-side as 'fair pests.' But in the house, if 'faither was in,' they were quiet as mice. In short, Hob moved through life in a great peace—the reward of any one who shall have killed his man, with any formidable and figurative circumstance, in the midst of a country gagged and swaddled with civilisation.

It was a current remark that the Elliotts were 'guid and bad, like sanguishes'; and certainly there was a curious distinction, the men of business coming alternately with the dreamers. The second brother, Gib, was a weaver by trade, had gone out early into the world to Edinburgh, and come home again with his wings singed. There was an exaltation in his nature which had led him to embrace with enthusiasm the principles of the French Revolution, and had ended by bringing him under the hawse* of my Lord Hermiston in that furious onslaught of his upon the Liberals, which sent Muir and Palmer* into exile and dashed the party into chaff. It was whispered that my lord, in his great scorn for the movement, and prevailed upon a little by a sense of neighbourliness, had given Gib a hint. Meeting him one day in the Potterrow, my lord had stopped in front of him: 'Gib, ye eediot,' he had said, 'what's this I hear of you? Poalitics, poalitics, poalitics, weaver's poalitics, is the way of it, I hear. If ye arena a'thegither dozened with eediocy, ye'll gang your ways back to Cauldstaneslap, and ca' your loom, and ca' your loom, man!' And Gilbert had taken him at the word and returned, with an expedition almost to be called flight, to the house of his father. The clearest of his inheritance was that family gift of prayer of which Kirstie had boasted; and the baffled politician now turned his attention to religious matters—or, as others said, to heresy and schism. Every Sunday morning he was in Crossmichael, where he had gathered together, one by one, a sect of about a dozen persons, who called themselves 'God's Remnant of the True Faithful,' or, for short, 'God's Remnant.' To the profane, they were known as 'Gib's Deils.' Bailie Sweedie, a noted humorist in the town, vowed that the proceedings always opened to the tune of 'The Deil Fly Away with the Exciseman,' and that the sacrament was dispensed in the form of hot whisky-toddy; both wicked hits at the evangelist, who had been suspected of smuggling in his youth, and had been overtaken (as the phrase went) on the streets of Crossmichael one Fair day. It was known that every Sunday they prayed for a blessing on the arms of Bonaparte. For this, 'God's Remnant,' as they were 'skailing' from the cottage that did duty for a temple, had been repeatedly stoned by the bairns, and Gib himself hooted by a squadron of Border volunteers in which his own brother, Dand, rode in a uniform and with a drawn sword. The 'Remnant' were believed, besides, to be 'antinomian* in principle,' which might otherwise have been a serious charge, but the way public opinion then blew it was quite swallowed up and forgotten in the scandal about Bonaparte. For the rest, Gilbert had set up his loom in an outhouse at Cauldstaneslap, where he laboured assiduously six days of the week. His brothers, appalled by his political opinions, and willing to avoid dissension in the household, spoke but little to him; he less to them, remaining absorbed in the study of the Bible and almost constant prayer. The gaunt weaver was dry-nurse at Cauldstaneslap, and the bairns loved him dearly. Except when he was carrying an infant in his arms, he was rarely seen to smile—as, indeed, there were few smilers in that family. When his sister-in-law rallied him, and proposed that he should get a wife and bairns of his own, since he was so fond of them, 'I have no clearness of mind upon that point,' he would reply. If nobody called him in to dinner, he stayed out. Mrs Hob, a hard, unsympathetic woman, once tried the experiment. He went without food all day, but at dusk, as the light began to fail him, he came into the house of his own accord, looking puzzled. 'I've had a great gale of prayer upon my speerit,' said he. 'I canna mind sae muckle's what I had for denner.' The creed of God's Remnant was justified in the life of its founder. 'And yet I dinna ken,' said Kirstie. 'He's maybe no more stockfish than his neeghbours! He rode wi' the rest o' them, and had a good stamach to the work, by a' that I hear! God's Remnant! The deil's clavers! There wasna muckle Christianity in the way Hob guided Johnny Dickieson, at the least of it; but Guid kens! Is he a Christian even? He might be a Mahommedan or a Deevil or a Fireworshipper, for what I ken.'

The third brother had his name on a door-plate, no less, in the city of Glasgow, 'Mr Clement Elliott,' as long as your arm. In his case, that spirit of innovation which had shown itself timidly in the case of Hob by the admission of new manures, and which had run to waste with Gilbert in subversive politics and heretical religions, bore useful fruit in many ingenious mechanical improvements. In boyhood, from his addiction to strange devices of sticks and string, he had been counted the most eccentric of the family. But that was all by now; and he was a partner of his firm, and looked to die a bailie. He too had married, and was rearing a plentiful family in the smoke and din of Glasgow; he was wealthy, and could have bought out his brother, the cock-laird, six times over, it was whispered; and when he slipped away to Cauldstaneslap for a well-earned holiday, which he did as often as he was able, he astonished the neighbours with his broadcloth, his beaver hat, and the ample plies of his neckcloth. Though an eminently solid man at bottom, after the pattern of Hob, he had contracted a certain Glasgow briskness and *aplomb* which set him off. All the other Elliotts were as lean as a rake, but Clement was laying on fat, and he panted sorely when he must get into his boots. Dand said, chuckling: 'Ay, Clem has the elements of a corporation.' 'A provost and corporation,' returned Clem. And his readiness was much admired.

The fourth brother, Dand, was a shepherd to his trade, and by starts, when he could bring his mind to it, excelled in the business. Nobody could train a dog like Dandie; nobody, through the peril of great storms in the winter time, could do more gallantly. But if his dexterity were exquisite, his diligence was but fitful; and he served his brother for bed and board, and a trifle of pocket-money when he asked for it. He loved money well enough, knew very well how to spend it, and could make a shrewd bargain when he liked. But he preferred a vague knowledge that he was well to windward to any counted coins in the pocket; he felt himself richer so. Hob would expostulate: 'I'm an amature herd.' Dand would reply, 'I'll keep your sheep to you when I'm so minded, but I'll keep my liberty too. Thir's no man can coandescend on what I'm worth.' Clem would expound to him the miraculous result of compound interest, and recommend investments. 'Ay, man?' Dand would say; 'and do you think, if I took Hob's siller, that I wouldna drink it or wear it on the lassies? And, anyway, my kingdom is no of this world. Either I'm a poet or else I'm nothing.' Clem would remind him of old age. 'I'll die young, like Robbie Burns,'* he would say stoutly. No question but he had a certain accomplishment in minor verse. His 'Hermiston Burn,' with its pretty refrain—

> 'I love to gang thinking whaur ye gang linking,
> Hermiston burn, in the howe;'

his 'Auld, auld Elliotts, clay-cauld Elliots, dour, bauld Elliotts of auld,' and his really fascinating piece about the Praying Weaver's Stone, had gained him in the neighbourhood the reputation, still possible in Scotland, of a local bard; and, though not printed himself, he was recognised by others who were and who had become famous. Walter Scott owed to Dandie the text of the 'Raid of Wearie' in the *Minstrelsy*;* and made him welcome at his house, and appreciated his talents, such as they were, with all his usual generosity. The Ettrick

Shepherd* was his sworn crony; they would meet, drink to excess, roar out their lyrics in each other's faces, and quarrel and make it up again till bedtime. And besides these recognitions, almost to be called official, Dandie was made welcome for the sake of his gift through the farmhouses of several contiguous dales, and was thus exposed to manifold temptations which he rather sought than fled. He had figured on the stool of repentance, for once fulfilling to the letter the tradition of his hero and model. His humorous verses to Mr Torrance on that occasion—'Kenspeckle here my lane I stand'—unfortunately too indelicate for further citation, ran through the country like a fiery cross; they were recited, quoted, paraphrased, and laughed over as far away as Dumfries on the one hand and Dunbar on the other.

These four brothers were united by a close bond, the bond of that mutual admiration—or rather mutual hero-worship—which is so strong among the members of secluded families who have much ability and little culture. Even the extremes admired each other. Hob, who had as much poetry as the tongs, professed to find pleasure in Dand's verses; Clem, who had no more religion than Claverhouse, nourished a heartfelt, at least an open-mouthed, admiration of Gib's prayers; and Dandie followed with relish the rise of Clem's fortunes. Indulgence followed hard on the heels of admiration. The laird, Clem, and Dand, who were Tories and patriots of the hottest quality, excused to themselves, with a certain bashfulness, the radical and revolutionary heresies of Gib. By another division of the family, the laird, Clem, and Gib, who were men exactly virtuous, swallowed the dose of Dand's irregularities as a kind of clog or drawback in the mysterious providence of God affixed to bards, and distinctly probative of poetical genius. To appreciate the simplicity of their mutual admiration it was necessary to hear Clem, arrived upon one of his visits, and dealing in a spirit of continuous irony with the affairs and personalities of that great city of Glasgow where he lived and transacted business. The various personages, ministers of the church, municipal officers, mercantile big-wigs, whom he had occasion to introduce, were all alike denigrated, all served but as reflectors to cast back a flattering side-light on the house of Cauldstaneslap. The Provost, for whom Clem by exception entertained a measure of respect, he would liken to Hob. 'He minds me o' the laird there,' he would say. 'He has some of Hob's grand, whunstane sense, and the same way with him of steiking his mouth when he's no very pleased.' And Hob, all unconscious, would draw down his upper lip and produce, as if for comparison, the formidable grimace referred to. The unsatisfactory incumbent of St Enoch's Kirk was thus briefly dismissed: 'If he had but twa fingers o' Gib's, he would waken them up.' And Gib, honest man! would look down and secretly smile. Clem was a spy whom they had sent out into the world of men. He had come back with the good news that there was nobody to compare with the Four Black Brothers, no position that they would not adorn, no official that it would not be well they should replace, no interest of mankind, secular or spiritual, which would not immediately bloom under their supervision. The excuse of their folly is in two words: scarce the breadth of a hair divided them from the peasantry. The measure of their sense is this: that these symposia of rustic vanity were kept entirely within the family, like some secret ancestral practice. To the world their serious faces were never deformed by the suspicion of any simper of self-contentment. Yet it was known. 'They hae a guid pride o' themsel's!' was the word in the country-side.

Lastly, in a Border story, there should be added their 'to-names.' Hob was The Laird. 'Roy ne puis, prince ne daigne';* he was the laird of Cauldstaneslap—say fifty acres—*ipsissimus.** Clement was Mr Elliott, as upon his door-plate, the earlier Dafty having beeen discarded as no longer applicable, and indeed only a reminder of misjudgment and the imbecility of the public; and the youngest, in honour of his perpetual wanderings, was known by the sobriquet of Randy Dand.

It will be understood that not all this information was communicated by the aunt, who had too much of the family failing herself to appreciate it thoroughly in others. But as time went on, Archie began to observe an omission in the family chronicle.

'Is there not a girl too?' he asked.

'Ay: Kirstie. She was named for me, or my grandmother at least—it's the same thing,' returned the aunt, and went on again about Dand, whom she secretly preferred by reason of his gallantries.

'But what is your niece like?' said Archie at the next opportunity.

'Her? As black's your hat! But I dinna suppose she would maybe be what you would ca' *ill-looked* a'thegither. Na, she's a kind of a handsome jaud—a kind o' gipsy,' said the aunt, who had two sets of scales for men and women—or perhaps it would be more fair to say that she had three, and the third and the most loaded was for girls.

'How comes it that I never see her in church?' said Archie.

''Deed, and I believe she's in Glesgie with Clem and his wife. A heap good she's like to get of it! I dinna say for men folk, but where weemen folk are born, there let them bide. Glory to God, I was never far'er from here than Crossmichael.'

In the meanwhile it began to strike Archie as strange, that while she thus sang the praises of her kinsfolk, and manifestly relished their virtues and (I may say) their vices like a thing creditable to herself, there should appear not the least sign of cordiality between the house of Hermiston and that of Cauldstaneslap. Going to church of a Sunday, as the lady housekeeper stepped with her skirts kilted, three tucks of her white petticoat showing below, and her best India shawl upon her back (if the day were fine) in a pattern of radiant dyes, she would sometimes overtake her relatives preceding her more leisurely in the same direction. Gib of course was absent: by skreigh of day he had been gone to Crossmichael and his fellow-heretics; but the rest of the family would be seen marching in open order: Hob and Dand, stiff-necked, straight-backed six-footers, with severe dark faces, and their plaids about their shoulders; the convoy of children scattering (in a state of high polish) on the wayside, and every now and again collected by the shrill summons of the mother; and the mother herself, by a suggestive circumstance which might have afforded matter of thought to a more experienced observer than Archie, wrapped in a shawl nearly identical with Kirstie's, but a thought more gaudy and conspicuously newer. At the sight, Kirstie grew more tall—Kirstie showed her classical profile, nose in air and nostril spread, the pure blood came in her cheek evenly in a delicate living pink.

'A braw day to ye, Mistress Elliott,' said she, and hostility and gentility were nicely mingled in her tones. 'A fine day, mem,' the laird's wife would reply with a miraculous curtsey, spreading the while her plumage—setting off, in other words, and with arts unknown to the mere man, the pattern of her India shawl. Behind her, the whole Cauldstaneslap contingent marched in closer order, and with an indescribable air of being in the presence of the foe; and while Dandie saluted his aunt with a certain familiarity as of one who was well in court, Hob marched on in awful immobility. There appeared upon the face of this attitude in the family the consequences of some dreadful feud. Presumably the two women had been principals in the original encounter, and the laird had probably been drawn into the quarrel by the ears, too late to be included in the present skin-deep reconciliation.

'Kirstie,' said Archie one day, 'what is this you have against your family?'

'I dinna complean,' said Kirstie, with a flush. 'I say naething.'

'I see you do not—not even good-day to your own nephew,' said he.

'I hae naething to be ashamed of,' said she. 'I can say the Lord's prayer with a good grace. If Hob was ill, or in preeson or poverty, I would see to him blithely. But for curtchying and complimenting and colloguing, thank ye kindly!'

Archie had a bit of a smile: he leaned back in his chair. 'I think you and Mrs Robert are not very good friends,' says he slyly, 'when you have your India shawls on?'

She looked upon him in silence, with a sparkling eye but an indecipherable expression; and that was all that Archie was ever destined to learn of the battle of the India shawls.

'Do none of them ever come here to see you?' he inquired.

'Mr Archie,' said she, 'I hope that I ken my place better. It would be a queer thing, I think, if I was to clamjamfry up your faither's house—that I should say it!—wi' a dirty, black-a-vised clan, no ane o' them it was worth while to mar soap upon but just mysel'! Na, they're all damnifeed wi' the black Ellwalds. I have nae patience wi' black folk.' Then, with a sudden consciousness of the case of Archie, 'No that it maitters for men sae muckle,' she made haste to add, 'but there's naebody can deny that it's unwomanly. Long hair is the ornament o' woman ony way; we've good warrandise for that—it's in the Bible—and wha can doubt that the Apostle had some gowden-haired lassie in his mind—Apostle and all, for what was he but just a man like yersel'?'

CHAPTER VI

A LEAF FROM CHRISTINA'S PSALM-BOOK

ARCHIE was sedulous at church. Sunday after Sunday he sat down and stood up with that small company, heard the voice of Mr Torrance leaping like an ill-played clarionet from key to key, and had an opportunity to study his moth-eaten gown and the black thread mittens that he joined together in prayer, and lifted up with a reverent solemnity in the act of benediction. Hermiston pew was a little square box, dwarfish in proportion with the kirk itself, and enclosing a table not much bigger than a footstool. There sat Archie, an apparent prince, the only undeniable gentleman and the only great heritor in the parish, taking his ease in the only pew, for no other in the kirk had doors. Thence he might command an undisturbed view of that congregation of solid plaided men, strapping wives and daughters, oppressed children, and uneasy sheep-dogs. It was strange how Archie missed the look of race; except the dogs, with their refined foxy faces and inimitably curling tails, there was no one present with the least claim to gentility. The Cauldstaneslap party was scarcely an exception; Dandie perhaps, as he amused himself making verses through the interminable burden of the service, stood out a little by the glow in his eye and a certain superior animation of face and alertness of body; but even Dandie slouched like a rustic. The rest of the congregation, like so many sheep, oppressed him with a sense of hob-nailed routine, day following day—of physical labour in the open air, oatmeal porridge, peas bannock, the somnolent fireside in the evening, and the night-long nasal slumbers in a box-bed. Yet he knew many of them to be shrewd and humorous, men of character, notable women, making a bustle in the world and radiating an influence from their low-browed doors. He knew besides they were like other men; below the crust of custom, rapture found a way; he had heard them beat the timbrel before Bacchus—had heard them shout and carouse over their whisky-toddy; and not the most Dutch-bottomed and severe faces among them all, not even the solemn elders themselves, but were capable of singular gambols at the voice of love. Men drawing near to an end of life's adventurous journey—maids thrilling with fear and curiosity on the threshold of entrance—women who had borne and perhaps buried children, who could remember the clinging of the small dead hands and the patter of the little feet now silent—he marvelled that among all those faces there should be no face of expectation, none that was mobile, none into which the rhythm and poetry of life had entered. 'O for a live face,' he thought; and at times he had a memory of Lady Flora; and at times he would study the living gallery before him with despair, and would see himself go on to waste his days in that joyless, pastoral place, and death come to him, and his grave be dug under the rowans, and the Spirit of the Earth laugh out in a thunder-peal at the huge fiasco.

On this particular Sunday, there was no doubt but that the spring had come at last. It was warm, with a latent shiver in the air that made the warmth only the more welcome. The shallows of the stream glittered and tinkled among bunches of primrose. Vagrant scents of the earth arrested Archie by the way with moments of ethereal intoxication. The grey, Quakerish dale was still only awakened in places and patches from the sobriety of its winter colouring; and he wondered at its beauty; an essential beauty of the old earth it seemed to him, not resident in particulars but breathing to him from the whole. He surprised himself by a sudden impulse to write poetry—he did so sometimes, loose, galloping octosyllabics in the vein of Scott—and when he had taken his place on a boulder, near some fairy falls and shaded by a whip of a tree that was already radiant with new leaves, it still more surprised him that he should find nothing to write. His heart perhaps bent in time to some vast indwelling rhythm of the universe. By the time he came to a corner of the valley and could see the kirk, he had so lingered by the way that the first psalm was finishing. The nasal psalmody, full of turns and trills and graceless graces, seemed the essential voice of the kirk itself upraised in thanksgiving. 'Everything's alive,' he said; and again cries it aloud, 'thank God, everything's alive!'

He lingered yet a while in the kirk-yard. A tuft of primroses was blooming hard by the leg of an old, black table tombstone, and he stopped to contemplate the random apologue. They stood forth on the cold earth with a trenchancy of contrast; and he was struck with a sense of incompleteness in the day, the season, and the beauty that surrounded him—the chill there was in the warmth, the gross black clods about the opening primroses, the damp earthy smell that was everywhere intermingled with the scents. The voice of the aged Torrance within rose in an ecstasy. And he wondered if Torrance also felt in his old bones the joyous influence of the spring morning; Torrance, or the shadow of what once was Torrance, that must come so soon to lie outside here in the sun and rain with all his rheumatisms, while a new minister stood in his room and thundered from his own familiar pulpit? The pity of it, and something of the chill of the grave, shook him for a moment as he made haste to enter.

He went up the aisle reverently, and took his place in the pew with lowered eyes, for he feared he had already offended the kind old gentleman in the pulpit, and was sedulous to offend no further. He could not follow the prayer, not even the heads of it. Brightness of azure, clouds of fragrance, a tinkle of falling water and singing birds, rose like exhalations from some deeper, aboriginal memory, that was not his, but belonged to the flesh on his bones. His body remembered; and it seemed to him that his body was in no way gross, but ethereal and perishable like a strain of music; and he felt for it an exquisite tenderness as for a child, an innocent, full of beautiful instincts and destined to an early death. And he felt for old Torrance—of the many supplications, of the few days—a pity that was near to tears. The prayer ended. Right over him was a tablet in the wall, the only ornament in the roughly masoned chapel—for it was no more; the tablet commemorated, I was about to say the virtues, but rather the existence of a former Rutherford of Hermiston; and Archie, under the trophy of his long descent and local greatness, leaned back in the pew and contemplated vacancy with the shadow of a smile between playful and sad, that became him strangely. Dandie's sister, sitting by the side of Clem in her new Glasgow finery, chose that moment to observe the young laird. Aware of the stir of his entrance, the little formalist had kept her eyes fastened and her face prettily composed during the prayer. It was not hypocrisy, there was no one further from a hypocrite. The girl had been taught to behave: to look up, to look down, to look unconscious, to look seriously impressed in church, and in every conjuncture to look her best. That was the game of female life, and she played it frankly. Archie was the one person in church who was of interest, who was somebody new, reputed eccentric, known to be young, and a laird, and still unseen by Christina. Small wonder that, as she stood there in her attitude of pretty decency, her mind should run upon him! If he spared a glance in her direction, he should know she was a well-behaved young lady who had been to Glasgow. In reason he must admire her clothes, and it was possible that he should think her pretty. At that her heart beat the least thing in the world; and she proceeded, by way of a corrective, to call up and dismiss a series of fancied pictures of the young man who should now, by rights, be looking at her. She settled on the plainest of them,—a pink short young man with a dish face and no figure, at whose admiration she could afford to smile; but for all that, the consciousness of his gaze (which was really fixed on Torrance and his mittens) kept her in something of a flutter till the word Amen. Even then, she was far too well-bred to gratify her curiosity with any impatience. She resumed her seat languidly—this was a Glasgow touch—she composed her dress, rearranged her nosegay of primroses, looked first in front, then behind upon the other side, and at last allowed her eyes to move, without hurry, in the direction of the Hermiston pew. For a moment, they were riveted. Next she had plucked her gaze home again like a tame bird who should have meditated flight. Possibilities crowded on her; she hung over the future and grew dizzy; the image of this young man, slim, graceful, dark, with the inscrutable half-smile, attracted and repelled her like a chasm. 'I wonder, will I have met my fate?' she thought, and her heart swelled.

Torrance was got some way into this first exposition, positing a deep layer of texts as he went along, laying the foundations of his discourse, which was to deal with a nice point in divinity, before Archie suffered his eyes to wander. They fell first of all on Clem, looking insupportably prosperous, and patronising Torrance with the favour of a modified attention, as of one who was used to better things in Glasgow. Though he had never before set eyes on him, Archie had no difficulty in identifying him, and no hesitation in pronouncing him vulgar, the worst of the family. Clem was leaning lazily forward when Archie first saw him. Presently he leaned nonchalantly back; and that deadly instrument, the maiden, was suddenly unmasked in profile. Though not quite in the front of the fashion (had anybody cared!), certain artful Glasgow mantua-makers, and her own inherent taste, had arrayed her to great advantage. Her accoutrement was, indeed, a cause of heart-burning, and almost of scandal, in that infinitesimal kirk company. Mrs Hob had said her say at Cauldstaneslap. 'Daft-like!' she had pronounced it. 'A jaiket that'll no meet! Whaur's the sense of a jaiket that'll no button upon you, if it should come to be weet? What do ye ca thir things? Demmy brokens, d'ye say? They'll be brokens wi' a vengeance or ye can win back! Weel, I have naething to do wi'it—it's no good taste.' Clem, whose purse had thus metamorphosed his sister, and who was not insensible to the advertisement, had come to the rescue with a 'Hoot, woman! What do you ken of good taste that has never been to the ceety?' And Hob, looking on the girl with pleased smiles, as she timidly displayed her finery in the midst of the dark kitchen, had thus ended the dispute: 'The cutty looks weel,' he had said, 'and it's no very like rain. Wear them the day, hizzie; but it's no a thing to make a practice o'.' In the breasts of her rivals, coming to the kirk very conscious of white under-linen, and their faces splendid with much soap, the sight of the toilet had raised a storm of varying emotion, from the mere unenvious admiration that was expressed in a long-drawn 'Eh!' to the angrier feeling that found vent in an emphatic 'Set her up!' Her frock was of straw-coloured jaconet muslin, cut low at the bosom and short at the ankle, so as to display her *demi-broquins* of Regency violet, crossing with many straps upon a yellow cobweb stocking. According to the pretty fashion in which our grandmothers did not hesitate to appear, and our great-aunts went forth armed for the pursuit and capture of our great-uncles, the dress was drawn up so as to mould the contour of both breasts, and in the nook between, a cairngorm brooch maintained it. Here, too, surely in a very enviable position, trembled the nosegay of primroses. She wore on her shoulders—or rather, on her back and not her shoulders, which it scarcely passed—a French coat of sarsenet, tied in front with Margate braces, and of the same colour with her violet shoes. About her face clustered a disorder of dark ringlets, a little garland of yellow French roses surmounted her brow, and the whole was crowned by a village hat of chipped straw. Amongst all the rosy and all the weathered faces that surrounded her in church, she glowed like an open flower—girl and raiment, and the cairngorm that caught the daylight and returned it in a fiery flash, and the threads of bronze and gold that played in her hair.

Archie was attracted by the bright thing like a child. He looked at her again and yet again, and their looks crossed. The lip was lifted from her little teeth. He saw the red blood work vividly under her tawny skin. Her eye, which was great as a stag's, struck and held his gaze. He knew who she must be—Kirstie, she of the harsh diminutive, his housekeeper's niece, the sister of the rustic prophet, Gib—and he found in her the answer to his wishes.

Christina felt the shock of their encountering glances, and seemed to rise, clothed in smiles, into a region of the vague and bright. But the gratification was not more exquisite than it was brief. She looked away abruptly, and immediately began to blame herself for that abruptness. She knew what she should have done, too late—turned slowly with her nose in the air. And meantime his look was not removed, but continued to play upon her like a battery of cannon constantly aimed, and now seemed to isolate her alone with him, and now seemed to uplift her, as on a pillory, before the congregation. For Archie continued to drink her in with his eyes, even as a wayfarer comes to a well-head on a mountain, and stoops his face, and drinks with thirst unassuageable. In the cleft of her little breasts the fiery eye of the topaz and the pale florets of primrose fascinated him. He saw the breasts heave, and the flowers shake with the heaving, and marvelled what should so much discompose the girl. And Christina was conscious of his gaze—saw it, perhaps, with the dainty plaything of an ear that peeped among her ringlets; she was conscious of changing colour, conscious of her unsteady breath. Like a creature tracked, run down, surrounded, she sought in a dozen ways to give herself a countenance. She used her handkerchief—it was a really fine one—then she desisted in a panic: 'He would only think I was too warm.' She took to reading in the metrical psalms, and then remembered it was sermon-time. Last she put a 'sugar-bool' in her mouth, and the next moment repented of the step. It was such a homely-like thing! Mr Archie would never be eating sweeties in kirk; and, with a palpable effort, she swallowed it whole, and her colour flamed high. At this signal of distress Archie awoke to a sense of his ill-behaviour. What had he been doing? He had been exquisitely rude in church to the niece of his housekeeper; he had stared like a lackey and a libertine at a beautiful and modest girl. It was possible, it was even likely, he would be presented to her after service in the kirkyard, and then how was he to look? And there was no excuse. He had marked the tokens of her shame, of her increasing indignation, and he was such a fool that he had not understood them. Shame bowed him down, and he looked resolutely at Mr Torrance; who little supposed, good worthy man, as he continued to expound justification by faith, what was his true business: to play the part of derivative to a pair of children at the old game of falling in love.

Christina was greatly relieved at first. It seemed to her that she was clothed again. She looked back on what had passed. All would have been right if she had not blushed, a silly fool! There was nothing to blush at, if she *had* taken a sugar-bool. Mrs MacTaggart, the elder's wife in St Enoch's, took them often. And if he had looked at her, what was more natural than that a young gentleman should look at the best-dressed girl in church? And at the same time, she knew far otherwise, she knew there was nothing casual or ordinary in the look, and valued herself on its memory like a decoration. Well, it was a blessing he had found something else to look at! And presently she began to have other thoughts. It was necessary, she fancied, that she should put herself right by a repetition of the incident, better managed. If the wish was father to the thought, she did not know or she would not recognise it. It was simply as a manœuvre of propriety, as something called for to lessen the significance of what had gone before, that she should a second time meet his eyes, and this time without blushing. And at the memory of the blush, she blushed again, and became one general blush burning from head to foot. Was ever anything so indelicate, so forward, done by a girl before? And here she was, making an exhibition of herself before the congregation about nothing! She stole a glance upon her neighbours, and behold! they were steadily indifferent, and Clem had gone to sleep. And still the one idea was becoming more and more potent with her, that in common prudence she must look again before the service ended. Something of the same sort was going forward in the mind of Archie, as he struggled with the load of penitence. So it chanced that, in the flutter of the moment when the last psalm was given out, and Torrance was reading the verse, and the leaves of every psalm-book in church were rustling under busy fingers, two stealthy glances were sent out like antennæ among the pews and on the indifferent and absorbed occupants, and drew timidly nearer to the straight line between Archie and Christina. They met, they lingered together for the least fraction of time, and that was enough. A charge as of electricity passed through Christina, and behold! the leaf of her psalm-book was torn across.

Archie was outside by the gate of the graveyard, conversing with Hob and the minister and shaking hands all round with the scattering congregation, when Clem and Christina were brought up to be presented. The laird took off his hat and bowed to her with grace and respect. Christina made her Glasgow curtsey to the laird, and went on again up the road for Hermiston and Cauldstaneslap, walking fast, breathing hurriedly with a heightened colour, and in this strange frame of mind, that when she was alone she seemed in high happiness, and when any one addressed her she resented it like a contradiction. A part of the way she had the company of some neighbour girls and a loutish young man; never had they seemed so insipid, never had she made herself so disagreeable. But these struck aside to their various destinations or were out-walked and left behind; and when she had driven off with sharp words the proffered convoy of some of her nephews and nieces, she was free to go on alone up Hermiston brae, walking on air, dwelling intoxicated among clouds of happiness. Near to the summit she heard steps behind her, a man's steps, light and very rapid. She knew the foot at once and walked the faster. 'If it's me he's wanting, he can run for it,' she thought, smiling.

Archie overtook her like a man whose mind was made up. 'Miss Kirstie,' he began.

'Miss Christina, if you please, Mr Weir,' she interrupted. 'I canna bear the contraction.'

'You forget it has a friendly sound for me. Your aunt is an old friend of mine, and a very good one. I hope we shall see much of you at Hermiston?'

'My aunt and my sister-in-law doesna agree very well. Not that I have much ado with it. But still when I'm stopping in the house, if I was to be visiting my aunt, it would not look considerate-like.'

'I am sorry,' said Archie.

'I thank you kindly, Mr Weir,' she said. 'I whiles think myself it's a great peety.'

'Ah, I am sure your voice would always be for peace!' he cried.

'I wouldna be too sure of that,' she said. 'I have my days like other folk, I suppose.'

'Do you know, in our old kirk, among our good old grey dames, you made an effect like sunshine.'

'Ah, but that would be my Glasgow clothes!'

'I did not think I was so much under the influence of pretty frocks.'

She smiled with a half look at him. 'There's more than you!' she said. 'But you see I'm only Cinderella. I'll have to put all these things by in my trunk; next Sunday I'll be as grey as the rest. They're Glasgow clothes, you see, and it would never do to make a practice of it. It would seem terrible conspicuous.'

By that they were come to the place where their ways severed. The old grey moors were all about them; in the midst a few sheep wandered; and they could see on the one hand the straggling caravan scaling the braes in front of them for Cauldstaneslap, and on the other, the contingent from Hermiston bending off and beginning to disappear by detachments into the policy gate. It was in these circumstances that they turned to say farewell, and deliberately exchanged a glance as they shook hands. All passed as it should, genteelly; and in Christina's mind, as she mounted the first steep ascent for Cauldstaneslap, a gratifying sense of triumph prevailed over the recollection of minor lapses and mistakes. She had kilted her gown, as she did usually at that rugged pass; but when she spied Archie still standing and gazing after her, the skirts came down again as if by enchantment. Here was a piece of nicety for that upland parish, where the matrons marched with their coats kilted in the rain, and the lasses walked barefoot to kirk through the dust of summer, and went bravely down by the burn-side, and sat on stones to make a public toilet before entering! It was perhaps an air wafted from Glasgow; or perhaps it marked a stage of that dizziness of gratified vanity, in which the instinctive act passed unperceived. He was looking after! She unloaded her bosom of a prodigious sigh that was all pleasure, and betook herself to run. When she had overtaken the stragglers of her family, she caught up the niece whom she had so recently repulsed, and kissed and slapped her, and drove her away again, and ran after her with pretty cries and laughter. Perhaps she thought the laird might still be looking! But it chanced the little scene came under the view of eyes less favourable; for she overtook Mrs Hob marching with Clem and Dand.

'You're shürely fey, lass!' quoth Dandie.

'Think shame to yersel', miss!' said the strident Mrs Hob. 'Is this the gait to guide yersel' on the way hame frae kirk? You're shürely no sponsible the day! And anyway I would mind my guid claes.'

'Hoot!' said Christina, and went on before them head in air, treading the rough track with the tread of a wild doe.

She was in love with herself, her destiny, the air of the hills, the benediction of the sun. All the way home, she continued under the intoxication of these sky-scraping spirits. At table she could talk freely of young Hermiston; gave her opinion of him off-hand and with a loud voice, that he was a handsome young gentleman, real well mannered and sensible-like, but it was a pity he looked doleful. Only—the moment after—a memory of his eyes in church embarrassed her. But for this inconsiderable check, all through meal-time she had a good appetite, and she kept them laughing at table, until Gib (who had returned before them from Crossmichael and his separative worship) reproved the whole of them for their levity.

Singing 'in to herself' as she went, her mind still in the turmoil of a glad confusion, she rose and tripped upstairs to a little loft, lighted by four panes in the gable, where she slept with one of her nieces. The niece, who followed her, presuming on 'Auntie's' high spirits, was flounced out of the apartment with small ceremony, and retired, smarting and half tearful, to bury her woes in the byre among the hay. Still humming, Christina divested herself of her finery, and put her treasures one by one in her great green trunk. The last of these was the psalm-book; it was a fine piece, the gift of Mistress Clem, in a distinct old-faced type, on paper that had begun to grow foxy in the warehouse—not by service—and she was used to wrap it in a handkerchief every Sunday after its period of service was over, and bury it end-wise at the head of her trunk. As she now took it in hand the book fell open where the leaf was torn, and she stood and gazed upon that evidence of her bygone discomposure. There returned again the vision of the two brown eyes staring at her, intent and bright, out of that dark corner of the kirk. The whole appearance and attitude, the smile, the suggested gesture of young Hermiston came before her in a flash at the sight of the torn page. 'I was surely fey!' she said, echoing the words of Dandie, and at the suggested doom her high spirits deserted her. She flung herself prone upon the bed, and lay there, holding the psalm-book in her hands for hours, for the more part in a mere stupor of unconsenting pleasure and unreasoning fear. The fear was superstitious; there came up again and again in her memory Dandie's ill-omened words, and a hundred grisly and black tales out of the immediate neighbourhood read her a commentary on their force. The pleasure was never realised. You might say the joints of her body thought and remembered, and were gladdened, but her essential self, in the immediate theatre of consciousness, talked feverishly of something else, like a nervous person at a fire. The image that she most complacently dwelt on was that of Miss Christina in her character of the Fair Lass of Cauldstaneslap, carrying all before her in the straw-coloured frock, the violet mantle, and the yellow cobweb stockings. Archie's image, on the other hand, when it presented itself was never welcomed—far less welcomed with any ardour, and it was exposed at times to merciless criticism. In the long vague dialogues she held in her mind, often with imaginary, often with unrealised interlocutors, Archie, if he were referred to at all, came in for savage handling. He was described as 'looking like a stirk,' 'staring like a caulf,' 'a face like a ghaist's.' 'Do you call that manners?' she said; or, 'I soon put him in his place.' ' "*Miss Christina if you please, Mr Weir!*" says I, and just flyped up my skirt tails.' With gabble like this she would entertain herself long whiles together, and then her eye would perhaps fall on the torn leaf, and the eyes of Archie would appear again from the darkness of the wall, and the voluble words deserted her, and she would lie still and stupid, and think upon nothing with devotion, and be sometimes raised by a quiet sigh. Had a doctor of medicine come into the loft, he would have diagnosed a healthy, well-developed, eminently vivacious lass lying on her face in a fit of the sulks; not one who had just contracted, or was just contracting, a mortal sickness of the mind which should yet carry her towards death and despair. Had it been a doctor of psychology, he might have been pardoned for divining in the girl a passion of childish vanity, self-love *in excelsis*, and no more. It is to be understood that I have been painting chaos and describing the inarticulate Every lineament that appears is too precise, almost every word used too strong. Take a finger-post in the mountains on a day of rolling mists; I have but copied the names that appear upon the pointers, the names of definite and famous cities far distant, and now perhaps basking in sunshine; but Christina remained all these hours, as it were, at the foot of the post itself, not moving, and enveloped in mutable and blinding wreaths of haze.

The day was growing late and the sunbeams long and level, when she sat suddenly up, and wrapped in its handkerchief and put by that psalm-book which had already played a part so decisive in the first chapter of her love-story. In the absence of the mesmerist's eye, we are told nowadays that the head of a bright nail may fill his place, if it be steadfastly regarded. So that torn page had riveted her attention on what might else have been but little, and perhaps soon forgotten; while the ominous words of Dandie—heard, not heeded, and still remembered—had lent to her thoughts, or rather to her mood, a cast of solemnity, and that idea of Fate—a pagan Fate, uncontrolled by any Christian deity, obscure, lawless, and august—moving indissuadably in the affairs of Christian men. Thus even that phenomenon of love at first sight, which is so rare and seems to simple and violent, like a disruption of life's tissue, may be decomposed into a sequence of accidents happily concurring.

She put on a grey frock and a pink kerchief, looked at herself a moment with approval in the small square of glass that served her for a toilet mirror, and went softly downstairs through the sleeping house that resounded with the sound of afternoon snoring. Just outside the door, Dandie was sitting with a book in his hand, not reading, only honouring the Sabbath by a sacred vacancy of mind. She came near him and stood still.

'I'm for off up the muirs, Dandie,' she said.

There was something unusually soft in her tones that made him look up. She was pale, her eyes dark and bright; no trace remained of the levity of the morning.

'Ay, lass? Ye'll have ye're ups and downs like me, I'm thinkin',' he observed.

'What for do ye say that?' she asked.

'O, for naething,' says Dand. 'Only I think ye're mair like me than the lave of them. Ye've mair of the poetic temper, tho' Guid kens little enough of the poetic taalent. It's an ill gift at the best. Look at yoursel'. At denner you were all sunshine and flowers and laughter, and now you're like the star of evening on a lake.'

She drank in this hackneyed compliment like wine, and it glowed in her veins.

'But I'm saying, Dand'—she came nearer him—'I'm for the muirs. I must have a braith of air. If Clem was to be speiring for me, try and quaiet him, will ye no?'

'What way?' said Dandie. 'I ken but the ae way, and that's leein'. I'll say ye had a sair heed, if ye like.'

'But I havena,' she objected.

'I daursay no',' he returned. 'I said I would say ye had; and if ye like to nay-say me when ye come back, it'll no mateerially maitter, for my chara'ter's clean gane a'ready past reca'.'

'O, Dand, are ye a leear?' she asked, lingering.

'Folks say sae,' replied the bard.

'Wha says sae?' she pursued.

'Them that should ken the best,' he responded. 'The lassies, for ane.'

'But, Dand, you would never lee to me?' she asked.

'I'll leave that for your pairt of it, ye girzie,' said he. 'Ye'll lee to me fast eneuch, when ye hae gotten a jo. I'm tellin' ye and it's true; when you have a jo, Miss Kirstie, it'll be for guid and ill. I ken: I was made that way mysel', but the deil was in my luck! Here, gang awa wi' ye to your muirs, and let me be; I'm in an hour of inspiraution, ye upsetting tawpie!'

But she clung to her brother's neighbourhood, she knew not why.

'Will ye no gie's a kiss, Dand?' she said. 'I aye likit ye fine.'

He kissed her and considered her a moment; he found something strange in her. But he was a libertine through and through, nourished equal contempt and suspicion of all womankind, and paid his way among them habitually with idle compliments.

'Gae wa' wi' ye!' said he. 'Ye're a dentie baby, and be content wi' that!'

That was Dandie's way; a kiss and a comfit to Jenny—a bawbee and my blessing to Jill—and good-night to the whole clan of ye, my dears! When anything approached the serious, it became a matter for men, he both thought and said. Women, when they did not absorb, were only children to be shoo'd away. Merely in his character of connoisseur, however, Dandie glanced carelessly after his sister as she crossed the meadow. 'The brat's no that bad!' he thought with surprise, for though he had just been paying her compliments, he had not really looked at her. 'Hey! what's yon?' For the grey dress was cut with short sleeves and skirts, and displayed her trim strong legs clad in pink stockings of the same shade as the kerchief she wore round her shoulders, and that shimmered as she went. This was not her way in undress; he knew her ways and the ways of the whole sex in the country-side, no one better; when they did not go barefoot, they wore stout 'rig and furrow' woollen hose of an invisible blue mostly, when they were not black outright; and Dandie, at sight of this daintiness, put two and two together. It was a silk handkerchief, then they would be silken hose; they matched—then the whole outfit was a present of Clem's, a costly present, and not something to be worn through bog and briar, or on a late afternoon of Sunday. He whistled. 'My denty May, either your heid's fair turned, or there's some ongoings!' he observed, and dismissed the subject.

She went slowly at first, but ever straighter and faster for the Cauldstaneslap, a pass among the hills to which the farm owed its name. The Slap opened like a doorway between two rounded hillocks; and through this ran the short cut to Hermiston. Immediately on the other side it went down through the Deil's Hags, a considerable marshy hollow of the hill tops, full of springs, and crouching junipers, and pools where the black peat-water slumbered. There was no view from here. A man might have sat upon the Praying Weaver's stone a half century, and seen none but the Cauldstaneslap children twice in the twenty-four hours on their way to the school and back again, an occasional shepherd, the irruption of a clan of sheep, or the birds who haunted about the springs, drinking and shrilly piping. So, when she had once passed the Slap, Kirstie was received into seclusion. She looked back a last time at the farm. It still lay deserted except for the figure of Dandie, who was now seen to be scribbling in his lap, the hour of expected inspiration having come to him at last. Thence she passed rapidly through the morass, and came to the farther end of it, where a sluggish burn discharges, and the path for Hermiston accompanies it on the beginning of its downward path. From this corner a wide view was opened to her of the whole stretch of braes upon the other side, still sallow and in places rusty with the winter, with the path marked boldly, here and there by the burn-side a tuft of birches, and—two miles off as the crow flies—from its enclosures and young plantations, the windows of Hermiston glittering in the western sun.

Here she sat down and waited, and looked for a long time at these far-away bright panes of glass. It amused her to have so extended a view, she thought. It amused her to see the house of Hermiston—to see 'folk'; and there was an indistinguishable human unit, perhaps the gardener, visibly sauntering on the gravel paths.

By the time the sun was down and all the easterly braes lay plunged in clear shadow, she was aware of another figure coming up the path at a most unequal rate of approach, now half running, now pausing and seeming to hesitate. She watched him at first with a total suspension of thought. She held her thought as a person holds his breathing. Then she consented to recognise him. 'He'll no be coming here, he canna be; it's no possible.' And there began to grow upon her a subdued choking suspense. He *was* coming; his hesitations had quite ceased, his step grew firm and swift; no doubt remained; and the question loomed up before her instant: what was she to do? It was all very well to say that her brother was a laird himself; it was all very well to speak of casual intermarriages and to count cousinship, like Auntie Kirstie. The difference in their social station was trenchant; propriety, prudence, all that she had ever learned, all that she knew, bade her flee. But on the other hand the cup of life now offered to her was too enchanting. For one moment, she saw the question clearly, and definitely made her choice. She stood up and showed herself an instant in the gap relieved upon the sky line; and the next, fled trembling and sat down glowing with excitement on the Weaver's stone. She shut her eyes, seeking, praying for composure. Her hand shook in her lap, and her mind was full of incongruous and futile speeches. What was there to make a work about? She could take care of herself, she supposed! There was no harm in seeing the laird. it was the best thing that could happen. She would mark a proper distance to him once and for all. Gradually the wheels of her nature ceased to go round so madly, and she sat in passive expectation, a quiet, solitary figure in the midst of the grey moss. I have said she was no hypocrite, but here I am at fault. She never admitted to herself that she had come up the hill to look for Archie. And perhaps after all she did not know, perhaps came as a stone falls. For the steps of love in the young, and especially in girls, are instinctive and unconscious.

In the meantime Archie was drawing rapidly near, and he at least was consciously seeking her neighbourhood. The afternoon had turned to ashes in his mouth; the memory of the girl had kept him from reading and drawn him as with cords; and at last, as the cool of the evening began to come on, he had taken his hat and set forth, with a smothered ejaculation, by the moor path to Cauldstaneslap. He had no hope to find her; he took the off chance without expectation of result and to relieve his uneasiness. The greater was his surprise, as he surmounted the slope and came into the hollow of the Deil's Hags, to see there, like an answer to his wishes, the little womanly figure in the grey dress and the pink kerchief sitting little, and low, and lost, and acutely solitary, in these desolate surroundings and on the weatherbeaten stone of the dead weaver. Those things that still smacked of winter were all rusty about her, and those things that already relished of the spring had put forth the tender and lively colours of the season. Even in the unchanging face of the deathstone, changes were to be remarked; and in the channeled lettering, the moss began to renew itself in jewels of green. By an afterthought that was a stroke of art, she had turned up over her head the back of the kerchief; so that it now framed becomingly her vivacious and yet pensive face. His feet were gathered under her on the one side, and she leaned on her bare arm, which showed out strong and round, tapered to a slim wrist, and shimmered in the fading light.

Young Hermiston was struck with a certain chill. He was reminded that he now dealt in serious matters of life and death. This was a grown woman he was approaching, endowed with her mysterious potencies and attractions, the treasury of the continued race, and he was neither better nor worse than the average of his sex and age. He had a certain delicacy which had preserved him hitherto unspotted, and which (had either of them guessed it) made him a more dangerous companion when his heart should be really stirred. His throat was dry as he came near; but the appealing sweetness of her smile stood between them like a guardian angel.

For she turned to him and smiled, though without rising. There was a shade in this cavalier greeting that neither of them perceived; neither he, who simply thought it gracious and charming as herself; nor yet she, who did not observe (quick as she was) the difference between rising to meet the laird, and remaining seated to receive the expected admirer.

'Are ye stepping west, Hermiston?' said she, giving him his territorial name after the fashion of the country-side.

'I was,' said he, a little hoarsely, 'but I think I will be about the end of my stroll now. Are you like me, Miss Christina? The house would not hold me. I came here seeking air.'

He took his seat at the other end of the tombstone and studied her, wondering what was she. There was infinite import in the question alike for her and him.

'Ay,' she said. 'I couldna bear the roof either. It's a habit of mine to come up here about the gloaming when it's quaiet and caller.'

'It was a habit of my mother's also,' he said gravely. The recollection half startled him as he expressed it. He looked around. 'I have scarce been here since. It's peaceful,' he said, with a long breath.

'It's no like Glasgow,' she replied. 'A weary place, yon Glasgow! But what a day have I had for my hame-coming, and what a bonny evening!'

'Indeed, it was a wonderful day,' said Archie. 'I think I will remember it years and years until I come to die. On days like this—I do not know if you feel as I do—but everything appears so brief, and fragile, and exquisite, that I am afraid to touch life. We are here for so short a time; and all the old people before us—Rutherfords of Hermiston, Elliotts of the Cauldstaneslap—that were here but a while since riding about and keeping up a great noise in this quiet corner—making love too, and marrying—why, where are they now? It's deadly commonplace, but, after all, the commonplaces are the great poetic truths.'

He was sounding her, semi-consciously, to see if she could understand him; to learn if she were only an animal the colour of flowers, or had a soul in her to keep her sweet. She, on her part, her means well in hand, watched, womanlike, for any opportunity to shine, to abound in his humour, whatever that might be. The dramatic artist, that lies dormant or only half awake in most human beings, had in her sprung to his feet in a divine fury, and chance had served her well. She looked upon him with a subdued twilight look that became the hour of the day and the train of thought; earnestness shone through her like stars in the purple west; and from the great but controlled upheaval of her whole nature there passed into her voice, and rang in her lightest words, a thrill of emotion.

'Have you mind of Dand's song?' she answered. 'I think he'll have been trying to say what you have been thinking.'

'No, I never heard it,' he said. 'Repeat it to me, can you?'

'It's nothing wanting the tune,' said Kirstie.

'Then sing it me,' said he.

'On the Lord's Day? That would never do, Mr Weir!'

'I am afraid I am not so strict a keeper of the Sabbath, and there is no one in this place to hear us, unless the poor old ancient under the stone.'

'No that I'm thinking that really,' she said. 'By my way of thinking, it's just as serious as a psalm. Will I sooth it to ye, then?'

'If you please,' said he, and, drawing near to her on the tombstone, prepared to listen.

She sat up as if to sing. 'I'll only can sooth it to ye,' she explained. 'I wouldna like to sing out loud on the Sabbath. I think the birds would carry news of it to Gilbert,' and she smiled. 'It's about the Elliotts,' she continued, 'and I think there's few bonnier bits in the book-poets, though Dand has never got printed yet.'

And she began, in the low, clear tones of her half voice, now sinking almost to a whisper, now rising to a particular note which was her best, and which Archie learned to wait for with growing emotion:—

'O they rade in the rain, in the days that are gane,
In the rain and the wind and the lave,
They shoutit in the ha' and they routit on the hill,
But they're a' quaitit noo in the grave.
Auld, auld Elliotts, clay-cauld Elliotts, dour, bauld
Elliotts of auld!'

All the time she sang she looked steadfastly before her, her knees straight, her hands upon her knee, her head cast back and up. The expression was admirable throughout, for had she not learned it from the lips and under the criticism of the author? When it was done, she turned upon Archie a face softly bright, and eyes gently suffused and shining in the twilight, and his heart rose and went out to her with boundless pity and sympathy. His question was answered. She was a human being tuned to a sense of the tragedy of life; there were pathos and music and a great heart in the girl.

He arose instinctively, she also; for she saw she had gained a point, and scored the impression deeper, and she had wit enough left to flee upon a victory. They were but commonplaces that remained to be exchanged, but the low, moved voices in which they passed made them sacred in the memory. In the falling greyness of the evening he watched her figure winding through the morass, saw it turn a last time and wave a hand, and then pass through the Slap; and it seemed to him as if something went along with her out of the deepest of his heart. And something surely had come, and come to dwell there. He had retained from childhood a picture, now half obliterated by the passage of time and the multitude of fresh impressions, of his mother telling him, with the fluttered earnestness of her voice, and often with dropping tears, the tale of the 'Praying Weaver,' on the very scene of his brief tragedy and long repose. And now there was a companion piece; and he beheld, and he should behold for ever, Christina perched on the same tomb, in the grey colours of the evening, gracious, dainty, perfect as a flower, and she also singing—

> 'Of old, unhappy far off things,
> And battles long ago,'*

of their common ancestors now dead, of their rude wars composed, their weapons buried with them, and of these strange changelings, their descendants, who lingered a little in their places, and would soon be gone also, and perhaps sung of by others at the gloaming hour. By one of the unconscious arts of tenderness the two women were enshrined together in his memory. Tears, in that hour of sensibility, came into his eyes indifferently at the thought of either; and the girl, from being something merely bright and shapely, was caught up into the zone of things serious as life and death and his dead mother. So that in all ways and on either side, Fate played his game artfully with this poor pair of children. The generations were prepared, the pangs were made ready, before the curtain rose on the dark drama.

In the same moment of time that she disappeared from Archie, there opened before Kirstie's eyes the cup-like hollow in which the farm lay. She saw, some five hundred feet below her, the house making itself bright with candles, and this was a broad hint to her to hurry. For they were only kindled on a Sabbath night with a view to that family worship which rounded in the incomparable tedium of the day and brought on the relaxation of supper. Already she knew that Robert must be within-sides at the head of the table, 'waling the portions'; for it was Robert in his quality of family priest and judge, not the gifted Gilbert, who officiated. She made good time accordingly down the steep ascent, and came up to the door panting as the three younger brothers, all roused at last from slumber, stood together in the cool and the dark of the evening with a fry of nephews and nieces about them, chatting and awaiting the expected signal. She stood back; she had no mind to direct attention to her late arrival or to her labouring breath

'Kirstie, ye have shaved it this time, my lass?' said Clem. 'Whaur were ye?'

'O, just taking a dander by mysel',' said Kirstie.

And the talk continued on the subject of the American War,* without further reference to that truant who stood by them in the covert of the dusk, thrilling with happiness and the sense of guilt.

The signal was given, and the brothers began to go in one after another, amid the jostle and throng of Hob's children.

Only Dandie, waiting till the last, caught Kirstie by the arm. 'When did ye begin to dander in pink hosen, Mistress Elliott?' he whispered slyly.

She looked down; she was one blush. 'I maun have forgotten to change them,' said she; and went into prayers in her turn with a troubled mind, between anxiety as to whether Dand should have observed her yellow stockings at church, and should thus detect her in a palpable falsehood, and shame that she had already made good his prophecy. She remembered the words of it, how it was to be when she had gotten a jo, and that that would be for good and evil. 'Will I have gotten my jo now?' she thought with a secret rapture.

And all through prayers, where it was her principal business to conceal the pink stockings from the eyes of the indifferent Mrs Hob—and all through supper, as she made a feint of eating and sat at the table radiant and constrained—and again when she had left them and come into her chamber, and was alone with her sleeping niece, and could at last lay aside the armour of society—the same words sounded within her, the same profound note of happiness, of a world all changed and renewed, of a day that had been passed in Paradise, and of a night that was to be heaven opened. All night she seemed to be conveyed smoothly upon a shallow stream of sleep and waking, and through the bowers of Beulah;* all night she cherished to her heart that exquisite hope; and if, towards morning, she forgot it a while in a more profound unconsciousness, it was to catch again the rainbow thought with her first moment of awaking.

CHAPTER VII

ENTER MEPHISTOPHELES

TWO days later a gig from Crossmichael deposited Frank Innes at the doors of Hermiston. Once in a way, during the past winter, Archie, in some acute phase of boredom, had written him a letter. It had contained something in the nature of an invitation, or a reference to an invitation—precisely what, neither of them now remembered. When Innes had received it, there had been nothing further from his mind than to bury himself in the moors with Archie; but not even the most acute political heads are guided through the steps of life with unerring directness. That would require a gift of prophecy which has been denied to man. For instance, who could have imagined that, not a month after he had received the letter, and turned it into mockery, and put off answering it, and in the end lost it, misfortunes of a gloomy cast should begin to thicken over Frank's career? His case may be briefly stated. His father, a small Morayshire laird with a large family, became recalcitrant and cut off the supplies; he had fitted himself out with the beginnings of quite a good law library, which, upon some sudden losses on the turf, he had been obliged to sell before they were paid for; and his bookseller, hearing some rumour of the event, took out a warrant for his arrest. Innes had early word of it, and was able to take precautions. In this immediate welter of his affairs, with an unpleasant charge hanging over him, he had judged it the part of prudence to be off instantly, had written a fervid letter to his father at Inverauld, and put himself in the coach for Crossmichael. Any port in a storm! He was manfully turning his back on the Parliament House and its gay babble, on porter and oysters, the racecourse and the ring; and manfully prepared, until these clouds should have blown by, to share a living grave with Archie Weir at Hermiston.

To do him justice, he was no less surprised to be going than Archie was to see him come; and he carried off his wonder with an infinitely better grace.

'Well, here I am!' said he, as he alighted. 'Pylades has come to Orestes* at last. By the way, did you get my answer? No? How very provoking! Well, here I am to answer for myself, and that's better still.'

'I am very glad to see you, of course,' said Archie. 'I make you heartily welcome, of course. But you surely have not come to stay, with the Courts still sitting; is that not most unwise?'

'Damn the Courts!' says Frank. 'What are the Courts to friendship and a little fishing?'

And so it was agreed that he was to stay, with no term to the visit but the term which he had privily set to it himself—the day, namely, when his father should have come down with the dust, and he should be able to pacify the bookseller. On such vague conditions there began for these two young men (who were not even friends) a life of great familiarity and, as the days drew on, less and less intimacy. They were together at meal times, together o' nights when the hour had come for whisky-toddy; but it might have been noticed (had there been any one to pay heed) that they were rarely so much together by day. Archie had Hermiston to attend to, multifarious activities in the hills, in which he did not require, and had even refused, Frank's escort. He would be off sometimes in the morning and leave only a note on the breakfast table to announce the fact; and sometimes, with no notice at all, he would not return for dinner until the hour was long past. Innes groaned under these desertions; it required all his philosophy to sit down to a solitary breakfast with composure, and all his unaffected good-nature to be able to greet Archie with friendliness on the more rare occasions when he came home late for dinner.

'I wonder what on earth he finds to do, Mrs Elliott?' said he one morning, after he had just read the hasty billet and sat down to table.

'I suppose it will be business, sir,' replied the housekeeper dryly, measuring his distance off to him by an indicated curtsy.

'But I can't imagine what business!' he reiterated.

'I suppose it will be *his* business,' retorted the austere Kirstie.

He turned to her with that happy brightness that made the charm of his disposition, and broke into a peal of healthy and natural laughter.

'Well played, Mrs Elliott!' he cried; and the housekeeper's face relaxed into the shadow of an iron smile. 'Well played indeed!' said he. 'But you must not be making a stranger of me like that. Why, Archie and I were at the High School together, and we've been to college together, and we were going to the Bar together, when—you know! Dear, dear me! what a pity that was! A life spoiled, a fine young fellow as good as buried here in the wilderness with rustics; and all for what? A frolic, silly, if you like, but no more. God, how good your scones are, Mrs Elliott!'

'They're no mines, it was the lassie made them,' said Kirstie; 'and, saving your presence, there's little sense in taking the Lord's name in vain about idle vivers that you fill your kyte wi'.'

'I daresay you're perfectly right, ma'am,' quoth the imperturbable Frank. 'But as I was saying, this is a pitiable business, this about poor Archie; and you and I might do worse than put our heads together, like a couple of sensible people, and bring it to an end. Let me tell you, ma'am, that Archie is really quite a promising young man, and in my opinion he would do well at the Bar. As for his father, no one can deny his ability, and I don't fancy any one would care to deny that he has the deil's own temper—'

'If you'll excuse me, Mr Innes, I think the lass is crying on me,' said Kirstie, and flounced from the room.

'The damned, cross-grained, old broomstick!' ejaculated Innes.

In the meantime, Kirstie had escaped into the kitchen, and before her vassal gave vent to her feelings.

'Here, ettercap! Ye'll have to wait on yon Innes! I canna haud myself in. "Puir Erchie!" I'd "puir Erchie" him, if I had my way! And Hermiston with the deil's ain temper! God, let him take Hermiston's scones out of his mouth first. There's no a hair on ayther o' the Weirs that hasna mair spunk and dirdum to it than what he has in his hale dwaibly body! Settin' up his snash to me! Let him gang to the black toon where he's mebbe wantit—birling in a curricle—wi' pimatum on his heid—making a mess o' himsel' wi' nesty hizzies—a fair disgrace!' It was impossible to hear without admiration Kirstie's graduated disgust, as she brought forth, one after another, these somewhat baseless charges. Then she remembered her immediate purpose, and turned again on her fascinated auditor. 'Do ye no hear me, tawpie? Do ye no hear what I'm tellin' ye? Will I have to shoo ye in to him? If I come to attend to ye, mistress!' And the maid fled the kitchen, which had become practically dangerous, to attend on Innes' wants in the front parlour.

*Tantaene irae?** Has the reader perceived the reason? Since Frank's coming there were no more hours of gossip over the supper tray! All his blandishments were in vain; he had started handicapped on the race for Mrs Elliott's favour.

But it was a strange thing how misfortune dogged him in his efforts to be genial. I must guard the reader against accepting Kirstie's epithets as evidence; she was more concerned for their vigour than for their accuracy. Dwaibly, for instance; nothing could be more calumnious. Frank was the very picture of good looks, good humour, and manly youth. He had bright eyes with a sparkle and a dance to them, curly hair, a charming smile, brilliant teeth, an admirable carriage of the head, the look of a gentleman, the address of one accustomed to please at first sight and to improve the impression. And with all these advantages, he failed with every one about Hermiston; with the silent shepherd, with the obsequious grieve, with the groom who was also the ploughman, with the gardener and the gardener's sister—a pious, down-hearted woman with a shawl over her ears—he failed equally and flatly. They did not like him, and they showed it. The little maid, indeed, was an exception; she admired him devoutly, probably dreamed of him in her private hours; but she was accustomed to play the part of silent auditor to Kirstie's tirades and silent recipient of Kirstie's buffets, and she had learned not only to be a very capable girl of her years, but a very secret and prudent one besides. Frank was thus conscious that he had one ally and sympathiser in the midst of that general union of disfavour that surrounded, watched, and waited on him in the house of Hermiston; but he had little comfort or society from that alliance, and the demure little maid (twelve on her last birthday) preserved her own counsel, and tripped on his service, brisk, dumbly responsive, but inexorably unconversational. For the others, they were beyond hope and beyond endurance. Never had a young Apollo been cast among such rustic barbarians. But perhaps the cause of his ill-success lay in one trait which was habitual and unconscious with him, yet diagnostic of the man. It was his practice to approach any one person at the expense of some one else. He offered you an alliance against the some one else; he flattered you by slighting him; you were drawn into a small intrigue against him before you knew how. Wonderful are the virtues of this process generally; but Frank's mistake was in the choice of the some one else. He was not politic in that; he listened to the voice of irritation. Archie had offended him at first by what he had felt to be rather a dry reception, had offended him since by his frequent absences. He was besides the one figure continually present in Frank's eye; and it was to his immediate dependants that Frank could offer the snare of his sympathy. Now the truth is that the Weirs, father and son, were surrounded by a posse of strenuous loyalists. Of my lord they were vastly proud. It was a distinction in itself to be one of the vassals of the 'Hanging Judge,' and his gross, formidable joviality was far from unpopular in the neighbourhood of his home. For Archie they had, one and all, a sensitive affection and respect which recoiled from a word of belittlement.

Nor was Frank more successful when he went farther afield. To the Four Black Brothers, for instance, he was antipathetic in the highest degree. Hob thought him too light, Gib too profane. Clem, who saw him but for a day or two before he went to Glasgow, wanted to know what the fule's business was, and whether he meant to stay here all session time! 'Yon's a drone,' he pronounced. As for Dand, it will be enough to describe their first meeting, when Frank had been whipping a river and the rustic celebrity chanced to come along the path.

'I'm told you're quite a poet,' Frank had said.

'Wha tell 't ye that, mannie?' had been the unconciliating answer.

'O, everybody!' says Frank.

'God! Here's fame!' said the sardonic poet, and he had passed on his way.

Come to think of it, we have here perhaps a truer explanation of Frank's failures. Had he met Mr Sheriff Scott he could have turned a neater compliment, because Mr Scott would have been a friend worth making. Dand, on the other hand, he did not value sixpence, and he showed it even while he tried to flatter. Condescension is an excellent thing, but it is strange how one-sided the pleasure of it is! He who goes fishing among the Scots peasantry with condescension for a bait will have an empty basket by evening.

In proof of this theory Frank made a great success of it at the Crossmichael Club, to which Archie took him immediately on his arrival; his own last appearance on that scene of gaiety. Frank was made welcome there at once, continued to go regularly, and had attended a meeting (as the members ever after loved to tell) on the evening before his death. Young Hay and young Pringle appeared again. There was another supper at Windielaws, another dinner at Driffel; and it resulted in Frank being taken to the bosom of the county people as unreservedly as he had been repudiated by the country folk. He occupied Hermiston after the manner of an invader in a conquered capital. He was perpetually issuing from it, as from a base, to toddy parties, fishing parties, and dinner parties, to which Archie was not invited, or to which Archie would not go. It was now that the name of The Recluse became general for the young man. Some say that Innes invented it; Innes, at least, spread it abroad.

'How's all with your Recluse to-day?' people would ask.

'O, reclusing away!' Innes would declare, with his bright air of saying something witty; and immediately interrupt the general laughter which he had provoked much more by his air than his words, 'Mind you, it's all very well laughing, but I'm not very well pleased. Poor Archie is a good fellow, an excellent fellow, a fellow I always liked. I think it small of him to take his little disgrace so hard and shut himself up. "Grant that it is a ridiculous story, painfully ridiculous," I keep telling him. "Be a man! Live it down, man!" But not he. Of course it's just solitude, and shame, and all that. But I confess I'm beginning to fear the result. It would be all the pities in the world if a really promising fellow like Weir was to end ill. I'm seriously tempted to write to Lord Hermiston, and put it plainly to him.'

'I would if I were you,' some of his auditors would say, shaking the head, sitting bewildered and confused at this new view of the matter, so deftly indicated by a single word. 'A capital idea!' they would add, and wonder at the *aplomb* and position of this young man, who talked as a matter of course of writing to Hermiston and correcting him upon his private affairs.

And Frank would proceed, sweetly confidential: 'I'll give you an idea, now. He's actually sore about the way that I'm received and he's left out in the county—actually jealous and sore. I've rallied him and I've reasoned with him, told him that every one was most kindly inclined towards him, told him even that *I* was received merely because I was his guest. But it's no use. He will neither accept the invitations he gets, nor stop brooding about the ones where he's left out. What I'm afraid of is that the wound's ulcerating. He had always one of those dark, secret, angry natures—a little underhand and plenty of bile—you know the sort. He must have inherited it from the Weirs, whom I suspect to have been a worthy family of weavers somewhere; what's the cant phrase?—sedentary occupation. It's precisely the kind of character to go wrong in a false position like what his father's made for him, or he's making for himself, whichever you like to call it. And for my part, I think it a disgrace,' Frank would say generously.

Presently the sorrow and anxiety of this disinterested friend took shape. He began in private, in conversations of two, to talk vaguely of bad habits and low habits. 'I must say I'm afraid he's going wrong altogether,' he would say. 'I'll tell you plainly, and between ourselves, I scarcely like to stay there any longer; only, man, I'm positively afraid to leave him alone. You'll see, I shall be blamed for it later on. I'm staying at a great sacrifice. I'm hindering my chances at the Bar, and I can't blind my eyes to it. And what I'm afraid of is that I'm going to get kicked for it all round before all's done. You see, nobody believes in friendship nowadays.'

'Well, Innes,' his interlocutor would reply, 'it's very good of you, I must say that. If there's any blame going, you'll always be sure of *my* good word, for one thing.'

'Well,' Frank would continue, 'candidly, I don't say it's pleasant. He has a very rough way with him; his father's son, you know. I don't say he's rude—of course, I couldn't be expected to stand that—but he steers very near the wind. No, it's not pleasant; but I tell ye, man, in conscience I don't think it would be fair to leave him. Mind you, I don't say there's anything actually wrong. What I say is that I don't like the looks of it, man!' and he would press the arm of his momentary confidant.

In the early stages I am persuaded there was no malice. He talked but for the pleasure of airing himself. He was essentially glib, as becomes the young advocate, and essentially careless of the truth, which is the mark of the young ass; and so he talked at random. There was no particular bias, but that one which is indigenous and universal, to flatter himself and to please and interest the present friend. And by thus milling air out of his mouth, he had presently built up a presentation of Archie which was known and talked of in all corners of the county. Wherever there was a residential house and a walled garden, wherever there was a dwarfish castle and a park, wherever a quadruple cottage by the ruins of a peel-tower showed an old family going down, and wherever a handsome villa with a carriage approach and a shrubbery marked the coming up of a new one—probably on the wheels of machinery—Archie began to be regarded in the light of a dark, perhaps a vicious mystery, and the future developments of his career to be looked for with uneasiness and confidential whispering. He had done something disgraceful, my dear. What, was not precisely known, and that good kind young man, Mr Innes, did his best to make light of it. But there it was. And Mr Innes was very anxious about him now; he was really uneasy, my dear; he was positively wrecking his own prospects because he dared not leave him alone. How wholly we all lie at the mercy of a single prater, not needfully with any malign purpose! And if a man but talks of himself in the right spirit, refers to his virtuous actions by the way, and never applies to them the name of virtue, how easily his evidence is accepted in the court of public opinion!

All this while, however, there was a more poisonous ferment at work between the two lads, which came late indeed to the surface, but had modified and magnified their dissensions from the first. To an idle, shallow, easy-going customer like Frank, the smell of a mystery was attractive. It gave his mind something to play with, like a new toy to a child; and it took him on the weak side, for like many young men coming to the Bar, and before they have been tried and found wanting, he flattered himself he was a fellow of unusual quickness and penetration. They knew nothing of Sherlock Holmes* in those days, but there was a good deal said of Talleyrand.* And if you could have caught Frank off his guard, he would have confessed with a smirk that, if he resembled any one, it was the Marquis de Talleyrand-Périgord. It was on the occasion of Archie's first absence that this interest took root. It was vastly deepened when Kirstie resented his curiosity at breakfast, and that same afternoon there occurred another scene which clinched the business. He was fishing Swingleburn, Archie accompanying him, when the latter looked at his watch.

'Well, good-bye,' said he. 'I have something to do. See you at dinner.'

'Don't be in such a hurry,' cries Frank. 'Hold on till I get my rod up. I'll go with you; I'm sick of flogging this ditch.' And he began to reel up his line.

Archie stood speechless. He took a long while to recover his wits under this direct attack; but by the time he was ready with his answer, and the angle was almost packed up, he had become completely Weir, and the hanging face gloomed on his young shoulders. He spoke with a laboured composure, a laboured kindness even; but a child could see that his mind was made up.

'I beg your pardon, Innes; I don't want to be disagreeable, but let us understand one another from the beginning. When I want your company, I'll let you know.'

'O!' cries Frank, 'you don't want my company, don't you?'

'Apparently not just now,' replied Archie. 'I even indicated to you when I did, if you'll remember—and that was at dinner. If we two fellows are to live together pleasantly—and I see no reason why we should not—it can only be by respecting each other's privacy. If we begin intruding——'

'O, come! I'll take this at no man's hands. Is this the way you treat a guest and an old friend?' cried Innes.

'Just go home and think over what I said by yourself,' continued Archie, 'whether it's reasonable, or whether it's really offensive or not; and let's meet at dinner as though nothing had happened. I'll put it this way, if you like—that I know my own character, that I'm looking forward (with great pleasure, I assure you) to a long visit from you, and that I'm taking precautions at the first. I see the thing that we—that I, if you like—might fall out upon, and I step in and *obsto principiis*.* I wager you five pounds you'll end by seeing that I mean friendliness, and I assure you, Francie, I do,' he added, relenting.

Bursting with anger, but incapable of speech, Innes shouldered his rod, made a gesture of farewell, and strode off down the burn-side. Archie watched him go without moving. He was sorry, but quite unashamed. He hated to be inhospitable, but in one thing he was his father's son. He had a strong sense that his house was his own and no man else's; and to lie at a guest's mercy was what he refused. He hated to seem harsh. But that was Frank's look-out. If Frank had been commonly discreet, he would have been decently courteous. And there was another consideration. The secret he was protecting was not his own merely; it was hers: it belonged to that inexpressible she who was fast taking possession of his soul, and whom he would soon have defended at the cost of burning cities. By the time he had watched Frank as far as the Swingleburnfoot, appearing and disappearing in the tarnished heather, still stalking at a fierce gait but already dwindled in the distance into less than the smallness of Lilliput, he could afford to smile at the occurrence. Either Frank would go, and that would be a relief—or he would continue to stay, and his host must continue to endure him. And Archie was now free—by devious paths, behind hillocks and in the hollow of burns—to make for the trysting-place where Kirstie, cried about by the curlew and the plover, waited and burned for his coming by the Covenanter's stone.

Innes went off down-hill in a passion of resentment, easy to be understood, but which yielded progressively to the needs of his situation. He cursed Archie for a cold-hearted, unfriendly, rude dog: and himself still more passionately for a fool in having come to Hermiston when he might have sought refuge in almost any other house in Scotland. But the step once taken, was practically irretrievable. He had no more ready money to go anywhere else; he would have to borrow from Archie the next club-night; and ill as he thought of his host's manners, he was sure of his practical generosity. Frank's resemblance to Talleyrand strikes me as imaginary; but at least not Talleyrand himself could have more obediently taken his lesson from the facts. He met Archie at dinner without resentment, almost with cordiality. You must take your friends as you find them, he would have said. Archie couldn't help being his father's son, or his grandfather's, the hypothetical weaver's, grandson. The son of a hunks, he was still a hunks at heart, incapable of true generosity and consideration; but he had other qualities with which Frank could divert himself in the meanwhile, and to enjoy which it was necessary that Frank should keep his temper.

So excellently was it controlled that he awoke next morning with his head full of a different, though a cognate subject. What was Archie's little game? Why did he shun Frank's company? What was he keeping secret? Was he keeping tryst with somebody, and was it a woman? It would be a good joke and a fair revenge to discover. To that task he set himself with a great deal of patience, which might have surprised his friends, for he had been always credited not with patience so much as brilliancy; and little by little, from one point to another, he at last succeeded in piecing out the situation. First he remarked that, although Archie set out in all the directions of the compass, he always came home again from some point between the south and west. From the study of a map, and in consideration of the great expanse of untenanted moorland running in that direction towards the sources of the Clyde, he laid his finger on Cauldstaneslap and two other neighbouring farms, Kingsmuirs and Polintarf. But it was difficult to advance farther. With his rod for a pretext, he vainly visited each of them in turn; nothing was to be seen suspicious about this trinity of moorland settlements. He would have tried to follow Archie, had it been the least possible, but the nature of the land precluded the idea. He did the next best, ensconced himself in a quiet corner, and pursued his movements with a telescope. It was equally in vain, and he soon wearied of his futile vigilance, left the telescope at home, and had almost given the matter up in despair, when, on the twenty-seventh day of his visit, he was suddenly confronted with the person whom he sought. The first Sunday Kirstie had managed to stay away from kirk on some pretext of indisposition, which was more truly modesty; the pleasure of beholding Archie seemed too sacred, too vivid for that public place. On the two following, Frank had himself been absent on some of his excursions among the neighbouring families. It was not until the fourth, accordingly, that Frank had occasion to set eyes on the enchantress. With the first look, all hesitation was over. She came with the Cauldstaneslap party; then she lived at Cauldstaneslap. Here was Archie's secret, here was the woman, and more than that—though I have need here of every manageable attenuation of language—with the first look, he had already entered himself as rival. It was a good deal in pique, it was a little in revenge, it was much in genuine admiration; the devil may decide the proportions! I cannot, and it is very likely that Frank could not.

'Mighty attractive milkmaid,' he observed, on the way home.

'Who?' said Archie.

'O, the girl you're looking at—aren't you? Forward there on the road. She came attended by the rustic bard; presumably, therefore, belongs to his exalted family. The single objection!

for the four black brothers are awkward customers. If anything were to go wrong, Gib would gibber, and Clem would prove inclement; and Dand fly in danders,* and Hob blow up in gobbets. It would be a Helliott of a business!'

'Very humorous, I am sure,' said Archie.

'Well, I am trying to be so,' said Frank. 'It's none too easy in this place, and with your solemn society, my dear fellow. But confess that the milkmaid has found favour in your eyes, or resign all claim to be a man of taste.'

'It is no matter,' returned Archie.

But the other continued to look at him, steadily and quizzically, and his colour slowly rose and deepened under the glance, until not impudence itself could have denied that he was blushing. And at this Archie lost some of his control. He changed his stick from one hand to the other, and—'O, for God's sake, don't be an ass!' he cried.

'Ass? That's the retort delicate without doubt,' says Frank. 'Beware of the homespun brothers, dear. If they come into the dance, you'll see who's an ass. Think now, if they only applied (say) a quarter as much talent as I have applied to the question of what Mr Archie does with his evening hours, and why he is so unaffectedly nasty when the subject's touched on——'

'You are touching on it now,' interrupted Archie, with a wince.

'Thank you. That was all I wanted, an articulate confession,' said Frank.

'I beg to remind you——' began Archie.

But he was interrupted in turn. 'My dear fellow, don't. It's quite needless. The subject's dead and buried.'

And Frank began to talk hastily on other matters, an art in which he was an adept, for it was his gift to be fluent on anything or nothing. But although Archie had the grace or the timidity to suffer him to rattle on, he was by no means done with the subject. When he came home to dinner, he was greeted with a sly demand, how things were looking 'Cauldstaneslap ways.' Frank took his first glass of port out after dinner to the toast of Kirstie, and later in the evening he returned to the charge again.

'I say, Weir, you'll excuse me for returning again to this

affair. I've been thinking it over, and I wish to beg you very seriously to be more careful. It's not a safe business. Not safe, my boy,' said he.

'What?' said Archie.

'Well, it's your own fault if I must put a name on the thing; but really, as a friend, I cannot stand by and see you rushing head down into these dangers. My dear boy,' said he, holding up a warning cigar, 'consider! What is to be the end of it?'

'The end of what?'—Archie, helpless with irritation, persisted in this dangerous and ungracious guard.

'Well, the end of the milkmaid; or, to speak more by the card, the end of Miss Christina Elliott of the Cauldstaneslap.'

'I assure you,' Archie broke out, 'this is all a figment of your imagination. There is nothing to be said against that young lady; you have no right to introduce her name into the conversation.'

'I'll make a note of it,' said Frank. 'She shall henceforth be nameless, nameless, nameless, Gregarach!* I make a note besides of your valuable testimony to her character. I only want to look at this thing as a man of the world. Admitted she's an angel—but, my good fellow, is she a lady?'

This was torture to Archie. 'I beg your pardon,' he said, struggling to be composed, 'but because you have wormed yourself into my confidence——'

'O, come!' cried Frank. 'Your confidence? It was rosy but unconsenting. Your confidence, indeed? Now, look! This is what I must say, Weir, for it concerns your safety and good character, and therefore my honour as your friend. You say I wormed myself into your confidence. Wormed is good. But what have I done? I have put two and two together, just as the parish will be doing to-morrow, and the whole of Tweeddale in two weeks, and the black brothers— well, I won't put a date on that; it will be a dark and stormy morning! Your secret, in other words, is poor Poll's. And I want to ask of you as a friend whether you like the prospect? There are two horns to your dilemma, and I must say for myself I should look mighty ruefully on either. Do you see yourself explaining to the four Black Brothers? or do you see yourself presenting the milkmaid to papa as the future lady of Hermiston? Do you? I tell you plainly, I don't!'

Archie rose. 'I will hear no more of this,' he said, in a trembling voice.

But Frank again held up his cigar. 'Tell me one thing first. Tell me if this is not a friend's part that I am playing?'

'I believe you think it so,' replied Archie. 'I can go as far as that. I can do so much justice to your motives. But I will hear no more of it. I am going to bed.'

'That's right, Weir,' said Frank heartily. 'Go to bed and think over it; and I say, man, don't forget your prayers! I don't often do the moral—don't go in for that sort of thing—but when I do there's one thing sure, that I mean it.'

So Archie marched off to bed, and Frank sat alone by the table for another hour or so, smiling to himself richly. There was nothing vindictive in his nature; but, if revenge came in his way, it might as well be good, and the thought of Archie's pillow reflections that night was indescribably sweet to him. He felt a pleasant sense of power. He looked down on Archie as on a very little boy whose strings he pulled—as on a horse whom he had backed and bridled by sheer power of intelligence, and whom he might ride to glory or the grave at pleasure. Which was it to be? He lingered long, relishing the details of schemes that he was too idle to pursue. Poor cork upon a torrent, he tasted that night the sweets of omnipotence, and brooded like a deity over the strands of that intrigue which was to shatter him before the summer waned.

CHAPTER VIII

A NOCTURNAL VISIT

KIRSTIE had many causes of distress. More and more as we grow old—and yet more and more as we grow old and are women, frozen by the fear of age—we come to rely on the voice as the single outlet of the soul. Only thus, in the curtailment of our means, can we relieve the straitened cry of the passion within us; only thus, in the bitter and sensitive shyness of advancing years, can we maintain relations with those vivacious figures of the young that still show before us and tend daily to become no more than the moving wall-paper of life. Talk is the last link, the last relation. But with the end of the conversation, when the voice stops and the bright face of the listener is turned away, solitude falls again on the bruised heart. Kirstie had lost her 'Cannie hour at e'en'; she could no more wander with Archie, a ghost if you will, but a happy ghost, in fields Elysian. And to her it was as if the whole world had fallen silent; to him, but an unremarkable change of amusements. And she raged to know it. The effervescency of her passionate and irritable nature rose within her at times to bursting point.

This is the price paid by age for unseasonable ardours of feeling. It must have been so for Kirstie at any time when the occasion chanced; but it so fell out that she was deprived of this delight in the hour when she had most need of it, when she had most to say, most to ask, and when she trembled to recognise her sovereignty not merely in abeyance but annulled. For, with the clairvoyance of a genuine love, she had pierced the mystery that had so long embarrassed Frank. She was conscious, even before it was carried out, even on that Sunday night when it began, of an invasion of her rights; and a voice told her the invader's name. Since then, by arts, by accident, by small things observed, and by the general drift of Archie's humour, she had passed beyond all possibility of doubt. With a sense of justice that Lord Hermiston might have envied, she had that day in church considered and admitted the attractions of the young Kirstie; and with the profound humanity and sentimentality of her nature, she had recognised the coming of fate. Not thus would she have chosen. She had seen, in imagination, Archie wedded to some tall, powerful, and rosy heroine of the golden locks, made in her own image, for whom she would have strewed the bride-bed with delight; and now she could have wept to see the ambition falsified. But the gods had pronounced, and her doom was otherwise.

She lay tossing in bed that night, besieged with feverish thoughts. There were dangerous matters pending, a battle was toward, over the fate of which she hung in jealousy, sympathy, fear, and alternate loyalty and disloyalty to either side. Now she was reincarnated in her niece, and now in Archie. Now she saw, through the girl's eyes, the youth on his knees to her, heard his persuasive instances with a deadly weakness, and received his overmastering caresses. Anon, with a revulsion, her temper raged to see such utmost favours of fortune and love squandered on a brat of a girl, one of her own house, using her own name—a deadly ingredient—and that 'didna ken her ain mind an' was as black's your hat.' Now she trembled lest her deity should plead in vain, loving the idea of success for him like a triumph of nature; anon, with returning loyalty of her own family and sex, she trembled for Kirstie and the credit of the Elliotts. And again she had a vision of herself, the day over for her old-world tales and local gossip, bidding farewell to her last link with life and brightness and love; and behind and beyond, she saw but the blank butt-end where she must crawl to die. Had she then come to the lees? she, so great, so beautiful, with a heart as fresh as a girl's and strong as womanhood? It could not be, and yet it was so; and for a moment her bed was horrible to her as the sides of the grave. And she looked forward over a waste of hours, and saw herself go on to rage, and tremble, and be softened, and rage again, until the day came and the labours of the day must be renewed.

Suddenly she heard feet on the stairs—his feet, and soon after the sound of a window sash flung open. She sat up with her heart beating. He had gone to his room alone, and he had not gone to bed. She might again have one of her night cracks; and at the entrancing prospect, a change came over her mind; with the approach of this hope of pleasure, all the baser metal became immediately obliterated from her thoughts. She rose, all woman, and all the best of woman, tender, pitiful, hating the wrong, loyal to her own sex—and all the weakest of that dear miscellany, nourishing, cherishing next her soft heart, voicelessly flattering, hopes that she would have died sooner than have acknowledged. She tore off her nightcap, and her hair fell about her shoulders in profusion. Undying coquetry awoke. By the faint light of her nocturnal rush, she stood before the looking-glass, carried her shapely arms above her head, and gathered up the treasures of her tresses. She was never backward to admire herself; that kind of modesty was a stranger to her nature; and she paused, struck with a pleased wonder at the sight. 'Ye daft auld wife!' she said, answering a thought that was not; and she blushed with the innocent consciousness of a child. Hastily she did up the massive and shining coils, hastily donned a wrapper, and with the rushlight in her hand, stole into the hall. Below stairs she heard the clock ticking the deliberate seconds, and Frank jingling with the decanters in the dining-room. Aversion rose in her, bitter and momentary. 'Nesty, tippling puggy!' she thought; and the next moment she had knocked guardedly at Archie's door and was bidden enter.

Archie had been looking out into the ancient blackness, pierced here and there with a rayless star; taking the sweet air of the moors and the night into his bosom deeply; seeking, perhaps finding, peace after the manner of the unhappy. He turned round as she came in, and showed her a pale face against the window-frame.

'Is that you, Kirstie?' he asked. 'Come in!'

'It's unco late, my dear,' said Kirstie, affecting unwillingness.

'No, no,' he answered, 'not at all. Come in, if you want a crack. I am not sleepy, God knows!'

She advanced, took a chair by the toilet table and the candle, and set the rushlight at her foot. Something—it might be in the comparative disorder of her dress, it might be the emotion that now welled in her bosom—had touched her with a wand of transformation, and she seemed young with the youth of goddesses.

'Mr Erchie,' she began, 'what's this that's come to ye?'

'I am not aware of anything that has come,' said Archie, and blushed, and repented bitterly that he had let her in.

'O, my dear, that'll no dae!' said Kirstie. 'It's ill to blend the eyes of love. O, Mr Erchie, tak a thocht ere it's ower late. Ye shouldna be impatient o' the braws o' life, they'll a' come in their saison, like the sun and the rain. Ye're young yet; ye've mony cantie years afore ye. See and dinna wreck yersel' at the outset like sae mony ithers! Hae patience—they telled me aye that was the owercome o' life—hae patience, there's a braw day coming yet. Gude kens it never cam to me; and here I am, wi' nayther man nor bairn to ca' my ain, wearying a' folks wi' my ill tongue, and you just the first, Mr Erchie!'

'I have a difficulty in knowing what you mean,' said Archie.

'Weel, and I'll tell ye,' she said. 'It's just this, that I'm feared. I'm feared for ye, my dear. Remember, your faither is a hard man, reaping where he hasna sowed and gaithering where he hasna strawed. It's easy speakin', but mind! Ye'll have to look in the gurly face o'm, where it's ill to look, and vain to look for mercy. Ye mind me o' a bonny ship pitten oot into the black and gowsty seas—ye're a' safe still, sittin' quait and crackin' wi' Kirstie in your lown chalmer; but whaur will ye be the morn, and in whatten horror o' the fearsome tempest, cryin' on the hills to cover ye?'

'Why, Kirstie, you're very enigmatical tonight—and very eloquent,' Archie put in.

'And, my dear Mr Erchie,' she continued, with a change of voice, 'ye mauna think that I canna sympathise wi' ye. Ye mauna think that I havena been young mysel'. Lang syne, when I was a bit lassie, no twenty yet——' She paused and sighed. 'Clean and caller, wi' a fit like the hinney bee,' she continued. 'I was aye big and buirdly, ye maun understand; a bonny figure o' a woman, though I say it that suldna—built to rear bairns—braw bairns they suld hae been, and grand I would hae likit it! But I was young, dear, wi' the bonny glint o' youth in my e'en, and little I dreamed I'd ever be tellin' ye this, an auld, lanely, rudas wife! Weel, Mr Erchie, there was a lad cam' courtin' me, as was but naetural. Mony had come before, and I would nane o' them. But this yin had a tongue to wile the birds frae the lift and the bees frae the foxglove bells. Deary me, but it's lang syne! Folk have dee'd sinsyne and been buried, and are forgotten, and bairns been born and got merrit and got bairns o' their ain. Sinsyne woods have been plantit, and have grawn up and are bonny trees, and the joes sit in their shadow, and sinsyne auld estates have changed hands, and there have been wars and rumours of wars on the face of the earth. And here I'm still—like an auld droopit craw—lookin' on and craikin'! But, Mr Erchie, do ye no think that I have mind o' it a' still? I was dwalling then in my faither's house; and it's a curious thing that we were whiles trysted in the Deil's Hags. And do ye no think that I have mind of the bonny simmer days, the lang miles o' the bluid-red heather, the cryin' o' the whaups, and the lad and the lassie that was trysted? Do ye no think that I mind how the hilly sweetness ran about my hairt? Ay, Mr Erchie, I ken the way o' it—fine do I ken the way—how the grace o' God takes them, like Paul of Tarsus, when they think it least, and drives the pair o' them into a land which is like a dream, and the world and the folks in 't are nae mair than clouds to the puir lassie, and heeven nae mair than windle-straes, if she can but pleesure him! Until Tam dee'd—that was my story,' she broke off to say, 'he dee'd, and I wasna at the buryin'. But while he was here, I could take care o' mysel'. And can yon puir lassie?'

Kirstie, her eyes shining with unshed tears, stretched out her hand towards him appealingly; the bright and the dull gold of her hair flashed and smouldered in the coils behind her comely head, like the rays of an eternal youth; the pure colour had risen in her face; and Archie was abashed alike by her beauty and her story. He came towards her slowly from the window, took up her hand in his and kissed it.

'Kirstie,' he said hoarsely, 'you have misjudged me sorely. I have always thought of her, I wouldna harm her for the universe, my woman!'

'Eh, lad, and that's easy sayin',' cried Kirstie, 'but it's nane sae easy doin'! Man, do ye no comprehend that it's God's wull we should be blendit and glamoured, and have nae command over our ain members at a time like that? My bairn,' she cried, still holding his hand, 'think o' the puir lass! have pity upon her, Erchie! and O, be wise for twa! Think o' the risk she rins! I have seen ye, and what's to prevent ithers! I saw ye once in the Hags, in my ain howf, and I was wae to see ye there—in pairt for the omen, for I think there's a weird on the place—and in pairt for pure nakit envy and bitterness o' hairt. It's strange ye should forgather there tae! God! but yon puir, thrawn, auld Covenanter's seen a heap o' human natur since he lookit his last on the musket barrels, if he never saw nane afore,' she added, with a kind of wonder in her eyes.

'I swear by my honour I have done her no wrong,' said Archie. 'I swear by my honour and the redemption of my soul that there shall none be done her. I have heard of this before. I have been foolish, Kirstie, not unkind and, above all, not base.'

'There's my bairn!' said Kirstie, rising. 'I'll can trust ye noo, I'll can gang to my bed wi' an easy hairt.' And then she saw in a flash how barren had been her triumph. Archie had promised to spare the girl, and he would keep it; but who had promised to spare Archie? What was to be the end of it? Over a maze of difficulties she glanced, and saw, at the end of every passage, the flinty countenance of Hermiston. And a kind of horror fell upon her at what she had done. She wore a tragic mask. 'Erchie, the Lord peety you, dear, and peety me! I have buildit on this foundation'—laying her hand heavily on his shoulder—'and buildit hie, and pit my hairt in the buildin' of it. If the hale hypothec were to fa', I think, laddie, I would dee! Excuse a daft wife that loves ye, and that kenned your mither. And for His name's sake keep yersel' frae inordinate desires; haud your heart in baith your hands, carry it canny and laigh; dinna send it up like a bairn's kite into the collieshangie o' the wunds! Mind, Maister Erchie dear, that this life's a' disappointment, and a mouthfu' o' mools is the appointed end.'

'Ay, but Kirstie, my woman, you're asking me ower much at last,' said Archie, profoundly moved, and lapsing into the broad Scots. 'Ye're asking what nae man can grant ye, what only the Lord of heaven can grant ye if He see fit. Ay! And can even He? I can promise ye what I shall do, and you can depend on that. But how I shall feel—my woman, that is long past thinking of!'

They were both standing by now opposite each other. The face of Archie wore the wretched semblance of a smile; hers was convulsed for a moment.

'Promise me ae thing,' she cried, in a sharp voice. 'Promise me ye'll never do naething without telling me.'

'No, Kirstie, I canna promise ye that,' he replied. 'I have promised enough, God kens!'*

'May the blessing of God lift and rest upon ye, dear!' she said.

'God bless ye, my old friend,' said he.

CHAPTER IX

AT THE WEAVER'S STONE

IT was late in the afternoon when Archie drew near by the hill path to the Praying Weaver's stone. The Hags were in shadow. But still, through the gate of the Slap, the sun shot a last arrow, which sped far and straight across the surface of the moss, here and there touching and shining on a tussock, and lighted at length on the gravestone and the small figure awaiting him there. The emptiness and solitude of the great moors seemed to be concentred there, and Kirstie pointed out by that figure of sunshine for the only inhabitant. His first sight of her was thus excruciatingly sad, like a glimpse of a world from which all light, comfort, and society were on the point of vanishing. And the next moment, when she had turned her face to him and the quick smile had enlightened it, the whole face of nature smiled upon him in her smile of welcome. Archie's slow pace was quickened; his legs hasted to her though his heart was hanging back. The girl, upon her side, drew herself together slowly and stood up, expectant; she was all languor, her face was gone white; her arms ached for him, her soul was on tip-toes. But he deceived her, pausing a few steps away, not less white than herself, and holding up his hand with a gesture of denial.

'No, Christina, not to-day,' he said. 'To-day I have to talk to you seriously. Sit ye down, please, there where you were. Please!' he repeated.

The revulsion of feeling in Christina's heart was violent. To have longed and waited these weary hours for him, rehearsing her endearments—to have seen him at last come—to have been ready there, breathless, wholly passive, his to do what he would with—and suddenly to have found herself confronted with a grey-faced, harsh schoolmaster—it was too rude a shock. She could have wept, but pride withheld her. She sat down on the stone, from which she had arisen, part with the instinct of obedience, part as though she had been thrust there. What was this? Why was she rejected? Had she ceased to please? She stood here offering her wares, and he would none of them! And yet they were all his! His to take and keep, not his to refuse though! In her quick petulant nature, a moment ago on fire with hope, thwarted love and wounded vanity wrought. The schoolmaster that there is in all men, to the despair of all girls and most women, was now completely in possession of Archie. He had passed a night of sermons, a day of reflection; he had come wound up to do his duty; and the set mouth, which in him only betrayed the effort of his will, to her seemed the expression of an averted heart. It was the same with his constrained voice and embarrassed utterance; and if so—if it was all over—the pang of the thought took away from her the power of thinking.

He stood before her some way off. 'Kirstie, there's been too much of this. We've seen too much of each other.' She looked up quickly and her eyes contracted. 'There's no good ever comes of these secret meetings. They're not frank, not honest truly, and I ought to have seen it. People have begun to talk; and it's not right of me. Do you see?'

'I see somebody will have been talking to ye,' she said sullenly.

'They have, more than one of them,' replied Archie.

'And whae were they?' she cried. 'And what kind o' love do ye ca' that, that's ready to gang round like a whirligig at folk talking? Do ye think they havena talked to me?'

'Have they indeed?' said Archie, with a quick breath. 'That is what I feared. Who were they? Who has dared——?'

Archie was on the point of losing his temper.

As a matter of fact, not any one had talked to Christina on the matter; and she strenuously repeated her own first question in a panic of self-defence.

'Ah, well! what does it matter?' he said. 'They were good folk that wished well to us, and the great affair is that there are people talking. My dear girl, we have to be wise. We must not wreck our lives at the outset. They may be long and happy yet, and we must see to it, Kirstie, like God's rational creatures and not like fool children. There is one thing we must see to before all. You're worth waiting for, Kirstie!

worth waiting for a generation; it would be enough reward.'—And here he remembered the schoolmaster again, and very unwisely took to following wisdom. 'The first thing that we must see to, is that there shall be no scandal about for my father's sake. That would ruin all; do ye no see that?'

Kirstie was a little pleased, there had been some show of warmth of sentiment in what Archie had said last. But the dull irritation still persisted in her bosom; with the aboriginal instinct, having suffered herself, she wished to make Archie suffer.

And besides, there had come out the word she had always feared to hear from his lips, the name of his father. It is not to be supposed that, during so many days with a love avowed between them, some reference had not been made to their conjoint future. It had in fact been often touched upon, and from the first had been the sore point. Kirstie had wilfully closed the eye of thought; she would not argue even with herself; gallant, desperate little heart, she had accepted the command of that supreme attraction like the call of fate and marched blindfold on her doom. But Archie, with his masculine sense of responsibility, must reason; he must dwell on some future good, when the present good was all in all to Kirstie; he must talk—and talk lamely, as necessity drove him—of what was to be. Again and again he had touched on marriage; again and again been driven back into indistinctness by a memory of Lord Hermiston. And Kirstie had been swift to understand and quick to choke down and smother the understanding; swift to leap up in flame at a mention of that hope, which spoke volumes to her vanity and her love, that she might one day be Mrs Weir of Hermiston; swift, also, to recognise in his stumbling or throttled utterance the death-knell of these expectations, and constant, poor girl! in her large-minded madness, to go on and to reck nothing of the future. But these unfinished references, these blinks in which his heart spoke, and his memory and reason rose up to silence it before the words were well uttered, gave her unqualifiable agony. She was raised up and dashed down again bleeding. The recurrence of the subject forced her, for however short a time, to open her eyes on what she did not wish to see; and it had invariably ended in another disappointment. So now again, at the mere wind of its coming, at the mere mention of his father's name—who might seem indeed to have accompanied them in their whole moorland courtship, an awful figure in a wig with an ironical and bitter smile, present to guilty consciousness—she fled from it head down.

'Ye havena told me yet,' she said, 'who was it spoke?

'Your aunt for one,' said Archie.

'Auntie Kirstie?' she cried. 'And what do I care for my Auntie Kirstie?'

'She cares a great deal for her niece,' replied Archie, in kind reproof.

'Troth, and it's the first I've heard of it,' retorted the girl.

'The question here is not who it is, but what they say, what they have noticed,' pursued the lucid schoolmaster. 'That is what we have to think of in self-defence.'

'Auntie Kirstie, indeed! A bitter, thrawn auld maid that's fomented trouble in the country before I was born, and will be doing it still, I daur say, when I'm deid! It's in her nature; it's as natural for her as it's for a sheep to eat.'

'Pardon me, Kirstie, she was not the only one,' interposed Archie. 'I had two warnings, two sermons, last night, both most kind and considerate. Had you been there, I promise you you would have grat, my dear! And they opened my eyes. I saw we were going a wrong way.'

'Who was the other one?' Kirstie demanded.

By this time Archie was in the condition of a hunted beast. He had come, braced and resolute; he was to trace out a line of conduct for the pair of them in a few cold, convincing sentences; he had now been there some time, and he was still staggering round the outworks and undergoing what he felt to be a savage cross-examination.

'Mr Frank!' she cried. 'What nex', I would like to ken?'

'He spoke most kindly and truly.'

'What like did he say?'

'I am not going to tell you; you have nothing to do with that,' cried Archie, startled to find he had admitted so much.

'O, I have naething to do with it!' she repeated, springing to her feet. 'A'body at Hermiston's free to pass their opinions upon me, but I have naething to do wi' it! Was this at prayers like? Did ye ca' the grieve into the consultation? Little wonder if a'body's talking, when ye make a'body ye're confidants! But as you say, Mr Weir,—most kindly, most considerately, most truly, I'm sure—I have naething to do with it. And I think I'll better be going. I'll be wishing you good evening, Mr Weir.' And she made him a stately curtsey, shaking as she did so from head to foot, with the barren ecstasy of temper.

Poor Archie stood dumbfounded. She had moved some steps away from him before he recovered the gift of articulate speech.

'Kirstie!' he cried. 'O, Kirstie woman!'

There was in his voice a ring of appeal, a clang of mere astonishment that showed the schoolmaster was vanquished.

She turned round on him. 'What do ye Kirstie me for?' she retorted. 'What have ye to do wi' me? Gang to your ain freends and deave them!'

He could only repeat the appealing 'Kirstie!'

'Kirstie, indeed!' cried the girl, her eyes blazing in her white face. 'My name is Miss Christina Elliott, I would have ye to ken, and I daur ye to ca' me out of it. If I canna get love, I'll have respect, Mr Weir. I'm come of decent people, and I'll have respect. What have I done that ye should lightly me? What have I done? What have I done? O, what have I done?' and her voice rose upon the third repetition. 'I thocht—I thocht—I thocht I was sae happy!' and the first sob broke from her like the paroxysm of some mortal sickness.

Archie ran to her. He took the poor child in his arms, and she nestled to his breast as to a mother's, and clasped him in hands that were strong like vices. He felt her whole body shaken by the throes of distress, and had pity upon her beyond speech. Pity, and at the same time a bewildered fear of this explosive engine in his arms, whose works he did not understand, and yet had been tampering with. There arose from before him the curtains of boyhood, and he saw for the first time the ambiguous face of woman as she is. In vain he looked back over the interview; he saw not where he had offended. It seemed unprovoked, a wilful convulsion of brute nature. . . .

APPENDIX A

THE CONTINUATION OF *WEIR OF HERMISTON* FROM SIR SIDNEY COLVIN'S EDITORIAL NOTE

WITH the words last printed, 'a wilful convulsion of brute nature,' the romance of *Weir of Hermiston* breaks off. They were dictated, I believe, on the very morning of the writer's sudden seizure and death. *Weir of Hermiston* thus remains in the work of Stevenson what *Edwin Drood* is in the work of Dickens or *Denis Duval* in that of Thackeray: or rather it remains relatively more, for if each of those fragments holds an honourable place among its author's writings, among Stevenson's the fragment of *Weir* holds certainly the highest.

Readers may be divided in opinion on the question whether they would or they would not wish to hear more of the intended course of the story and destinies of the characters. To some, silence may seem best, and that the mind should be left to its own conjectures as to the sequel, with the help of such indications as the text affords. I confess that this is the view which has my sympathy. But since others, and those almost certainly a majority, are anxious to be told all they can, and since editors and publishers join in the request, I can scarce do otherwise than comply. The intended argument, then, so far as it was known at the time of the writer's death to his step-daughter and devoted amanuensis, Mrs Strong, was nearly as follows:—

Archie persists in his good resolution of avoiding further conduct compromising to young Kirstie's good name. Taking advantage of the situation thus created, and of the girl's unhappiness and wounded vanity, Frank Innes pursues his purpose of seduction; and Kirstie, though still caring for Archie in her heart, allows herself to become Frank's victim. Old Kirstie is the first to perceive something amiss with her, and believing Archie to be the culprit, accuses him, thus making him aware for the first time that mischief has happened. He does not at once deny the charge, but seeks out and questions young Kirstie, who confesses the truth to him; and he, still loving her, promises to protect and defend her in her trouble. He then has an interview with Frank Innes on the moor, which ends in a quarrel, and in Archie killing Frank beside the Weaver's Stone. Meanwhile the Four Black Brothers, having become aware of their sister's betrayal, are bent on vengeance against Archie as her supposed seducer. They are about to close in upon him with this purpose when he is arrested by the officers of the law for the murder of Frank. He is tried before his own father, the Lord Justice-Clerk, found guilty, and condemned to death. Meanwhile the elder Kirstie, having discovered from the girl how matters really stand, informs her nephews of the truth; and they, in a great revulsion of feeling in Archie's favour, determine on an action after the ancient manner of their house. They gather a following, and after a great fight break the prison where Archie lies confined, and rescue him. He and young Kirstie thereafter escape to America. But the ordeal of taking part in the trial of his own son has been too much for the Lord Justice-Clerk, who dies of the shock. 'I do not know,' adds the amanuensis, 'what becomes of old Kirstie, but that character grew and strengthened so in the writing that I am sure he had some dramatic destiny for her.'

In addition to Sir Sidney Colvin's Editorial Note, the Rev. S. R. Lysaght who, encouraged by George Meredith, went to see R.L.S. at Vailima on Easter Sunday, 1894 writes:

> He [R.L.S.] expressed to me, as I believe he wrote to Sir Sidney Colvin, his opinion that in this story he had touched his high-water mark; he told me something of its outline, and as in one, and that an important, point it differed from the notes furnished by Mrs Strong, it will be heard with interest. The strongest scene in the book, he said—the strongest scene he had ever conceived or would ever write—was one in which the younger Kirstie came to her lover when he was in prison and confessed to him that she was with child by the man he had murdered. His eyes flashed with emotion as he spoke about it, and I cannot think that he had abandoned this climax. It is a climax, too, which would seem to be much more in harmony with the genius and conception of the story and characters than the ending sketched in the notes, which was no doubt an alternative with which he coquetted. (*TLS*, 4 December 1919, pp. 713–14.)

APPENDIX B

A CHAPTER ON DREAMS

THE past is all of one texture—whether feigned or suffered—whether acted out in three dimensions, or only witnessed in that small theatre of the brain which we keep brightly lighted all night long, after the jets are down, and darkness and sleep reign undisturbed in the remainder of the body. There is no distinction on the face of our experiences; one is vivid indeed, and one dull, and one pleasant, and another agonising to remember; but which of them is what we call true, and which a dream, there is not one hair to prove. The past stands on a precarious footing; another straw split in the field of metaphysic, and behold us robbed of it. There is scarce a family that can count four generations but lays a claim to some dormant title or some castle and estate: a claim not prosecutable in any court of law, but flattering to the fancy and a great alleviation of idle hours. A man's claim to his own past is yet less valid. A paper might turn up (in proper story-book fashion) in the secret drawer of an old ebony secretary, and restore your family to its ancient honours, and reinstate mine in a certain West Indian islet (not far from St Kitt's, as beloved tradition hummed in my young ears) which was once ours, and is now unjustly some one else's, and for that matter (in the state of the sugar trade) is not worth anything to anybody. I do not say that these revolutions are likely; only no man can deny that they are possible; and the past, on the other hand, is lost for ever: our old days and deeds, our old selves, too, and the very world in which these scenes were acted, all brought down to the same faint residuum as a last night's dream, to some incontinuous images, and an echo in the chambers of the brain. Not an hour, not a mood, not a glance of the eye, can we revoke; it is all gone, past conjuring. And yet conceive us robbed of it, conceive that little thread of memory that we trail behind us broken at the pocket's edge; and in what naked nullity should we be left! for we only guide ourselves, and only know ourselves, by these air-painted pictures of the past.

Upon these grounds, there are some among us who claim to have lived longer and more richly than their neighbours; when they lay asleep they claim they were still active; and among the treasures of memory that all men review for their amusement, these count in no second place the harvests of their dreams. There is one of this kind whom I have in my eye, and whose case is perhaps unusual enough to be described. He was from a child an ardent and uncomfortable dreamer. When he had a touch of fever at night, and the room swelled and shrank, and his clothes, hanging on a nail, now loomed up instant to the bigness of a church, and now drew away into a horror of infinite distance and infinite littleness, the poor soul was very well aware of what must follow, and struggled hard against the approaches of that slumber which was the beginning of sorrows. But his struggles were in vain; sooner or later the night-hag would have him by the throat, and pluck him, strangling and screaming, from his sleep. His dreams were at times commonplace enough, at times very strange: at times they were almost formless, he would be haunted, for instance, by nothing more definite than a certain hue of brown, which he did not mind in the least while he was awake, but feared and loathed while he was dreaming; at times, again, they took on every detail of circumstance, as when once he supposed he must swallow the populous world, and awoke screaming with the horror of the thought. The two chief troubles of his very narrow existence—the practical and everyday trouble of school tasks and the ultimate and airy one of hell and judgment—were often confounded together into one appalling nightmare. He seemed to himself to stand before the Great White Throne; he was called on, poor little devil, to recite some form of words, on which his destiny depended; his tongue stuck, his memory was blank, hell gaped for him; and he would awake, clinging to the curtain-rod with his knees to his chin.

These were extremely poor experiences, on the whole; and at that time of life my dreamer would have very willingly parted with his power of dreams. But presently, in the course of his growth, the cries and physical contortions passed away, seemingly for ever; his visions were still for the most part miserable, but they were more constantly supported; and he would awake with no more extreme symptom than a flying heart, a freezing scalp, cold sweats, and the speechless midnight fear. His dreams, too, as befitted a mind better stocked with particulars, became more circumstantial, and had more the air and continuity of life. The look of the world beginning to take hold on his attention, scenery came to play a part in his sleeping as well as in his waking thoughts, so that he would take long, uneventful journeys and see strange towns and beautiful places as he lay in bed. And, what is more significant, an odd taste that he had for the Georgian costume and for stories laid in that period of English history, began to rule the features of his dreams; so that he masqueraded there in a three-cornered hat, and was much engaged with Jacobite conspiracy between the hour for bed and that for breakfast. About the same time, he began to read in his dreams—tales, for the most part, and for the most part after the manner of G. P. R. James, but so incredibly more vivid and moving than any printed book, that he has ever since been malcontent with literature.

And then, while he was yet a student, there came to him a dream-adventure which he has no anxiety to repeat; he began, that is to say, to dream in sequence and thus to lead a double life—one of the day, one of the night—one that he had every reason to believe was the true one, another that he had no means of proving to be false. I should have said he studied, or was by way of studying, at Edinburgh College, which (it may be supposed) was how I came to know him. Well, in his dream-life, he passed a long day in the surgical theatre, his heart in his mouth, his teeth on edge, seeing monstrous malformations and the abhorred dexterity of surgeons. In a heavy, rainy, foggy evening he came forth into the South Bridge, turned up the High Street, and entered the door of a tall *land*, at the top of which he supposed himself to lodge. All night long, in his wet clothes, he climbed the stairs, stair after stair in endless series, and at every second flight a flaring lamp with a reflector. All night long, he brushed by single persons passing downward—beggarly women of the street, great, weary, muddy labourers, poor scarecrows of men, pale parodies of women—but all drowsy and weary like himself, and all single, and all brushing against him as they passed. In the end, out of a northern window, he would see day beginning to whiten over the Firth, give up the ascent, turn to descend, and in a breath be back again upon the streets, in his wet clothes, in the wet, haggard dawn, trudging to another day of monstrosities and operations. Time went quicker in the life of dreams, some seven hours (as near as he can guess) to one; and it went, besides, more intensely, so that the gloom of these fancied experiences clouded the day, and he had not shaken off their shadow ere it was time to lie down and to renew them. I cannot tell how long it was that he endured this discipline; but it was long enough to leave a great black blot upon his memory, long enough to send him, trembling for his reason, to the doors of a certain doctor; whereupon with a simple draught he was restored to the common lot of man.

The poor gentleman has since been troubled by nothing of the sort; indeed, his nights were for some while like other men's, now blank, now chequered with dreams, and these sometimes charming, sometimes appalling, but except for an occasional vividness, of no extraordinary kind. I will just note one of these occasions, ere I pass on to what makes my dreamer truly interesting. It seemed to him that he was in the first floor of a rough hill-farm. The room showed some poor efforts at gentility, a carpet on the floor, a piano, I think, against the wall; but, for all these refinements, there was no mistaking he was in a moorland place, among hillside people, and set in miles of heather. He looked down from the window upon a bare farmyard, that seemed to have been long disused. A great, uneasy stillness lay upon the world. There was no sign of the farm-folk or of any live stock, save for an old, brown, curly dog of the retriever breed, who sat close in against the wall of the house and seemed to be dozing. Something about this dog disquieted the dreamer; it was quite a nameless feeling, for the beast looked right enough—indeed, he was so old and dull and dusty and broken-down, that he should rather have awakened pity; and yet the conviction came and grew upon the dreamer that this was no proper dog at all, but something hellish. A great many dozing summer flies hummed about the yard; and presently the dog thrust forth his paw, caught a fly in his open palm, carried it to his mouth like an ape, and looking suddenly up at the dreamer in the window, winked to him with one eye. The dream went on, it matters not how it went; it was a good dream as dreams go; but there was nothing in the sequel worthy of that devilish brown dog. And the point of interest for me lies partly in that very fact: that having found so singular an incident, my imperfect dreamer should prove unable to carry the tale to a fit end and fall back on indescribable noises and indiscriminate horrors. It would be different now; he knows his business better!

For, to approach at last the point: This honest fellow had long been in the custom of setting himself to sleep with tales, and so had his father before him; but these were irresponsible inventions, told for the teller's pleasure, with no eye to the crass public or the thwart reviewer: tales where a thread might be dropped, or one adventure quitted for another, on fancy's least suggestion. So that the little people who manage man's internal theatre had not as yet received a very rigorous training; and played upon their stage like children who should have slipped into the house and found it empty, rather than like drilled actors performing a set piece to a huge hall of faces. But presently my dreamer began to turn his former amusement of story-telling to (what is called) account; by which I mean that he began to write and sell his tales. Here was he, and here were the little people who did that part of his business, in quite new conditions. The stories must now be trimmed and pared and set upon all fours, they must run from a beginning to an end and fit (after a manner) with the laws of life; the pleasure, in one word, had become a business; and that not only for the dreamer, but for the little people of his theatre. These understood the change as well as he. When he lay down to prepare himself for sleep, he no longer sought amusement, but printable and profitable tales; and after he had dozed off in his box-seat, his little people continued their evolutions with the same mercantile designs. All other forms of dream deserted him but two: he still occasionally reads the most delightful books, he still visits at times the most delightful places; and it is perhaps worthy of note that to these same places, and to one in particular, he returns at intervals of months and years, finding new field-paths, visiting new neighbours, beholding that happy valley under new effects of noon and dawn and sunset. But all the rest of the family of visions is quite lost to him: the common, mangled version of yesterday's affair, the raw-head-and-bloody-bones nightmare, rumoured to be the child of toasted cheese—these and their like are gone; and, for the most part, whether awake or asleep, he is simply occupied—he or his little people—in consciously making stories for the market. This dreamer (like many other persons) has encountered some trifling vicissitudes of fortune. When the bank begins to send letters and the butcher to linger at the back gate, he sets to belabouring his brains after a story, for that is his readiest money-winner; and, behold! at once the little people begin to bestir themselves in the same quest, and labour all night long, and all night long set before him truncheons of tales upon their lighted theatre. No fear of his being frightened now; the flying heart and the frozen scalp are things bygone; applause, growing applause, growing interest, growing exultation in his own cleverness (for he takes all the credit), and at last a jubilant leap to wakefulness, with the cry, 'I have it, that'll do!' upon his lips: with such and similar emotions he sits at these nocturnal dramas, with such outbreaks, like Claudius in the play, he scatters the performance in the midst. Often enough the waking is a disappointment: he has been too deep asleep, as I explain the thing; drowsiness has gained his little people, they have gone stumbling and maundering through their parts; and the play, to the awakened mind, is seen to be a tissue of absurdities. And yet how often have these sleepless Brownies done him honest service, and given him, as he sat idly taking his pleasure in the boxes, better tales than he could fashion for himself.

Here is one, exactly as it came to him. It seemed he was the son of a very rich and wicked man, the owner of broad acres and a most damnable temper. The dreamer (and that was the son) had lived much abroad, on purpose to avoid his parent;

and when at length he returned to England, it was to find him married again to a young wife, who was supposed to suffer cruelly and to loathe her yoke. Because of this marriage (as the dreamer indistinctly understood) it was desirable for father and son to have a meeting; and yet both being proud and both angry, neither would condescend upon a visit. Meet they did accordingly, in a desolate, sandy country by the sea; and there they quarrelled, and the son, stung by some intolerable insult, struck down the father dead. No suspicion was aroused; the dead man was found and buried, and the dreamer succeeded to the broad estates, and found himself installed under the same roof with his father's widow, for whom no provision had been made. These two lived very much alone, as people may after a bereavement, sat down to table together, shared the long evenings, and grew daily better friends; until it seemed to him of a sudden that she was prying about dangerous matters, that she had conceived a notion of his guilt, that she watched him and tried him with questions. He drew back from her company as men draw back from a precipice suddenly discovered; and yet so strong was the attraction that he would drift again and again into the old intimacy, and again and again be startled back by some suggestive question or some inexplicable meaning in her eye. So they lived at cross purposes, a life full of broken dialogue, challenging glances, and suppressed passion; until, one day, he saw the woman slipping from the house in a veil, followed her to the station, followed her in the train to the seaside country, and out over the sandhills to the very place where the murder was done. There she began to grope among the bents, he watching her, flat upon his face; and presently she had something in her hand—I cannot remember what it was, but it was deadly evidence against the dreamer—and as she held it up to look at it, perhaps from the shock of the discovery, her foot slipped, and she hung at some peril on the brink of the tall sand-wreaths. He had no thought but to spring up and rescue her; and there they stood face to face, she with that deadly matter openly in her hand—his very presence on the spot another link of proof. It was plain she was about to speak, but this was more than he could bear—he could bear to be lost, but not to talk of it with his destroyer; and he cut her short with trivial conversation. Arm in arm, they returned together to the train, talking he knew not what, made the journey back in the same carriage, sat down to dinner, and passed the evening in the drawing-room as in the past. But suspense and fear drummed in the dreamer's bosom. 'She has not denounced me yet'—so his thoughts ran—'when will she denounce me? Will it be to-morrow?' And it was not to-morrow, nor the next day, nor the next; and their life settled back on the old terms, only that she seemed kinder than before, and that, as for him, the burthen of his suspense and wonder grew daily more unbearable, so that he wasted away like a man with a disease. Once, indeed, he broke all bounds of decency, seized an occasion when she was abroad, ransacked her room, and at last, hidden away among her jewels, found the damning evidence. There he stood, holding this thing, which was his life, in the hollow of his hand, and marvelling at her inconsequent behaviour, that she should seek, and keep, and yet not use it; and then the door opened, and behold herself. So, once more, they stood, eye to eye, with the evidence between them; and once more she raised to him a face brimming with some communication; and once more he shied away from speech and cut her off. But before he left the room, which he had turned upside down, he laid back his death-warrant where he had found it; and at that, her face lighted up. The next thing he heard, she was explaining to her maid, with some ingenious falsehood, the disorder of her things. Flesh and blood could bear the strain no longer; and I think it was the next morning (though chronology is always hazy in the theatre of the mind) that he burst from his reserve. They had been breakfasting together in one corner of a great, parqueted, sparely-furnished room of many windows; all the time of the meal she had tortured him with sly allusions; and no sooner were the servants gone, and these two protagonists alone together, than he leaped to his feet. She too sprang up, with a pale face; with a pale face, she heard him as he raved out his complaint: Why did she torture him so? she knew all, she knew he was no enemy to her; why did she not denounce him at once? what signified her whole behaviour? why did she torture him? and yet again, why did she torture him? And when he had done, she fell upon her knees, and with outstretched hands: 'Do you not understand?' she cried. 'I love you!'

Hereupon, with a pang of wonder and mercantile delight, the dreamer awoke. His mercantile delight was not of long endurance; for it soon became plain that in this spirited tale there were unmarketable elements; which is just the reason why you have it here so briefly told. But his wonder has still kept growing; and I think the reader's will also, if he consider it ripely. For now he sees why I speak of the little people as of substantive inventors and performers. To the end they had kept their secret. I will go bail for the dreamer (having excellent grounds for valuing his candour) that he had no guess whatever at the motive of the woman—the hinge of the whole well-invented plot—until the instant of that highly dramatic declaration. It was not his tale; it was the little people's! And observe: not only was the secret kept, the story was told with really guileful craftsmanship. The conduct of both actors is (in the cant phrase) psychologically correct, and the emotion aptly graduated up to the surprising climax. I am awake now, and I know this trade; and yet I cannot better it. I am awake, and I live by this business; and yet I could not outdo—could not perhaps equal—that crafty artifice (as of some old, experienced carpenter of plays, some Dennery or Sardou) by which the same situation is twice presented and the two actors twice brought face to face over the evidence, only once it is in her hand, once in his—and these in their due order, the least dramatic first. The more I think of it, the more I am moved to press upon the world my question: Who are the Little People? They are near connections of the dreamer's, beyond doubt; they share in his financial worries and have an eye to the bank-book; they share plainly in his training; they have plainly learned like him to build the scheme of a considerate story and to arrange emotion in progressive order; only I think they have more talent; and one thing is beyond doubt, they can tell him a story piece by piece, like a serial, and keep him all the while in ignorance of where they aim. Who are they, then? and who is the dreamer?

Well, as regards the dreamer, I can answer that, for he is no less a person than myself;—as I might have told you from the beginning, only that the critics murmur over my consistent egotism;—and as I am positively forced to tell you now, or I could advance but little farther with my story. And for the Little People, what shall I say they are but just my Brownies, God bless them! who do one-half my work for me while I am fast asleep, and in all human likelihood, do the rest for me as well, when I am wide awake and fondly suppose I do it for myself. That part which is done while I am sleeping is the Brownies' part beyond contention; but that which is done when I am up and about is by no means necessarily mine, since all goes to show the Brownies have a hand in it even then. Here is a doubt that much concerns my conscience. For myself—what I call I, my conscious ego, the denizen of the pineal gland unless he has changed his residence since Descartes, the man with the conscience and the variable bank-account, the man with the hat and the boots, and the privilege of voting and not carrying his candidate at the general elections—I am sometimes tempted to suppose he is no story-teller at all, but a creature as matter of fact as any cheesemonger or any cheese, and a realist bemired up to the ears in actuality; so that, by that account, the whole of my published fiction should be the single-handed product of some Brownie, some Familiar, some unseen collaborator, whom I keep locked in a back garret, while I get all the praise and he but a share (which I cannot prevent him getting) of the pudding. I am an excellent adviser, something like Molière's servant; I pull back and I cut down; and I dress the whole in the best words and sentences that I can find and make; I hold the pen, too; and I do the sitting at the table, which is about the worst of it; and when all is done, I make up the manuscript and pay for the registration; so that, on the whole, I have some claim to share, though not so largely as I do, in the profits of our common enterprise.

I can but give an instance or so of what part is done sleeping and what part awake, and leave the reader to share what laurels there are, at his own nod, between myself and my collaborators; and to do this I will first take a book that a number of persons have been polite enough to read, the

Strange Case of Dr Jekyll and Mr Hyde. I had long been trying to write a story on this subject, to find a body, a vehicle, for that strong sense of man's double being which must at times come in upon and overwhelm the mind of every thinking creature. I had even written one, *The Travelling Companion*, which was returned by an editor on the plea that it was a work of genius and indecent, and which I burned the other day on the ground that it was not a work of genius, and that *Jekyll* had supplanted it. Then came one of those financial fluctuations to which (with an elegant modesty) I have hitherto referred in the third person. For two days I went about racking my brains for a plot of any sort; and on the second night I dreamed the scene at the window, and a scene afterward split in two, in which Hyde, pursued for some crime, took the powder and underwent the change in the presence of his pursuers. All the rest was made awake, and consciously, although I think I can trace in much of it the manner of my Brownies. The meaning of the tale is therefore mine, and had long pre-existed in my garden of Adonis, and tried one body after another in vain; indeed, I do most of the morality, worse luck! and my Brownies have not a rudiment of what we call a conscience. Mine, too, is the setting, mine the characters. All that was given me was the matter of three scenes, and the central idea of a voluntary change becoming involuntary. Will it be thought ungenerous, after I have been so liberally ladling out praise to my unseen collaborators, if I here toss them over, bound hand and foot, into the arena of the critics? For the business of the powders, which so many have censured, is, I am relieved to say, not mine at all but the Brownies'. Of another tale, in case the reader should have glanced at it, I may say a word: the not very defensible story of *Olalla*. Here the court, the mother, the mother's niche, Olalla, Olalla's chamber, the meetings on the stair, the broken window, the ugly scene of the bite, were all given me in bulk and detail as I have tried to write them; to this I added only the external scenery (for in my dream I never was beyond the court), the portrait, the characters of Felipe and the priest, the moral, such as it is, and the last pages, such as, alas! they are. And I may even say that in this case the moral itself was given me; for it arose immediately on a comparison of the mother and the daughter, and from the hideous trick of atavism in the first. Sometimes a parabolic sense is still more undeniably present in a dream; sometimes I cannot but suppose my Brownies have been aping Bunyan, and yet in no case with what would possibly be called a moral in a tract; never with the ethical narrowness; conveying hints instead of life's larger limitations and that sort of sense which we seem to perceive in the arabesque of time and space.

For the most part, it will be seen, my Brownies are somewhat fantastic, like their stories hot and hot, full of passion and the picturesque, alive with animating incident; and they have no prejudice against the supernatural. But the other day they gave me a surprise, entertaining me with a love-story, a little April comedy, which I ought certainly to hand over to the author of *A Chance Acquaintance*, for he could write it as it should be written, and I am sure (although I mean to try) that I cannot.—But who would have supposed that a Brownie of mine should invent a tale for Mr Howells?

me; for it arose immediately on a comparison of the mother and the daughter, and from the hideous trick of atavism in the first. Sometimes a parabolic sense is still more undeniably present in a dream; sometimes I cannot but suppose my Brownies have been aping Bunyan, and yet in no case with what would possibly be called a moral in a tract; never with the ethical narrowness; conveying hints instead of life's larger limitations and that sort of sense which we seem to perceive in the arabesque of time and space.

For the most part, it will be seen, my Brownies are somewhat fantastic, like their stories hot and hot, full of passion and the picturesque, alive with animating incident; and they have no prejudice against the supernatural. But the other day they gave me a surprise, entertaining me with a love-story, a little April comedy, which I ought certainly to hand over to the author of *A Chance Acquaintance*, for he could write it as it should be written, and I am sure (although I mean to try) that I cannot.—But who would have supposed that a Brownie of mine should invent a tale for Mr Howells?

EXPLANATORY NOTES

Volume numbers of Stevenson's works and letters refer to the Swanston Edition unless otherwise stated.

Balfour = Graham Balfour, *The Life of Robert Louis Stevenson*, 2 vols. (1901).
Maixner = Paul Maixner (ed.), *Robert Louis Stevenson: The Critical Heritage* (1981).
Swearingen = Roger G. Swearingen, *The Prose Writings of Robert Louis Stevenson: A Guide* (1980).

THE STRANGE CASE OF DR JEKYLL AND MR HYDE

Katharine de Mattos: the sister of R.L.S.'s cousin and close friend, Bob Stevenson. She caused a family scandal by marrying and later divorcing Sydney de Mattos, a 'Cambridge Atheist'. R.L.S. dedicated two of the poems in *Underwoods* to her as well as *Jekyll and Hyde*.

7 *Cain's heresy*: the reference is to Genesis 4.

9 *Juggernaut*: Hindi *Jagannath*, 'lord of the world', the title of Krishna, the eighth avatar of Vishnu: specifically, the uncouth idol of this deity at Puri in Orissa, annually dragged in procession on an enormous car, under the wheels of which many devotees are said to have formerly thrown themselves to be crushed.

11 *Queer Street*: an imaginary street where people in difficulties are supposed to reside; hence any difficulty, fix, or trouble, bad circumstances, debt, illness, etc. *OED* records three uses: Bulwer Lytton in *Ernest Maltravers* (1837), Dickens in *Our Mutual Friend* (1866) and R.L.S. here.

14 . . . *without further delay*: Dr Jekyll's will called forth some criticism; Rider Haggard commented that it was the one 'blot upon an otherwise perfect story'. On 26 January 1886, he wrote furthermore that: 'probate would not have been allowed to issue for a period of years. It would have been necessary to produce overwhelming evidence in support of the presumption of Jekyll's death.'

E. T. Cook in the *Athenaeum* on 16 January 1886 remarked, too, that:

the terms of Dr Jekyll's will would have been inoperative. Mr Stevenson has overlooked the fact that a man's will does not come into force until he is dead, and that the fact that he has not been heard of for three months would not enable his executor to carry out his testamentary directions. [Maixner, pp. 202–3.]

15 *Damon and Pythias*: Damon was a Pythagorean famous for his friendship with Phintias (not, as here, Pythias, a frequent misspelling of the name). Phintias was sentenced to death by Dionysius (I or II), then reprieved. He returned at the last moment to save Damon who had gone bail for him.

19 *Dr Fell*: although Dr John Fell (1625–86) was quite a respected person, Dean of Christ Church, Oxford, Bishop of Oxford, and patron of Oxford University Press, he is remembered mainly for his place in this translation of Martial, *Epigrams*, i. 32:

> I do not love you, Dr Fell;
> But why I cannot tell;
> But this I know full well,
> I do not love you, Dr Fell.

The phrase 'Dr Fell' is used to signify a vaguely unamiable person against whom it is not possible to specify the ground of dislike or distaste.

20 *pede claudo*: on halting foot.

28 *from Henry Jekyll*: this picture raised queries from F. W. H. Myers who commented extensively on the novel in letters to R.L.S. of 21 and 27 February 1886. Myers wrote, 'Would Jekyll have sent a picture there? Would he not have concealed the house from his servants?' R.L.S. replied that he had 'rather meant that Hyde had bought it himself.' Myers, still not satisfied, rejoined, 'Would Hyde have bought a picture? I think—and friends of weight support my view—that such an act would have been altogether unworthy of him' (Maixner, pp. 215, 219).

44 . . . *drug is wanted bitter bad, sir*: Balfour comments that R.L.S.'s immediate, family audience felt that the powder was 'too material an agency, but this he could not eliminate, because in the dream it had made so strong an impression upon him' (Balfour, II, p. 14). See also Appendix B: A Chapter on Dreams, p. 208 above.

58 . . . *the unbelief of Satan*: Myers made a just comment here: 'Style too elevated for Hyde . . . These are not remarks that fit the husky broken voice of Hyde—they are Jekyllian. Surely Hyde's admirable style [p. 18] should be retained for him.'

R.L.S. replied agreeing with 'almost every word' of Myers's detailed criticisms:

> . . . much of it, I must confess, would never have been, if I had been able to do what I like, and lay the thing by for the matter of a year. But the wheels of Byles the Butcher drive exceeding swiftly . . . Nothing but this white-hot haste would explain the gross error of Hyde's speech at Lanyon's (Maixner, pp. 216, 219)

64 *agonies of death and birth*: the birth motif links up with Jekyll's assertions that Hyde is his son (e.g. p. 68), and is a variation of the father-son theme that recurs in R.L.S.'s fiction.

captives of Philippi: an earthquake at Philippi (Acts 16) burst open the doors of the prison where Paul and Silas were held captive. Philippi was also the site of two battles in 42 BC, in which Octavianus and Antony defeated Brutus and Cassius.

67 *Babylonian finger on the wall*: the reference is to Daniel 5, Daniel's interpretation of the writing on the wall prophesying the end of King Belshazzar.

68 *a son's indifference*: again, there is the reference to Jekyll and Hyde as father and son; their uneasy relationship as such looks forward to the fuller portrayal of the filial relationship in *Catriona* (1893) and, especially, in *Weir of Hermiston*. Cf. p. 69 where Jekyll insists that his crime was in 'no more reasonable spirit than that in which a sick child may break a plaything'.

71 *to growl for license*: Jekyll consistently describes Hyde in bestial language in his 'Statement'. See Introduction, p. xii and cf. pp. 18, 45, 47, 48, 49, 67, 71, 75.

73 *I cannot say, I*: Jekyll's confusion with 'I', and his refusal to own 'the brute that slept within' [him], contributes to the sense of uncertainty that the text creates. See Introduction, p. xiii

75 *destroying the portrait of my father*: R.L.S. here brings in the idea of the three generations as Hyde, as Jekyll's 'son', destroys his grandfather. This section reminds the reader of R.L.S.'s uneasy relationship with his own father.

WEIR OF HERMISTON

83 *Claverhouse*: John Graham of Claverhouse, Viscount Dundee (1648–89). In 1678 he was commissioned to act against the Covenanting conventicles then meeting in south-western Scotland. Famed for his cruelty in this 'Killing Time', John

Graham lives in Scots memory as 'Bloody Clavers' and also as 'Bonnie Dundee'. Scots writers of the nineteenth century are divided as to his true part in the Covenanting troubles: see Walter Scott's *Old Mortality* (1816), James Hogg's *The Brownie of Bodsbeck* (1818) and John Galt's *Ringan Gilhaize* (1823).

Balweary: this village is also the setting of Stevenson's story 'Thrawn Janet' and of the fragment *Heathercat*.

Old Mortality: the name given to Robert Paterson (1715–1801), an ardent Covenanter who spent his life travelling round south-western Scotland looking after Covenanting monuments. Walter Scott's novel of 1816 takes its title from this character.

The Covenanters were so called from the National Covenant (1638), a document in which the Scottish people expressed their grievances against Charles I's popish tendencies and religious innovations. A second Covenant was drawn up in 1643. See especially, Gordon Donaldson, *Scotland: James V–James VII* (Edinburgh, 1965).

Cameronian: the name applied to an extreme Covenanter, a follower of Richard Cameron (1648–80). He broke away totally from the majority of Presbyterians, went to Holland and was ordained there by some exiled ministers. In 1680 he returned as a field preacher, and on 20 June 1680 he made a public renunciation of the King's authority. He was defeated and killed at Airds Moss on 20 July 1680.

Francie's cairn: named persumably after Frank Innes who was to meet his death nearby (see Appendix A, pp. 195–6 above).

84 *Lord Justice-Clerk*: originally the clerk of the central criminal court; then, a judge.

Flodden: a famous defeat of the Scots by the English in 1513.

James the Fifth: James V (1512–42) was stringent with those who challenged his authority. The Borders were particularly unruly during his reign, and some rebellious persons from that area were hanged at his instigation, including the ballad hero, Johnnie Armstrong.

Tom Dalyell: General Sir Thomas, of the Binns (*c.*1599–1685) had a varied military career. In 1628 he joined the English expedition against La Rochelle, and then held a number of appointments in Ireland and elsewhere. In 1651 he was captured by the Cromwellians but he escaped from the Tower of London. He served in Russia but was then recalled by Charles II and given command of the forces in Scotland. He, too, like Claverhouse (see note to p. 83), was involved in suppressing Covenanting recusants and, in 1666, he defeated the Covenanters at Rullion Green. He was also a Commissioner of Justiciary for dealing with the Covenanters after their second major rebellion at Bothwell Brig.

Hell-Fire Club: an association of reckless young men who were mainly active in the eighteenth century.

The heredity of Jean Rutherford has something in common with that of Stevenson's own mother: see *Records of a Family of Engineers* (1896).

85 *Lord-Advocate*: the Crown Prosecutor.

. . . haangit: Stevenson's Judge Hermiston is modelled on Robert MacQueen, Lord Braxfield (1722–99). He became an advocate in 1744 and, in 1766, was appointed a Lord of Session; in 1788 he became Justice-Clerk, in effect head of the Criminal Court in Scotland. He was known for being particularly harsh with political offenders, and was noted for his brutality and insulting treatment of such plaintiffs as appeared before him. He was, however, also thought of as a man of considerable skill and courage; and Stevenson is clearly well aware of the complexities of the man. In *Virginibus Puerisque* (1881) he writes of Raeburn's portrait of Braxfield:

> So sympathetically is the character conceived by the portrait-painter, that it is hardly possible to avoid some movement of sympathy on the part of the spectator. And sympathy is a thing to be encouraged, apart from humane considerations, because it supplies us with the materials for wisdom. It is probably more instructive to entertain a sneaking kindness for any unpopular person, and among the rest, for Lord Braxfield, than to give way to perfect raptures of moral indignation against his abstract vices. He was the last judge on the Scots bench to employ the pure Scots idiom. His opinions, thus given in Doric, and conceived in a lively, rugged, conversational style, were full of point and authority. Out of the bar, or off the bench, he was a convivial man, a lover of wine, and one who 'shone peculiarly' at tavern meetings. He has left behind him an unrivalled reputation for rough and cruel speech; and to this day his name smacks of the gallows. [II, 389.]

The sympathy mentioned by R.L.S. in this essay is that which Archie Hermiston fails to feel for the Judge; and that which, only towards the end of his life and many miles away from Scotland, R.L.S. can feel for his own father.

88 *Rutherford's Letters*: this refers to the letters of Samuel Rutherford (1600–61) which were well-known religious reading in Scotland; although they undoubtedly have spiritual insight, the florid style,

emotionalism and inappropriately erotic imagery has caused the *Letters* (1664) to be ridiculed as, for instance, in Gilbert Crokatt's *The Scotch Presbyterian Eloquence* (1692).

Scougal's Grace Abounding: Henry Scougal (1650–78), one of the Saints of the Scottish church who became Professor of Divinity at Aberdeen University at a very young age. His *The Life of God in the Soul of Man* was published in 1677, the year before his untimely death from consumption.

89 *Rullion Green*: see note to p. 84.

Bloody MacKenzie: Sir George MacKenzie of Rosehaugh (1636–91) became an advocate in 1659; in 1661 he was appointed a justice for criminal cases and in 1669 he became a Member of Parliament for the Sherrifdom of Ross; initially he was opposed to the administration of Lauderdale although he later supported it and was made Lord Advocate in 1677. He is mainly associated with prosecutions of the Covenanters and his boast made in 1680 was that he never lost a case for the King. He rejected the policy of toleration of James VII and was removed from the Advocacy in May 1686 to be reinstated, however, from February 1688 to May 1689. At the Revolution he was one of five Jacobite members who opposed the resolution that James VII had forfeited his throne; he then, however, went to England and died on 8 May 1691. His 'bloody' reputation is now thought by historians to be something of a distortion; and it should be noted that he was also founder of the Advocates' Library in Edinburgh (now the National Library of Scotland) and that he was well known in his day as a writer of considerable versatility. His divided nature is similar to that of R.L.S.'s Hermiston.

Lauderdale: John Maitland, 2nd Earl and 1st Duke of Lauderdale (1616–82) took part in the negotiations with the Covenanters with Charles II at Ripon in 1642; in 1643 he helped draw up the Solemn League and Covenant and he became a Scottish Commissioner to the Westminster Assembly; he gradually, however, moved towards the Royalists and in 1651, he sailed with Charles II to Scotland and was amongst those captured at Worcester. After the Restoration he was made Secretary of State and was involved in this office with dealing with his former Covenanting associates.

Rothes: John Leslie, 7th Earl and 1st Duke of Rothes (1630–81), began his career as a Covenanting leader although his allegiance was consistently to the Royalist section of the Covenanters. He gained the favour of Charles II, fought with him and was captured at Worcester. After the Restoration he became King's Commissioner to the Scottish Parliament in 1633. He is remembered for his licentious nature and for the severity of his treatment of the Covenanters which contributed in large part to the Pentland Rising of 1666. In 1673–4 he opposed Lauderdale who remained in office as Commissioner until 1681.

poleetical: Jean Rutherford's Scots pronunciation features are shared with and imitated by her son, Archie. See p. 92 and note.

90 *hills of Naphtali*. See Matthew 4. The lines including this phrase were important to R.L.S. in childhood. In the essay 'Rosa Quo Locorum' he quotes:

> Behind the hills of Naphatali
> The sun went slowly down,
> Leaving on mountain, tower and tree,
> A tinge of golden brown.
>
> [See Tusitala Edition, XXX, 2.]

92 *justifeed in staying with him*: here Archie takes up his mother's Scots speech and pronunciation features. Cf. p. 89 and note.

'The Hanging Judge': sobriquet used of Lord Braxfield. Also the title of a play written by R.L.S. in collaboration with Fanny. The play was not directly inspired by Braxfield but, according to W. E. Henley, was suggested by a story in Sheridan Le Fanu's *Through a Glass Darkly* (1872). Fanny, however, states that the play was based on her idea. See Swearingen, p. 112.

97 *Corderius, Papinian and Paul*: Corderius is the Latin form of the French Cordier (*c.*1480–1564), a French schoolmaster from Normandy or Perche who wrote several books for children, the best known of which is his *Colloquia*, which went into successive editions and was used in schools for three centuries. Papinian and Paul are two of the greatest of Roman jurists, much more sophisticated texts than Corderius; Papinian, in particular, is considered difficult because of the conciseness of his style.

99 *Forbes of Culloden*: Duncan Forbes (1685–1747) became Laird of Culloden in 1734; studied law at Leyden and became an advocate in 1709; in 1715 he acted against the Jacobites; but he also insisted that Scots arrested at this time should not be tried in England. In 1725, he was appointed Lord Advocate. The allusion to Forbes here is particularly apposite because of his role in the Porteous Riots of 1736: an Edinburgh mob hanged

John Porteous, Captain of the City Guard, after he opened fire on Edinburgh men who had raised a disturbance after the execution of a smuggler. The Porteous episode is linked with Archie's attitude towards the hanging of Duncan Jopp. In 1737 Duncan Forbes became Lord President and he was said to have transformed the courts of law into courts of justice. In the Jacobite Rising of 1745 he persuaded many of the northern clans of Scotland not to join Jacobite forces. Despite his services Forbes was insulted by the victorious Cumberland who remarked on the law: 'The laws of the country! My Lord, I'll make a brigade give laws, by God,' and later referred to Forbes as 'that old woman who talked to me about humanity'. (As quoted in Gordon Donaldson and Robert S. Morpeth, *Who's Who in Scottish History* [Oxford, 1973], p. 166.) The latter comment could be made by Hermiston about Lord Glenalmond.

In the *Master of Ballantrae*, R.L.S. also compares his character, William Johnson, with Duncan Forbes in terms of the way both men have to deal with very awkward situations and act as mediators.

100 *Cato and Brutus*: Cato refers to Cato the Censor (234–149 BC), who was well known for his opposition to prevalent fashions of luxury and licentiousness. He was of the firm conviction that Rome would never be safe until Carthage was destroyed and his final words in the Senate on every occasion he was called upon to vote were, 'Delenda est Carthage' (Carthage must be destroyed).

Brutus: Lucius Junius Brutus, first consul of Rome. His brother was murdered by Tarquinius Superbus and he escaped this fate by pretending idiocy. After the death of Lucretia, he incited the Romans to expel the Tarquins and was elected to the consulship. He put his two sons to death for conspiring to restore the Tarquins. This reference looks forward to the conclusion of the novel that was never written: see pp. 195–7. Archie's radical and unacceptable views are comparable with those of Brutus's sons. (Cf. the allusion to his being 'Frenchifeed', p. 114.)

the Speculative Society: a students' debating society at Edinburgh University, founded in 1764, of which Stevenson was a noted member. See also his comments in 'A College Magazine', *Memories and Portraits*, IX, pp. 36–45. Cf. p. 106f.

101 *Rhadamanthus*: the son of Zeus and Europa, and brother of King Minos of Crete. After his death he became one of the Judges in Hades.

104 *Obiter dictum*: something said by the way.

105 *Holyrood*: the palace of Holyroodhouse in Edinburgh.

Queen Mary: Mary Queen of Scots (1542–87).

Prince Charlie: The Young Pretender held court at Holyroodhouse after defeating General Cope at Prestonpans on 21 September 1745.

hooded stag: the life of King David (*c.*1084–1153) was endangered when he was hunting, by a large stag. Legend has it that, by a miracle, a piece of the Holy Rood appeared in the King's hand and saved him.

107 *the Spec*: see note to p. 100. On one occasion R.L.S. tried to organize a debate on capital punishment but the plan foundered from lack of support.

109 *Dr Gregory*: James Gregory (1753–1821), Professor of the Practice of Medicine at Edinburgh University and Chief of the Edinburgh Medical School.

114 *the Peninsula*: this refers to the Peninsula War (1804–14), fought in opposition to Napoleon's plans in the Iberian Peninsula.

118 *in apicibus juris*: at the height of his judicial powers.

119 *Ay*: the very rare use of the Scots word by Archie suggests the degree of intimacy between him and Lord Glenalmond.

120 *sclamber*: similarly, the genteel Glenalmond does not usually employ Scots words, and the Scots term here signals his warmth of feeling for Archie.

major and sui juris: has attained his majority and is not subject to the power of a father (in Roman Law).

121 *Tigris ut aspera*: as a fierce tiger. 'Atqui non ego te, tigris ut aspera' (Horace, *Odes*, I. xxiii, 'To Chloe').

125 *At Hermiston*: In his Editorial Note, Sidney Colvin writes:

> If the reader seeks, further, to know whether the scenery of Hermiston can be identified with any one special place familiar to the writer's early experience, the answer, I think, must be in the negative. Rather it is distilled from a number of different haunts and associations among the moorlands of southern Scotland. In the dedication and in a letter to me he indicates the Lammermuirs as the scene of his tragedy. And Mrs Stevenson (his mother) tells me that she thinks he was inspired by recollections of a visit paid in boyhood to an uncle living at a remote farmhouse in that district called Overshiels, in the parish of Stow. But though he may have thought of the Lammermuirs in the first instance,

we have already found him drawing his description of the kirk and manse from another haunt of his youth, namely, Glencorse in the Pentlands; while passages in chapter v. and viii. point explicitly to a third district, that is, Upper Tweeddale, with the country stretching thence towards the wells of Clyde. With this country also holiday rides and excursions from Peebles had made him familiar as a boy: and this seems certainly the most natural scene of the story, if only from its proximity to the proper home of the Elliotts, which of course is in the heart of the Border, especially Teviotdale and Ettrick. Some of the geographical names mentioned are clearly not meant to furnish literal indications. The Spango, for instance, is a water running, I believe, not from the Tweed but into the Nith, and Crossmichael as the name of a town is borrowed from Galloway. [*Weir of Hermiston*, 1896, pp. 284–85.]

126 *Mr Sherriff Scott*: Sir Walter Scott (1771–1832) was sherriff-depute of Selkirkshire from 1799. Scott had a life-long interest in the Borders and was responsible for the publication of *Minstrelsy of the Scottish Border* (1802–3) to which James Hogg (see note to p. 141) also contributed.

128 *when Byronism was new*: Byron, George Gordon, 6th Baron (1788–1824), Romantic poet, at the height of his popularity from *c.*1818–24, the year he was drowned at Missolonghi in Greece. His poetry, although censured on moral grounds, was hugely successful at home and on the Continent owing to his rejection of 'cant, political, religious, and moral'. Some Scottish writers (this reference to Byron adds one further important name to the roll of honour of Scots writers in this text) disapproved of Byronism, or as George MacDonald called it, 'Byron fever'. The Byronic hero with whom Archie Weir is compared is usually an outcast, an exile, a darkly mysterious character who is often believed to have committed some nameless crime. Cf. p. 175.

130 *lever de rideau*: curtain up; the raising of the curtain at the start of a performance.

132 *Lyon King of Arms*: the official in control of Scottish heraldry.

133 *Camperdown and Cape St Vincent*: both of these are British naval victories, the first a defeat of the Dutch, the second of the Spanish.

137 *Barbarossa*: the nickname of Frederick I (red-beard), emperor of the Holy Roman Empire (1152–90). He was drowned during the Third Crusade but the legend survives that he still sleeps in a cavern in the Kyffhauser mountains until such time as his country needs him.

. . . *under the hawse*: there has been some textual controversy about this phrase as to whether it should, in fact, read *tawse* (a leather strap formerly used in schools as a form of punishment) or *hawse* (the bow of a ship). M. R. Ridley comments in favour of *tawse*, suggesting that, 'the compositor was, once again, baffled by an unfamiliar word . . . Stevenson wrote "tawse" which gives just the sense required' (*TLS*, 28 August 1959, p. 495 and see also *TLS*, 16 October 1959, p. 593). For the argument in favour of *hawse* (the bow of a ship), see Douglas G. Browne's letter, *TLS*, 11 September, 1959, p. 519.

Muir and Palmer: Thomas Muir (1765–98), an advocate in Edinburgh who, at the time of the French Revolution, became a member of the Convention of Delegates of Friends of the People. In 1793 he was arrested on a charge of sedition, but allowed bail. After a time in France, he returned to Edinburgh and was tried in the High Court. He was sentenced to fourteen years in the Colonies but was rescued by an American ship after only two years in Australia.

Thomas Fyshe Palmer (1747–1802), a Unitarian minister; like Muir, Palmer was associated with revolutionary societies and was sentenced to twelve years transportation to Botany Bay.

138 *antinomian*: member of an extreme group which holds that under the gospel the moral law is not obligatory.

140 *Robbie Burns*: Robert Burns (1759–96). Stevenson had a divided attitude to Burns. Whilst he loved and admired the poetry, he was angered by Burns's adoption of the mask of a professional Don Juan. He records his mixed feelings in the essay 'Some Aspects of Robert Burns' (1879), III, 43–76. This piece did not endear R.L.S. further to Edinburgh Society which was inclined, with some hypocrisy, to turn a blind eye to Burns's licentiousness.

the Minstrelsy: see note to p. 126.

141 *the Ettrick Shepherd*: James Hogg (1770–1835), poet and novelist. Hogg, the son of a farmer, entered farm service with almost no formal education in 1777, on his father's bankruptcy. His own life was frequently beset with financial difficulties and he twice lost his savings in farming ventures. He contributed songs to Scott's *Minstrelsy* and after their meeting in 1802, Scott and Hogg became life-long friends. In 1810 Hogg went to Edinburgh and there tried to make a literary living editing his own magazine, *The Spy*. In 1813 he gained fame with the

publication of *The Queen's Wake*; and, in the same year, he met Wordsworth, Shelley and other important literary figures of the day. He is best known for poetry, such as *The Queen's Wake* and *Kilmeny*, collections of *Jacobite Relics*, and for his great novel, *The Private Memoirs and Confessions of a Justified Sinner* (1824). Hogg is one of Scotland's divided characters and portrays himself both as rough, untaught Ettrick shepherd and as genteel litterateur about Edinburgh. See especially, James Hogg, *Memoirs of The Author's Life* and *Familiar Anecdotes of Sir Walter Scott*, ed. Douglas S. Mack (Edinburgh, 1972).

142 *Roy ne puis, prince ne daigne*: King I cannot be, Prince (or Duke) I would not be. Motto of the House of Rohan, an ancient Breton family.

ipsissimus: one's very self.

166 *And battles long ago*: the lines come from Wordsworth's 'The Solitary Reaper'.

167 *the American War*: this refers to the Anglo-American war, 1812–14.

Beulah: see Isaiah, 62: 4. In Bunyan's *Pilgrim's Progress* the pilgrims when they reached Beulah were in sight of the Heavenly City and 'beyond the valley of the shadow of death'.

169 *Pylades . . . Orestes at last*: Orestes, son of Agamemnon and Clytemnestra, was brought up and educated with his cousin, Pylades. The two men are associated with the deepest and most loyal friendship. Frank Innes's allusion to them is grimly ironic.

171 *Tantaene irae*? Cf. 'Tantaene animis coelestibus irae?'—'Can heavenly natures nourish hate?' (Virgil, *Aeneid*, i. 11.)

176 *Sherlock Holmes*: the famous private detective in novels by A. Conan Doyle, another Scottish writer. The character of Holmes was partly inspired by an Edinburgh surgeon, Dr Joseph Bell. Sherlock Holmes appears in Conan Doyle's work from 1887 onwards.

Talleyrand: Charles Maurice de Talleyrand (1754–1838). A Frenchman who occupied a high position during the Revolution and under Napoleon. He is generally remembered for his complete lack of principle and his enormous egotism. The reference here is a danger sign, warning the reader just how potentially dangerous Frank Innes really is.

177 *obsto principiis*: resist the first beginnings (root out the evil before it becomes too strong).

180 *danders*: this is a rare occasion in the existing fragment of *Weir* on which Frank Innes uses a Scots word. See Introduction, p. xxi.

181 *nameless, Gregarach*: the reference is to the Clan MacGregor whose name was proscribed in Scotland in 1693. The most famous Clan member was Rob Roy and R.L.S. introduces other MacGregors in *Kidnapped* (1886) and *Catriona* (1893).

189 *God kens*: this 'lapse' into Scots shows the depth of Archie's feeling and is commented upon by, e.g., Norman Page, *Speech in the English Novel* (1973), p. 59.

GLOSSARY

Note: this glossary of Scots words in *Weir of Hermiston* is indebted to the *Scottish National Dictionary* and the *Concise Scots Dictionary*. It replaces the shorter glossary included at the end of the First Edition.

ae, one
ain, own
aith, oath
amang, among
ane, one
arena, are not
a'thegither, altogether
auld, old
Auld Hornie, the Devil
awa, away
ay, yes; always
ayther, either

bailie, magistrate
bairn, child
baith, both
ballants, ballads, songs
bauchle, old shoe, loose slipper
bauld, bold
bawbee, copper coin
bethankit, God be thanked
birling, whirling
black-a-vised, black-faced
blagyard, blackguard
blendit, windswept
bluid, blood
bonnet-laird, man who farms his own property, a yeoman
bool, round sweet
braith, breath
braw, good, well, fine
braws (o' life), pleasures, good things (of life)
brewst, brewing
brig, bridge
brither, brother
brocken, broken
broughten, brought
buff, to play, make a fool of
buirdly, burly; rough
burn, stream
butt end, kitchen, outer room of a house
byre, cowshed

ca', drive; call
cairn, pile of stones (as a memorial or marking a grave)
caller, fresh
canna, cannot
canny (-ie), cautious, careful, prudent; of good omen
canty (-ie), lively, pleasant, cheerful
carline, old woman
cauld, cold
caulf, calf
chalmer, private room, bedroom
claes, clothes
clamjamfry, crowd, clutter up
clavers, gossip
cock-laird, small landed proprietor
collieshangie, noisy dispute, uproar
colloguing, chatting; scheming
complean, complain

corp, body
crack, joke, gossip
craikin, croaking, clamouring
craw, crow
cuddies, donkeys, asses
cuist, cast
cutty, mischievous or disobedient girl

dander, stroll
danders, cinders, refuse of a smith's fire
daur, dare
daurna, dare not
daursay, daresay
deave, deafen
deevil/deil, devil
deid, dead
denner, dinner
dentie, dainty
didna/dinna, did not
dirdum, spirit, vigour
disjaskit, untidy, dilapidated
doer, agent
dour, sullen, dull, humourless
dozened, dazed, stupefied
dram, drink
dreid, dread
dreidful, dreadful
droopit, weak, infirm
drumlie, muddy, gloomy
dule-tree, gallows-tree
dunting, knocking
dwaibly, infirm, shaky

earrand, errand
e'en, even, evening
eneuch, enough
ettercap, spider; spiteful person

faither, father
fechting, fighting
feck, quantity, number
feckless, weak, incompetent
fell, very, extremely
fey, unlike oneself; strange, as persons are observed to be in the hour approaching death or calamity
fit, foot
fleering, mocking
flit, move (esp. to move house), depart
flyped, folded back, turned inside out
forby, besides, in addition
forgather, meet, fall in with
fower, four
frae, from
fushionless, spiritless, faint-hearted
fyled, made dirty, defiled
fylement, defilement, dirt

gae, go
gaed, went
gaithering, gathering
gane, gone
gang, go
gey an, very
ghaist, ghost
gie, give
gigot, leg of mutton
girzie (dim. of Grizel), maidservant
glamoured, dazzled, deceived
glaur, mud, slime
gloaming, twilight
gowden, golden
gowsty, wild, stormy
grat, cried
grieve, the overseer or head-workman on a farm; steward
grund, ground
grunding, grinding

guddling, catching fish with the hands
guid, good
gumption, common-sense, native wit
gurley, stormy, threatening
gyte, mad

ha/hae, have
ha', hall
haddit, held
hags, marshy ground, bog
hairm, harm
hairt/hert, heart
hale, whole
hame, home
hasna, has not
haud, hold
havena, have not
hazelnit, hazelnut
heed/heid, head
heels-ower-hurdie, heels over head
hinney, honey
hirstle, drive, harrass
hizzie, wench, servant girl
hosen, stockings
howe, hollow
howf, shelter
hunkered, crouched
hunks, a lazy slut, indolent woman; a thick piece, lump
hypothec (Sc. law), the right of a creditor to hold the effects of a debtor as security for a claim without taking possession of them
    the hale hypothec: the whole business

idleset, idleness
infeftment (Sc. law), the investing of a new owner with a real right in, or legal possession of, land or a heritage
isna, is not
ithers, others

jaiket, jacket
jaud, jade
jeely piece, piece of bread with jam
jennipers, juniper
jo, sweetheart
jyle, jail

kebbuck, cheese
kenspeckle, easily recognizable, conspicuous
kilted, tucked up (of clothes, esp. women's)
kye, cattle
kyte, belly

laigh, low
lane, alone
lanely, lonely
lang, long
lang syne, long since, long ago
lave, rest, remainder
leear, liar
leein', lying
linking, walking arm in arm
lown, sheltered, snug
lynn, pool below a waterfall

ma, my
macer, an officer of the crown who delivered Royal commands and summonses and uttered public proclamations
mainner, manner
mair, more

maist, most
maitter, matter
maun, must
mauna, must not
menseful, polite, sensible
micht, might
mirk, dark
misbegowk, disappointment
mither, mother
mony, many
mools, mould, earth
muckle, much, great, big
muir, moor
my lane, by myself

nae/na, no
naebody, nobody
naething/nawthing, nothing
nane, none
nayther, neither
nesty, nasty
nicht, night
noo, now
nowt, ox

o', of
ongoings, goings on (usu. in a disreputable sense)
ony, any
onybody, anybody
oot, out
ower, too much, excessively

pairt, part
palmering, sauntering, wandering about aimlessly
panel (Sc. law), the accused
peat-hag, peat bog
peel, fortified house or small defensive tower
pimatum, pomatum
pitten (oot), setting out, embarking
plew-stilts, plough-shafts
policy, enclosed grounds of a large house, park
pouder, powder
preeson, prison
puddock, frog
puggy, monkey (gen. term of disrespect)
puir, poor

quaiet, quiet
quatit, quietened; calmed
quean, young woman (usu. unmarried)

rade, rode
raired, roared
rig and furrow, ribbed (stockings)
rin, run
risping, grinding, grating
routh, plenty, abundance
rowt, rant, roar
rudas, coarse, masculine-looking
runt, old or decayed tree stump; withered stalk; short, thickset person

sab, sob
sae, so
sair, sore, sorely
saison, season
sanguishes, sandwiches
sasine (Sc. law), the act of giving possession of feudal property
sax, six
saxt, sixth
sclamber, clamber
sculduddery, obscene or indecent conversation
seeven, seven

shauchling, shuffling, walking clumsily
shurely, surely
siller, silver
simmer, summer
sinsyne, from that time, since then
skailing, dispersing (esp. from church)
skelp, strike, hit
skirling, shrieking, making a shrill noise
skreigh (o' day), dawn
snash, abuse, impudence
sneisty, arrogant, contemptuous
sodger, soldier
sooth, hum, sing under the breath
sough, noise, sound
spak', speak
spier, ask
splairging, running wild, squandering one's resources or talents
spledering, sprawling
spunk and dirdum, spirit and vigour
stamach, stomach
stanes, stones
steik, shut
stirk, young bullock; stupid, oafish fellow
sugar bool, round boiled sweet
suld, should
suldna, should not
swalled, swollen
syne, since, then

tae, to, two
ta'en, taken
tak, take
tawpie, giddy careless person (esp. a young woman)
thir, these
thocht, thought
thrawn, twisted, crooked
to-names, forenames, first names
toon, town
triced, arranged, made an appointment
twa, two
tyke, dog

unchancy, unlucky
unco, strange, extraordinary, uncanny; very
uncoly, strangely
upsetting, forward, ambitious
upsitten, callous, indifferent

vennel, narrow lane between houses; the Vennel: a narrow lane in Edinburgh running out of the Grassmarket
vivers, provisions

wae, sad, woeful
waling, choosing
warrandise, guarantee, undertaking to protect another person
wasna, was not
waur, worse
weel, well
weemen, women
weet, wet
weird, fate, destiny
wha/whae, who, whom
whammles, upsets
whatten, what, which
whaup, curlew
whaur, where
wheeped, whistled, squeaked

whiles, sometimes
whunstane, whinstone
whure, whore
wi', with
win, reach
windlestrae, withered stalk of grass
wishen, washed
wouldna, would not
wull, will
wund, wind

yersel, yourself
yin, one
yon, that (one), those over there

THE WORLD'S CLASSICS

A Select List

HANS ANDERSEN: Fairy Tales
Translated by L. W. Kingsland
Introduction by Naomi Lewis
Illustrated by Vilhelm Pedersen and Lorenz Frølich

LUDOVICO ARIOSTO: Orlando Furioso
Translated by Guido Waldman

ARISTOTLE: The Nicomachean Ethics
Translated by David Ross

JANE AUSTEN: Emma
Edited by James Kinsley and David Lodge

HONORÉ DE BALZAC: Père Goriot
Translated and Edited by A. J. Krailsheimer

CHARLES BAUDELAIRE: The Flowers of Evil
Translated by James McGowan
Introduction by Jonathan Culler

R. D. BLACKMORE: Lorna Doone
Edited by Sally Shuttleworth

MARY ELIZABETH BRADDON: Lady Audley's Secret
Edited by David Skilton

CHARLOTTE BRONTË: Jane Eyre
Edited by Margaret Smith

EMILY BRONTË: Wuthering Heights
Edited by Ian Jack

GEORG BÜCHNER:
Danton's Death, Leonce and Lena, Woyzeck
Translated by Victor Price

JOHN BUNYAN: The Pilgrim's Progress
Edited by N. H. Keeble

FRANCES HODGSON BURNETT: The Secret Garden
Edited by Dennis Butts

LEWIS CARROLL: Alice's Adventures in Wonderland
and Through the Looking Glass
Edited by Roger Lancelyn Green
Illustrated by John Tenniel

MIGUEL DE CERVANTES: Don Quixote
Translated by Charles Jarvis
Edited by E. C. Riley

GEOFFREY CHAUCER: The Canterbury Tales
Translated by David Wright

ANTON CHEKHOV: The Russian Master and Other Stories
Translated by Ronald Hingley

Ward Number Six and Other Stories
Translated by Ronald Hingley

WILKIE COLLINS: Armadale
Edited by Catherine Peters

No Name
Edited by Virginia Blain

JOSEPH CONRAD: Chance
Edited by Martin Ray

Lord Jim
Edited by John Batchelor

Youth, Heart of Darkness, The End of the Tether
Edited by Robert Kimbrough

THOMAS DE QUINCEY:
The Confessions of an English Opium-Eater
Edited by Grevel Lindop

CHARLES DICKENS: Christmas Books
Edited by Ruth Glancy

Oliver Twist
Edited by Kathleen Tillotson

FEDOR DOSTOEVSKY: Crime and Punishment
Translated by Jessie Coulson
Introduction by John Jones

ARTHUR CONAN DOYLE:
Sherlock Holmes: Selected Stories
Introduction by S. C. Roberts

THEODORE DREISER: Jennie Gerhardt
Edited by Lee Clark Mitchell

ALEXANDRE DUMAS *fils*:
La Dame aux Camélias
Translated by David Coward

MARIA EDGEWORTH: Castle Rackrent
Edited by George Watson

GEORGE ELIOT: Daniel Deronda
Edited by Graham Handley

Felix Holt, The Radical
Edited by Fred C. Thompson

Selected Critical Writings
Edited by Rosemary Ashton

GUSTAVE FLAUBERT: Madame Bovary
Translated by Gerard Hopkins
Introduction by Terence Cave

A Sentimental Education
Translated by Douglas Parmée

ELIZABETH GASKELL: Cousin Phillis and Other Tales
Edited by Angus Easson

My Lady Ludlow and Other Stories
Edited by Edgar Wright

GEORGE GISSING: The Nether World
Edited by Stephen Gill

WILLIAM GODWIN: Caleb Williams
Edited by David McCracken

J. W. VON GOETHE: Faust, Part One
Translated by David Luke

H. RIDER HAGGARD: King Solomon's Mines
Edited by Dennis Butts

THOMAS HARDY: A Pair of Blue Eyes
Edited by Alan Manford

Tess of the D'Urbervilles
Edited by Juliet Grindle and Simon Gatrell

NATHANIEL HAWTHORNE:
Young Goodman Brown and Other Tales
Edited by Brian Harding

WILLIAM HAZLITT: Selected Writings
Edited by Jon Cook

HESIOD: Theogony *and* Works and Days
Translated by M. L. West

JAMES HOGG: The Private Memoirs and
Confessions of a Justified Sinner
Edited by John Carey

HOMER: The Iliad
Translated by Robert Fitzgerald
Introduction by G. S. Kirk

THOMAS HUGHES: Tom Brown's Schooldays
Edited by Andrew Sanders

HENRIK IBSEN: An Enemy of the People, The Wild Duck, Rosmersholm
Edited and Translated by James McFarlane

Four Major Plays
Translated by James McFarlane and Jens Arup
Introduction by James McFarlane

HENRY JAMES: The Ambassadors
Edited by Christopher Butler

The Bostonians
Edited by R. D. Gooder

The Spoils of Poynton
Edited by Bernard Richards

M. R. JAMES: Casting the Runes and Other Ghost Stories
Edited by Michael Cox

JOCELIN OF BRAKELOND:
Chronicle of the Abbey of Bury St. Edmunds
Translated by Diana Greenway and Jane Sayers

GWYN JONES (Transl.):
Eirik the Red and Other Icelandic Sagas

BEN JONSON: Five Plays
Edited by G. A. Wilkes

JUVENAL: The Satires
Translated by Niall Rudd
Notes and Introduction by William Barr

RUDYARD KIPLING: Stalky & Co.
Edited by Isobel Quigly

MADAME DE LAFAYETTE: The Princesse de Clèves
Translated and Edited by Terence Cave

J. SHERIDAN LE FANU: Uncle Silas
Edited by W. J. McCormack

CHARLOTTE LENNOX: The Female Quixote
Edited by Margaret Dalziel
Introduction by Margaret Anne Doody

LEONARDO DA VINCI: Notebooks
Edited by Irma A. Richter

MATTHEW LEWIS: The Monk
Edited by Howard Anderson

JACK LONDON:
The Call of the Wild, White Fang, and Other Stories
Edited by Earle Labor and Robert C. Leitz III

KATHERINE MANSFIELD: Selected Stories
Edited by D. M. Davin

KARL MARX AND FRIEDRICH ENGELS:
The Communist Manifesto
Edited by David McLellan

CHARLES MATURIN: Melmoth the Wanderer
Edited by Douglas Grant
Introduction by Chris Baldick

HERMAN MELVILLE: The Confidence-Man
Edited by Tony Tanner

PROSPER MÉRIMÉE: Carmen and Other Stories
Translated by Nicholas Jotcham

MICHELANGELO: Life, Letters, and Poetry
Translated by George Bull with Peter Porter

JOHN STUART MILL: On Liberty and Other Essays
Edited by John Gray

MOLIÈRE: Don Juan and Other Plays
Translated by George Graveley and Ian Maclean

GEORGE MOORE: Esther Waters
Edited by David Skilton

E. NESBIT: The Railway Children
Edited by Dennis Butts

ORIENTAL TALES
Edited by Robert L. Mack

OVID: Metamorphoses
Translated by A. D. Melville
Introduction and Notes by E. J. Kenney

EDGAR ALLAN POE: Selected Tales
Edited by Julian Symons

JEAN RACINE: Britannicus, Phaedra, Athaliah
Translated by C. H. Sisson

ANN RADCLIFFE: The Italian
Edited by Frederick Garber

THE MARQUIS DE SADE:
The Misfortune of Virtue and Other Early Tales
Translated and Edited by David Coward

PAUL SALZMAN (Ed.):
An Anthology of Elizabethan Prose Fiction

OLIVE SCHREINER: The Story of an African Farm
Edited by Joseph Bristow

SIR WALTER SCOTT: The Heart of Midlothian
Edited by Claire Lamont

MARY SHELLEY: Frankenstein
Edited by M. K. Joseph

STENDHAL: The Red and the Black
Translated by Catherine Slater

TOBIAS SMOLLETT: The Expedition of Humphry Clinker
Edited by Lewis M. Knapp
Revised by Paul-Gabriel Boucé

ROBERT LOUIS STEVENSON: Kidnapped and Catriona
Edited by Emma Letley

Treasure Island
Edited by Emma Letley

BRAM STOKER: Dracula
Edited by A. N. Wilson

JONATHAN SWIFT: Gulliver's Travels
Edited by Paul Turner

WILLIAM MAKEPEACE THACKERAY: Barry Lyndon
Edited by Andrew Sanders

LEO TOLSTOY: Anna Karenina
Translated by Louise and Aylmer Maude
Introduction by John Bayley

War and Peace
Translated by Louise and Aylmer Maude
Edited by Henry Gifford

ANTHONY TROLLOPE: The American Senator
Edited by John Halperin

Dr. Thorne
Edited by David Skilton

Dr. Wortle's School
Edited by John Halperin

Orley Farm
Edited by David Skilton

IVAN TURGENEV: First Love and Other Stories
Translated by Richard Freeborn

MARK TWAIN: Pudd'nhead Wilson and Other Tales
Edited by R. D. Gooder

GIORGIO VASARI: The Lives of the Artists
Translated and Edited by Julia Conaway Bondanella and Peter Bondanella

JULES VERNE: Journey to the Centre of the Earth
Translated and Edited by William Butcher

VIRGIL: The Aeneid
Translated by C. Day Lewis
Edited by Jasper Griffin

The Eclogues and The Georgics
Translated by C. Day Lewis
Edited by R. O. A. M. Lyne

HORACE WALPOLE : The Castle of Otranto
Edited by W. S. Lewis

IZAAK WALTON and CHARLES COTTON:
The Compleat Angler
Edited by John Buxton
Introduction by John Buchan

OSCAR WILDE: Complete Shorter Fiction
Edited by Isobel Murray

The Picture of Dorian Gray
Edited by Isobel Murray

MARY WOLLSTONECRAFT:
Mary *and* The Wrongs of Woman
Edited by Gary Kelly

VIRGINIA WOOLF: Mrs Dalloway
Edited by Claire Tomalin

ÉMILE ZOLA:
The Attack on the Mill and Other Stories
Translated by Douglas Parmée

Nana
Translated and Edited by Douglas Parmée